THE TURQUOISE SUN

"What's wrong?" Tanya asked sharply. "Have they found out the truth? Are they going to kill us now?"

Swift Blade's eyes darted nervously. "No. They have requested a dance from you and Keane. It would be purely for entertainment, Miss Darrow."

Keane stood up with no hesitation and held out his hand to Tanya. "I was sorta getting the hankering to move around a little anyway. Make it something primitive. Listen to the beat of the drums. Let it flow into your soul."

His gaze held hers like a magnet, keeping them connected even as he began lifting his feet to the beat and moving around her. She followed his movements, holding to his eyes as if they were her lifeline. He spoke to her through the lithe, uninhibited movements of his body and through the subtle, sexual suggestion in his eyes. Without a touch, or a word, she felt as if he were making love to her.

Desire was born. Tanya began to match his movements, his erotic mood. The drumbeats picked up tempo to match the intensity of the mood consuming her, as if the players now felt the same sensual beat flowing hotly in her veins.

THE TURQUOISE SUN

Linda Sandifer

Zebra Books
Kensington Publishing Corp.

http://www.zebrabooks.com

ZEBRA BOOKS are published by

Kensington Publishing Corp.
850 Third Avenue
New York, NY 10022

First Printing: January, 1997
10 9 8 7 6 5 4 3 2 1

Printed in the United States of America

Prologue

Southwestern Colorado, 1896

Never let it be said that Keane Trevalyan ever passed up a good deal, or lost a card game if big winnings were at stake. And this time was certainly no exception. With pearly white teeth flashing beneath a satisfied grin, he reached across the weathered, round table and scooped up the pile of money and trinkets from the center.

Clamping his cigar between his teeth, he gathered up the worn cards and took in the glum expressions of his drunk and unhappy opponents. Of course, they didn't actually realize they were drunk, and he doubted it had ever occurred to them that while they were putting away free whiskey he hadn't drunk but two shots himself. All he really knew was that he'd never known an Indian who wouldn't gamble until he was down to nothing but his breechcloth. There were some who would even gamble that. And he had no intention of ending this friendly little game of poker until his three Ute friends were bare to the boards. They had something he wanted, and he wasn't going to leave until he got it.

"Well, what'll it be, boys?" He flashed them another congenial smile. "Want to call it a day?"

Three sets of black eyes glinted at him like chunks of shiny, sharp obsidian. A man of lesser confidence might have been uneasy under their ominous perusals, but Keane had won all their knives in the poker game, so all he really had to worry about was the three of them taking after him with their fists. That didn't bother him too much either because his horse was right outside, ready for a quick flight.

The biggest Ute, a barrel-chested fellow by the name of Buffalo Belly, was the one who finally spoke, mainly because he could speak English considerably better than the other two. "We want a chance to get our things back, Trevalyan."

"Then you shall have your chance, my friend." He took a draw on his cigar and blew a puff of smoke to the center of the table. It billowed out and slowly enveloped their solemn faces. If he wasn't mistaken, their scowls deepened. "That is," he continued, "if you can come up with something to put in the pot. For as much fun as this game is, boys, I don't play it for matches."

They didn't act as if they knew exactly what he was talking about. Finally Buffalo Belly said, motioning toward the chattel at Keane's elbows, "You have everything, Trevalyan. Everything we have with us."

Keane's crystal-clear, green-eyed gaze slid to the necklace around Hooting Owl's neck. The Indian was as tall and skinny as Buffalo Belly was short and fat, and Keane had him exactly where he wanted him. It had taken a few hours, but he'd known for years that patience could be a very profitable virtue. Hooting Owl had already lost his shirt, all his shell necklaces and hair paraphernalia, his belt, boots, hat, and knife. Basically, all he had left was his pants and the necklace. Even in the back room of the dimly lit reservation trading post, its gems whispered wealth. Keane believed the necklace had an Aztecan origin. If he sold it to the right buyer, he would probably never have to work again for the rest of his life.

At the thought, he was unexpectedly struck by a momentary stab of guilt and the fleeting, gorgeous image of his long-legged fellow archaeologist, Tanya Darrow. He could see her now, chiding him about not "donating" the necklace to a museum. It seemed that every time he found himself in her company she didn't miss the chance to chastise him for his "sleazy" ways. But the blond-haired, blue-eyed brain wasn't here, now was she?

No, he was here all by himself, just him and his con-science. And his conscience, impure that it was, told him repeatedly that the necklace was worth a bundle and he'd be a damn fool to pass up the opportunity of a lifetime.

The necklace gleamed on Hooting Owl's naked bronze chest in all its exquisite glory: over two dozen strands of turquoise beads, four strands of pearls, three strands of jade, and five smaller strands—graduating in size toward the throat—made of solid gold ball beads. All of these valuable gems were interspersed with beads and shells of lesser value in shades of white and coral, and each strand was arranged one beneath the other in graduating size so it fanned out across his chest in a half-circle. Larger gold balls, on string-ers, hung from the last strand of turquoise beads at intervals that gave the effect of the shooting rays of the sun. It was held at Hooting Owl's neck by long, wide bar clasps of solid gold. What a shame to have it go to waste decorating such a bony neck.

Keane removed the cigar from his mouth and used it as a pointer. "How about that necklace that Hooting Owl's wearing?"

The Utes' glazed brains took a minute to respond, but when they did, Hooting Owl's skinny hand came up to cover the necklace in a protective gesture. "No can gamble the Turquoise Sun. It has been passed down . . . many times. It is very old and very sacred."

Keane took a couple more puffs on his cigar, anticipating initial rebellion. Finally he leaned back in his chair and fingered the old deck of cards. "I guess the game's over then. I won't accept credit."

With concise movements, he began placing the coins and trinkets in the pockets of his coat. The larger items he would sell to the trading post owner, and the Utes would probably get them back through trade, or credit.

He heard Buffalo Belly and the other Indian, Talon Hunter, speaking in low, insistent voices to Hooting Owl, whose responses were short and clipped and very stubborn-sounding. Keane could only understand a few words of their language, but he knew that the two were pressuring the one to gamble the Turquoise Sun so they could get their money and belongings back. They were probably telling him that whoever won the game would return everything to its rightful owner, thus assuring Hooting Owl that he would get his necklace back. They were probably also telling him that they couldn't possibly lose *again.*

Keane stood up, tugging his hat down firmly onto his head. Buffalo Belly stood, too; the top of his head barely reached the top of Keane's chest. He placed a hand on Keane's forearm in a detaining gesture while glancing down at Hooting Owl.

"What is your answer, Hooting Owl?" Buffalo Belly asked.

Hooting Owl didn't look happy about it, but he had to stay in good stead with his friends. After all, his reputation might be ruined if he proved to be spineless on such a manly pursuit as gambling. He would be able to tell a great tale around the campfire later of how he had gambled the Sun and had won everything the White Eyes owned, even his horse. Keane knew the nature of the natives, and he was counting on his assumptions to help him get what he wanted.

Hooting Owl slowly reached behind his skinny neck and unhooked the gold bar clasps that held the ornament in place. At last, looking very sad and quite ill, he carefully laid the necklace on the table. The sheer weight of it made a solid thud against the old wood. With a loving gesture and long, skeletal fingers, he fanned the many gem-laden strands into a perfect half-circle. Then he looked up into Keane's greedy gaze.

"We play," he said. "You deal."

One

The Utes claimed the cliff dwellings were haunted by the Anasazi, the ancient ones who had come before, and they shunned them even though the ruins were on their traditional lands.

Tanya Darrow's archaeological digs had taken her all over the world, and through the years she had experienced many strange and unusual phenomena while relieving the earth of its past. But as she stood at the base of the silent Indian ruins, an unexpected and penetrating chill rushed through her. It could have been caused by the cool breeze pushing past her canvas jacket, or the excitement of reaching her destination after a long and arduous horseback ride. But it could be, too, that the Utes were right.

Midway up the canyon wall, constructed in the mouth of a tremendous, yawning cave, rose scores of multistoried, buff-colored cliff dwellings. Their architectural structure was a complex creation of shaped and fitted sandstone whose squares and curves adhered gracefully to the surrounding rock walls and massive rock roof arching protectively overhead. The open cave gave the appearance of a huge amphitheater with the dwellings, built on terraces, taking center stage and filling it from end to end and from top to bottom.

Down the center of the canyon, winding through a congestion of pinyon, juniper, brush, and aspen, ran the shallow but dependable river that had once been the lifeblood of the vanished people. Now, its sandy shores would be the camping site for Tanya's field crew until fall.

Her gaze lifted to the great green mesa above the silent ruins. Scored by a labyrinth of rugged canyons and runnels, it stretched in all directions as far as the eye could see. There were remnants of adobe walls up there, too, and Tanya wondered why the people had abandoned those early villages built on level ground, to mortar their homes instead into precarious crevices of the canyon walls like flocks of nervous mud daubers seeking sanctuary. And why had they then left the cozy and secure dwellings that had obviously taken tremendous labor to build, not to mention years— probably decades—to construct? Where had the people gone? What had caused them to scatter to the four winds like autumn leaves, vanishing forever?

The silent dwellings called to Tanya, as if the voices of the ancient people were on the wind, beckoning her to join them and learn their secrets. Yet, despite the mystery of the place, there was also something disturbingly familiar about it. As if she had been here before.

She shook away the peculiar, unsettling sensation of *déjà vu*. If she hurried, she would be able to make a quick investigation before dark. She had waited too long for this moment and ridden too far to delay until tomorrow. She knew she would never sleep until she had set foot inside the ruins.

She swung from the saddle with ease, virtually unaffected by the grueling horseback ride that had taken her expedition across thirty miles of wilderness and then down the steep, winding trail from the mesa top to the canyon floor, a descent of seven hundred feet. She went directly to the mule that carried her personal belongings and began disassembling the pack. In her anxious enthusiasm to get into the dwellings before dark, she turned a deaf ear to the moans and groans coming from the shovel hands and the college students who had signed on for the dig. They obviously weren't used to extreme physical exertion and primitive conditions, but they would adjust in a couple of weeks. Only the old cook, a former cowboy named Zeke, and the Hopi Indians who had come along to assist, seemed unaffected by the journey.

The lead guide, a man by the name of Miles Rule, sauntered over, chewing on a wad of tobacco. He squatted down on his haunches and watched Tanya struggle with the pack ropes, making no move to assist. But she didn't expect any man to hold her hand. Since she'd been a motherless child, she had accompanied her busy father on digs all over the world. In the early days it was to ancient sites of European, Egyptian, and Middle Eastern civilizations. In the last decade, it had been to Central America where archaeologists were beginning to unearth mysterious civilizations that had nearly been lost forever by the overgrowth of near-impenetrable jungles.

Miles, graying and fifty, had been greatly annoyed when he'd found Tanya in charge of this Southwestern expedition. He'd been expecting to lead the internationally famous Prof. J. D. Darrow, and he hadn't been happy to learn that Darrow was back in Boston recuperating from a near-fatal bout of pneumonia and had sent his daughter. The fact that Tanya was an experienced archaeologist herself, and the head of the history department at Wellesley College, had made little difference to Miles, at least at first. Then he'd seen that she was capable of taking care of herself, and his respect had quadrupled. He'd even taken a shine to her and had started teasing her, mostly about the trousers she always wore when she went on a field expedition. Their growing friendship still hadn't made him any more eager to give assistance of any kind, though. Miles simply didn't do anything if he could relegate a task to someone else.

At last Tanya had the ropes off and pulled her packs to the ground. Tossing her long braid over her shoulder, she quickly found what she was looking for—her Colt revolver.

There was no telling what wild animals she might flush out of the ruins on her first visit, and she wanted to be prepared. The rifle on her saddle would be better protection against large predators, like mountain lions, but she needed both hands free to climb the trail—*if* she could find it.

"Expectin' trouble, Miss Darrow?" Miles asked, spatting a glob of tobacco on the ground between his boots.

"Maybe," Tanya replied, checking the load in the revolver. "I'm going up to the ruins for a quick look."

He chuckled. "You figure that Colt will stop those ghosts I hear are up there?"

"It's not ghosts I'm worried about, Miles." She flashed him a tolerant smile.

"Want me to come along and protect you?" Of course he made the offer because he knew she would decline.

Tanya buckled the holster to her hip. "Kid me, Miles, but not yourself. The last thing you want to do is climb up to those dwellings. Besides, I need you to stay here and make sure the others get camp set up before dark. Have Swift Blade take care of my horse, would you?"

"Will do, Missy. And be careful. You never know what you'll disturb in those ruins besides loose rocks and blood-suckin' bats."

Tanya pulled on her well-worn leather gloves and watched him return to his duties, wondering if he truly believed all the nonsense that passed across his weathered lips. Then, adjusting her dusty, narrow-brimmed, brown hat over her eyes, she set off for the ruins. The members of her party might not approve of her leaving them to set up camp, but she seriously doubted any of them would want to come with her after all the whining they'd done today about chafed knees, saddle sores, and aching backs.

After initially struggling through the tangle of under-brush, she found a game trail winding through the thick growth of trees in the canyon bottom. She followed it, keeping her eye on her destination. The trail brought her out at the base of the ruins, where her progress was impeded by a break in the earth and a huge talus slope. She saw another trail descending from one side of the mammoth cave, and after a brief upward struggle through more brush and a crawl across the talus slope on hands and knees, she emerged onto the final trail.

The shadows had deepened here. The sun, resting on the western rim of the mesa, lit the foreground of the great cave, but the farther reaches of the cliff dwellings slumbered in shadow. Tanya glanced back down to where the others had set up camp in the canyon, but the spot was obscured by the bushy heads of a thick, isolated stand of aspens. She could not even hear the field crew; the only sound reaching her ears was the wind quivering the aspen leaves, making their semiround leaves flutter noisily.

She wondered how long she had before darkness obliterated the path. Forty minutes? An hour, perhaps? The distance through the trees and along the tangled path had been deceptive. It had taken longer to get here than she had thought it would. But despite the threat of darkness, her eyes were drawn back to the silent, beckoning ruins. They loomed above her now, so much larger than the doll-like structures they had appeared to be from a distance. She was too close to turn back now.

Her booted feet moved forward on the path, crunching pieces of sandstone and twigs that had collected there with the help of time and the wind. She paused under the great red half-dome of the cave, feeling the weight of it penetrate her imagination. She wondered how the Anasazi could have lived beneath it without fear of its collapse. What stopped a small tremor of the earth from bringing it down, crushing the ancient dwellings?

But it had stood for millions of years, so she proceeded onward along the outskirts of the structures, picking her way slowly and carefully through the rubble of fallen sandstone bricks piled up in corridors and strewn in courtyards.

In the foreground plaza area were many kivas—recessed, circular chambers where dutiful priests had once carried out their religious ceremonies, ensuring the safety and prosperity of the people. Most of the roof timbers of both the kivas and the other buildings had rotted and collapsed, taking with them the withes, thatching, and the three to four inches of adobe that had covered them.

Tanya wound her way over rubble to the fourth terrace which opened out onto a large plaza. Her footsteps across the plaza were muffled by centuries of dirt and disintegrating clay mortar. So silent were the ruins that she could hear her own breathing. She wasn't totally alone of course. There were numerous trashy occupants. Rat nests filled the corners, and their builders scurried in dark shadows unseen. The beautiful handiwork of spiders stretched in gossamer patterns over almost every wall, and the flutter of wings overhead alerted her to a departing swallow, winging its way from its hidden nest of mud.

With the ancient walls towering over her on either side now, she climbed up over mounds of rubble to peer into the tiny, abandoned rooms that had once been living quarters for those who had been here so long ago. The rooms, plaster peeling from the walls, were small and couldn't have measured more than six feet by eight feet, with low ceilings only as high as the builder's head. There were seldom windows in the apartments, no chimneys, and hence no firepits. Only T-shaped openings served as doors barely large enough to crawl through and with sills three feet off the ground in most places. Apparently the women must have done their cooking on the plaza, and they must have worn heavy robes to stay warm in the winter.

Inside the dim, shadowed apartments, she saw beautiful pieces of pottery, some broken, some not, as well as stone *manos* and *metates* in the positions they had probably last been used. Her fingers itched to pick the objects up, study them. But they should not be disturbed until she had her materials to record each piece. Unfortunately further exploration would have to wait until morning. It was simply getting too dark in these back rooms to stay any longer.

She was pleased, however, to see that nothing appeared to have been disturbed since the departure of the occupants so long ago. Many dwellings had been discovered in the canyons of the plateau region by the Wetherill brothers, and many had already been stripped of their artifacts by both treasure-seekers and archaeologists. But when Richard Wetherill had recently stumbled onto this two-hundred-room ruin, the one he had named *Castillo Blanco,* he had guarded his find religiously. He had secured Prescott Institute of Natural History in New Mexico to back a major excavation, requesting it be headed by her father. The location had been kept secret to keep unauthorized individuals from looting. Wetherill's efforts had been successful. She was satisfied that her field crew would be the first to explore this ancient civilization.

Reluctantly she turned back to the plaza. As she did, a sound far back in the ruins—like that of wood splitting under weight—suddenly made her scalp prickle and a chill race down her spine. Unconsciously holding her breath, she cocked her head to listen. But the only noises she heard now were the scampering of mice, the brush of birds' wings in flight, the ruffle of aspen leaves touched by the wind, and the not-completely-silent tick of time.

Time. In this ghostly place, it seemed to take on the watchful personality of a living entity.

She released the breath she'd been holding and mentally collected herself, shaking off her foolish thoughts. The wind could be blamed for many strange things, especially in a place such as this one where it could whistle and bend its way through all sorts of cracks and crevices.

Out on the open plaza, she saw darkness swiftly spreading over the canyon. She started across the plaza to the fading trail, but another sound, much fainter than the first, brought her up short again. This time it had the distinctive quality of a human moan. Afraid of what she might see in the empty dwellings behind her, she turned. But there was nothing there.

She was reminded of the words of the old Ute Indian she had met outside of Durango, Colorado, their last stop before embarking into the wilderness. She had been looking for Indian volunteers to join the expedition as aides and advisors. The Ute had been very uneasy about her request. "No go there," he had said, his black eyes gleaming with fear. "Ghosts of the Old Ones still linger." Then he had hurried away, refusing to speak further on the matter.

He had started the ghost stories, and Miles and the students had kept them alive, titillating themselves around the campfires at night. The place truly had an eerie quality, but Tanya refused to attribute it to ghosts. No, if something was here, it had to be alive. And from the sound of the moan, probably hurt. Maybe even dying.

She debated whether to get Miles and Swift Blade and some of the other men to come up and investigate. But with darkness quickly filling the canyon and the cliff dwellings, there was really only time to do one thing.

Drawing her revolver, she turned back to the ruins.

Retracing her steps across the fourth terrace's plaza, she moved cautiously along the stone-paved courtyard to a dark and winding corridor that led to the rear section of the dwellings. Her gaze slid up to the second floor of the square, three-story tower building in center front and the maze of multistoried apartments surrounding it. Again she was struck with the unnerving feeling of *déjà vu*. But it was fleeting, and in another instant had winged beyond her grasp as elusive as the call of a nightbird in a dusky mountain forest.

She moved on. Through the darkness of the back rooms she could see very little but looming walls and narrow doorways. All she could rely on were her five senses, and that elusive sixth sense that guided her, as if she'd walked these corridors before, and at the same time told her she was foolishly heading toward danger.

Shortly the sound came again, closer now, not too far ahead. With heart hammering, she stepped over the high sill of the first tiny room, progressing warily through three more that were lined up one behind the other, their doors looking like picture frames within picture frames. Twice she felt the brush of cobwebs on her face; once the frantic bolt of a mouse across her boot toe. An owl watched her from his perch on a high wall, moving nothing but his head and eyes as he followed her movement.

The sound was not continual, nor always the same. Now it sounded like movement of some sort, mixed with groaning.

Behind the apartment buildings, just under the eave of the great cave, she came to another kiva, a small one probably only twelve or fourteen feet in circumference. Protected from the wind and rain by the cave's dome, the heavy juniper timbers were still intact in the roof, along with a good portion of the brush and mud covering it. She was not foolish enough to believe, though, that the timbers would hold her weight. She suspected that the slightest pressure would send the ancient beams crashing to the floor below.

Hovering on the edge of the ceremonial chamber, she sensed that this was the place whence the sounds had originated, although all was utterly silent now. Had the person heard her approach? This isolated kiva built at the very back of the cave was not a place where someone would have gone in hopes of being found. It was a place where someone would have gone to hide.

An old ladder had been dropped into the kiva through a ragged hole in the side of the roof rather than through the traditional hatchway in the center. She lowered herself to hands and knees and peered down into the kiva through the gaps in the timber and thatch. The interior was in complete darkness; she could see nothing. And yet, something—or someone—was down there. Just as she had sensed the ticking of an invisible clock in this place, so did she sense the presence of life.

"Hello," she said in a nervous whisper. "Is someone there?"

The silence below seemed to deepen as if all sound had been cast into a black abyss. Fear began to press in on her. The scent of danger was potent here; the scent of Death more elusive, but detectable. She glanced over her shoulder into the darkness. Only crumbling sandstone walls stared back. She considered running from the ruins as swiftly as a gazelle flees a lion. Instead she elevated her voice and repeated the question.

This time she heard a rustling sound, as if a coarse item of clothing had brushed against a rock wall.

"Yes." A deep male voice, brittle with the trace of pain, came back to her through the hole. "Can you help me? I'm . . . hurt."

The voice didn't seem to be directly below her in the kiva, but filtering into that area from some other place. Another kiva perhaps? But she saw none in the shadowy surroundings. Only a refuse pile beneath the cave's wall.

She seriously questioned her sanity, wondering if going into the kiva would be stepping into a trap that would ultimately be her doom. But whoever was down there needed help, or seemed to, and regardless of how he had gotten there or why, she must do something to save his life.

With her heart in her throat, she removed her gloves and tucked them into her belt. Holding her revolver in her right hand, she grabbed the ladder with her left and swung one foot from solid ground onto the first rung. She had barely done so when the pained voice came up to her, "The third rung is broken . . . and the fifth as well. Step lightly."

Cautiously she put part of her weight onto the first rung. When it held, she shifted both feet to it and started down into the dark hole, testing each rung as she went. The deeper she went, the more the walls of the kiva seemed to close in around her. She found the first broken rung and stretched her long legs down to the next. The ladder was indeed old, but she seriously doubted it had been here as long as the cliff dwellings. Someone else, an explorer perhaps, had probably left it behind.

At last she felt solid, packed earth beneath her boots. In the darkness of the ceremonial chamber, she could see nothing, but could feel the confines of the circular wall. She could smell the coolness of the place, the dust of centuries being faintly stirred by the intrusion of her feet, and the very faint whiff of tobacco. But she felt no human presence in the kiva and it was too dark to see anything. The chill crept down her spine again. Ghosts?

"Where are you?" she asked, her voice sounding a touch too fearful in its demand. She expected an assault from the person who might be able to see her even though she couldn't see him. Because flight might be necessary, she kept one hand on the ladder and the other on her revolver.

"There's another kiva," came the man's raspy reply from a greater distance yet. "A short tunnel to your right joins the two kivas. The entrance to it is a couple of feet off the floor."

Tanya was down to groping her way now. She left the security of the ladder and inched along the wall, stumbling over debris, until she felt the opening to the tunnel. She gauged the size of it by feel alone and, with rocks gouging her hands and knees, and hoping the man had flushed out any snakes, she crawled blindly, feeling every inch of her way. Luckily it was a short distance, no more than five or six feet, and she came out hands first onto a cool, earthen floor in the second kiva. It was as dark as the one she'd left and she couldn't see a thing. It felt cool and damp as well, or perhaps that was only due to the fear crawling all over her like billions of lice. Suddenly she realized the full extent of her folly. What if there was more than one man in here?

"You ask for help and yet you sit in the darkness." She stayed close to the tunnel, preparing for escape. "How is anyone to find you, let alone help you?"

"I can't build a fire. Can't move . . . much." He took a breath that sounded staggered and pained. "My God, but your voice is like the songs of angels, T. D. I was beginning to think you'd cancelled the expedition."

Tanya's thumping heart suddenly seemed to stop. Her senses, previously blocked by fear, began to work amazingly well. Instantly she recognized the deep, husky voice, the distinct aroma of his cigars, and that annoying sobriquet he'd insisted on using for years. As clearly as if someone had struck a match to a lantern wick, she could see him in her mind's eye in all his handsome but irritating arrogance.

Keane Trevalyan.

Damn the man and his infernal interference in her life! She didn't know what sort of game he was playing this time, but he wouldn't win. He would leave her dig—immediately—even if it meant using the gentle persuasion of her Colt revolver to accomplish it.

Two

"I have half a notion to head right back up that ladder and leave you to your own no-good devices, Keane Trevalyan." Her tone was low and barely contained her fury. "Perhaps you'd like to explain what you're doing at my dig—and hidden all the way back here in this kiva."

There was a moment of silence in the darkness, then, "How did you know it was me?"

"It's not hard to recognize the stench of a polecat."

He groaned again, but this time it was more a sound of emotional pain than physical. "Oh, come on, T. D. Don't be so hostile for just once in your life. I really need your help."

With frustrated anger, she leaned in the direction of his voice, even though she still couldn't see anything. "Why do you need my help? Have you been shot or something?"

He attempted a chuckle, but it faded into another groan. "Sorry to disappoint you, sweetheart, but it's nothing quite that fatal. At least I don't think so. Just a little accident that's left me feeling like a punching bag."

Tanya took a deep breath intended to cool her temper. A punching bag is exactly what she would like to use him for. Unscrupulous, undeniably handsome, and exhaustively charming—Keane Trevalyan was the last person on the face of the earth she wanted to see at her dig. His notoriety as a fortune-hunting adventurer and playboy had long preceded him. His reckless habits tended to land him, and everybody around him, into all sorts of trouble. The most recent example had been just last year. While deep in Central America unearthing the temple of an ancient civilization, he had been observed paying too much attention to the daughter of an important local dignitary who was assisting their efforts. Keane had found himself on the road to marriage, and the entire excavating party, of which she was a member, had had to come to his rescue. They had been forced to flee through the jungle, pursued by the dignitary's personal army of assassins, and had barely escaped with their lives.

The thing that upset her the most about Keane, though, was his habit of embarking on lone adventures to unearth legendary artifacts of great monetary value. He didn't care about putting the items in museums. All he cared about was finding the highest bidder and banking the money in his own pockets. On his many escapades he usually took along only a few guides and never asked for financing from any individual or institution that might demand the donation of what he unearthed. By doing this, he kept his conscience free of loyalty to anyone but himself. He was what was known—and frowned upon—by other archaeologists and anthropologists as a "thief of time."

In Tanya's estimation, it was highly unprofessional behavior for a Harvard-educated individual, although rumor had it he'd paid his way through college with money obtained from the sale of artifacts, since his wealthy father had refused to finance his interest in archaeology. Apparently his father and two brothers were upstanding businessmen and jointly owned a successful carriage company in Connecticut. His mother and sisters-in-law were saints of high society. His father and he had had a falling-out when Keane had shown no interest in going into the family business. It was rumored the entire family had disowned him after that. If it bothered him, he never let on. He had plenty of money, it seemed, and everyone talked about his beautiful country estate in New Hampshire.

How she wished he was there now instead of here at her dig. She couldn't believe her incredible bad luck. How many artifacts had he already pilfered? Had he wiped the place clean of everything of value?

She took a second deep breath, but still her temper crackled. It was hard to remind herself that he was hurt, or claimed to be. It might be just another of his endless ploys to get something he wanted. All she could think of was how her entire summer excavations might have already been undermined. Furthermore, he had no right to be here, since he had declined to officially join the expedition.

Despite his less than professional behavior, Tanya grudgingly admitted she still found him devastatingly attractive, even to the point of distraction. In that sense, she was as foolish as every other female who had ever crossed his path. It seemed every time she turned around he was there, smiling that irresistible smile and being charming. The number of ladies' hearts he'd been rumored to have broken was a staggering amount. He would have broken hers, too, if she had been gullible enough to succumb to his numerous attempts of seduction. But she had learned her lesson about men like him long ago, thanks to another rogue named Frankie Locke to whom she'd naively given her heart, and her virginity, at the age of eighteen.

If Keane's attempted seductions weren't enough, he had actually considered himself a cut above Frankie. He'd had the audacity, even back then, to act like a big brother and caution her against getting involved with the "sort" who would take advantage of her.

Who better to know the moves of a rogue, than a rogue?

She had never discussed Frankie's jilting of her with anyone, but she had seen in Keane's eyes a certain knowledge. She was positive he knew, or surmised, the outcome of that disastrous love affair. And, for some reason, she was always reminded of it when he was around, even though he never said a word one way or the other. The biggest problem with

Keane was that he simply knew too much about her. And maybe she also knew too much about him.

"Light a match so I can see you," she finally commanded in an irritable, but conceding growl. "The sooner I can get you out of this kiva, the quicker you can be on your way. Why were you here anyway? Were you nosing around and fell through that roof? You didn't want to come with the rest of us on this dig, so I want you out of here. You're not going to reap the rewards of my labor, Keane Trevalyan. Do you have those matches yet?"

"No, I don't have the matches, and for your information I didn't come to reap the rewards of your labor."

"Just get the matches, Keane. I have no desire to hear your explanations because they would probably just be a bunch of poppycock anyway."

She heard the rustling noise and visualized him digging into his pocket for matches. "God, Tanya," he said finally, and slightly out of breath. "I hurt like hell. Can you help me?"

It had always seemed a dangerous thing to get too close to Keane Trevalyan, and even though other women did it at every opportunity, Tanya avoided it at all costs. But it didn't look as though getting him on his way was going to be done without her assistance, so she advanced through the darkness toward him, setting each foot down cautiously until the toe of her boot bumped up against his body. He was apparently flat on his back. Kneeling down next to him, she realized she was going to have to touch him in order to get the matches.

In all the years she'd known him—eight to be exact—she had only touched him once, on purpose, and that had been when he'd asked her to dance at a fund-raising ball. Even now she remembered how he had held her and smiled at her too familiarly, how he'd told her she was gorgeous in the blue silk gown she'd had made especially for the occasion. No man had ever told her she was beautiful, let alone gorgeous. Not Frankie. Not her father. Not even her fiancé, Edward Chatham. So she hadn't known whether Keane really meant it, or if he was just spreading on the charm in yet another attempt to get her to bed.

She'd been sorely tempted, too. The years had passed since then, but not the memory of his hands and body touching hers, scorching her with a heat equivalent to that of the Cairo sun. Being in his arms had made her mind swirl away from common sense, as if dulled by sweet brandy wine, into something no more substantial than pure, primeval desire.

Realizing she could fall more hopelessly in love with him than she had with Frankie, she had ever since concealed her attraction behind a facade of annoyance, so that he might never know the struggle she experienced each time he appeared in her life. Which, lately, was more often than she deemed necessary.

Now, apprehensive about what part of him her hand would fall upon first, she reached out tentatively into the darkness and groped. Her fingers found the buttons on his vest and the rock-hard expanse of his chest. She felt the steady thumping of his heart beneath her hand and would have withdrawn it except that, of all his body parts, his chest seemed about the safest to be in physical contact with.

"Where are the matches?" she asked with an affected tone of impatient crankiness.

"My pants pocket," he replied. "The one on the right."

She'd have to reach across him to get to it. If she didn't know better, the insufferable rogue was purposely trying to unsettle her. "For heaven's sake, Keane, don't you have some matches in a more logical place, such as your vest pocket or your coat pocket?"

"No," came his almost-too-hasty reply. "All I have left are what's in my pants pocket."

She groped her hands from the buttons on his vest down to the tautness of his stomach. She found his belt and belt buckle. Her fingers inched down toward the right until she found the edge of his pocket, and the protrusion of his hip bone. The heat emanating from his body scorched a path from her palms and right up her arms to engulf her. She was suddenly very thankful for the darkness and all the things it hid; the heat burning her cheeks, the shaking hands, and his probing eyes that, had it been light, would have mockingly read every telltale thought in her head.

How was it possible he could unnerve her when she knew him for exactly what he was? Granted his six-foot-two physique, laughing eyes, and dark, wavy hair were commendable physical attributes. And he *was* a good archaeologist. If only he would put his knowledge to some honest—possibly even some scholarly—use. But all Keane Trevalyan really seemed interested in at the age of twenty-eight was money and women, and not necessarily in that order.

She slid her hand inside his pocket and felt him tense beneath her. "Am I hurting you?" she asked, still impatiently anxious to find out what was wrong with him and send him on his way. It would be the only way to bring order and serenity back to her life, and to this dig.

He sucked in a ragged breath. "No . . . ah . . . you're not hurting me. Not at all."

From the sound of him, that was hardly an honest statement, but she proceeded with her task, found the matches, and pulled out several, trying to force steadiness to her hands. She reached over him again, found the kiva's stone wall and struck the match across it. The flame leaped and parted the darkness. She moved its feeble, wavering tip closer to his face.

"My God, Keane!" she gasped, nearly jerking back at the sight of him. "What happened to you?"

Gingerly he touched a purple and swollen eye, caked with dried blood. "I fell from a cliff."

Her gaze narrowed suspiciously. "The truth, Keane."

He maintained a long moment of silence. "I thought you didn't want to hear all my poppycock."

Her lips pursed. "I suppose it's necessary."

After a moment of studying her face, and with hesitation showing on his own, he finally relented to her interrogation. "All right, Tanya. I tangled with a trio of guys over at the Ute Reservation. Seems I had something they wanted."

"And what could you possibly have that some Indians would want?"

He tried his old rakish smile, but winced from the effort and immediately reached a hand up to gingerly mollify his cut lip. "Oh, nothing much. Just my life."

"Humph. Well, it wouldn't be the first time somebody wanted that. Be more specific. *Why* did they want your life?"

The match burned her finger and she dropped it; it flickered out when it hit the dirt. She lit another, but knew it wouldn't last. Keane saw the problem, too, and suggested she build a fire. He made a move to get up, as if he intended to help her, but he clutched his midsection and collapsed back to the ground, groaning in pain.

"What is it?" she asked warily, afraid of what the answer might be.

"A broken rib. I think. Or maybe it's just cracked."

Her brow knotted with genuine concern. The fool had really gotten himself hurt this time. What if he was hurt internally? What if he was going to die? For as much as he annoyed her, she didn't want to see that happen. It was true that he always seemed to be disrupting the equilibrium of her life, but he always managed to keep things from getting too dull, too.

"Then stay put," she said a bit more gently. "I'll build the fire."

With Keane keeping the matches lit to provide light, she collected tinder and wood from the debris that had fallen into the kiva from the thatch roof, heaped it into the old fire pit, and touched a match to it. Soon the flames' wavering light pushed the darkness back to the circular, soot-blackened walls.

She could better see the extent of Keane's injuries now, which were so alarming that if she hadn't recognized his voice in the dark, she might not have recognized his face in the light. Several deep cuts marred his rugged but handsome visage. Bruises had spread to ugly proportions on both jaws. His right eye seemed to have escaped damage, but the other one was swollen completely shut, and another gash cut across just above the eyelid. It was the source of all the blood that had spilled down on that side of his face and dried. A cut on his forehead and a split upper lip completed the extent of visible facial damage.

Dropping to her knees next to him, she looked at his one good eye, scanned his injuries, and felt genuine sympathy for him, possibly for the first time since she'd known him. But there were still things he needed to explain.

"You said something about some Indians," she prodded. "What happened? Honestly."

She could see now he was speaking carefully to avoid opening the cut on his lip again. "I met 'em at the Ute trading post. Struck up a game of poker in the back room. Indians love to gamble, you know."

"So I've heard," she responded dryly, encouraged that his spirits still seemed relatively high.

"Anyway, I ended up with everything they owned," he continued. "They figured I'd cheated."

"Did you?"

His head swiveled toward her, and if she wasn't mistaken, his good eye glared. "It's always nice having your confidence, sweetheart."

Her gaze wandered from the battered face to the broad shoulders and down to the narrow hips that would stir any woman's mental meanderings of men and the physical pleasures they could offer. But the thoughts those hips gave her were more dangerous than anything she would ever encounter in this canyon. It was a shame he had to play every woman he met for a potential conquest. That's why she'd determined years ago that she wouldn't be one of them. Too bad she hadn't known as much about Frankie.

"Why did you come here to the ruins, Keane?"

He moistened his lips and tried to change positions, but it wasn't without pain searing through him again. "Because I . . . needed some help," he said through deep breaths. "And I knew you would be arriving soon."

"Why not just go to Durango and find a doctor?"

"They would have followed me. But I knew they wouldn't come into these dwellings."

"Then you're saying they might be waiting for you outside the canyon somewhere?"

He nodded. "Unfortunately. But they'll get tired of that after a while. They'll cool down, sober up, and realize they lost that card game fair and square. They got all their belongings back anyway after they beat me up, so they really don't have a reason to come after me."

Tanya studied his battered face. He wasn't telling her all of the story, as usual. If they had gotten all their belongings back, then why were they still after him? Just because they figured he'd cheated? It didn't seem plausible, unless they just liked to beat up on white adventurers.

"You know, Keane," she said contemplatively. "I'll help you in whatever way I can, but I honestly don't want you on this dig."

"I wouldn't have guessed," he replied dryly, giving her that eye again. "But just to ease your mind, sweetheart, I'd like you to know I didn't come out here to join it."

"No, I don't suppose you did. You just came out to carry off what you could before I got here. There's absolutely no other reason for you to be here. And, in the meantime, you just thought you'd kill a little time over a card game with the natives. But you overstepped the bounds, got beaten up, and now you need my help."

"If I told you I came out West to satisfy a touch of gold fever, would you believe that?"

"No."

"All right. I came to the ruins for several reasons, Tanya. One because I knew the Utes wouldn't come in here, especially into a kiva. Two, because I knew you would be here and you could help me. And three, I really did come out West looking for gold. Of course, I was hoping for some that had already been minted."

"Of course. And your being in this part of the country had nothing whatsoever to do with this new discovery and the lure of what you might find?"

He closed his eyes and continued to grip his midsection. She hated it when he closed his eyes; she could never tell if he was lying when he did that. "Well, sure it interested me, T. D. But I wasn't going to step on your toes. I know this is the first expedition you've headed without your father."

"You could have come with us, you know."

"I know. But you know me . . ."

"Yes, I'm afraid I do. A little too well."

She stood up, refusing to listen to any more of his flimsy explanations. She needed to go back to camp, get a lantern, some medical supplies, and some assistance to get him out of here. It would have helped if he hadn't burrowed himself so far back in this hole. How he'd gotten here in the first place amazed her. He must have suffered a great deal, and probably did himself more damage in the process. He must have really wanted to make sure those Utes didn't find him. But the sooner she could get him back on his feet, the quicker he could he gone.

He caught her hand in a sudden action that surprised her. She was brought back down to her knees next to his side with a strength she hadn't thought he could possess in his present condition. His good eye beseeched her. "Hey, you're not leaving, are you?"

His fingers closing tightly over her hand scattered her intent and nearly made her forget what it had been. He didn't sound desperate, but he did sound anxious. He needed her, and she felt her heart soften again. Quickly she bolstered it.

"I know you don't like me, Tanya," he continued in a pleading voice that played on her emotions. "But how about a little compassion just this once? I need your help. I've spent one night in this kiva already, and believe me, it gets cold. There's a terrible draft slipping in here from somewhere. I can walk, but this rib makes it awfully painful. I'd like to stay in here until tomorrow, but I need some firewood and a couple of blankets. I was trying to climb up the ladder to find some firewood when that third rung broke."

"So that's the noise I heard."

"Probably. But you can understand why I don't want to go back up that ladder tonight and make my way to camp in the dark. I'm just worn out. I need some rest."

His hoarse, whispered plea, and the gentle rubbing of his thumb over the back of her hand, reminded her of how well he knew a woman's weaknesses. But as long as she knew his tactics, she could stay one step ahead of him, and then he wouldn't be able to find any of *her* weaknesses.

"I'm just going for some medical supplies," she finally replied in the firmest voice she could muster. "And some blankets. I won't be long. But I want you to be fully aware of where I stand on this, Keane. I'll let you stay until you can ride, but then I want you on your horse—wherever you've got him hidden—and I want you out of here. You got yourself into this mess, as usual, and if those Utes come in here and disrupt my dig or hurt somebody, so help me I'll make your other eye purple. *And,*" she continued, gaining momentum, "if you so much as put one sherd in your pocket while you're here, I'll personally hang you from the nearest tree that has a sturdy limb."

"It's nice to know I mean so much to you, sweetheart. But I wouldn't dream of doing such an underhanded thing as to steal your potsherds."

Tanya decided he could have crossed his heart and hoped to die, even stuck a needle in his eye, and she still wouldn't have believed him. "Just make sure you don't."

With that being her final word, Tanya left the kiva the way she'd entered it.

Keane Trevalyan watched the play of the firelight flickering over Tanya's well-rounded bottom as she crawled through the short tunnel to the outer kiva. The fact that she had always worn trousers on her digs was something he enjoyed immensely. Little did she know that she'd supplied the male students with endless hours of entertainment. Of course, modest Tanya would have died of mortification if she'd known her pretty little fanny had been the topic of more fireside conversations than a bunch of old broken pots ever had.

He wiggled himself into a semicomfortable position on the cold, bumpy ground. At least the fire was warming things up. Now, if the pain in his ribs would just subside.

As a sort of consolation to his agony, he slipped his hand inside his coat pocket and ran his fingers over the contents. Tanya didn't have to worry about him taking any of her precious potsherds. He didn't need to. His pocket was already amply filled . . . with the Turquoise Sun.

Three

"Oh, no you don't, Tanya," Keane protested, gripping his aching ribs. "There's no point in badgering me. I won't wear that thing and that's final. A man has his pride. Don't you agree, Swift Blade?"

Keane turned to the young Hopi who had come with Tanya on the second trip to the kiva to offer his assistance. He had been standing quietly, gnawing on a piece of jerky, indifferent to their discussion until his name had been spoken. He was dressed more like a cowboy than an Indian, except he wore no hat over his long hair, and carried a knife at his hip instead of a revolver. His black eyes stared with definite confusion. Should he be loyal to Tanya, his employer? Or Keane, a fellow male? While he was trying to make up his mind, Tanya continued.

"For heaven's sake, Keane," she admonished, "it's only a corset. And it will be the perfect thing to bind your ribs so you can move about without so much pain."

"So you can put me on my horse and send me out of here, you mean. You're heartless, T. D. And you have no regard for how you humiliate me in the process. It's not just a corset. My god, it's a *yellow silk* corset with a bunch of lace and rosettes and . . . and *frills!*"

"It's the latest fashion. And I doubt that with even the corset you could sit a horse for a few days. But you can't stay in this kiva and rot."

"Tanya—*sweetheart.* In case you hadn't noticed, I'm a

lot like you. I tend to do anything I please, and if I feel like rotting in this kiva, I'll rot. I've helped a number of women out of those things, but I'm certainly not going to allow you to help me into one. Especially not a yellow silk one. Don't you have something else you can bind my ribs with?"

Her patience vanished. She dropped the corset on his chest. "I'm only trying to help you, which is what you wanted me to do, if I recall. But if you're going to be bull-headed because of vanity, then you can just do the best you can on your own. I'm going back to camp."

In brusque movements, she gathered the lantern she'd brought and started for the short tunnel to the outer kiva. Swift Blade looked from one to the other, his consternation and anxiety deepening. His jerky was clutched in his hand, momentarily forgotten.

"Wait, Miss Darrow. I'll stay here with your friend. That is, if you can spare me from camp for the night."

"He's not my friend, and there's no sense in you staying anyway, Swift Blade. Keane's going to stay there on his back until he mummifies."

In a rumble of moaning and groaning, Keane rolled to his side and then struggled to his knees, all the while gripping his midsection. With one hand, he groped for the corset that had fallen behind him, and then dragged it around in front of him.

"Is it yours, Tanya?"

She backed away from the tunnel, satisfied to see him up but irritated by his remark. "I would never humiliate myself by flashing my undergarments around. Of course it's not mine!"

His cut lip curled into a sardonic smile. "I didn't think so. It's much too . . . big."

"For your information, I only wear a riding corset when I'm working in the field. Anything else would be pointless and painful."

His good eye raked her from bosom to waist, as if he could see the garment hidden beneath the loose man's shirt, attesting to her declaration of feminine semi-independence. Then, with a disgruntled expression, he again scrutinized the boned contraption dangling from his fingertips. "Don't tell me. It belongs to Georgia Murphy."

Tanya stabbed him with narrowing, suspicious blue eyes. "So you recognize it?"

A derisive chuckle slipped from his swollen lips. "I haven't yet had the opportunity to remove it or any other garment from Miss Georgia Murphy, if that's what you're insinuating. I was merely guessing by the sheer size of the thing."

"Georgia gladly offered it, Keane, so you should show your appreciation of her generosity by wearing it."

He lashed the feminine underthing with one more disapproving glance. Then, still on his knees, he finally held it out to Tanya. "All right. You win. Help me put it on."

Tanya started for the tunnel again. "Swift Blade can help you."

"But, Miss Darrow," Swift Blade hastily interjected, "I do not know how this . . . this *corset* thing works." His coal-colored eyes, resembling those of a frightened and lost puppy, darted from one to the other while they decided his fate.

Tanya released a defeated sigh and a murmured curse. Keane's unexpected appearance was becoming very disruptive to the orderly and professional management of her dig. Keane was really taking up too much of her time. She wouldn't be a bit surprised if one of the students reported back to Wellesley that she was being negligent in her duties.

Seeing no other way to get the chore done, she kneeled in front of Keane. Taking the corset in hand, she instructed him to remove his jacket, vest, and shirt. His first attempt to obey her command sent him grabbing for his ribs in pain again.

Tanya didn't know what came over her just then, but he

looked so utterly pathetic, so vulnerable, and genuinely in pain. His poor face was a mess, and . . . well, her heart just went out to him. She had the overwhelming, and somewhat ridiculous urge to actually pull him into her arms and comfort him. Of course, she couldn't do that—she might hurt him—so she opted for helping him out of his jacket, gently sliding it off his shoulders and down over his arms. Mindful of his ribs, she undid the buttons on his vest and shirt and slid those off in the same manner.

Somewhere in the process of disrobing him, she became aware of the hot, smooth flesh of his shoulders, burning her palms into uncomfortable awareness of his masculinity. And then she felt the watchful gaze of his good eye focused intently upon her. She refused to meet the disturbing probe of that eye, choosing to concentrate on the firelight's mesmerizing red shadow dance over his muscled form. She found herself feeling the appalling need to slide her hands into the patch of black hair that curled snugly against his bronzed, taut chest.

"I'll have to see how much we need to adjust this," she said softly, feeling suddenly subdued by the broad expanse of naked male skin. "It might hurt, tightening it. Can you tell me where the pain is the worst?"

Keane wasn't sure he could at the moment. The pain from his face and his ribs seemed to have been drawn to a new and delicious discomfort in his loins. It was Tanya kneeling in front of him that was the cause of it; the blond hair dangling from beneath her brown hat in one long braid over her shoulder, shimmering like a rope of spun gold in the firelight's glow; the fullness of pink lips that had softened considerably while she cared for him; the upthrust of her bosom, only inches away, molded softly but fully against the tan cotton workshirt; the gentleness of her hands as they slid sensuously over his skin; and last but not least, the sky blue eyes that actually gazed at him for a fleeting moment with what had to be sympathy.

Did she know what she was doing to him? Was she doing it on purpose just to inflict more pain? He knew she didn't like him.

He lifted a hand and placed his fingers to the left side of his rib cage. "The worst of it is here."

He removed his hand when her fingertips began a tentative exploration of the spot. "There doesn't seem to be any misalignment," she announced. "Maybe they're only cracked. Can you breathe without pain?"

"Not completely, but moving is what hurts the most."

"I think the corset will help hold the ribs in place enough that it'll relieve the pain caused from movement."

"Go ahead then," he said. "Help me into it."

She tossed her hat aside to better see in the poor light, gathered the corset, and set to work loosening the stays up the back of it as much as she could.

He held his breath while she leaned closer. He felt her breasts brush against his chest, and he inhaled sharply. She mistook it for pain and apologized. She slid the corset around his back and drew it up in the front, having to put both arms around him to do so. He caught the perfumed scent of her hair and watched the way her slender fingers deftly hooked the front corset fastenings. He had the urge to place a kiss to the creamy length of her neck. As if she'd read his mind, she lifted her eyes to his. For just a moment, he thought his better judgment would fall into those blue pools and he would succumb to desire. But hastily, at the last possible second, he reached in and rescued himself.

"Hold the corset in place, Keane," she said softly with no trace of irritation this time and with her gaze holding his for a second more. "I'll need to tighten the stays from behind."

Little by little, she adjusted the stays, loosening and tightening according to his shape that was so different from Georgia's. When she was done, it wasn't a perfect fit and

never would be, but after she had drawn the garment as
snugly as she dared, she made the final tie.

"When you want to take it off, all you'll have to do is
release the front closures."

She knelt in front of him again to check the fit, sitting
back on her heels to survey the finished product. The compassion that had softened her face suddenly faded, and
Keane saw an unexpected gleam of devilment. She was staring at the ruching that stood straight up along the top of
the corset, tickling his man nipples. Slowly a giggle bubbled
up from her throat, and even her hand clamping over her
mouth wasn't quick enough to suppress it.

Keane's piercing gaze warned her that while she was
amused, he wasn't. He reached for his shirt so suddenly he
winced with pain. "Dang it, Tanya, don't laugh at me. It's
bad enough prancing around dressed in women's under-
wear."

She took the shirt from him. "Let me help you put this
back on," she offered in a rare moment of generosity, but
the smile still toyed with the corners of her lips.

Keane actually found himself not minding her ridicule
overly much. In all the years he'd known Tanya, he couldn't
remember a time when she hadn't had a smile for other
people. But never for him. He'd always thought of her as
attractive in a classic way, but the smile transformed her
into a beautiful goddess and gave his heart a lurch that
reverberated all the way to his loins.

She was greatly enjoying herself at his expense, but she
did help him put his vest back on. When it came to his
coat, however, Keane was afraid she'd notice the weight in
the pocket. The last thing he needed was for honorable and
dedicated Miss Darrow to get her hands on the Turquoise
Sun. He didn't need her railing on him again for his sleazy
ways. He'd won the necklace, fair and square. Those Utes
were just sore losers. Of course, Tanya would never believe
he hadn't cheated.

He rescued the coat from her. "It's okay, Tanya. It's plenty warm in here now."

She rose slowly to her feet, seemingly as reluctant to leave her position in front of him as he was to have her leave. He'd never seen her so mellow. If Swift Blade wasn't watching the entire procedure, he'd have been tempted to see if she was mellow enough to receive a kiss in gratitude. But perhaps it was a good thing Swift Blade was with them. Keane didn't need any more cracked ribs or black eyes, and he never doubted for a minute that Tanya wouldn't light into him with both feet if he so much as touched her in an intimate way. She really didn't like him. He wished he could change her mind about that, just for the space of a night. But apparently it was one of those wishes that he would just have to accept as never coming true. At least not in this lifetime.

The kiva's fire flickered over Swift Blade's young, handsome face and cast a blue sheen to the length of raven hair that fell down past his shoulders. The glow touched on uncertainty in the center of his black eyes, wavering there like candle flames.

"You don't have to tell me if you don't want to," Tanya said. "But if it's true that the Hopi believe they are direct descendants of the Anasazi, then your customs and beliefs would surely help me understand the people who once lived in these ruins. It would help me to better understand this kiva that I know only as a ceremonial chamber."

Tanya had elected to sleep in the kiva that first night, not only because she didn't want to hike back to camp a second time, but because she wanted to experience firsthand the way the cliff dwellers had lived. She had always felt that if she could experience something herself it would make her job of deciphering the vestiges of the past an easier and more rewarding job.

It hadn't taken much to convince Swift Blade to stay with her in the kiva. He seemed to be very comfortable here, preferring it to the tents on the river, as if he had lived here in the dwellings all his life. But he had informed her that women were forbidden in the kivas of his people unless they were participants in certain ceremonies, or unless they were given the "privilege" of plastering the kiva walls. And he could not share sleeping quarters with her because she was not his wife, nor a member of his clan. Keane had come to her rescue, saying that since he would be staying, too, the three of them would share the abandoned kiva as friends on a quest for answers.

"Consider Tanya just one of the boys," Keane had said, giving her a wicked grin. "That's the way she likes it."

Swift Blade had agreed to the arrangement then. But he had said that even though he could adjust to many of the peculiar ways of the white man, he honestly didn't think he could treat Tanya like one of the boys.

Tanya liked eighteen-year-old Swift Blade. Educated back East, but preferring his family's home on Black Mesa, he had the spirit of adventure she truly liked in the people who joined her digs. He'd signed on to help with the horses, but she had hired him mainly because he spoke four languages—Hopi, English, Ute, and Navajo. She had engaged him to teach her his language, as well as standard sign language, and often the two of them carried on entire conversations without using but a few words of English. The only problem she had with Swift Blade was keeping his stomach full. Built like a willow, he was always searching for something to eat. Tonight, however, he sat quietly for a change, his hunger abated after the large supper prepared by Zeke.

"I don't know if it is for me to tell you the origin of our people," Swift Blade continued solemnly. "It would be for one of the elders of our tribe to make that decision."

"But I have no elder from your tribe here," Tanya continued doggedly. "And if I'm to know about the Anasazi, you must help me."

He was terribly reluctant, evading her eyes to focus on the fire. Finally he rose lithely and moved to a spot opposite the fire pit. Down on hands and knees, he brushed aside debris and dirt until he had uncovered a small hole in the kiva floor. Its width was about three inches; its depth about four. He took a deep breath and began to speak with the typical shyness of youth. But soon he was telling his story like a master, and, like children at bedtime, Keane and Tanya leaned eagerly forward to listen.

"My people have followed the rules set down by the Creator since our emergence into the Fourth World, this world we now live in. This hole," he said, placing a brown finger to its edge, "is what we call the *sipapuni*. It is very important to the priests who conduct the ceremonial prayers. The hole is only a symbol. But to the Hopi, and probably the Anasazi before us, it represents the entrance to the underworld, the opening used by all mankind and all living creatures to come forth from the womb of Mother Earth and into this—the Fourth World of our existence." He held his arms out in an all-encompassing gesture that seemed to take in not just the kiva but the entire world. He continued. "In the beginning, our Father, the sun, and our Mother, the earth, made a union. All creatures from that union existed in a dark cave in the center of the earth. They moved from that dark cave to the world of twilight through the *sipapuni*, and from there to the world of dawn. The last world they entered was the present one, crossing a great body of water to get here.

"The three worlds before this one were each, in turn, destroyed when the people became wicked and evil and forgot to live by the laws of He who had created them. Only the people of good heart were allowed to leave each world before it was destroyed and journey into the next. The First

World was destroyed by fire; the Second by earthquakes and ice; the Third by water.

"The Fourth World was made differently than the three that had gone before. It gave man a choice, but it was not as easy as the previous worlds. This Fourth World offered barrenness as well as lushness; it offered a changing climate of heat and cold. Wherever the people chose to live would effect how they carried out the plan of Creation that had been laid out to them upon the Emergence. It would effect whether they would succeed in what the Creator had intended for them, or whether they would fail as the three worlds before them had failed.

"The Creator did not want the People to forget that he was their creator, but those people who went to the good lands with good soil, abundant rains, and warm weather soon became wealthy, fat, and lazy, and they forgot their Creator. They took credit for every aspect of their own existence, and they glorified themselves for the abundance in their lives and in their magnificent cities. As before, evil came and consumed them. Their minds were no longer focused on survival and on the Creator's purpose for them. Instead, they dwelled on things of pleasure. Ultimately the great civilizations destroyed themselves as the people weakened in mind and body. Others came and conquered them.

"But the Hopi were led here to this harsh and barren land and here they have stayed, because here they are never allowed to forget the power of the Creator and his supremacy over them. Here they have no choice but to depend on a rainfall that must be brought forth by prayer. Here the Hopi can never grow complacent, for to do so would mean death, not just to the individual, but to the tribe."

Swift Blade paused, staring into the mesmerizing flames of the fire. Forever solemn and contemplative, he watched the fire's shadow play on the kiva walls and upon his companions who listened to his story with rapt attention.

"Go on," Tanya urged. "Tell us more, Swift Blade."

The youth, as before, seemed reluctant, but finally allowed himself to drift back into the history of his people. "Many gods live in the underworld, and the *sipapuni* is not only the symbolic entrance to the Fourth World, but it is the entrance to the spirit world as well. Muyingwa, god of germination and growth, lives beneath the kivas. The prayers of our medicine men can reach Muyingwa and the other gods through the *sipapuni.* During ceremonies, the medicine men place offerings in the hole and around it. And, too, when a person dies, his spirit returns to Earth Mother through the *sipapuni.* It is the center of all our ceremonies, of our life, of our very existence.

"The people who came before, the Shadow People of these dwellings, prayed in this kiva where we sit, just as the Hopi does today in his kivas on Black Mesa. I can feel their presence even as I sit here. They called upon the power of their Creator for their every need. In this kiva they chanted their prayers, and the rains came and their crops grew—or failed, depending on whether they had conducted themselves properly in the eyes of the Creator."

Swift Blade returned to his blankets spread out against the kiva wall. Silent in thought now, moved by his own story and its significance in his life, he offered no more.

"But why did they leave here, Swift Blade?" Tanya persisted, wanting to know more.

He lifted his eyes to hers. "Because it was time," he said simply.

Tanya was about to interrogate him further when Keane interceded. "And now I'd say it's time we all slept. You'll have months to wring the answers from him, T. D. You don't need to do it all the first night."

Swift Blade seemed relieved to have been pardoned from further story-telling. Like Keane, he burrowed down on his blankets. In a matter of minutes, Tanya heard the Hopi breathing heavily in the full throes of sleep. She wondered how he could possibly feel like sleeping when his story had brought to life the essence of the supernatural forces that had dictated every move the Anasazi had made. And they had called those forces to work right here in this very kiva!

At last she sighed in resignation. It would all have to wait until tomorrow, and how she hated to wait until tomorrow when she was on the threshold of new and fascinating information!

She placed more sticks on the fire and settled back on her blankets. The flames made the interior of the old kiva cozy. It was no wonder Swift Blade had been more than eager to spend the night here. Occasionally the beams overhead creaked, and dust and bits of dirt trickled down, but Tanya felt that if the juniper timbers had held for centuries, they would hold for one more night.

She studied the interior of the kiva closer now. Swift Blade had told her that kiva meant "world below." A kiva was usually built cylindrical to represent a womb, and sunk deep into the ground which was the body of Mother Earth, for all men spring from the earth and are nourished by it. The ladder was symbolic of the emergence to the world above. The four masonry pillars that helped to hold up the roof represented the four successive worlds. Even the poles positioned crosswise in the roof had meaning. They symbolized the reeds that had been woven into the rafts on which the people crossed from the Third World to the present World.

The knowledge warmed her internally, but outwardly she was chilled by a draft of cold air coming from the wall behind her. The only thing on the other side of the kiva was the cave wall itself. Surely there could be no air penetration there. But it was as if the icy fingers of a cold wind had found a crevice and tunneled through to curl around every limb of her body. She ran a hand over the wall. On closer inspection she saw that the wall of the kiva had been built around a big rock, probably one that the people had not been able to move. It had been chiseled away and smoothed to blend in with the rest of the wall, but the mortar that had once formed a seal around the rock had all but fallen out.

"Cold, Tanya?" Keane whispered from across the kiva, snapping her attention from her discomfort to him. "Maybe you should come over here and we could share blankets."

The sound of her name, rather than a sobriquet, sounded almost caressing to her ear, and his suggestion was certainly tempting. Nonetheless, she wouldn't be undone by him and managed a glare as icy as the breeze skating up her back. "I'm perfectly fine where I am."

He lifted up on one elbow, wincing with pain, but trying nevertheless to fluff the coat he'd been using for a pillow. "Suit yourself. But I've spent a couple of nights in here and it's always chilly up against that wall. You might have to move closer to the fire if you don't want to catch a cold and come down sick. That could put a screeching halt to your excavations. Why, someone else might even have to take over your responsibilities."

Tanya's chest suddenly tightened. "If that should happen, don't think I'll appoint you to the position so you can walk off with everything in these ruins that will bring you a buck."

He settled back onto the pillow with another groan, but if she wasn't mistaken, one corner of his mouth managed to move beyond the swelling and into the semblance of a satisfied smile. "Power is taken, T. D.," he said. "Not given. And with old Miles as your head guide, who else but me could possibly be qualified to keep this expedition from turning into chaos? Besides, Prescott might appoint me to that position themselves since they've offered me a job as their director."

Tanya blanched. "I can't imagine anyone offering you an honest job. You didn't accept?"

He gave her a maddening grin. "No . . . not yet."

Burning with the very idea of Keane taking over her expedition, Tanya grabbed her blankets up tighter around her body, thinking that once he was asleep she would move closer to the fire.

He chuckled at her stubborn determination, then pulled his hat down over his face. "Well, good night, sweetheart. Let me know if you change your mind about sharing blankets."

It was with visions of brown-skinned priests dressed in ritualistic costumes, chanting and waving strange fetishes, that Tanya opened her eyes several hours later. The only light in the kiva was supplied by a few glowing embers. The images vanished, but the chanting lingered, seeming to come from some place far away and deeper than the corners of her imagination. Almost from inside the canyon walls themselves, as if the sound had somehow penetrated the rock centuries ago and remained through time, replaying like echoes just before nightfall.

And then the sound was gone.

She sat up, listening, expecting to hear it again. A disturbing dark wind rustled past her for the second time. She knew she hadn't imagined it either, because it touched the fire's embers and lifted them to red, glowing coals. She would have thought the breeze had come down through the main kiva, swirling down the short connecting tunnel and into the inner kiva. But the sparks were lifted by an air current that seemed to come from the opposite direction, from out of the canyon wall that formed one side of the kiva.

She tossed her blanket back and went to the fire, arranging more dry sticks carefully over the coals. They caught quickly and soon the flames were once again opening the darkness of the ceremonial chamber.

Settling back on her blankets, she pulled them snugly around her shoulders, glancing at Keane and thinking that it probably *would* be warmer nestled against his solid frame. And safer, too.

Sleep was gone, so she studied the still figures of her companions. She couldn't even be angry with Keane at the moment. No, she was actually thankful he was here with her in the kiva. He and Swift Blade offered security that she suddenly felt she needed. She didn't know why, but she couldn't shake the feeling that the chanting hadn't come from her mind, or a dream, but from a place faraway and yet near. It was almost as if she were hearing the drumbeats of another world that existed just beyond her reach, separated from her by nothing more than the thin, but unbreachable, barrier of time.

Four

Keane struggled out of the kiva the next day and allowed a few of the muscle-bound shovel hands to load him onto a stretcher made of ropes, blankets, and green aspen poles. Everyone had ventured up to the ruins that morning to get their first look at where they'd be working for the next three months, and to see what had happened to Keane. Most of them already knew him from other digs, or at least knew *of* him. Their surprised reaction to his appearance was expected, and they bombarded him with questions about what happened.

"Oh, I just tried to climb up along that wall over there and some rock crumbled out from under me." He glanced at Tanya, giving her the look that said he hoped she'd keep his secret. She did.

The college girls clustered around him, offering sympathy and assistance. All Tanya offered was a look of disdain. "Get him back to camp, boys," she said. "I'd like to get started on this dig before sundown."

"He needs someone to look after him," Georgia said, her voice more high-pitched and grating than usual. She laid a hand possessively on his shoulder, as if she might have a special claim to him simply because it was her corset he was wearing.

Tanya secretly admitted to more than just annoyance at Georgia's behavior, but actually to a twinge of jealousy. "That won't be necessary," she replied, effectively keeping her feelings hidden. "Keane insisted that he didn't want his injuries to interfere with the work we have ahead of us. He knows I need every one of you on the job. Rest assured, if he needs anything, Miles or Zeke will be in camp to assist him."

Several of the female students continued to fawn over him all the way back to camp and until the shovel hands lowered him to the shade of somebody's tent flap. Ultimately they had to leave his side, but not before making sure he had two full canteens of water nearby, a pillow, some books, and anything else they thought he might need in their absence.

With growing irritation, Tanya watched their schoolgirl silliness out of the corner of her eye while preparing her own pack for the day of work ahead. They'd probably be tittering all day long now over Keane, and she'd be lucky to get them to focus on anything. They'd be careless, possibly damaging anything they unearthed. She wondered why women couldn't see through Keane's exterior charm to the true philanderer beneath. Any one of them could conquer him for a night—she could do that herself—but didn't they know a stallion would never be happy with just one mare?

She hoisted her pack onto her back, straightened her hat, and started for the ruins, having to walk right past Keane's spot of shade to do so. She found her feet slowing until they had stopped completely in front of him. She knew she should walk on to keep from appearing as giddy over him as the other women had, but she found herself lowering to her haunches next to him anyway, balancing on the balls of her feet while giving his bruised face a more thorough scrutiny in the light of day. If anything, it looked worse than it had in the shadows of the kiva last night.

A knot of worry formed inside her mind again. She would hate to see complications set in when they were so far from town. But she kept these thoughts to herself. He might misconstrue her compassion for personal feelings of a deeper nature.

"With all this feminine attention, Keane, you should recover quicker than I originally thought," she gibed. "You might even be able to leave by the end of the week. Won't that be nice?"

He looked at her with his good eye, then placed his fingertip against her chin. The caressing contact sent a jolt of weakness somersaulting through her all the way to her toes, but she would die before she would let him know it.

He managed a half-smile—the swollen half wouldn't move. Likewise, his tone was half serious, half insouciant. "Beneath it all I know you love me, Tanya. And I think you would really hate to see me go. Now, isn't that true?"

"Humph." She pushed to her full height of five-foot-seven. "I think I'll have Zeke check you for delirium."

"Zeke?" A chuckle came from his throat, but he was careful not to part his lips too much. "He's so danged brittle that if that scowl on his face turned to a smile he'd probably fall apart like one of your precious potsherds. And Miles. If he moved any slower it would take him 'til sundown to get his socks on. Are you sure you can't spare one of those girls?" He glanced to where they were just shrugging on their packs and pulling on hats to protect their faces from the sun.

Tanya followed his gaze to the girls dressed in an array of divided riding skirts and white shirtwaists that wouldn't remain white for long. "No. I really can't, Keane. You know that. Zeke and Miles are all right. You just need to get to know them. They were recommended by Richard Wetherill. They both used to be cowboys around here."

"That explains why Zeke doesn't look as if he's enjoying being a cook."

"Zeke would complain no matter what he did."

"Well, I think I'm running a fever. Why don't you check

me yourself before you leave? All you'd have to do is lay your hand on my forehead to see how hot I am."

Tanya gave him a long, hard scrutiny. The man *never* gave up. She was beginning to think she'd have to bed him just to get him to lose interest and leave her alone. But even one night with him could result in ramifications that might last a lifetime. No, this particular problem didn't have a solution quite so simple.

Finally she glanced at the sun, then back to him. "I hate to be the one to break the news to you, sugar, but you're probably going to get a lot hotter before the day's over." She repositioned her pack and took a step or two away before stopping again and glancing over her shoulder at him. "Oh, by the way, do you have your gun handy? Now that you're out in the open, those Utes might come back and finish what they started."

He shifted, trying to find a more comfortable position. Pain creased his face. "You almost sound as if you'd like to see that happen."

Tanya spared a sardonic smile. "Not at all, Keane. If they kill you, I'd have to ask Miles to dig a hole for you. And, well . . . there might be nothing left of you by the time he gets that done."

"At least you'd try, T. D. I'd have been afraid you might just feed me to the scavengers."

"That *is* a thought."

Having his fill of her barbs, he pulled his hat down over his face, attempting to end the conversation.

Amused that she was getting to him, she said, "I'll have Swift Blade retrieve your horse and gear from its hiding place and bring them to camp."

"Thanks." The word was muffled from beneath his hat and didn't sound entirely sincere. "Have a good day, sweetheart. Dig up a few old bones for me, would you?"

"I'll save you the female ones."

He lifted his hat and glared. Laughing, she left for the ruins.

Tanya spent the first few days establishing a routine and the procedures she wanted followed for keeping a record of every item found. Involved in this procedure was mapping of the area, sketches, photographs, tagging, and listing each item. The artifacts were carefully spread out in a cleared spot where they would later be bundled for the long haul back to civilization and further study to determine their age.

When she had the students squared away, she began spending time in the kiva where she'd first found Keane, and where she'd heard the chanting that first night. In the quiet of the small, inner kiva, she listened again. She lingered each evening after the students had returned to camp, until darkness fell. And each day, just at dark, she once again heard that haunting, distant sound that seemed so close and yet so faraway. She said nothing to anyone, though, because she didn't want them to think she was crazy. Nor did she want to frighten some of the Hopis who might consider the chanting a bad omen and then leave the expedition.

On the fifth day, Keane crawled out of the shade of the tent flap and made his way to the ruins. He had changed into his work clothes—khakis and tall, brown boots worn outside his pants in the manner of cavalrymen. The holster and revolver he wore on his hip while traveling had been replaced with a scabbard and Bowie knife.

He was obviously still in pain, but tired of his convalescence. It didn't surprise Tanya to see him out and about. She figured curiosity was one of the driving forces behind his actions—that and greed. He was probably afraid all the good stuff would be gone if he tarried too long.

For the week after that she tried to keep an eye on him.

So far he'd taken nothing that she knew of, but she didn't doubt he might hide his finds and come back for them later.

Nearly two weeks after his accident, she found him in the very back part of the cave, behind the dwellings. He was kneeling, with a lantern sitting next to him that cast an oval light over the mounds of dirt. Like the others he was carefully prodding and brushing dirt from something. Here the cave's overhanging rock roof was too low for dwellings, too low to stand up in. So, bending from the waist, she eased her way into the tight quarters where he was. His broad-shouldered presence seemed to make the area smaller than normal.

He heard her approach and flashed her a smile overflowing with excitement. "How did you know I was wishing you would show up, T. D.? I think we'll find some good things back here. I've already found something just under this first layer of dirt. From what I can tell, this area was the garbage dump."

She knelt next to him. "Isn't it just like you to sniff out the garbage dump."

"A good archaeologist knows where the treasures are, sweetheart."

"It looks as if this was the roosting place for some chickens or something. Look at the splotches on the rocks."

"Turkey dung. They kept turkeys. See, here's a feather."

He gave it to her for examination. "From the mess on the rocks, it looks like the turkeys might have kept them," she replied. "Anyway, I'm going back out to check on the students. *I'll* keep the feather."

"Everything I find is yours. You know that."

"Yeah. Right."

He grinned at her knowing smirk and went back to his vigilant search. He was so engrossed in the garbage dump, it worried her. What did he hope to find back here? She would have to keep a close eye on him indeed.

She returned to sunlight, wondering if she was making

a mistake by telling him he would have to leave soon. He was good. He had honed in on the location of the garbage dump immediately, knowing it would be the right place to start unearthing the bulk of the items the Anasazi had left behind. She should have gone there first herself, but the kiva had kept pulling her back. Just as it did now.

She descended the ladder into the quiet interior, then crawled through the short tunnel that connected it to the inner kiva. Swift Blade had explained to her that it wasn't unusual for kivas to be connected by tunnels. It was all part of the Anasazi rituals and used for theatrical purposes during ceremonies.

The chanting she'd heard here, and here alone, unnerved her. But her curiosity, and her desire for a logical explanation, drove her beyond her initial fear.

She settled herself cross-legged on the earthen floor, leaned her head back against the wall, and closed her eyes. She must have sat there for over an hour, focusing her thoughts on the room and its essence. Then, just at nightfall, the chanting came again. Distantly at first, then louder as it had done the times before. But it never reached beyond a certain level in volume and always seemed to remain just beyond the edge of her mind, tenuous and impossible to locate or to grasp.

"T. D., there you are. We've found the most incredible thing! You've got to come and see."

Keane's emergence from the tunnel, followed by Swift Blade pushing a lantern in front of him, startled her from her meditation. She had been so entranced by the chanting that she hadn't even heard them enter the outer kiva. She put her hand over her heart now to try and ease the sudden burst of frightened thumping.

"You two nearly scared me into the next life. Don't sneak up on me like that again."

Keane settled on his haunches next to her. His grin deepened with that distinct trace of flirtation she had come to expect. "We didn't sneak up on you," he said. "But whatever you were dreaming about must have been good. Want to let us in on it?"

Tanya didn't particularly want them to know what kept calling her back to this kiva that lay shadowed by the spine of the great rock amphitheater. The idea of chanting sounded silly anyway now that they were here and Keane's close proximity shifted the focus of her attention.

She turned the question back around to him. "You said you found something incredible? What was it?"

The excitement in his eyes made them gleam as pure and bright as polished emeralds. "I found a body in that garbage dump," he said. "Three of the students are working at exhuming it. But it's not just a bunch of bones, T. D. It's a mummy, and it's in practically perfect condition from what we can see so far. The hair's intact, the skin, even the clothing hasn't rotted completely away. It looks like an old man. And gauged by what was found in the hole with him, he was an important old man."

Tanya's heart began to thump wildly. This was the sort of thing that brought an archaeologist respect and acclaim. It was just what she needed to step out of her father's shadow.

She leaped to her feet and headed for the tunnel, but Keane caught her arm. "The mummy can wait for a few more minutes, sweetheart. You never did say why you've been spending so much time down here. Do you really prefer this dark, dusty old hole to the sunshine of my company?"

She sighed. The man was impossible. But would he be open-minded enough to take into her confidence on the matter of the chanting? She already knew how Swift Blade would react.

"Oh, I've just been digging around in here."

Keane glanced at the floor. It had not been disturbed by anything but their feet. He couldn't be fooled that easily and he let her know it with the sardonic tone in his voice. "You're making a lot of progress, I see."

"Well, I dig a little, then cover up the holes," she replied lamely.

"Uh-huh. And those Utes out there beyond the mesa don't want me dead."

After a few moments of consideration and glancing back and forth between the two, she finally said. "All right, I'll tell you why I've been here, if you promise not to laugh at me, or to send me to an asylum for crazy people."

She clearly had their attention and curiosity. They both told her to proceed. She took a deep breath for courage. "I've been down here because I keep hearing something in this kiva. Noises. Noises that sound like . . . like chanting of some sort."

Swift Blade suddenly took a step back toward the tunnel, his black eyes bursting with fear. Afraid he'd cut and run, Keane said, "I didn't hear anything. How about you, Swift Blade?"

The Hopi shook his head and took another step backward. "Maybe it is ghosts of the Old Ones. Maybe they do not want us here."

"You don't really believe that stuff, do you?" Keane said, grinning at the young man. "It was just the wind. You've heard the songs it makes when it whistles through barbed wire, haven't you? What's to say it doesn't make similar noises when it infiltrates tunnels and kivas and cracks in rock walls?"

Swift Blade wasn't convinced. Neither was Tanya. Perhaps it was just her imagination working overtime, but she could clearly hear the monotone syllables of the chant, the thump of drums, the clatter of rattles. Wind couldn't have produced that sound. But to keep Keane from thinking she was crazy, and to keep Swift Blade from fleeing like a man with wolves at his heels, she said, "There seems to be a crack in the wall over there, around that boulder. So I suppose the wind could be responsible."

Keane, ducking his head in the low-roofed kiva, moved to the boulder and the crack. "There's a definite draft in here. I wonder if there's some sort of room behind this kiva. Maybe a secret place where the valuable items were kept from marauding enemy tribes. Let's see if we can find out where the draft is coming from. Would you bring the lantern closer, Swift Blade?"

Apprehension was clearly written on Swift Blade's young, handsome face. It didn't take a wizard to see that he would have preferred leaving the kiva entirely. Tanya figured pride was the only thing that kept him with them.

"What do you make of this, Swift Blade?" Keane insisted on drawing him into the investigation. "You're the expert on kiva construction. Could there be a room behind here?"

"It is not likely." Swift Blade put his hand next to Keane's over the crack, but drew it back as sharply as if he'd touched fire. After a second of hesitation, he slowly extended it again to the crack. "I do not understand this. The canyon wall wherein these dwellings were built is clearly solid rock. Because of that, the kivas have been constructed differently than originally designed. Normally, a kiva is dug into the ground and the roof covered over to ground level. But here, because of the rock base, no holes can be dug. To compensate, the people assembled the rock walls and brought the plaza up level with the kiva roof, giving the appearance that the kiva was beneath the ground and thus satisfying the required symbolism. This boulder indicates that this wall of the kiva is made, at least partially, of the cave's granite wall itself. Still, I feel the draft. But where could it be coming from?"

Keane removed his Bowie and began chipping the mortar and plaster away from the boulder. It had apparently been put there to blend the rock into the rest of the wall. As he dug, a large crack began to appear, and then small stones and finally larger rocks began to fall out with the mortar. To Tanya, the arrangement looked to be that of Mother Nature, not man. But Keane continued on.

"There's a hole here behind these rocks," he announced a moment later. "The draft is stronger now. Come on, Swift Blade. Help me get this stuff out so we can see what's hidden back here."

Swift Blade, still skeptical that they were doing the right thing, removed the big hunting knife from his belt scabbard and squatted next to Keane. Soon their efforts revealed a hole a foot wide. Behind it were more rocks.

"It's nothing, Keane," Tanya said. "Just an irregularity in the rocks, possibly a small cave back in there."

Keane had returned the knife to his scabbard and used his hands now to remove the rocks. The outer hole became wide enough for a man's shoulders. "I want to see where it goes. There might be something really valuable in here."

"If there is, it belongs to the expedition."

"I know, I know," he added impatiently.

By now he was into the hole up past his shoulders. If his ribs hurt he was ignoring the pain in his enthusiasm to find the source of the mystery wind. Debris came spitting out behind him as he crawled in up to his waist. Then quickly he pushed himself back out.

"That's the last of the rocks and sticks," he said. "There's nothing now but air, or maybe another tunnel. Only this one doesn't look man-made. I'm going in. Give me the lantern."

"Do you think that's safe?" Tanya's voice rose with alarm.

"Maybe not, but we'll never know what's in there if we don't investigate. You know me; I've never been any good at resisting dangling carrots."

"I've never known a jackass who could."

Accustomed to her gibes, he merely returned her smile.

"And I've never known you to pass up an opportunity, T. D."

Swift Blade overlooked their bickering, having come to accept it as everyone else had. "There could be snakes," he reminded them nervously. "Maybe even a whole den of them."

That gave Keane a moment's pause, but ultimately he reached for the lantern anyway. "No, I'll bet it's too cold in there for snakes."

Pushing the lantern ahead of him, he eased his body back into the hole that appeared barely large enough to accommodate him. He swore a few times as they watched his legs vanish from sight. Tanya peered into the hole after him. "Is something wrong?"

"Just my ribs. It's making this one hell of a painful exploration."

"Maybe you should wait."

There was no response. He burrowed himself farther and farther from sight. Then the light began to fade and finally all she saw was darkness.

"Keane? Are you all right?"

His voice came back, quite distant now. "Yes! The tunnel just took a slight curve and it's getting bigger."

Tanya decided he was completely crazy to be in there. What if he got stuck? Or the rock collapsed? Or he ran into that den of snakes? She'd been in some uncomfortable situations and tight places during her expeditions with her father, and she had never been one to back down to a challenge. But between Swift Blade's story about the *sipapuni,* and the chanting she'd been hearing, she was left with a very eerie feeling about this tunnel.

"Keane?" She called his name several times. No answer.

"He must be out of earshot," Swift Blade said, his young brow creased with worry.

"He's a fool," Tanya muttered, her brow knotting with worry.

Swift Blade gave a slight shake of his head. "Maybe, but he is very brave."

"He's going to get himself killed. What could this tunnel have been used for anyway?"

"I do not know, Miss Darrow. From the way it looks, I would say the Anasazi did not even know it was here."

"Tanya! Swift Blade!" Came Keane's excited voice from far off. "You've got to see this!"

They exchanged dubious glances, neither wanting to see anything if they had to get to it via the tunnel.

The light appeared again and behind it came Keane, pulling himself toward them on his forearms. "Come on. It's not bad in here, and it widens up right around the bend. You won't believe this!"

Tanya decided she had no choice if she wanted to ensure that whatever was at the other end of the passageway ended up in her hands and not in Keane Trevalyan's pockets. But she had never liked tight, confining spaces.

She finally tugged her hat down tighter on her head, took a deep breath to steady her nerves, and climbed into the hole. It wasn't as tight a fit for her as it had been for Keane, but she still had to pull herself along on her forearms, inch by difficult inch. Pebbles dug through her long-sleeved shirt into her forearms and gouged her elbows and knees. To her surprise, Swift Blade came behind her, fearful, but bit by the curiosity bug.

She staved off the suffocating encroachment of claustrophobia, concentrating instead on the end of the tunnel and trying not to think she would have to go back the way she'd come. At the bend, Keane backed up, taking the lantern with him, inching his way backward. As he'd promised, the tunnel widened. He sat up, pushed his hat to the back of his head, and waited for them to join him in a little pocket big enough for all three of them to sit up in.

Still wearing his grin of excitement, he proceeded to lead the way on hands and knees, lantern in hand for the next twenty feet or so. The smell of wet earth touched Tanya's nostrils. Completely intrigued now, she crawled quickly after him, keeping his narrow buttocks in full view at all times. He finally came to a ledge in the tunnel that dropped down to another level three feet below. When his feet touched bottom, he was standing straight up. He held out a hand for Tanya and held the light for Swift Blade.

They emerged from the tunnel onto a new level of rock. The lantern light did not reach far into the darkness. Still, Tanya sensed they were no longer in a confining space, but one of huge proportions.

Keane led the way, and they walked on either side of him. The light began to move across an eerie landscape of stalactites, stalagmites, even a subterranean pool where water from somewhere overhead dripped into it in a slow, steady rhythm. The dark ceiling of the cavern rose beyond the light, and the rock walls she felt surrounding them were likewise lost to darkness.

Then the light reflected off an object about twenty feet away—a mesmerizing, black and shiny "something" that pulled them deeper into the cave. When they stopped a few feet from it, they recognized it as a tall and elegant vase, sitting on a table of stone. It was not made of glass or any substance they recognized, but of some material that appeared as black and slick as oil, as shiny as glass, and as sturdy as steel. Inside the vase, an obsidian mirror stood on its slender, carved handle of teakwood. The two objects were an odd contrast to each other. The mirror was ancient, and yet the vase looked almost . . . futuristic.

Keane and Tanya reached for the mirror's handle simultaneously and neither was about to relinquish it. Together they lifted it free of the vase.

"It belongs to my expedition, Keane."

"This cave isn't part of your dig, Tanya. This cave is my discovery."

"You found it only because I said I heard chanting and felt a cool breeze in the kiva. So unhand it."

"Not on your life, sweetheart."

Swift Blade, glancing about nervously, stepped between them. "You both must put it back. I do not have a good feeling about our being in this place. I fear this cavern is the underground dwelling of the gods. The mirror surely is an instrument of great power. It might even belong to Great Bear."

"And who is Great Bear?" Keane wanted to know.

Swift Blade licked his lips, peering again over his shoulder into the dark reaches of the cavern beyond the glow of the feeble lamplight. "Great Bear is a shape-changing wizard who sees all in his obsidian mirror. He rules the night sky, and great power lies in his mirror. The legends of the Great Bear's existence originated among the Aztlans. It is not really part of the Hopi beliefs, but tales of it are sometimes still told around campfires. The Aztlans came from this area. They were bands of people who left the villages and went south, seeking a richer life. After hundreds of years they gained numbers and strength and eventually became the most powerful people in what is now Mexico. Their legend of the Great Bear says the mirror is buried in a cave far to the north, but no one has ever found it."

Keane and Tanya considered the explanation. Then Keane found what he felt was a plausible explanation that would allow him to proceed with his own plans. "Well, I don't believe in legends. Besides, if the Great Bear rules the night sky, he wouldn't have buried his mirror underground where he couldn't see anything but darkness."

Swift Blade placed a hand on the mirror's long, graceful handle. "Please, let me put the mirror back. You must believe me. I know the powers that exist in the worlds that lie beyond our knowledge and experience."

Suddenly a cold wind rushed over them from the impenetrable darkness beyond the light, blowing out the lantern in its flight to an unknown and unseen destination. The trio's only connection to each other in the cimmerian surroundings were their hands on the mirror's handle, and they clung to it in that moment of perplexing disorientation.

A feeling of suspension swirled down around Tanya, leaving her with a strange sense of separation from the earth and everything on it. The feeling was even more frightening than the darkness. Once again she heard the chanting on the other side of her mind, just beyond physical grasp.

"Keane? Swift Blade?" she whispered urgently. "Do you hear it now? The chanting?"

The Hopi's answer came swiftly. "Yes. I hear it."

Keane's response was slower, perplexed but affirmative.

Then as swiftly as it had swirled down upon them, the eerie moment passed. Tanya's head cleared, and she wondered if the others had felt that peculiar interruption in time and space.

"I'm going to let go of the mirror to get a match," Keane said. "Make sure you have it."

"I do." Both she and Swift Blade replied.

Keane fumbled in his pocket and shortly a scraping noise brought forth a flame. He relit the lantern, and everything in its faint yellow glow looked normal and felt normal again. Tanya relinquished the mirror to Swift Blade and reverently he returned it to its place inside the mysterious black vase.

"I think we'd better get more light and maybe some jackets before we explore any further," Keane suggested.

"You should not take these objects from here," Swift Blade insisted, and the fear in his eyes was enough to make them wonder if they should heed his warning. "Something could happen. They could be part of an ancient curse."

Both Keane and Tanya had been around enough different societies to know that many still took curses seriously. Many even still performed acts of witchcraft that defied scholars to dispute their power. But beyond common respect, neither took the supernatural seriously. The bottom line was that they both wanted the vase and mirror in their possession, and each would do whatever it took to accomplish that goal.

"We'll discuss it tomorrow," Tanya said, starting for the tunnel. "But they're both too valuable to leave here."

Swift Blade quickly followed her, more than eager to leave the subterranean cave. Keane was slower, glancing back at the mirror and the vase. Tanya knew that if he could sneak it out without her interference, he'd be gone like the wind.

At the tunnel entrance she stopped, forgetting about Keane's likely attempts to make off with the discoveries. She could hear the chanting again. This time it was so tangible it sent a chill clear to her toes.

"I can hear it again," she whispered, bemused. "It's louder and closer than before. It doesn't seem to be just in my head anymore."

"It isn't in your head," Swift Blade replied in a voice as serious as death. Newfound fear lit his black eyes. "I hear it, too, Miss Darrow. It seems to be at the end of the tunnel, back in the kiva. And I recognize the chant. It is a plea to the gods for rain. Is this what you have been hearing all along?"

Tanya nodded.

"Come on, you two," Keane cut in impatiently. "It's only the other Hopi guides putting on a performance for the students, or something like that. Don't make mountains out of molehills."

"The other guides are not qualified to summon the gods for rain," Swift Blade countered. "Only the high priests are granted such power. If they had wanted to put on a performance, they would never have chosen such a sacred, and private, ritual."

Keane shrugged. "I'm sure there's an explanation for it."

Tanya and Swift Blade exchanged glances, unable to

shake the eerie feeling that something was definitely amiss, but they said no more about it and followed Keane back into the tunnel. The chanting grew closer all the while. Tanya was even able to decipher a few of the words that were being sung, thanks to the weeks of Swift Blade's tutoring in the Hopi language.

Just before they reached the entrance to the kiva, Keane stopped short. "Now, how in the hell did this happen?"

"What?" Tanya worriedly asked from behind him.

"The tunnel's closed up. I'm going to have to clear these rocks out of the way again. They must have fallen in behind us. Maybe there was a little tremor in the earth, something that caused this to happen at the same time that the lantern was blown out."

Tanya suddenly felt very trapped. An invisible weight pressed down on her lungs and she found it difficult to breathe. What if the rest of the tunnel caved in before they got out?

Keane handed rocks back to her and she in turn handed them to Swift Blade, who set them out of the way in the tunnel behind him. The quarters were tight and the going slow. Tanya had to admire Keane for keeping his cool despite a sheen of sweat that appeared on his face. His ribs had to hurt, too, but he made no complaints.

"I think I can push the rest of it into the kiva," he said.

Tanya noticed then how deathly silent the passageway had become. The chanting had stopped. Only the scraping and falling of the rocks being cleared from the passage could be heard.

"We're through," Keane announced matter-of-factly.

He wiggled free of the tunnel with Tanya and Swift Blade close behind, all coming out into the inner kiva on their hands and knees, face down. When they got to their feet, they found they weren't alone. A fire burned brightly in the kiva's center, and sitting slump-shouldered on the seating ledge around the altar were six Indians. They were not the young Hopis who had come with them on the expedition, but old men with thin chests and deep-sunk eyes filled with fear. Indians attired in nothing but breechcloths, paint, feathers, and primitive jewelry.

Suddenly the old men fell to their knees, muttering a frenzy of indecipherable words that sounded very much like frantic prayers.

Tanya's mouth felt as dry as the mesa soil after a fourteen-year drought, and her heart threatened to pound a hole all the way through her chest. The look of confusion on Keane's face, and the utter shock on Swift Blade's, did nothing to allay her fears.

"I don't suppose these fellows are friends of either one of you?" she asked.

They shook their heads simultaneously.

"Well, whoever they are," she continued as nonchalantly as she could, "I hope they're *somebody's* friends. Because if they aren't, we could be in big trouble."

Five

Keane never took his eyes from the Indians, still down on their knees, bowing fervently before them. His mind went through some rapid deductions and conclusions of its own and suddenly came up with a plausible explanation. He visibly relaxed and gave Tanya a strained smile that held absolutely no humor.

"Don't play the innocent with me, T. D. You did all this to see if you could scare me off your dig, didn't you? You probably knew that tunnel was there all along, and all you had to do was toss me a bone and I'd grab it. Of all the stupid things . . . chanting! And you almost had me believing you. Now level with me. Who are these adoring gents and how much did you have to pay them to dress up and prance around in some beads and breechcloths and kick up dust?"

She stared at him, looking genuinely stupefied. "I had no idea we were going to find that tunnel, Keane. And I have no idea who these men are. I surely didn't pay them good money to pull a prank on you."

His eyebrows dove together in hard scrutiny of his fair-haired associate while he debated whether to believe her. He was still considering it a moment later when her eyes suddenly popped open to the size of teacup platters.

"Oh, my God. I hope they haven't massacred my field crew."

A few of the Indians were now sneaking peeks at the

three intruders between their bouts of frantic mutterings. They seemed transfixed with Tanya, staring at her with unconcealed awe as if she were an angel just stepped down from Heaven. Keane vaguely wondered why they would do that, unless it was all part of the nasty prank, and he still wasn't convinced it wasn't one. But drawing attention to herself was not Tanya's nature. She seemed totally ignorant of her own beauty, and he sincerely doubted she would purposefully make herself the center of some primitive adoration for the sake of a joke.

"They seem to speak Hopi," she said. "Let's see if we can communicate with them."

"It *is* Hopi, Miss Darrow—" Swift Blade began.

"How convenient," Keane cut in, folding his arms across his chest and taking on a bored, arrogant stance. "Let's see if we can come up with some more coincidences."

Swift Blade ignored his flippant interruption. "The language is Hopi, but sounds somewhat different . . . as if it might be a very old form of it. These people are different, too, from those who come from Black Mesa. Their attire, their ornaments . . . it all looks very crude, very ancient. Almost as if they stepped out of the past. And I wonder why they would be out here in this land that now belongs to the Utes."

The Indians had finally ceased their praying and had lifted their heads to stare at the three intruders who were exchanging conjectures in a language they obviously did not understand. The look in their eyes seemed to translate into a belief that they could be struck down by lightning at any second.

Swift Blade spoke again. "I will tell them we are here in peace, and I'll ask them where they came from and what they call themselves."

Keane studied Swift Blade's actions closely, expecting to see through the joke, but the young Hopi's black eyes surprisingly reflected true fear and apprehension. It was unsettling, and Keane found it difficult to retain his forced air of indifference.

The Indians responded to Swift Blade's questions only with blank stares. Swift Blade repeated the questions, embellishing on them with more words and hand signs. Tanya and Keane found that even with their limited knowledge of the language, they were able to follow the exchange somewhat.

Finally the old man with hair the color of iron, and who easily looked to be a century old, struggled stiffly to his feet. He was the most adorned of the kiva's occupants with fancy necklaces and bracelets, and with feathers of every kind tied into his hair. His face resembled the runnels of the mesa itself and only a half dozen of his teeth remained. With his bony knees trembling, he bowed respectfully. Fear that struck Keane as genuine flickered in his jet black eyes. He began to speak in an unusually strong voice for someone so old, and soon his uncertainty was replaced with confidence. He gestured slowly and precisely with gnarled, brown hands, and he pointed once to himself with the air of great pride. His head was fully elevated now, accentuating a strong, square chin that jutted resolutely. His tone and his attitude revealed a great deference towards the new arrivals. Although Keane had never seen him before, there was still something disturbingly familiar about him.

At the conclusion of the interchange, Swift Blade translated again. "His name is Ten-Moon, and he is the high priest among the Red Sand People. He is a *túhikya,* a medicine man. He knows we come in peace for it was he who brought us here from the world of the gods. There is much power in his songs, he says."

"The chanting I've been hearing has been coming from him?" Tanya asked, perplexed. "Why did they come here to these ruins? Have they been camped near here, maybe up on the mesa? Did they see my field crew when they came into the kiva?"

Swift Blade relayed the questions, but the old man looked extremely perplexed this time, shook his head, and began to intone a longer monologue than the one before.

At his completion, uncertainty deepened in Swift Blade's eyes. "He says there is no one here but his people. And there hasn't been for many, many months, since the last attack by the People of the North. He does not understand what I mean by ruins. He says he has lived here in this village all his life with his people."

"But the village is in ruins."

"It was when we left it, Miss Darrow, but somehow I think we have not returned to the place we left."

"What do you mean?" Tanya asked guardedly.

"I have no explanation for my feelings," he replied. "But the old man also says he is very honored that the gods have sent Kachina People again. They have not walked among the mortals for centuries now, and he is happy we will be able to assist in bringing the rain they so desperately need."

"Kachinas? Rain?" A distinct uneasiness shivered down Tanya's spine.

Swift Blade nodded. "His prayers successfully reached to the gods through the *sipapuni,* the symbolic Place of Emergence. Because we came from inside the mountain, they believe we are Kachina People, intermediaries who deliver the people's prayers to the gods. Kachinas are the spirits of plant, animal, bird, mineral, and human entities, of the stars and clouds and every invisible force of life.

"Upon the Emergence into this Fourth World, spirits from other planets and stars took human form and lived here on the earth with the people, and they danced in the villages and brought rain. After the siege of Palátkwapi, the Red City of the South, where they saved the clans from a siege by the evil Spider Clan, they did not continue with the clans on their migrations, but retreated to a high mountain that we know as San Francisco Mountain, southwest of Oraibi, to await their messages of need.

"Apparently we have arrived shortly after the tribe's usual Niman Kachina ceremonies, but those ceremonies brought no rain, probably because of the evil power of witches working against them. So Ten-Moon and the high priests were making a private plea to the gods when we appeared."

Tanya could find no words; she could only stare in utter disbelief. There was much Swift Blade was going to have to explain, but of course he couldn't do it now.

Keane merely shifted his weight from one leg to the other, growing weary of the charade. He did notice in that instant, however, with an odd flash of realization, that his ribs no longer pained him. Nevertheless, he shrugged his shoulders with an air of indifference and played along with the massive joke being played on him.

"If they think we're messengers of the gods, then it would be very rude of us—possibly even dangerous—not to accept their hospitality for a few days," Keane said. "Maybe we could even leave here with something more substantial than some broken potsherds."

Tanya handed Keane a healthy dose of sarcasm. "Unless you know how to do a rain dance, sugar, I think you'd better be thinking of preserving your life instead of filling your pockets with treasures."

He shrugged. "Never pass up an opportunity. That's my motto. As for making rain, we'll get away before they start demanding we perform miracles."

"And where will we go? I agree with Swift Blade. We're in the same kiva that we left from . . . and yet we're not. Something's happened that I don't understand, but—"

"It *is* the same kiva," Keane replied stubbornly, losing patience with the entire scenario. "And I'll prove it to you by heading up that ladder. I'm sure once I'm up there, I'll find your field crew ready to make me a laughingstock. But they'll find out quick enough that their little prank didn't work."

"I'm telling you, Keane, this isn't a joke. Something's terribly wrong here."

"Oh, enough, Tanya! You're trying to make it look like we've gone back in time to the age of Anasazi—or something equally stupid. Well, have your little laugh. I'm going back to camp and pack my stuff. I'll be out of here at first light, and you'll have your precious dig all to yourself."

With head down to keep from bumping it on the low roof, Keane moved past the Indians and into the connecting tunnel. They all stared after his sudden departure with dismay and confusion, then simultaneously they scrambled to their feet to follow him like lemmings after their leader. At a sharp word from Ten-Moon, they came to attention again and backed away from the tunnel. Ten-Moon motioned for Tanya and Swift Blade to go first. Tanya was more than anxious to follow Keane. Never before in her life had she been so desperate to be near him.

The three of them came out of the kiva to a dark plaza lit by campfires and primitive torches. Keane had honestly expected to see the field crew, laughing at the joke they'd played on him. But as Ten-Moon had said, they were not there. What he saw was a stately stone complex filling the huge rock cavern where just earlier in the day there had been nothing but rubble, abandonment, and silence.

It was the same cavern; the same set of cliff dwellings. But now they housed not eager young university students and indifferent shovel hands, but hundreds of scantily clothed, dark-skinned, black-haired people acting as if they truly belonged there. As a few of those people saw him and Tanya and Swift Blade, they stopped their work, whispered to others, until one by one everyone was moving toward them with caution and awe.

Keane gave a quick glance down into the canyon, searching again for the campfires and kerosene lamps of the field crew. He saw only fathomless darkness.

"I guess you weren't playing a joke after all," he said to Tanya, who stood touching shoulders with him.

"I tried to tell you."

"So what's the explanation for all of this?"

Swift Blade positioned himself on the other side of Tanya. His eyes were as large as two full moons. His voice sounded faint with fear. "You said it yourself, Mr. Trevalyan. We have found ourselves back in time among the Anasazi themselves. Ten-Moon's chant somehow reached out across space and time and captured us in the strains of the song, much in the way that a spider's web captures an unsuspecting fly."

Keane's usual complacency about challenging situations was replaced with an irritated frown. "That's all good and well from the aspect of discovery—and discovery is our business. But I'm a man who doesn't like to stay in one place too long, so where's the road out of here, in case I want to make a hasty exit?"

His companions, of course, had no answer.

Ten-Moon called for all his people to gather around closer. With the situation out of their control, and completely surrounded, the trio had little choice but to watch and listen and see what fate awaited them.

After the people were sufficiently assembled on the plazas and rooftops of the stone apartments, Ten-Moon explained in an eloquent speech who the visitors were. Even without Swift Blade's whispered translation, Keane and Tanya could gauge what was being said by the old man's boastful tone. In essence, he was taking credit for summoning them from the realm of the gods. The people, like the priests before them, fell to their knees in respectful fear.

After Ten-Moon had completed his speech, the people rose slowly. Whispering grew among them with the flavor of giddiness and excitement, even though the awe and wariness were still present as well. Tanya once again found most eyes focused on her. One child came forward and pointed to her, saying a few simple words which Tanya was able to understand. The child was fascinated with the color of her hair, for it resembled that of the sacred corn.

Children inched forward and touched the strange clothing, the knives in the scabbards on Keane's and Swift Blade's hips, the leather boots on their feet. They pointed at the hats Keane and Tanya wore. Others were pulled back by overly cautious mothers and clutched in bare-breasted, protective embraces.

A man in his middle forties and a head taller than most of the Indians pushed his way through the crowd with an air of authority. His eyes held wisdom, strength, and patience. Ten-Moon introduced him as Screaming Panther, tribal chief and leader of the Bear Clan. Through Swift Blade, Screaming Panther's words were translated.

"We People of the Red Sand are honored and humbled by the presence of the Kachina People. To show you our appreciation for your visit, we will prepare a great feast to be held tomorrow night. And now, I will see you to quarters where you can rest from your long journey and prepare yourselves for tomorrow's festivities."

He said something to his people which caused many of them to scamper off to their houses as if very intent on something. Another command brought him a small torch made of a resinous sort of wood. Carrying it to light the dark corridors, he summoned the three of them to follow. Before they had barely time to digest the situation or survey their dark surroundings, they were moving through a crowd that parted before them like the Red Sea before Moses.

Keane's hand circled Tanya's. Grateful for his nearness and the protective gesture, she gripped his fingers tightly.

"Squeeze tighter, sweetheart," he whispered in her ear. "If I'm dreaming, then maybe the pain will wake me up."

"You're not dreaming. My god, look at this place. It's incredible."

The narrow corridors they had walked just hours before

with their field crew and shovel hands were now swept clear
of fallen stones, mortar, and centuries of dust, twigs, and
leaves. The walls on either side of them stood high, straight,
and freshly plastered with buff-colored clay. No stones were
missing from the pathways. Only fresh turkey dung required
vigilant sidestepping. The turkeys themselves had vacated
for the night to the trash heap in the rear of the cave. Dogs,
lying by the tall, narrow apartment doorways, stood and
stretched and stared at their approach. One or two growled
and bared teeth until they were reprimanded by Screaming
Panther.

Some things were the same; an owl watching them from
a high perch; swallows fluttering in the rear of the cave;
mice skittering for cover.

On the fourth terrace, Screaming Panther stopped at the
ground-floor entrance of the square tower house. Each story,
or apartment, except the very top one, had two windows;
one facing east, and one facing south. He stepped over the
high-silled doorway and led the way inside the first apartment. This room, because it supported the upper floors of
the tower house, was slightly larger than the standard six
feet by eight feet.

The chief turned to Swift Blade. "The young man and
wife who lived here moved away just a few suns ago. Like
many, they left for an easier life in the land far to the south.
But it is not life they build there. Only eternal death." Bit-
terness clearly laced his tone, but when he spoke again it
was replaced with the polite deference of a host to his
guests. "No one has married since then and taken the room,
so my son, Pávati, who is sixteen, has been sleeping here
and keeping it clean. He will be pleased to share it with
the One of Many Words who has been sent to speak for
the kachinas."

He motioned for Keane and Tanya to follow him up the
ladder that led to the second-floor apartment. Swift Blade
followed to translate. Screaming Panther's explanation was

interrupted, however, by the sudden appearance of dozens of women, children, and a few men, each carrying something in their arms. The people took turns placing the items inside the two apartments and by the time they had left, the apartments had been furnished with clay pots, bowls, floor mats, skins, water jars, brooms of stiff grass, clothing, sandals, grass mattresses, necklaces, blankets, baskets. The men brought an array of tools; bows, arrows, digging sticks, hammerstones, mauls, axes, bone awls, drills, scrapers, knives—everything they would need for their sojourn. Corn cakes, jerky, berries, and fresh water were also brought for their evening meal.

"They are gifts from my people," Screaming Panther explained and Swift Blade translated. "Each has given you something that is very special to him or her. You will take these gifts with you when your visit here has ended."

"Now, there's a man of true generosity," Keane said, smiling at the chief who took the strange words as a compliment. "This stuff will bring a fortune back in New York."

Swift Blade was wise enough not to translate verbatim.

Tanya's eyes wandered over the gifts. These were the very things she and her crew had been searching for weeks in the rubble of *Castillo Blanco*. Now they were hers and in perfect condition. Imagine the look on her father's face when she returned to Boston with these.

If she returned.

Sobered by the reality of her situation, she forced her attention back to Screaming Panther who was now saying, via Swift Blade, "The upper room is small and you may use it for storage. I will go now and help my people prepare for the feast tomorrow. Rest well. And send word if there's anything you are without."

He slid the end of the torch into the top of a narrow-necked clay jar that stood next to the doorway so that they might have light. He had descended three rungs on the ladder to the lower apartment before the crux of what he'd said hit Tanya like a fist to the midriff, nearly knocking all the air from her lungs. With the last of it, she called, "Wait!" in such a frantic voice that Screaming Panther looked up, his black eyes ovaled with alarm.

"I'm afraid there's been a mistake. I can't stay in this room with this man," she frantically motioned toward Keane.

Of course, Screaming Panther understood absolutely nothing of what she had said. He stared at her blankly with a growing look of concern while glancing nervously at the gifts on the floor, clearly wondering if they were not adequate.

Keane was suddenly by her side, placing an arm around her shoulders, squeezing her fondly to him and smiling congenially at Screaming Panther. "It wouldn't be wise to insult him, Tanya. Maybe he doesn't have another room. I don't understand the kachina thing, but he apparently thinks you and I are together in some capacity, so we really should go along with it."

"I'm sure you think this is extremely amusing, Keane Trevalyan, but I refuse to stay with you in this—this tiny little space that is barely bigger than a . . . a . . ."

"A bed?"

His grin made her want to kill him, but she managed to calm the panic in her voice for Screaming Panther's sake. "Swift Blade, tell him we're not married and that Keane will just have to go elsewhere. Or I will."

Keane's smile changed to a dubious twist. "I don't know, T. D. If they think you're not with me, then you could end up drawing the attentions of some of the virile young men of the tribe. The next thing you know, you might find yourself on the road to marriage. Who knows, the chief himself might decide it would be wise to take a kachina as a second wife—or a fourth or fifth, depending on how many he has already. That would most certainly give him an 'outerworld' connection and assure future rain and plenty of power over this and other tribes."

Appalled, Tanya's mouth gaped. She caught herself and

clamped it shut, but it didn't stay shut for long. "They wouldn't do that. Would they?"

Keane shrugged. "Who knows what they might do in this society. These primitive people probably have some rather uncivilized customs."

"I doubt their customs are any different from those of the Hopi. Isn't that right, Swift Blade?"

"You're upsetting the chief," Keane continued, not giving the young guide a chance to respond. "See the look on his face. If you don't want to get us into trouble, Tanya, I suggest you go along."

"I'd rather die than share a room with you."

"Be careful of what you wish for, sweetheart. You know what they say."

Swift Blade finally intervened, assuring Tanya that it was not wise to insult the chief. His people had obviously given them their finest gifts, and gratitude should be given back. "You and Keane have shared quarters before, in the kiva," he concluded sensibly. "This should be no different."

Keane grinned, a look of amusement that infuriated her. But she grudgingly decided they were probably right. She surely wouldn't want to risk being separated from Swift Blade and Keane and possibly coupled—literally—with one of the males of the tribe. She remembered all too well how they'd looked at her. Regardless of how obnoxious Keane was, she felt she could at least keep him in line.

She finally managed a smile for Screaming Panther and proceeded to tell him how pleased she was and grateful for their hospitality. He seemed to know what she said simply by her actions and tone of voice, but Swift Blade translated.

The instant he was gone, Tanya's conciliatory smile vanished. "You can sleep up in the storage room."

Keane just wandered away from her side and squatted down on his haunches next to the gifts strewn around the room. He began picking each item up and examining it closely. "Look at this stuff. It'll bring a bundle back in New York."

"Don't ignore me, Keane Trevalyan."

He did. "Look at the craftsmanship in these pieces of cloth, Tanya. I wonder where they're getting their cotton. They can't grow it here. You should learn how to weave like this before we leave."

"It is the men who do the weaving," Swift Blade cut in.

Tanya looked from one to the other. "You may be using those things for your survival, Keane. Never mind selling them for big money back in New York. You may never see New York again."

Keane fingered an exquisitely designed clay bowl, painted in a black and white geometric pattern, as was most of the pottery they'd been given. "I've been thinking about that," he finally said. "Swift Blade, you'll need to try and set up a meeting with Ten-Moon. See if we can talk to him in private. We need to make him understand that we're not messengers of the gods and that he'll have to figure out a way to get us back to our own time. Tell him he's made a mistake, probably used the wrong chant or something. How do you think he'll take to that notion?"

Swift Blade was clearly skeptical. "I do not know. I can only approach him and ask."

Keane finally stood up. He still had to duck his head to keep from cracking it on the ceiling beams. "Well, we'd better do something real soon. He's old enough to die any second. With him dead, Tanya's right. We might be using these artifacts for survival. While I've never had a lovelier rooming companion, I've only got three cigars in my pocket. I doubt I can buy any around here for a few hundred years."

He picked up one of the grass mattresses, fluffed it up, and dropped it in a corner away from the doorway. He stretched out on it and his feet hung over by twelve inches. "We'll haul most of this stuff up to the storage room tomorrow."

"All you care about is your cigars?" Tanya stared at him incredulously. "Look at what we have around us, Keane. We can learn about these people's culture firsthand. What we can learn from this experience is beyond belief. Why, this is an archaeologist's dream come true!"

"Not if you can't get back to 1896 to tell all your friends about it, sweetheart."

"After the way you always carry on about your daring adventures, even to the point of bragging about the scrapes you've been in, I should think you would be ecstatic at this incredible circumstance."

"Adventure is one thing, Tanya. But the world I've come to know and love is probably—as near as I can calculate— about six or seven hundred years away. So, unless you'd consider becoming my woman, this 'experience' is hardly one to elicit ecstasy. Personally, I'd rather dig through the garbage dump after they're gone and make my own conjectures. It's more interesting not knowing for sure what happened. And it's a lot less dangerous."

"I guess that attitude is understandable. You've never cared about the people. All you've ever cared about is what they left behind that might bring you a buck."

He shrugged indifferently. "So all *you* care about is dead bodies and old pottery. I think you've even come to like your fiancé more since he disappeared and is believed to be dead." While she glared, he continued. "But I guess there is one good thing about going back in time."

"And what would that be?" she snapped.

"I think my ribs have miraculously healed. Since we came out of that kiva they haven't hurt at all. I could probably even get rid of this corset." He started unbuttoning his shirt. "So there *are* worse things than being stranded here."

"Yes, and I can think of at least one right now."

"And what would that be, sweetheart?"

"Being stranded here with you."

Six

Indeed, being stranded in pre-history America with Keane Trevalyan had to rank right up there with a horror story told around the campfire in the jungles of the Amazon. But to share a room with the rogue was Tanya's worst nightmare. Of all the men to be in this predicament with, why did it have to be him? She couldn't help but wonder if God was punishing her for something—she knew not what—to have allowed such a thing to happen.

She had immediately climbed the ladder to the third floor, deciding to stay there regardless of its size. To her chagrin, her appearance there had been met by a family of bats who hadn't had to do much squawking and swooping to make her retreat down the ladder in haste.

Keane, still fumbling with the clasps on Georgia Murphy's corset, grinned at her. "What seems to be the problem, sweetheart? Did you discover there's no maid service on the third floor?"

"There's a hole in the roof and the bats have taken the place over. It's not even suitable for storage in its present condition. I wonder why they haven't infiltrated this place, too."

Keane shrugged. "Maybe they prefer higher places."

"Well, Screaming Panther is going to have to smoke them out and then fix that hole, or we won't be able to put all this stuff up there."

"I'll mention it to him tomorrow." He patted the mattress

next to his own. "You've got no choice now but to share quarters with me. Don't look so distressed. Swift Blade's just a ladder away, and I promise I'll be a perfect gentleman. A saint even."

Tanya's lip curled sardonically. "I doubt you would know what a saint is."

She curled up on the grass mattress with her knees touching the rock and mortar wall of the small cubicle. She found a turkey feather blanket to cover herself with and another smaller blanket, made of cotton, to roll up for a pillow. Under normal conditions she would have been able to enjoy the fine craftsmanship that had gone into the blankets, but all she could focus on now was the man lying next to her, and all the virility that emanated from him as strongly as if he'd been drenched in a ton of expensive French perfume.

She had always hated being alone with him. Not that she was afraid of him; Keane Trevalyan would never harm a woman—he loved them all too much. Rather, she was afraid of her own disconcerting emotions and the sexual notions that his presence incited. She knew how vulnerable she was to both, having allowed them to rule her better judgment once before with Frankie Locke. It might have helped if she'd succeeded in making Keane angry by her remark, but, as usual, her barbs bounced off his head like dull arrowheads off the hide of an old bull buffalo.

She heard him rustling around and knew he was still trying to remove Georgia Murphy's corset. With only two feet separating them, she could practically feel the heat from his half-naked body. She tried to think of the clothed part, but the image of his slim hips and muscular thighs was as disturbing as that of his hairy chest.

She could understand why women sought the haven of his arms. She was tempted to turn to him herself in an effort to bring normalcy to this supernatural incident. She tried not to think of his nearness, his virility, and the way his rumpled black hair had such a devastating effect on her.

She tried not to think that he was the only secure thing she had to cling to right now in this primitive world of the Anasazi, where the two of them were very likely the first white people to step foot on this soil. This was one of the few times in her life when she had been at someone else's mercy. In this case, the mercy of an old medicine man whose life appeared to hang on the fragile threads of whim and time.

But she would do as she had always done. She wouldn't follow silly feminine weaknesses that made women reach out for men to protect them from their fears and from dangers. Instead, she would focus her mind away from those things, treat this situation as if it was an everyday occurrence, and put every bit of her energy into her work and what could be accomplished by it.

"Ah . . . it feels good to be free of this contraption," Keane said, flinging the corset aside. "How do you women stand to wear these things anyway?"

Tanya wouldn't have minded getting rid of the riding corset she wore either, although she would wait for Keane to fall asleep before she did. She went about making herself comfortable on her new bed, lifting up on one elbow and rearranging the blanket-pillow. She refused to turn to her other side, because it would mean facing him.

In the first-floor apartment, she heard Swift Blade talking in Hopi to Screaming Panther's son, Pávati. She wondered if he felt as vulnerable as she did, but after a few minutes she decided the experience wasn't troubling him much. She understood an occasional word and deduced from it, as well as from the sly male chuckling, that the two of them were discussing the tribe's eligible maidens. No, Swift Blade probably felt very much at home here. These people were his ancestors. He understood their language, their customs—or at least those that hadn't been lost to time. These quarters were probably not much different from those he had grown up with on Black Mesa.

"I think I've got it figured out," Keane was saying. "They make these rooms small to hold the heat in during the winter. Makes for a cozy little love nest, too. Don't you think?"

"I'll take your word for it," she replied dryly. "You're the expert."

Keane shifted around on his grass mattress, pondering why Tanya disliked him so much. While he was far from the saint he had claimed he would be, he had never done anything to her personally, and therefore did not think he warranted her contempt. True, he'd flirted outrageously with her, and frequently suggested that they become lovers, but she never appeared to take him seriously. He would have liked nothing better if she would have consented, of course, but he had figured out years ago that the prospect of that happening was virtually nil. He only continued to tease her because he wasn't one to easily give up hope.

Tanya's biggest problem was that she consistently became involved with men who weren't good for her, like that sleazy Frankie Locke for example. God knows, he'd warned her of that lowlife plenty of times, but like scores of women before her, she'd been blinded by his good looks and easy lies.

Keane had tried to convince himself that it was just as well that she ignored him. A love affair could likely destroy the friendly nature of their relationship, unless, of course, she was free to marry him, which she wasn't, being engaged to that egghead Eddie Chatham. Not that she would marry him anyway, even if she was unattached. But he had considered the arrangement on more than one occasion, and long ago had decided he wouldn't be adverse to spending the rest of his life with her. He knew no other woman who appealed to him so powerfully, and who would want to go into the wilds and dig around for lost artifacts. He was sure the two of them could share a life of unending pleasure and adventure. If only he could convince *her* of that.

There appeared to be no future for them as anything but associates. Still, he continued to show up at her digs, her workshops, her classroom door. He'd tried to stay away from her, but he couldn't deny the sexual attractiveness she held for him. It kept him coming back like an old stray dog who will suffer a kick in the butt if it's followed by a free meal. The free meal hadn't appeared yet, but he kept up the faith.

"There are dozens of women who would love to trade places with you, you know," he gibed, easily covering all the serious thoughts that had sifted through his mind.

He watched her try in vain to fluff the blanket she was using for a pillow. "And if they were here, I would gladly let them."

"Your voice sounds strained, T. D. You're not scared of all this, are you? Or of me, maybe? Well, you shouldn't be on either account. You and I have been through some life-threatening situations before—remember that time down in South America when we were looking for the gold of El Dorado? If worst comes to worst, we'll take off out to California or somewhere and start our own little tribe."

She glanced over her shoulder at him, her lip twisting disdainfully. She didn't have to say anything to let him know how she felt about that last idea. She addressed his other remark instead. "Naturally I'm frightened, Keane. I'd be a fool not to be. But I also see an opportunity here to learn things we could never hope to learn from digging through ruins. My only concern is whether Ten-Moon can get us back, but I wouldn't care if he didn't get around to it for a few days. Don't you agree?"

"Listen, sweetheart," he replied. "You know I like adventure better than most, but I prefer situations where the odds are better for high-tailin' it. And this isn't one of them. The only good thing about this is that I finally get to share a bedroom with you. I doubt you ever would have consented to that back in our time."

She released a throaty, sexy chuckle. "You're certainly right about that. It would have been a cold day in hell."

"Somehow that doesn't surprise me."

Her eyes, as clear as blue crystal, met his in the flickering light of the small torch. He decided in that instant that she was quite an incredible woman, not in just looks, but in everything about her. He knew of no other woman who wouldn't have gone into near-hysteria over the situation. But here she was, actually hoping to stay for a few days. His admiration for her deepened. There was just one thing about her that he wished was different.

"No, it doesn't surprise me at all that you're in hog heaven over this," he continued. "And I don't mean to downplay the importance of it, but for as long as I've known you, you were always more fascinated by the past than you were the present. More fascinated by previous lives than present ones."

He hadn't intended for his feelings to be so evident, but he heard the inflection of disappointment himself, and when she looked at him with eyes that had never searched his quite so intently before, he knew she hadn't missed it either.

"Are you suggesting I don't care about anything but my job?"

"It appears that way. The only man to ever turn your head was Frankie Locke. Oh, and I guess that Eddie Chatham. Although I wonder how he could turn any woman's head, since he always has his own stuck in the sand somewhere—literally."

He recognized the instant signs of denial and defiance flash across her lovely face. "You're just perturbed because I've never fallen all over you the way every other woman has. Besides, how do you know what's been in my heart toward other people?"

He finally had her full attention and he didn't want to lose it, even though it might be safer for his own heart if he returned to the insouciance that the majority of their conversations had had in common. And yet he couldn't. For once in his life he felt like being serious with Miss Tanya Darrow.

"You're not still waiting for Eddie, are you?"

She looked away, making an attempt to pull her turkey feather blanket up over her shoulders. When she did, she found her feet sticking out at the other end. She was a good six to eight inches taller than most of the Indian women in this complex, and the blanket was made for a shorter physique.

He reached down to the end of the room where the gifts they'd been given were stacked. He found another blanket and placed it over her feet. Their eyes locked again. Hers were filled with wariness of the gesture that had had a definite intimate undertone. She fussed with the blanket, rearranging it.

"What's the matter, Tanya?"

"You don't have to look after me as if I'm a helpless female."

"You're certainly not that, are you? But then I wouldn't want you to be, so how about just accepting a gesture meant in friendship?"

That idea clearly roiled through her mind. He never determined whether she would acquiesce to it, for she suddenly climbed from her bed and, using a clay cup, smothered the small flame at the end of the torch that had been keeping the room lit. For several minutes afterwards, the smell of smoke was strong before the last of it wafted out the windows. Now all he could do was read her thoughts and emotions through the inflection of her voice, and hope for some moonlight to give shape to her presence so near.

He knew she'd darkened the room on purpose. She hadn't wanted him delving into her mind, getting too close to the truth that she kept hidden inside herself. He wondered why she was protecting herself so fervently from involvement. Not just involvement with him, but involvement with anybody. She had never even appeared that involved with Chatham. He had watched the two of them together on numerous occasions, and they acted more like business associates than two people in love. Their behavior toward each other was so proper in fact that it made him wonder how they had ever come to be engaged in the first place.

Keane had known Tanya for years and had noticed the wall come up around her after Locke. The wall successfully kept everyone at arm's length, even female friends and associates. He tried and failed to break down that barrier. He wondered how Chatham had managed it, or if he had.

"You never answered my question, Tanya," he persisted. "Are you waiting for Eddie?"

In the silence that followed, they heard Swift Blade and Pávati still whispering in the apartment below. Keane wondered, during Tanya's contemplative silence, if Swift Blade would say more than he should. Had Screaming Panther put his son with the young Hopi to act as a spy of sorts?

Finally Tanya responded. "It shouldn't concern anyone if I'm still waiting for Edward. That's my business."

"Nobody's heard from him for two years, Tanya. I would say he must have had a run-in with the Mexican government. Either that or he got lost in the jungle, bit by a snake, died of malaria—"

"Yes, he could be dead, but Edward was one to get so totally involved in his work that he would forget time and everything that wasn't in his own immediate world. That lead he found on the legendary El Naranjal mines probably put him where he couldn't post a letter. If all his crew hadn't abandoned him, maybe this wouldn't have happened."

"They said they left because he was getting crazy over the idea. Obsessed. They were out of food and supplies and he wouldn't turn back."

"In the last letter I got he said he was close. He could feel it. Who knows, he could even be in prison down there.

The detective his family sent to investigate has been keeping us informed."

"Has he found anything?"

"Only resistance, which means the government probably knows something."

"Perhaps like us, he's down there lost on the other side of time."

"That's preposterous. We're here only because we were in the wrong place at the wrong time when an old medicine man was conducting a rain ceremony."

"What do you think the field crew and students will say about our disappearance? If we get back and tell them what happened, won't they think *we're* crazy? Considering what's happened to us, Tanya, how can we disallow something equally as strange happening to Eddie?"

There was silence from her side of the room. He'd never felt such a serious moment between them, but he wasn't going to end the conversation because of it. He didn't know what drove him on. Maybe he just wanted to make her see she might be waiting around forever for Chatham.

"There's one other possibility why Eddie never returned, Tanya. He might have found another woman."

"Let's just forget about Edward for now, shall we?" she snapped. "We have our own problems to contend with. I'd like to get some sleep, if you don't mind. I'm anxious to wake up and take a decent look around this place."

Keane had clearly succeeded in making her angry, although it hadn't been his intentions. He wasn't surprised by the reaction that seethed of denial. He listened to her squirming around on the grass-filled mattress, trying to get comfortable. The moon hadn't risen yet, and it was too dark for him to see anything of her exciting curves. He could only draw on memory and her nearness that was, by itself, almost tangible.

Then she spoke again. "Maybe all we'll have to do is return to the cavern, and we'll find ourselves back on the other side. Maybe we don't even need Ten-Moon's chant. Maybe there's something in the earth force itself that caused this—a magnetic field or something that we went through down there."

In the apartment below, the young men had fallen asleep; one snored softly. Across the canyons on the mesa rim, a coyote cried out his aloneness. Overhead, a mouse pattered noisily across the ceiling beams and, above them, the bats made funny little squeaking noises. It was easy for Keane to imagine himself back in the ruins with the field crew. It all sounded peaceful and safe, as it had before. But he knew how superstitious these primitive tribes could be. Knew what they could do when they got frightened of something they didn't understand. Peacefulness here could be very much an illusion.

He wasn't without fear, but he had learned that there was usually a way out of bad situations if a man stayed one jump ahead of his enemies. And he must treat these people as enemies until he knew for certain that they weren't, and until he found a way out. It didn't pay to trust anyone in a situation like this, to get complacent and content in your surroundings, to go around collecting information as Tanya intended on doing without keeping one eye over your shoulder.

He didn't agree that merely going back into the cavern would reverse the order of things either. No, he was firmly convinced that the old man's powerful prayer had somehow reached out and caught them, like the long darting tongue of a frog snaring a gnat. They might very well be swallowed here forever if a new chant couldn't send them back to their own world.

They needed to leave here as swiftly as Ten-Moon could send them. Like Tanya, he wouldn't mind having a few days here first. He wanted a chance to go back into the cavern alone. He wanted that obsidian mirror and black vase to go along with the Turquoise Sun. He would hide them and go back for them later. He felt a twinge of guilt at the thought of deceiving Tanya, but he didn't want those magnificent pieces to end up in a museum somewhere before he got his cut. He would have to be careful that she didn't know what he was up to.

"No, I don't think it would help to return to the cavern without Ten-Moon performing another ceremony," he finally replied. "In the meantime, it would be wise to stay away from the tunnel, even the kiva where the tunnel is. The truth might be suspected if the people here think we are trying to run away before accomplishing what they believe we were sent here to do. Now, get some sleep. Tomorrow we'll try and explain things to Ten-Moon . . . and hope the truth doesn't become our death warrant."

No one had entered the tunnel kiva since they had appeared there the day before. Ten-Moon explained to them that it was now a sacred place among the people and only the high priests and medicine men could enter. He met them there the next day and motioned for the three of them to settle around the fire pit with him. While they watched, he fed the fire a few more sticks of pinyon. The flames that leaped around the dry wood kept the kiva from being too dark. The smoke drifted out the ventilation shaft.

At the completion of the task, he gave his attention to Swift Blade, the interpreter, whom he and Screaming Panther both now referred to as One of Many Words. "You have called me here to discuss something of grave importance to you, for I see this in your eyes as well as hear it in your words. I am your servant in anything you desire. Please tell me what concerns you."

Swift Blade waited for Keane and Tanya to tell him what to say and how to say it. Tanya turned to Keane, a mocking smile playing at the corner of her lips. "Well, sugar, you got us into this mess. You can get us out."

Keane's green eyes narrowed; his dark brows pulled together. *"I* got us into this?"

"Isn't it always you that leads us into trouble? If you hadn't been determined to clear out that tunnel and 'explore,' we wouldn't be here right now."

"If I recall, sweetheart, you're the one who drew my attention to the crack in the wall. You could always have said no about going into the cavern with me."

"And let you claim anything and everything that might be of value in there for yourself?"

Swift Blade politely cleared his throat to remind them of the reason they were here.

"Then you want me to tell him?" Keane requested verification in a tone as derisive as the one she'd used. "I wouldn't want to do the wrong thing *again."*

"Please. Proceed. We're all waiting."

Keane chose his words carefully. "Swift Blade, tell him that we are very honored by the hospitality of his people, and we are greatly pleased by the gifts."

Swift Blade relayed the message in words and in sign, and Ten-Moon nodded, satisfied that they were satisfied. Then Keane continued. "We are also very honored to be here with his people. But he has made a mistake in believing we are messengers of the gods. Kachinas. Tell him . . . that we are merely people with no special powers who have come from the future. That it was *his* power and *his* prayers that broke through the barrier of time and brought us here. Tell him that we do not mind staying here and learning the ways of his people, so that we might go back to our own time and tell others about the Red Sand People. But eventually we will have to return to our own time, and only he will be able to send us back through a similar prayer ritual as the one that brought us here."

As Swift Blade's translation progressed, so did the shock on Ten-Moon's wrinkled face. At the completion of the explanation, the old medicine man was silent. Concern added new crevices to his brow. His response was so delayed, they were beginning to think he had nothing to say.

"Does he understand?" Keane prodded.

Swift Blade relayed the question and the old man nodded. "My power is greater than I thought," he finally said. Then he was silent again, clearly mulling over what he had done and how he was going to rectify it.

"My people will be disappointed," he said a moment later. "The spring rains came before the corn could be planted. We have had no rain since. Our crops will again die in the field if the rains do not come soon. Then our stomachs will be very empty when the cold wind brings snow."

"Tell him we understand this," Tanya put in, "but we cannot bring the rains, and he will have to speak to the gods again. Ask him when he can perform the ceremony that will send us back to our own time."

If they weren't mistaken, a rush of guilt and then helplessness marked the old man's features at this latest direct request. His old fingers nervously began to rise and fall on his bony knees. The crackling fire was the only sound in the quiet underground chamber.

An uneasy feeling crept over Tanya. "Ask him why our request has upset him."

Ten-Moon met her and Keane's waiting gaze. He spoke, and Swift Blade hastened to translate. "He says he does not know why you were caught in the strains of his song, like dust in the long shafts of sunlight. He thinks perhaps the gods really did send you to help his people with your superior knowledge. He sees by our clothes and our weapons that we are more advanced than his people. Maybe we know of something that will bring the rain. He says he would honor our request if he could, but he does not know what words to sing to send us back. He will pray to his Creator for guidance."

Icy fingers of fear shivered down Tanya's spine. Keane

was clearly unsettled, but, as was his nature, he didn't panic under duress.

"Tell him he must think of what he sang before," Keane said firmly. "If necessary, he must adjust the words accordingly. Asking for guidance from the Creator is wise as well."

Ten-Moon nodded when he got the word. "I will try, but I cannot promise success."

"Very well," Tanya put in. "Now, Swift Blade, tell him he must break the news to the others that we are not Kachina People and that we do not have the power to bring rain. Can they understand we have come from another time?"

Ten-Moon once again appeared disturbed. He finally went into a long monologue. "I am a *túhikya*. I have soared beyond this earthly world with my mind and roamed far into the outer world. I have communicated with the spirits and become one with the universal force. I have learned that nothing, and no one, stands alone. The secrets of the universe and mankind have been revealed to me.

"And yet, I have never gone into a time that was not my own. There is no time in the outer world. Time exists only here on earth. The road of time can be traveled—I know this—but it is the most elusive and difficult to find. Therefore, it is the one mystery of the universe that I have yet to solve.

"It is difficult for me to sit here, in this spot, and know that someone else sits here, too, on the other side of tomorrow. I believe in many things I cannot see, for I feel these things in my soul and in the invisible forces of the universe. But I do not feel other people in other times surrounding me. It puzzles me that I can weave myself into the universal force like a thread in a blanket, and yet I cannot reach beyond this moment and grasp what was, or what is yet to come."

Keane nodded, fully understanding the old man's confusion and inability to comprehend. "Nor do the future people see you, only the things your people left behind."

"Left behind?"

"Yes, after you went from this place."

"Where did we go?"

"We do not know. It was one of the things we had hoped to learn from the things you left behind."

Ten-Moon suddenly seemed very weary. "I am an old man. I have seen one hundred cycles of the earth's four seasons. There are those who have waited for me to die so they could take my place. The Sun Watcher told the people when to plant. He said it was by my recommendation, but that was not true. He tells them I do not remember anything I say, or anything anyone else says, and the younger ones believe him. I fear a *powáqa,* a witch, has gotten into the Sun Watcher's mind and is making him say and believe these things. I believe a witch has gotten into the minds of many of our people.

"If the people learn I have brought Future People instead of kachinas, the witch will use this against me. He will put thoughts in my people's heads, convincing them that I am old and cannot be trusted. He has much power among the young ones, for they have not lived long enough to recognize his lies."

"Do you know who this *powáqa* is?" Swift Blade lowered his voice and leaned toward Ten-Moon.

"No. I only see his evil at work. The lack of rain is surely his doing. Our people fight the invaders from the north, who try to take over our lands. We have also faced more years of drought than even I can remember. I fear we will be destroyed, not by the invaders, or even the drought, but from within by the power of this sorcerer."

"Why would he want to destroy his own people?" Tanya was clearly perplexed.

"Because that is the way of witches. They bring illness and misery. They steal people's hearts. Their powers are great. Their only desire is to harm and destroy, for they feed on the power of having everyone at their mercy. I battle this evil always, but more than ever these last few years. The evil is growing stronger, becoming more powerful. And I am becoming older and weaker. My strength is being taken by the constant battle with this evil. When I am gone, there are others in training to take my place, but I fear they will not have the power, the experience, and the knowledge to prevail.

"Therefore, I would ask that you pretend to be the gods' messengers for a few days, to give me time to prepare the ceremony that will take you back through this invisible cloud of time you speak of. I will continue to work also on my prayers for rain. I will have to do this alone or confide the truth of your identities to the other priests, something I do not want to do just yet. I am not sure the witch is not among them. I fear I could be thwarted by this witch whom, I suspect, is working to destroy me so he might assume my position among the people. If that happens, I fear the people will be doomed."

The three were uneasy at Ten-Moon's request. They discussed it among themselves. "I don't like what he's asking," Keane spoke first.

Tanya agreed. "If he is taken from power we may never get back. This witch may turn the entire tribe against us. Have us killed or something."

"Swift Blade, what do you think? You understand their ways."

Swift Blade hesitated, clearly not wanting to be the one to give advice. It was with a great deal of apprehension that he finally gave his opinion. "It is very dangerous to do as Ten-Moon requests. But Tanya is right in that if the people are upset with Ten-Moon, they could remove him from power and he would then not be able to perform the ritual that would allow us to go back."

Tanya's gaze caught Keane's. She thought she had probably never seen the fortune-hunter look so worried, and for a fleeting moment she almost felt a kinship with him. For the first time ever, they were working toward a common goal instead of working against each other.

"I prefer better odds," he said at last.

"It appears we have little choice," Tanya countered.

"Then we go along with him."

Seeing their decision was made, Swift Blade turned back to Ten-Moon. "We will trust in your judgment."

The old man's eyes glittered with relief. He gripped his knees firmly, forcing his old back into a straighter posture. "Everything will be all right," he said confidently. "You will see that I am a man of my word."

Seven

The sun sat two hours off the western rim of the Mancos Canyon when Keane paused at the base of the ladder that led to the second-story apartment he shared with Tanya. He could hear her rustling around up there, dressing for the big feast which had been in preparation all day. Since Pávati had gone to be of assistance, Keane had made his own preparations in Swift Blade's apartment.

The young Hopi had donned several of the items given to him by the people. A sleeveless, buckskin jerkin tied at the waist with an intricately woven sash made of dog hair; around his neck were numerous necklaces of stone, shell, and polished pieces of turquoise. Keane had decided he should honor the gifts, too, and was dressed in a similar jerkin, sash, and a dozen strands of necklaces. The items were all fine pieces and would bring big money back in New York.

The tower windows gave a clear view of people bustling about on the surrounding plazas, talking rapidly and excitedly. Their noise was mixed with the incessant gobble of the turkeys, who apparently thought it was their obligation to contribute, or compete.

Beyond was the steady, ominous sound of a drum that had been going all day long in the same rhythm. Swift Blade said it relayed the message up and down the canyon to other villages that special visitors had arrived. Runners, too, had been dispatched yesterday to assure that all isolated settlements received the word and an invitation to join the welcoming feast.

Keane, vaguely wondering if they were going to be the main course of the big meal, called to Tanya through the hatchway that led to the second floor. "Hey, sweetheart. Are you about ready to face the lions?"

"No, I'm not ready for this, *any* of it," came her exasperated reply from overhead. "It would help a lot if I had a mirror. A full-length one. I'd kill right now for that mirror in the cavern."

"So would I."

"What did you say?"

"I said, are you dressed?"

"I think so."

He climbed up the ladder and twisted his shoulders slightly sideways so they would fit through the narrow hatch. He slid an appreciative glance from the top of her head to the bottom of her sandaled feet. She'd pulled her hair up on one side with one of the decorated hair ornaments she'd been given. Her shirt and pants had been replaced by a soft, white buckskin shift that fell to mid-calf and was belted at the waist by a sash similar to the ones he and Swift Blade were wearing. Large earbobs made of red and black bird feathers offset her tanned face and blond hair. Numerous necklaces graced her slender neck and lay softly against the attractive curve of her bosom.

Naked ankles, shapely calves, and firm thighs were partially revealed through the shift's side slits. She had a tremendous effect on him, and almost instantly he felt the arousal of a familiar need in his loins. Thankfully she was too preoccupied to notice.

She tugged at the shift. "It's a little snug in the hips. Maybe I shouldn't wear it."

Keane thought it looked just fine, and her curves looked even finer clearly outlined beneath it, but he teasingly picked up another item from the stack of gifts on the floor.

"Personally I think you'd look good in this, T. D. And it's what all the other women are wearing."

She stared at the tiny apron made of yucca fiber stringers. It dangled from a leather cord that was strung around the waist and tied. It covered only the front of the wearer, leaving everything else exposed to the breeze. Most of the women didn't wear anything to cover their breasts either, which suited him and all the other men just fine.

She placed her hands on her hips. "And are you going to wear that buckskin loincloth you were given?" she countered sardonically.

"I will if you will."

She rolled her eyes and resumed fussing with her attire. "I should have known."

"Well?" The obscene scrap of attire still dangled from the end of his finger. His grin widened, challenging her.

"Don't be ridiculous."

"Hey, Swift Blade!" he suddenly called down the ladder. "Come up here. We need your opinion."

"Keane, don't—"

Swift Blade appeared in the hatch before Tanya could stop this asinine conversation from going farther.

"Tell me, Swift Blade," Keane hurried on. "Tanya wants to wear this, but she isn't sure it would be appropriate."

"I'm going to kill you, Keane Trevalyan," she grabbed for the string apron. "Some day. Some night. Maybe even tonight."

Swift Blade's young face reddened. "I do not think it would be appropriate for Miss Darrow."

"But all the other girls are wearing them," Keane insisted. "It's the latest fashion around here."

"*Here,* perhaps. But in our culture the women no longer dress this way. And since Miss Darrow does not come from this culture, I don't believe she should either. They consider her a kachina. I think it would be better if there remained an aura of mystery about her."

Keane reluctantly set the apron aside, greatly disappointed. "Well, it was worth a try."

Tanya, glad that the discussion was over—and that Swift Blade wasn't the derelict Keane was—turned to her young guide. "Thank you, Swift Blade. Now, is what I'm wearing appropriate for the dinner tonight? I would prefer my own clothes, but would they be insulted, or think that I didn't like their gifts?"

"What you are wearing will be fine, Miss Darrow. They will be honored that you are wearing it."

"You look the part you're supposed to be playing," Keane put in. "A messenger of the gods. Now, come on. I suspect someone will be here shortly to escort us to the shindig."

She led the way down the ladder, saying, "You referred to them as lions. You don't actually think we're going to be sacrificed or something?"

"Who knows what that old medicine man could have up his sleeve," he replied nonchalantly.

"There is no history of my ancestors ever engaging in human sacrifice or cannibalism," Swift Blade hastened to clarify. His tone was clearly defensive, but apprehension darted back and forth in his eyes as noticeable as the swings of a pendulum in a giant grandfather clock.

Keane stepped through the doorway that led from the ground floor to the plaza. Once outside, he extended his hand to assist Tanya over the high sill. She lifted her eyes to his and saw the sparkling gleam of flirtation against a background of sultry scrutiny. She realized he offered more than a helping hand. He offered a challenge for her to touch him with the physical awareness a woman has for a man.

She saw no way to gracefully sidestep the subtle, sexual invitation. Nor was she sure she even wanted to. Not only did his broad shoulders fill the narrow doorway, but she spotted Screaming Panther coming toward them across the plaza.

The tribal chief's quick eyes shifted to Keane's extended

hand. Then his gaze lifted to her, awaiting her reciprocation. The Anasazi leader had watched their behavior closely from the beginning, so it would not do to arouse suspicion now. He clearly had not acquired his position as leader by being dull-witted. With his son sharing quarters with Swift Blade, they would all three have to be doubly careful of their actions and words and how they might be interpreted.

Tanya placed her hand in Keane's and felt his fingers tighten around hers. The heat of his hand radiated through her flesh, shooting up her arm and into her body as swiftly and hotly as falling stars across the velvet night sky. His masculinity swept over her like a prairie fire, leaving a wasteland of smoldering emotions in its wake. In an effort to hide those shocking feelings, she kept her eyes averted and gracefully swung her legs over the sill.

Once through the squatty door frame, Keane's grip remained steady on her hand. She thought about tugging free of the disturbing virility, but Screaming Panther was still watching them closely. Because of his unsettling scrutiny, Tanya left her hand in the hard security of Keane's, finding it ironic that she should actually feel safer with him than without him, for a woman was never safe with Keane Trevalyan.

For the second time that day, they followed the tribal chief to the plaza. After their meeting with Ten-Moon, he had taken them around to be introduced personally to the high priests and clan leaders. He had then escorted them to the mesa so that they might see the toll that the drought was taking on the corn, squash, and beans. They'd been returned their quarters to rest during the heat of the afternoon, so they would be refreshed for the feast and dancing that was expected to continue on into the night.

Now, hundreds of people filled the terraces to capacity. People sat on rooftops and down on the rocks by the garbage dump. Children had found birds' eye views from the branches of aspen and juniper trees, and, like agile mountain goats, had clamored up onto jutting rocks into the sides of the cliffs themselves. The only clear spot was an area about the size of a small stage, perhaps twenty feet square and located on the third terrace.

At their appearance behind Chief Screaming Panther, silence moved through the crowd of black-haired people like a line of dominoes falling, until even the settling of a pin upon the sun-baked courtyard could have been heard. Screaming Panther lifted his arms in a needless gesture to get their attention. He began to speak, and Swift Blade automatically whispered the translation.

"He tells his people how honored he is by this visit from the Kachina People. He says that the strength of Ten-Moon's prayers, assisted by those of the other priests, have convinced the gods how desperate their situation is. The Kachina People have once again taken human form so that they might move among us with their superior wisdom and offer the assistance the Red Sand People need so that they might continue their lives and their migrations, as the Creator intended. All the members of all the clans will be expected to do everything possible to make their stay comfortable."

Upon the completion of his speech, Screaming Panther led them to a place of honor on the fourth terrace. It overlooked the "stage" just below them on the third terrace plaza.

Keane leaned close and whispered in Tanya's ear. "Well, sweetheart, I don't think they intend on making stew out of us tonight."

As during the day, the people's expressions were filled with awe and hope. The initial fear Tanya had felt now dissipated, and she began to feel the rhythm of the life surrounding her, filling her with an excitement that began to overflow. She wondered if the beat of the music contained some sort of hypnotic message, like an aphrodisiac of some sort, for she felt incredibly in tune with everything around her, even Keane. It was as if being by his side was as natural as being in this Anasazi village.

"Yes, it looks like they might put it off, at least until they learn who we really are."

"We'll have to make sure that never happens."

They were instructed by Screaming Panther to sit on grass mats in the company of the high priests, clan leaders, and the chiefs of all the secret societies. The most important were Ten-Moon, Medicine Chief; Bird That Falls, Town Chief; Rainbow In Winter Sky, War Chief; Man At Water, Sun Chief; Broken Spear, Hunt Chief, and He Who Runs, Crier Chief.

Delicious aromas of food filled the air. Bare-breasted young girls brought clay bowls heaped with multicolored ears of corn, baked squash, boiled beans, roots, roasted seeds, ground pinyon nuts, and corn cakes. Stews thick with fresh venison, rabbit, and wild onions came steamed in the finest pottery bowls of black and white geometric designs. Sweet bread—corn meal specially prepared by rolling in fresh corn leaves and boiled—was placed next to sparkling cold water in clay goblets. For a people suffering from drought, it appeared they had cleaned out their storage rooms to prepare the finest meal possible.

After the feasting was under way, groups of people, dressed in brilliant costumes of skins, feathers, furs, and jewelry took turns performing before the special guests. For the first time all day the beat of the drum was altered and the sounds of rattles and flutes and singing joined in.

As torches were lit to push back the coming darkness, the crowd's fervor grew to a deafening roar with each new dance. Tanya had never seen so much unrestrained joy coming from such simple proceedings.

"Look at them, Keane." She leaned close to his ear so he could hear above the din. "I think Ten-Moon was right when he said they would be disappointed to learn the truth about us. They are doing their best to impress and entertain."

His eyes slid over the jubilant faces of the dancers. "Yes, they truly seem to believe we're their salvation."

His tone suggested that this false impression troubled him deeply. It was unusual for Keane to worry about anything; his attitude had always seemed to be that a person could push his luck to the limit and, no matter what happened, everything would turn out in the end. To see him disturbed upset the equilibrium Tanya had begun to feel.

"Don't worry. Ten-Moon will do whatever is necessary to protect us."

Keane's eyes traveled over the crowd slowly. "Don't be so sure. He's looking out after his own hide."

Then the beat slowed and shifted tempo, returning to the steady, earlier rhythm that had worked on Tanya's body and mind in a primitively erotic way. Screaming Panther spoke to Ten-Moon, who in turn spoke to Swift Blade. By the time the young Hopi faced Keane and Tanya with an interpretation, his expression had taken on the appearance of one who might need to empty the contents of his stomach at any second.

"What's wrong?" Tanya asked sharply. "Have they found out the truth? Are they going to kill us now?"

Swift Blade's eyes darted nervously. "No. They have requested a dance from you and Keane." Seeing the color drain even further from Tanya's face, he hastened on. "It would be purely for entertainment, Miss Darrow. Do you know one?"

Keane stood up with no hesitation and held out a hand to Tanya. "I was sorta getting the hankering to move around a little anyway, and this will be like old times, sweetheart. Of course, a waltz won't do."

She placed her hand in his for the third time in less than twenty-four hours and allowed him to help her to her feet, but the horrified look was still on her face. "What then?"

"Make it something primitive. Listen to the beat of the drums. Let it flow into your soul. They'll never know the difference."

Despite Keane's encouraging words, Tanya still felt awkwardly self-conscious to be the center of attention. Keane led her onto the plaza stage. "Don't look so frightened, T. D. We'll make it through this like we have everything else. Let the rhythm speak to you."

He released her hand and she felt lost. Abandoned. But his gaze held hers like a magnet, keeping them connected even as he began lifting his feet to the beat and moving around her. She followed his movements, holding to his eyes as if they were her lifeline. The green gaze slowly shifted until it became a scorching glow, making her the focus of his dance. He spoke to her through the lithe, uninhibited movements of his body, and through the subtle, sexual suggestion in his eyes. Without a touch, or a word, she felt as if he was making love to her, and her body responded to the silent stimulus. She felt the rhythm of subdued passion rise and begin to course through her veins, settling in her loins with a throbbing beat that matched that of the drums.

Desire was born. The faces of the crowd faded away into the dark background beyond the level of her awareness. Soon all she saw was Keane. All she felt was the touch of his eyes, the suggestion of his body.

She began to match his movements, his erotic mood. Her feet soon matched his, too, beat for beat. She lifted her arms, swaying her hips and upper body in a subtle but provocative way that came from some wanton need deep inside her. He moved closer, closer, until barely a foot separated them. The drumbeats picked up tempo to match the intensity of the mood consuming her, as if the players now felt the same sensual beat flowing hotly in her veins.

She whirled away from Keane and continued to move farther with each step, but at the same time looking over her shoulder with eyes that enticed him to follow. He closed the distance again. His hands brushed her shoulders and glided provocatively down her arms to her wrists. At her fingertips, his hands fell away to her waist. He drew her to him, pressing his chest into her shoulder blades and his loins against her buttocks. She closed her eyes momentarily, fighting the urge to lean back into him even farther. She tried to refocus, to pull herself back into her surroundings and reality, but there was nothing real about either. She continued in the spell of his touch and of the music, of the darkness and the red glow of the torches.

Suddenly a shout went up from the rear of the crowd. Dogs began to bark furiously. The drumbeats stopped. The dance of the kachinas was forgotten as the people rose simultaneously, some with alarm on their faces, to look toward the trail coming up from the canyon. There were men who reached for bows and arrows, anticipating a raid.

For the space of a treasured moment, Keane and Tanya remained suspended in time with the echoes of the drums' last beats pulsing through their bodies. Keane leaned all the way against her. His words fell as lightly upon her ear as whispered kisses.

"It seems we've been upstaged, sweetheart."

Yes, and it is just as well, she thought, for she wondered where they would have gone from there. How would they have ended the dance? It had taken a purely sexual direction, and she could only hope the people would interpret it as a dance of fertility for their crops, or something of that nature. She fought for equilibrium, but all she could focus on was the heat of Keane's body burning the length of hers, and his hands on her waist slipping down onto the curve of her hips. His lips were just a kiss away from the corner of her mouth when he spoke again.

"Shall we see what the commotion is all about?"

She nodded, not truly caring, even that they might be under attack. Her dominant thought was that she would have preferred to return to their quarters in the tower house and continue this dance they had been drawn into. But Keane released her, and the magic spell that had fallen over them was broken. With the others, they turned their attention to the canyon.

Eight

The dancing sway of torches could be seen moving swiftly along the canyon bottom and toward the settlement as their carriers advanced on the village at a steady trot. The red glow of the torches turned the bronze skin of the runners a blood red in the afterglow. A group of young people leaped from the place they were occupying on the second terrace and ran out to meet the runners. Screaming Panther shouted at them in an angry tone. A few came back, but most ignored his order and kept going.

"What's going on?" Tanya queried worriedly.

"A visiting tribe maybe," Keane suggested.

"No. It is someone from this tribe," Swift Blade told them. "Apparently someone very important, but Screaming Panther does not seem happy about his untimely arrival. He has told the young men and women who attempted to run out and meet him that it is disrespectful of them to leave the feast that is being held in honor of the Kachina People. But as you can see, they seem to hold the approaching person in high regard."

"Higher regard than kachinas?" Tanya queried in dismay.

"I hear them saying something about this group returning from a trading expedition in the south."

Tanya wondered if the cities with whom the Anasazi traded were the same Mesoamerican cities being unearthed by archaeologists in her own time. She turned to Swift Blade. "Do you know who the people are that they trade with?"

The young Hopi kept his eyes on the approaching torches dancing along the river in the darkness. "The places you speak of were all settled by people who came to this Fourth World at the Emergence," he replied. "They spread out across the land as the Creator bade them to do. Leadership changed hands many times. The most powerful of all, the Aztlans, had a religion whose gods demanded human sacrifice to keep the universe revolving.

"It took centuries for the Aztlans to rise to power. But all mighty civilizations, regardless of power, eventually drift away like dust on the wind. The Aztlans were no exception. As you know, the Spaniards came to conquer them as they had conquered. One cannot depend on the power of the whole. A wise man minds his own destiny."

The runners thundered onto center stage then, and from their midst stepped a man who was tall compared to the other men of the tribe. He moved with a self-confident charisma that drew all eyes. In the light of the torches and the great fire, it was clearly seen how handsome he was as well, with high cheekbones in a thin face and alert black eyes that gleamed as brilliantly as obsidian in the sunlight.

Like the other men, he wore only a leather loincloth, and his muscular brown legs, hips, and taut buttocks gleamed in the fire's glow with a thin sheen of perspiration from the long run. Hair as black and shiny as a raven's wing was not styled in the traditional chin-length, blunt cut of the Anasazi. It had been allowed to grow long, hanging down his sun-bronzed back. Thin braids at the sides, and a leather band around his forehead, kept it out of his face. The only other things giving his body any degree of covering were leather sandals, a magnificent necklace of turquoise and gold fanning out across his chest like the rays of the sun itself, and more bands of gold circling his biceps.

"My god," Keane whispered in dismay. "That son of a bitch is wearing the Turquoise Sun."

Tanya could barely take her eyes off the man; his presence was completely mesmerizing. "The turquoise sun? What's that?"

Keane swallowed convulsively as the need for the necklace became so strong he could scarcely breathe. How could it have possibly appeared to entice him again? It was too incredible to be coincidental. Did it have some special significance in his life to be caught in this maddening circle of time that had trapped him, too? One way or the other, he knew he had to have it . . . *again*.

"The necklace. I've . . . heard about it. It's legendary. It would be worth thousands back in our time."

"It's the most beautiful thing I've ever seen," Tanya acknowledged. "It would definitely bring a lot of money if put in the hands of the right buyer. But it won't bring you anything here, except for maybe a slit throat."

He suffered her remark with a derisive smile. "Did I ever tell you you're such a pleasant one to have around, sweetheart?"

"Somebody has to remind you about the cold, hard facts of life, Keane."

Screaming Panther stepped forward again, trying to make the young people return to their positions, but the youths blatantly ignored his command for order. They clamored around the new arrival, not so interested in seeing what he had in his packs, but simply ecstatic that he had returned to them.

He spoke to them then, and finally they returned to their places on the terrace. Screaming Panther had a few words with the man and immediately his sharp gaze shot to Keane and Tanya and Swift Blade, a dark brow lifting with surprise and then a flash of open skepticism. When his gaze found Tanya, something in it softened; the wonder that had been seen on the faces of the others was now evident in his own eyes.

"Well, you've caught his attention," Keane said with a

bite of sarcasm. "And here I thought I finally had you to myself after all these years."

Tanya was flattered by the stranger's bold perusal, but didn't take his obvious interest seriously. "You may be the only white man around for centuries, Keane," she quipped, "but you're certainly not the only alternative."

"So I see. Well, he's only enamored by you because he's never seen blond hair before. As soon as he finds out how contentious you are, he'll see the light."

"If I'm so contentious, why are you upset that he's enamored?"

"Maybe I just don't want to lose my dance partner."

Tanya looked away, remembering all too well the feelings that dance had evoked. She was embarrassed by it now and thanked the torchlights for covering up the red glow creeping upward into her cheeks.

Screaming Panther proceeded with introductions, but his eyes had lost their earlier warmth. "This is Ocelot of the Four Winds," he said tersely, his jaw clenched. "He has been gone on a trading expedition to the great cities in the tropics and returns after a year's absence. With him, he brings many things our people cannot produce here." But something in the chief's tone suggested that he did not approve of the things Ocelot of the Four Winds brought back to his people.

When introductions were complete, Ocelot regally bowed before the three of them, although not in the complete deference the other people had given them on both knees with their heads on the ground and their arms stretched out before them. It was more the sort of bow one would give to a king rather than to messengers of the gods.

When he lifted his gaze, it drifted to Tanya's. He spoke, and the tone, the words, even the look in his eyes, left her feeling as if she'd been physically caressed. She could not suppress the shiver that trickled down her spine, unsettling her. Perhaps she should take him seriously after all.

"He wants to know if he can touch your hair," Swift Blade translated. "The only thing he has seen that rivals that color is the sun, the corn silk . . . and of course the gold that comes from the tropics."

His compliment warmed her; his charisma fascinated her. It was as if he possessed some sort of magical power that enabled him to hypnotize with nothing more than eye contact. She sensed that any touch he gave a woman would be an intimate one, including one as simple as touching her hair. Yet, to refuse him might mean offending both him and the Red Sand People. She was also very aware of Keane watching her closely, waiting for her response to the unorthodox request. The hard set of his jaw suggested he did not approve of the trader's boldness.

At last she nodded her consent, feeling there was no alternative if she wanted to stay in good stead with the tribe. At her nod of approval, Ocelot's lean, brown hand sensuously lifted a strand of her hair from off her breast, barely brushing the leather of her tunic with his long fingers. Even that whisper of contact sent a ripple of awareness through her. At the same time his eyes seemed to capture hers completely in a disturbingly erotic way. It did not seem to trouble him that she was one of the Kachina People. Either that, or he did not believe she actually was.

She fought the urge to look away from those probing black eyes that might too easily see into her soul and see that she was an impostor. But she held her ground, taking the role of a kachina to heart as if she were an actress on the stage.

Ocelot rubbed the strand of hair between his fingers and said a word that Swift Blade translated as "soft." He bowed once more—a stiff bend from the waist—and said, "I am honored by your visit to our humble village in answer to our prayers, as I am sure all the people are. We will eagerly await the rains that will come now, with your assistance, and save the corn and the people's future."

In an authoritative voice, he summoned one of the young men to bring his pack. From its bulging contents he carefully removed a piece of folded cloth, woven into a cream-and-rust-colored geometric design. The cloth alone caught Tanya's eye and she had the urge to touch it, to know its origin. It was all she could do to wait patiently while he held the item in one hand and with the other laid back the folds of the cloth to reveal an exotic-faced doll carved of teakwood. The doll wore a headdress fashioned from the iridescent green tail feathers of the quetzal bird, offset by tufts of brilliant blue cotinga feathers. A strip of leather, dotted with buttons of gold, held the feathers of the headdress together. The doll's clothing was of fine cotton woven into a green, gold, and blue pattern that matched the headdress. All details had been heeded, right down to the tiny leather sandals on the doll's carved feet.

Brushing his fingers against Tanya's, he reverently placed the doll in her hands.

"It's beautiful," she murmured, equally captivated by both doll and man.

A faint smile suggested that Ocelot needed no translation to understand her words, but he spoke again, and Swift Blade hurried to relay his message. "It is just a child's doll and holds no religious significance. Long ago it belonged to the daughter of a great ruler. Because of this, it commanded many things in trade. It is my gift to you, Kachina With Eyes of Sky."

His gaze held Tanya's in that mesmerizing way for another moment before he returned to his pack. This time he removed gifts for her companions; raw cotton weaving fibers for Swift Blade; a leather pouch filled with white seashells for Keane.

In another moment he had faded into the crowd and vanished from sight. He did not appear for the remainder of the celebration.

Much later, in Keane and Tanya's room, the trio discussed

the evening's events in whispers, even though no one would have been able to understand their language. While they conjectured on their situation, and the appearance of the strange but powerful Ocelot, Tanya removed the doll from its protective cloth and stared at it with renewed fascination.

"Can you believe this? This will help immensely in the studies being conducted on the Mesoamerican civilizations. I intend to get Ocelot to tell me all he can about the southern cities."

Keane's reply was thick with sarcasm. "While you're at it, maybe you could find out what year these lovely seashells are dated." With that he carelessly tossed the leather pouch aside. It landed at the foot of his grass mattress.

Tanya and Swift Blade looked up at him at the same time and with the same astounded expression on their faces.

"Did I say something wrong?"

"Seashells are very valuable here in the Mancos Canyon," Swift Blade said, a frown of confusion on his young face. "They are of the highest trading value. If you have them, you can trade for just about anything you want. The cotton fibers are also very valuable, because the plant cannot be grown here. The men prize these fibers and weave blankets and clothing. It is the custom for a young man to weave a special gift from them for his bride-to-be."

Keane was mildly appeased and retrieved the leather pouch. He opened it and took another look at the shells, trying with all his might to see some value in them while letting them sift through his fingers and back into the bag. "What did you make of that Ocelot guy anyway, Swift Blade? Why did he have so much influence over the younger people?"

A troubled look crossed Swift Blade's face, and even though Pávati had not returned from the celebration and couldn't have understood him anyway, he lowered his voice even more. "I don't know why he has so much influence over them, but I sense a strong rebellion brewing among them. It wasn't evident until his arrival, then it became very clear that he was the one they idolized, the one whom they would follow and listen to. And Screaming Panther knows his authority could be challenged."

"Screaming Panther looks to be a fine leader to me," Tanya said. "Why would the people want to replace him?"

"He *is* a fine leader, Miss Darrow," Swift Blade said. "I have no idea why some of them would think otherwise. But I suspect the longer we wait for Ten-Moon to produce a chant, the more likely we will be to find out."

All three silently considered the ramifications of what a rebellion could mean, especially if they were caught in the middle of it.

Swift Blade rose. "If you do not need me for anything else, Miss Darrow, I believe I will go to bed now."

Tanya, too, rose from her pallet and carefully placed the doll next to the pile of other gifts. Keane noticed she handled it as reverently as Ocelot had, and seemed incapable of removing her eyes from it.

"It'll bring a lot of money back in New York," he said. "But then I guess you'll probably give it to a museum."

She cocked her head, studying the doll. "I don't know. It's so . . . beautiful. I might just keep it for myself. After all, it was a gift."

Keane began peeling out of his jerkin. "I guess I wasn't wrong then."

The comment drew her full attention. "Wrong about what?"

"About you and that Indian falling in love at first sight."

She found that terribly amusing. "Love at first sight? You've got to be insane."

"I'd bet that pretty little doll over there that he fell head over heels for you. He's even given you a pet name—Kachina With Eyes of Sky. You might deny being attracted to him, but why else would you choose to pump him for information when Ten-Moon or Screaming Panther, or any-body else here, would do just as well? Swift Blade knows all the legends. Ask him."

She clicked her tongue in disgust. "Swift Blade knows the legends. Ocelot could tell me facts. Can you imagine what we could learn from him?"

"Always concerned with new knowledge, aren't you?"

"It's my job."

"Sorry, I forgot your job takes precedence over every-thing else. Just be careful what you ask, and how you ask it. A kachina would not be too curious; a kachina would already know about other civilizations."

Preferring not to get into an argument with him, Tanya snuffed out the small torch with the ceramic cup. At least in the darkness he could not see into her eyes and see that Ocelot of the Four Winds had indeed had an unusual effect on her. She didn't understand it herself. Those probing black eyes frightened her in a way, but they also mesmerized.

"Maybe tomorrow Ten-Moon will have the chant ready," she said, hoping to change the subject.

Keane slid under his turkey feather blanket and listened to her remove her jewelry, sandals, and earbobs, but not her leather shift. She would wait until he was asleep, as she had done last night. He kept thinking of the dance and the way she'd moved so sensuously. He felt the tightening in his loins again, stronger than ever.

"There was something about him I didn't like, Tanya," he said softly. "Swift Blade doesn't like him either. Or Screaming Panther. So be careful. Men like him can't be trusted."

"Oh? And I suppose you and Swift Blade have all the necessary credentials to be judges of that sort of thing."

Keane suddenly had the overwhelming urge to pull her into his arms and keep her there for no other reason than to protect her. Instead he just reached across the three feet of darkness that separated them and squeezed her arm.

"Just watch out for him, sweetheart," he whispered. "That's all I'm asking."

Nine

Tanya sifted the hot, red sandy soil through her fingers. The corn that had sprouted from it was small and spindly and looked as if a choking hand had a death grip on it. To Tanya, there seemed no hope for the wilted stalks to recover even if rain came today, and gauging by the unblemished blue sky, that was highly unlikely. She wanted to ask Screaming Panther if rain would even help at this point, but she was supposed to be the wise and powerful kachina with all the answers.

The summer ceremonies Swift Blade had spoken of were over, producing no rain. The failure had left the people adrift, not knowing what to do now or where to turn. Ten-Moon had told them that the Kachina People had come to search out the *powáqa*, who was doing the evil deed, and destroy his power. It was further explained to the people by Ten-Moon that the Kachina People did not wish to interfere with the ceremonies, or even to participate, but only to observe, in the hopes that they would detect the source of the evil. In the meantime, they would conduct their private appeals to the gods with Ten-Moon in the Sacred Kiva. The people were to do their part by being happy, for happiness ensured rain and the fruition of their crops.

The explanation had been readily accepted. The people, with renewed hope and unfaltering faith, returned to their work. But not without one eye on the sky.

Two days after the feast, Screaming Panther escorted

Tanya, Keane, and Swift Blade to the mesa at their request. What they found was disheartening at best. Tanya was glad they could continue to blame a witch for the drought, because it did not look as if rain clouds would ever appear on the horizon.

She felt the chief watching her and the others now as they wandered through the fields atop the mesa that contained not just corn but beans, squash, and tobacco. He followed behind, saying little, except that if rain didn't come soon it would be too late. To her eyes, it was already too late.

There were more weeds than crop, and, despite the heat and lack of water, they seemed to flourish. The men waged a constant battle with primitive hoes to hack them down so that they wouldn't steal from the crops what little moisture might remain deep in the soil.

In halting Hopi and sign language, Tanya told Screaming Panther that she and her companions would like to stay on the mesa for a time. He must have thought they needed time alone to perform some secret ritual over the dying plants, for he obligingly left the fields and returned to the cliff dwellings.

She found some shade on a sandstone rock beneath the branches of a large, very old juniper. Keane and Swift Blade joined her and they sat for a time in a silence that was broken only by the distant sounds of hoe against soil, by the young Hopi chewing on his omnipresent hunk of jerky, by insects in the grass, and by crows flying overhead, awaiting an opportunity to pick at an unguarded stalk of young corn.

Tanya studied the bent forms of the men with their hoes. She thought of the women and children below in the villages, who would perish if not for the men's vigilant work. Although she knew none of the people personally yet, she began to feel a genuine empathy for their situation and their future. She knew something would drive them away from these beautiful red and green canyonlands, and she wondered if this lack of rain would start a cycle of drought that would eventually force them to search for a new homeland. Would she, Keane, and Swift Blade be here to see them pack their turkey feather blankets and ceramic pots and wander off into the wilderness looking for a new start? Or would they watch them stay and die, one by one? Would the three of them be among those buried? Would her field crew find their bones?

That strange twist in the scheme of things was too much to comprehend, so she put it from her mind. She looked into the blazing sun and wondered why God sometimes gave no mercy. And then she said the words out loud.

It was Swift Blade who responded. "It is as I said before, the first night we spent in the kiva in the other world of our own time, Miss Darrow. The Hopi chose this unforgiving land so that they might never forget the power of the Creator and his supremacy over them. If God shows them no mercy now, it could be that there are some among them who are forgetting the Creator's purpose for them on this earth. Therefore, they are all suffering for those few."

"But how long will they stay? Until they perish?"

"They will stay until they receive a sign to move on. Then they will follow the sign to the place where the Creator wants them to go. It is all part of the migration plan set down at Emergence."

"I do not understand, Swift Blade," Tanya persisted. "Tell us about this migration plan."

The young Hopi chewed solemnly on a chunk of jerky for a moment, then swallowed it and began to speak. "Upon Emergence into this Fourth World called Túwaqachi, or World Complete, each clan was instructed to take a four-directional migration. At the end of which they would all come together again in a common and permanent home.

"This universal plan set down by the Creator was for them to go in all four directions to the ends of the land—

until their journeys were halted by water or ice. Clans joined other clans and set out from the place of Emergence, what we now know as Mexico. Some groups went north, some south. They spread out to the east and the west, sometimes retracing their routes. The migrations took generations. The clans stayed in a place until they were given a sign by the Creator to move on. If it was a sign in a cloud, or perhaps a star, they followed it until they were told to stop again. Some clans dwelled in the same places that the clans before them had dwelled.

"Finally, after many generations, the migrations slowed. The people were drawn back to Túwanasavi, here in this place of the San Juan River. The clans left their marks on the rock, showing they had been here and in what phase of their migration they were. These signs were like a signature that let the clans who followed know who had been there before them. The Bear Clan were the first to leave here and lead the way to Black Mesa, the permanent home. When the other clans completed their migrations, they followed."

"But what of all the people who did not settle at Black Mesa?" Tanya asked. "And what was the purpose of the migrations?"

"The migrations were like a cleansing ceremony to remove the evil that still dwelled in mankind from the previous three worlds. Over time, many clans forgot the commands of the Creator and settled in the tropical lands where life was easy. They built beautiful cities and were rich, but gradually they fell into decadence. The Creator's wish was for the people to never submit to indulgence, for he knew that when they did, they would lose their need for the Creator himself."

"Then that is why the people left this place? Because it was not their permanent home?"

Swift Blade tore off another chunk of jerky with his strong teeth. Chewing, he nodded his head and spoke around the meat. "No, it was not intended to be their final home."

Tanya looked out across the mesa, somehow disappointed that the mystery of the Anasazi's existence in this place had been uncovered so easily. It was such a simple explanation, but one that was completely plausible. And one that Swift Blade had known all along. She decided the white men could save themselves a lot of conjecturing and money if they would just sit around the campfires of the Old Ones and listen.

Keane sat down on the big red rock with Tanya, his shoulders brushing hers. His presence scattered her thoughts until the only thing she could focus on was him. She felt the strength in those shoulders and didn't move away. She needed his strength in a way she never had before. Whatever Keane Trevalyan was, he was an ally in this. Just this once, she thought it would do no harm to allow herself to be close to a man who could kindle that special, indefinable passion she'd felt only briefly so long ago with Frankie. Keane could make her remember that there was more to life than digging in lost cities for broken pieces of someone else's life, and searching for solutions to mysteries that weren't really mysteries at all because somebody, somewhere, had already solved them.

"You're not going to let this get you down, are you, sweetheart?" Keane gave her a conciliatory grin. "It's not like you're going to be able to change the course of things. What is meant to happen, will happen."

"Isn't that a little fatalistic?" Her smile softened the retort.

"No, it's realistic. We know the people left this place. We can't try to prevent it. We can't attempt to change history. At least now you know why they left."

Tanya rubbed a hand over the red rock, not wanting to look into his eyes that said he knew her thoughts better than he should. Her nervous fingers broke off a piece of the sandstone and she turned it over in her hands. Keane was right. They had to learn what they could, then leave as soon as they found a way.

Resigning herself to the weakness of her position, she held up the rock, rubbing a thumb over its fragile surface, watching the sandy substance easily crumble. "What is the Hopi word for this, Swift Blade?"

"For rock?"

She nodded.

"It is *owa*."

"Owa," she repeated, hoping to plant the word as deeply in her brain as the men had planted the precious kernels of corn in the red, sandy soil.

"What is the word for food?"

"Nöösioqa."

"For evil?"

"Nükpana."

"What's the word for big trouble?" Keane put in sardonically. "That's what we're going to be into up to our ears if Ten-Moon doesn't come through with the proper chant real soon."

Swift Blade smiled. "Yes, you are right about that. They need rain even worse than we thought, but we cannot bring it."

"We'll have to arrange another meeting with him to find out. If he can't get us back to our time, he'd darned well better be conjuring up some rain clouds."

"Maybe we'd better start saying our own prayers," Tanya suggested. "To our own God. And not just for ourselves, but for the sake of these poor people."

"The Sun Watcher is to blame for the crop failure," Swift Blade added. "He made them miss the first essential rains of the season. I know this country and its weather patterns, and it will be very unusual for rain to come in time to save the crops. When it does come, it will be a driving male rain that will strip the plants and wash them from the soil if they are not properly rooted."

"Do you think maybe he's the witch Ten-Moon was talking about?" Keane asked.

Swift Blade shrugged. "He is certainly trying to shift the blame of poor judgment from himself to Ten-Moon. But witches are good at concealing their identities. Only a very powerful *túhikya* can detect a witch. And Ten-Moon is getting old; it could be his senses are getting as weak as the rest of him."

Keane stood up, stretched, and readjusted his hat on his head. "Well, sitting here in the sun is making me drowsy. I'm going to head back down to the village and see if I can find something going on. You two go ahead and stay here and work on your words."

"You should learn the language better, too," Tanya said. "You might need it before this is all over."

Keane grinned. *"Owa;* rock. *Nöösiqua;* food. *Nükpana;* evil. I'm a fast learner. Besides, I've been around, sweetheart, and I know a lot of ways of communicating that don't include the spoken word. Like mingling. And mingling is the best way to disclose the source of *nükpana,* which we'd better find before it drains Ten-Moon of his power. We need that old man to get us out of here."

Tanya looked at him dubiously, knowing how easily it was for him to sniff out trouble and land right in the middle of it up to his ears. Knowing, too, that his mingling would probably be with the women and not the men. She hated to admit it, but that thought made her slightly jealous.

"You know a few words and phrases. Is that enough to communicate?"

"I've been communicating with natives all over the world for years, sweetheart." He grinned. "I have my ways."

Yes, and she knew his ways. But she wished he would stay with her and Swift Blade. She felt much safer, less vulnerable with him a few feet away. Swift Blade was still just a boy, and she didn't know if he could handle himself in dangerous situations the way she knew Keane could. No matter what Keane's flaws were, she had to admire the authority he commanded. An authority that had saved his neck as often as his nosiness had nearly severed it.

"All right, but don't do anything a kachina wouldn't do."

He gave her a mock salute. "Aye, aye, Captain. I'll do my best to be a saint."

She watched him leave the mesa and disappear over the cliff on one of the steep, but well-worn trails. She turned to Swift Blade. "Tell me, what is the word for foolish white man?"

The Sacred Kiva was empty, as Keane had hoped, but getting to it—and the vase and mirror—was going to be a problem. Outside the first kiva, a group of young men had gathered and were engaged in a game of some sort. From the looks of it, they were gambling. He had expected all the men to be in the corn fields during the day, but apparently there were some who found it unpalatable to labor in the heat of a midday sun. He was about to turn away and find entertainment elsewhere, when he came face to face with Ocelot. Or rather, face to face with the Turquoise Sun, shining brightly and enticingly on the Indian's brown chest.

The Indian glanced down at the ladder protruding from the kiva roof, almost as if he had known Keane had wanted to go back down. He began to speak and sign. Finally, when Keane couldn't understand anything he said, Ocelot simply smiled and took him by the arm, making him join the group of gamblers.

The men were more than eager to make room for him and Ocelot. At first, he sensed his presence put a damper on their spirits, but soon they seemed to forget he was there. By the end of the afternoon he understood the game and had a much better grasp of the language, at least the language used for this particular game. It didn't surprise him when after a time they asked him to join in. He saw many of them eyeing his few belongings; his knife, boots, hat, even his pants and shirt. He knew they would expect him to put these items up for grabs, and he had no intentions of doing that unless the Indians had more to offer. He held up a hand, indicating that he wanted them to wait. He hurried back to the room in the Tower House and returned shortly to the game with the seashells and Georgia Murphy's yellow silk corset.

His gaze met Ocelot's, expecting the Indian to be insulted that he would gamble away the shells he'd been given, but the Indian's enigmatic eyes brightened and he slapped Keane on the back, approving of his choice of gambling items. The corset was also a very intriguing item and passed from one hand to the other while they all conjectured on what it was and what it was used for. They marveled at the fine, soft material, exclaiming that it had surely come directly from the gods. After Keane showed them how the undergarment was worn, they became ecstatic and began immediate bidding.

The game was a simple one really and by the time the sun had fallen an hour off the mesa top, Keane had won a pile of goods that he was sure Tanya would be thoroughly impressed with. He had managed to retain most of the shells. He'd lost the corset to Ocelot, which he'd done on purpose, and with a great deal of satisfaction. The Indian, upon winning the undergarment, had immediately insisted that Keane help him into it. He was the envy of all the other men who had gambled for it and lost. Keane laughed aloud, enjoying how foolish Ocelot looked in the woman's undergarment and wondered how he would feel if he only knew the truth. Of course, Keane would never be the one to tell him.

Keane finally had everyone out of the game except Ocelot. As expected, the Indian wanted to continue—this time for everything they both had left, including Keane's knife, boots, and hat.

Keane leaned back against the warm sandstone wall and pulled out a cigar. He'd always been able to concentrate better when he had one in hand. The men in turn leaned forward with renewed interest, watching while he lit it with a burning stick from a nearby cook fire. He took a few puffs, allowing the smoke to settle gently over his audience, and he saw them all inhale it as if it were some new aphrodisiac. He passed it around. They were familiar with smoking and used a strong wild tobacco in their pipes. They clearly liked the flavor of his cigar better. Ocelot was the last to sample it. When he did, he suggested that Keane put his remaining cigars in the pot, too.

Keane, with the cigar back between his own fingers now, gave Ocelot his friendliest grin and pointed to the Turquoise Sun. "I'll put all this in the pot, but only if you will gamble the necklace."

Ocelot, like Hooting Owl before him, laid a protective hand over the necklace. Instead of refusing outright, however, he pondered the idea for a considerable length of time. The corset was definitely a prize, but he wanted Keane's knife, boots, hat, and very definitely the cigars. These were things he would never be able to duplicate in his lifetime, and he knew it. Plus, to say he had won the belongings of a kachina would bring him great status.

The others waited expectantly, sensing this would be a very important game, and the victor would be greatly honored for his gambling prowess.

Keane kept smiling, but he observed and absorbed every nuance of the Indian's demeanor, as he had been doing all afternoon. It was true that Ocelot was more clever than Hooting Owl had been, and he was more likely to cheat. But Keane was confident he could outwit him, even in his own game. He would have to be on his toes, and he had much more to lose than ever before. But he wanted the Sun. And he wanted it badly.

Finally, Ocelot's hands slid behind his neck and he released the heavy gold bar clasp that secured the necklace. He gently placed it atop the other items. Keane gathered it up, curious to know if there could possibly be two necklaces alike, or if this was the same one he'd gambled for and won the first time around. There was not a scratch or a flaw on it anywhere. He even recognized some of the peculiarities in the stones, assuring him that it had to be the same necklace. Finally he returned it to its place and added to the pot everything he had on except his pants and shirt.

Ocelot smiled in a cunning sort of way. "I will add a woman to the prizes, Trevalyan. Any woman you want can be arranged for."

Keane was getting quite familiar with the language, both verbal and sign. It took a moment or two, but he finally understood what the Indian was trying to tell him. Suddenly the friendly game became more than a mere battle for goods. Evil lurked beneath the surface of those black cat eyes. Eyes so black they reminded him of a tar pit—shiny on the surface, deadly beneath. He did not want to offend the man, but he honestly was not interested in any of the women, even though some were very pretty.

He retained his smile. "And what would you want me to put in that would be equal to this woman?"

Ocelot's sharp scrutiny of Keane intensified. *"Your* woman, of course."

Keane's congeniality faded. He reached for his belongings in the center of the playing area, retrieving his hat first. "We will continue this game, if you would like, on the previous terms. If not, it ends now."

Ocelot's smile wavered ever so slightly; his tone shifted to one of pacification. "I overestimated your desire for the necklace, Trevalyan. We will play on the previous terms. But, let me warn you, you will lose this time."

Sitting in his stocking feet, Keane's smile returned, but Ocelot had upset him and the bastard knew it. He also knew now how important Tanya was to him. Quite simply, Ocelot had dangled a rotten worm in front of him, and he'd been gullible enough to swallow it.

Keane watched Tanya return to the village from the canyon floor. She had been befriended by a young pregnant woman whom she was helping to carry some small jugs of water up from the lower springs. Their soft laughter sounded girlish and carefree and he wondered what they were discussing. It looked as if they'd been in the water themselves for their hair was still wet and droplets of water clung to the Anasazi woman's full, young breasts. To his amazement, however, the tightening that began in his loins came about by watching the sway of Tanya's hips beneath the soft, worn cotton of her trousers, and the rounded curve of her own full bosom enticingly hidden from view.

He had made a crucial mistake this afternoon. Granted, he'd won the Turquoise Sun and now had it safely hidden away in his packs, but he'd allowed Ocelot to know how much Tanya meant to him. He didn't know how the cat-eyed Indian would use that against him, but he was positive he would.

He had recognized Ocelot as a rival from the beginning, and the dislike that lay between them had deepened with the outcome of the game. Ocelot had not lost gracefully, even though he had pretended to take it all in good sport. He was preening even now over on the plaza, showing off the corset as if it were a greater prize than the necklace. Perhaps to these people, it was. They could never in all their wildest dreams duplicate such craftsmanship or such fine cloth. But for all his appearances, Keane sensed Ocelot really wasn't a gracious loser. He would get even. Somehow.

Someday. And Keane had the uneasy feeling that Tanya might become the object of his retaliation.

He moved to the edge of the first terrace where the dirt path came up from the canyon floor and offered a hand of assistance to them, the Anasazi woman being first. Tanya's laughter faded in her throat, but her smile and the twinkle in her warm blue eyes remained. She didn't hesitate this time to take his hand and he pulled her up that last little step, bringing her to within a few inches of his chest.

Her nearness made him feel as if he were falling backward, uncontrollably, into the sky; swallowed up by a force as powerful and invisible as the one that had brought them to this other side of time. In actuality, the only thing he was falling into was the depth of her eyes.

He felt light in the heart, like a boy touching a girl for the first time. His smile widened. "From the looks of you, you've been swimming. I didn't think there was enough water in this country to take a spit bath. Don't hold out on me, T. D. Where's the bathhouse?"

Her laughter rang out as clear and sweet as the trill of a songbird. She turned to the young woman standing silently, watching their exchange. In Hopi, she introduced the two of them. "This is She Who Sees Far, Keane. Her baby is due very soon."

"It is a pleasure to meet you." He smiled at the young woman, who lowered her eyes respectfully.

Tanya continued. "She took me down to the river where there's a small pool shaded by pinyons and junipers. It's only for women. The men go to a place upriver. The pool has been shaped a couple of feet deep by the women and then lined with rocks. The water there is crystal clear. She Who Sees Far showed me how to wash my hair with the soap from the yucca root."

Her hair sparkled like strands of gold in the heat of the afternoon sun. He resisted the urge to touch it, afraid that if he did it might destroy the rare moment of camaraderie between them. But he did comment, whispering, "I've never seen it more beautiful."

She touched it self-consciously. He realized, and perhaps she did, too, that it was possibly the first time he had complimented her without making it sound like blatant flirtation.

A moment later, she had collected herself and glanced up at the plaza where much laughing and clapping was going on. "What in the world is Ocelot doing wearing Georgia Murphy's corset?"

Keane followed her gaze, getting immense personal satisfaction again at having made an unsuspecting fool out of his opponent. "Modeling, I presume."

"Preening like a peacock is more like it."

"Yeah, isn't he making a complete ass out of himself?"

"He doesn't seem to realize how foolish he looks."

"Isn't that the beauty of it?"

She gave him a sidelong glance. "Does his wearing the corset have anything to do with that game you were playing over by the Sacred Kiva?"

"I was hoping to get back into the cavern and have a look around, but Ocelot waylaid me and got me involved in a gambling game with a bunch of the younger set. He won it. What can I say?"

Her brows knit together, but to his surprise she didn't start with her usual lecture on his corrupt nature. She didn't appear angry or annoyed, just concerned. "You were gambling? Is that wise? I mean, would a kachina do such a thing? They might see you as being too human, and it could jeopardize our position here."

"Will the women think less of you if they see you naked in the bathing pond?"

She reddened and looked away. "They . . . were surprised by the paleness of my skin," she admitted. "They all wanted to touch it, as if it were made of alabaster or something. If anything, they held me in higher regard."

"And I won the pot, sweetheart, which included the Turquoise Sun. In this world, that made me an even bigger celebrity than I was before."

"It'll bring you a fortune back in New York."

"It sure will. I'm hoping it'll set me up for life."

She frowned in that disapproving way he'd come to so easily recognize. He wished she could be happy and look at his good fortune in a more approving light. Maybe even be proud that his gaming expertise had won him such a prize. All she did was change the subject.

"Did you get a chance to talk to Ten-Moon?"

"No." He forced his smile to remain intact. He wasn't going to let her unreasonable morals put a dark cloud over his good fortune. "I haven't seen him, but I'll see if I can find out where he's gone to. Maybe I'll go find that pool that the men bathe in."

"Then I'll see you at supper time."

"You can count on it."

He watched her wind her way along the walkway behind Shé Who Sees Far, until the two of them disappeared into the corridor that led to the other woman's quarters. It was then that Keane noticed he wasn't the only one highly interested in her departure from the plaza. Ocelot had ceased his one-man fashion show and was leaning against a sun-baked wall. With arms folded across his corseted midsection, all smiles were gone now. He reminded Keane very much of a cat watching a mouse.

Ten

Dusk had been deepening in the canyon for over an hour by the time Keane and Swift Blade and several older men, who had accompanied them, returned from the river. They had gone to the men's swimming hole every day since they'd learned of its existence five days before. They were getting back much later tonight than usual. Fires danced now like twinkling stars in the shadows of the great rock amphitheater, turning the many small sandstone plazas to blood red.

Keane had wanted to return earlier. Since the day he'd seen Ocelot eyeing Tanya, he had begun to worry about her when they were separated for more than an hour or two. But the old men had wanted to talk, and it would have shown poor manners to rush them or to return to the dwellings before they were ready. There had been tense moments down by the pool for Keane and Swift Blade. The old men had begun asking questions about the "Other Side." Some said they had heard that there was a world that existed opposite this one, on a different sphere. They believed nothing separated the two worlds but a barrier no heavier than a spider's web, a mist, or a shaft of sunlight. They'd heard a person could go back and forth to the other side if he knew where the "door" was. They wanted to know if this Other Side was where the gods lived, or if there were just other people there like themselves.

Keane and Swift Blade had debated what to tell them, and had finally told them there were many secrets of the universe they were not at liberty to discuss. There were many things the Red Sand People would not understand, things that the gods were not ready for them to know. The elders of the tribe had shown disappointment in the response, but had accepted the wisdom of it. As superstitious as they were, Swift Blade said they would not press the point for fear there might be repercussions of some sort from the Creator himself.

Keane had been troubled by something else, too. Something that had nagged at his mind ever since the day he'd gambled Ocelot for the Turquoise Sun. It had not only kept him from fully enjoying the game that day and the friendliness of the other men, but had continued to trouble him, leaving a breach between him and the group who now seemed to have taken him into their fold. It was a fold he wasn't at all sure he wanted to be part of. He had the suspicion that the bunch of them were the tribe's slackers. Why else would they idle away their day in the shade of the cliffs while others, even women, worked their fingers to the bone up on the mesa top? And they clearly worshiped Ocelot. That bothered him most of all.

He needed to make sure Tanya was all right, that the black-eyed savage hadn't harmed her while he himself had spent too much time down by the river. He sought her out now and found her, looking safe and undisturbed. She sat cross-legged in the midst of a group of females who were either very young or very old. Awestruck toddlers with black hair to their shoulders crowded around her. One was brave enough to lean against her with an arm over her shoulder, as if Tanya had been a part of her life and her family forever. Another stood nearby, shyly fingering a strand of golden hair. The matrons, like the men who had gone to the river to while away an hour or two, were the ancient ones of the tribe. Their smooth faces had long ago been lost to furrows that had stolen their youthful beauty, but bespoke wisdom; and their graceful fingers had given way to gnarled, but experienced hands that painfully worked clay into beautiful pottery.

Tanya sat with a wad of clay in her hands and was constructing a water jar under the patient supervision of someone's iron-haired grandmother. The younger women bustled about the plaza, preparing the evening meals for their families over campfires. Those on the upper terrace cast glances toward Tanya occasionally. It was clear they would have preferred being with her, too, rather than dealing with the drudgery of cooking.

Keane purposefully looked for Ocelot. He was in his usual out-of-the-way corner where he could go virtually ignored, but where he could observe everything in the village. His interest was, as it had been these past few days, on Tanya. Intending to put a stop to it, Keane started across the plaza. But suddenly, as if finally sensing she was being watched, Tanya's head came up and her fingers halted on the clay mold before her. She turned her blond head back and forth, surveying the plaza and the dwellings bustling with evening activity. When she turned her eyes to the corner where Ocelot stood, nothing remained but shadows. The trader had vanished like a ghost . . . or like a man who has just stepped through the invisible door to the Other Side.

The firelight flickered over the solemn faces of the young men and women huddled close around it, sitting cross-legged on the ground. A thick clump of junipers secluded their meeting place on the mesa top. The people below, in the cliff dwellings, would be deep in slumber at this midnight hour and never hear the murmuring voices drifting away to the east and the north. They would feel confident in their rooms that the young men who guarded the cornfields were all at their posts. And that their young daughters dreamed sweet dreams beneath their turkey feather blankets.

Ocelot of the Four Winds sat among the young people.

Word had passed quickly among them that he would be on the mesa tonight, guarding the field of the Snake Clan, his mother's clan. They had come to clamor around him, seeking his attentions, his wisdom, and his tales of the great southern cities. They had waited a year for his return, and it had been easy to draw the boys away from the fields and the girls away from their beds. He had feared the Kachina People might have done something to change their minds, but the three had brought no rain, nor had they uncovered the identities of any witches. The young people were not patient in waiting for the kachinas to turn their powers into something substantial, so they turned, once again, to Ocelot.

Since he had lost the Turquoise Sun, he had replaced it with the corset and another necklace made of three strands of solid gold ball beads and polished jade stones. Although not as magnificent as the Sun, he wore it tonight because he wanted them to see the things they were missing. He wanted them to *want*. To *need*.

He knew the firelight reflected off the gold beads in a mesmerizing way. He knew the young people looked at the necklace often, a visible truth of the riches and wonders he'd seen. He spoke softly, and they hung on his every word like children at story time. They did not hear or see the small rodents slipping into the unprotected cornfields; the coyote slinking in the shadows just beyond the fire; the Great Horned Owl watching them from the highest juniper.

He passed out the precious peyotl buttons cut from the mescal's turniplike taproots. The youths here had never experienced the magic of the buttons before. Like Sacred Datura, peyotl was reserved for the medicine men to help them reach out to the spirit world. Naturally the youths were curious and eager, and they were not afraid because they trusted him.

"The peyotl will open your mind to a sphere of awareness otherwise blocked by the weight of your conscience," Ocelot intoned as he placed a small portion into each brown hand. "It will lift your mind out of this world and carry it into the Great Beyond where the Creator dwells. There you will be able to utilize powers you never thought possible. See things you were never able to see before. You will go where the kachinas go."

They did not need to know that the peyotl could not give special powers or insights to the person who was not naturally sensitive to spiritual and supernatural forces. For now, it would serve to dull their senses, even though they themselves would be under the delusion that their minds were lucid. The peyotl would give them visions and imaginary perceptions. It would weaken the wall they had around their thoughts and allow him to enter.

He tossed a little pebble into the fire, and they all watched the sparks scatter and rise into the midnight sky. He was getting closer to full control over their minds. Soon he would feed on the power they generated as a group, and it would make his own power that much greater.

He formulated an idea and used his telepathic abilities to insert it into their minds. In moments, the boldest young man, Sakngöisi, put that same thought into words.

"We are being ruled here by old men who are content to live the old ways," he said.

Now that one had opened the door, the others grew braver in voicing their grievances. Another named Tuwálanmomo added, "Our people have lived on this mesa for centuries in their pit houses and then inside their houses of clay and stone. One day someone told them to conserve the precious farm ground here on the mesa top and move their villages to the caves in the cliffs. The people were told they would be better protected by being hidden in the shadows of the canyon walls. This is true, but we cannot hide our fields from the Northern invaders who come at night, swooping down on our crops while we sleep like sparrows in our nests unaware. Some years we can plant corn on the river bottoms, but how many times has this failed because the rains have come and sent a torrent of water to destroy all? This is not a good place to dwell. The hardships are never ending."

Ocelot spoke softly, subtly injecting his poison. "In the southern cities they seldom have to worry about water. The rain is abundant there and falls when it should. They have slaves from other tribes to do the planting, hoe the weeds, do the harvesting."

The boldest young woman, Snow in Summer, daughter of the Sand Clan chief, spoke up. "They are powerful, these people? And wealthy?"

Ocelot nodded. "Very. Their clothing is of fine cloth, adorned with jewels, gold, and feathers of exotic birds. Their cities sprawl on wide, open plains, but are surrounded by thick forests and rivers. Rulers and leaders are not confined to tiny, cold rooms. They live in palaces with rich decorations on the walls and floors. They write their histories down on stones. They do not rely on the poor memories of old men who take liberties to change things to the way they want."

The youths stared into the fire with distant looks of yearning, and the peyotl helped them envision the fantastic things he spoke of.

Sakngöisi spoke again. "Our old men are blind to new things that would make our lives easier. They want to keep us uneducated, to fill our heads with old stories and old superstitions that came from primitive people."

"Yes," Ocelot murmured. "So they can keep you under their control."

"It is not they who slave up here on the mesa in the heat."

"No," replied another angry young voice. "It is not they who fight the enemies that come with their spears and arrows."

"It is not they who carry the jugs of water up the cliffs,

make the pottery, and tan the hides," Snow in Summer put in bitterly.

"They did once, when they were young," a meek voice cut in. It belonged to Pávati, son of Screaming Panther, leader of the village and of the Bear Clan.

The others glared at Pávati for defending the old ones, and they continued as if they hadn't heard.

"The Bear Clan leadership is holding us back," Tuwálan-momo said. "Their ideas are old, as old as the rock they make us live in. They've ruled the clans in this canyon for generations. They tell us we must stay here until a sign of some sort guides us to our permanent home. In the meantime, we wander around and around in our purifying migrations. Our people have been wandering since the Emergence into the Fourth World. When will it end so we can build the magnificent cities other people build? How do we know they will not someday come to conquer us with their superior power and knowledge?"

"They will if we remain here as complacent fools," Sakngöisi said angrily.

"I think the Bear Clan is lost in this dismal wilderness," sixteen-year-old Mochni said. "I wonder if we should trust these old men. I wonder if we should take control of our own lives? Take control of the Red Sand People?"

"Yes, we need new leadership," Kuwányauma of the Badger Clan said. "How do we know they are not all witches like Ten-Moon?"

"But he brought the Kachina People," Pávati spoke again. "How can he be a witch?"

They stared at him with glazed eyes, angry that he should constantly counter their growing rebellion from the Old Ones.

Snow in Summer lifted her pretty head haughtily. "Do you think you are special because you share quarters with the One of Many Words?"

"Maybe *you* are the witch, Pávati," Sakngöisi added to the attack. "Maybe you are the evil one among us."

Pávati's young face was stricken with horror. Desperation laced his words. "No! I . . . it was only a thought that I had. I just think that we should consider all things, both sides of all things. That is all I am saying."

Ocelot's gaze traveled over the young men and women. They were all waiting for guidance. He saw himself reflected in their dilated eyes, and he knew by now that they saw other things as well. Bright colors. Visions. Monsters. Witches. Witches that must be eliminated so that there would be no opposition to their goals of independence from the old ways and the old rulers. The Bear Clan rulers.

He kept his voice level, soothing. "How can we be sure that the Kachina People are not witches, too? I am not convinced that they were brought here to help us. Maybe they are here to put us under their spell, make us their slaves so that we might never get out of these fields. So that we might never see the splendor of the southern cities. So that we might never build those kinds of cities for ourselves."

"I have heard of people of light skin and fair hair who will come across the Great Water in large vessels," Pávati persisted, perhaps given courage by the powerful peyotl. "Even our legends speak of a lost white brother, Pahána, who will destroy those who harass us, and he will help us build a new peace for all mankind. Could Trevalyan be Pahána?"

Ocelot's eyes narrowed and wandered from the annoying Pávati to encompass each and every other young man individually. He had to be careful to hold onto his thoughts now. He did not want these trusting young men to sense that he feared Trevalyan's unseen powers. Ocelot was not easily intimidated, but just as the Great Bear of the Night Sky can see all in his obsidian mirror, Ocelot sensed that Trevalyan used his green puma's eyes to do the same thing. Every time Trevalyan looked at him, or spoke to him, he felt those eyes probing. He grew wary, for he sensed Trevalyan saw into his thoughts. Even though nothing had yet happened to suggest it, Ocelot knew that as surely as the Bear Clan and the Bow Clan were ancient enemies, so were he and Trevalyan.

"Trevalyan is not Pahána, our lost white brother from across the Great Water. When Pahána comes he will bring with him the lost piece of the Bear Clan tablet. Trevalyan has not produced it yet, has he?" A murmur of negative responses followed. When they settled to silence again, he continued. "I am more inclined to believe that he and the woman are clever witches from the Northern tribes who have come to spy on us so they will learn our weaknesses and come in great numbers to conquer us. Haven't you heard of the supernatural powers of the invaders? It is said their greatest *túhikyas* can change shape, even disappear. It is said they can be anything they choose to be. They can look any way they want to look. All they have to do is conjure an image in their minds, and they become that image."

"I say, let this Woman With Eyes of Sky and her companions prove their powers," Tuwálanmomo said. "Let us watch them with caution. Believe them with wariness."

"But they came from the earth, the rock itself." Pávati refused to go along with their ideas. "How can you explain that?"

"Tricks," Ocelot replied, growing angry. "It was all a trick. And who was in the kiva at the time?" Again he waited, but again no one answered. "It was Ten-Moon and his cronies. They could have told you anything. Are you gullible enough to believe him?"

"What can we do?" Sakngöisi's young eyes glittered with worry and the increasing paranoia induced by the peyotl.

"I will start by going into the kiva where they said the Kachina People came from," Ocelot offered. "I am sure I will find a tunnel to the outside to prove that they did not come from the inner world of the gods. I am asking at this time that you all cooperate with me so that I can get past the old men who sometimes sleep in the outer kiva. Snow in Summer, I have a special task for you so I will talk to you later."

"We will do anything you tell us to do," Mochni said, and everyone else nodded in agreement. Everyone but Pávati.

"What will you do if they are witches?"

"What is normally done with witches? With those who stand in the way of our progress?"

The shadow of fear fell over Pávati's face; he offered no reply.

Silence had them all now, but Ocelot was satisfied with the sanguinary gleam that entered their eyes. He rose to his feet and left them there, staring into the fire . . . and into their own faltering souls.

Eleven

The rain came sometime in the night. Tanya awoke
slowly, drawn to awareness by the faint murmur of rain-
drops against rock. She lay in the dark, listening, until her
mind gradually cleared and she remembered where she was.
She wished the darkness would lift and take with it the
uneasy feeling that something faceless and sinister was
crouching on the edge of her consciousness, trying to bur-
row its way into her mind. For a time, the peculiar sensation
clung there the way a spider's web clings to its maker's
victim.

Her next fragment of awareness was of something warm
against the calf of her leg. Something humanly warm, de-
cidedly male, and not at all unpleasant. She remembered
Keane lying next to her, but she did not pull away. Instead,
she lay perfectly still, absorbing the texture of his skin, the
heat, the strength, the rough hair, the essence of masculinity.
She turned her head on the blanket-pillow and peered
through the moonlit darkness, allowing her eyes to adjust
until she could make out facial features in slumbering innocence. What the darkness kept hidden from her, her memory supplied.

Without those disconcerting green eyes to tease her, she
allowed her gaze to settle on the firm, virile lips that had
tantalized females all over the world. They weren't perfect
lips. The bottom one was slightly fuller than the upper one,
which was pulled up as if he even found amusement in his

dreams. Keane had enjoyed life and every little adventure that came along, all the pleasures that could remotely be called pleasures. He possessed a levity of heart that was revealed on his lips. They were slightly parted now, and temptingly close.

Black stubble shadowed his jaw and chin. After that first day, he'd sharpened his knife to a razor-sharp edge and had been shaving with it. He'd nicked himself a few times, wishing for a straight-edged razor.

"What will you do if we don't ever get out of here?" she had asked while watching him smear the yucca soap on his jaw.

"Use my knife until it gives out, I guess."

"And then?"

"Grow a beard."

These little conversations and intimacies they'd been forced to share, along with the room, had brought them even closer on a personal level. They'd been around each other so much over the years that they'd always been relatively comfortable together—under normal conditions. Neither had ever concealed much from the other. They'd seen each other dirty, hungry, angry, and first thing in the morning with their hair standing on end. If she were to make comparisons, it would probably be safe to say that she was much more at ease with Keane than she was Edward or Frankie before him. She was certainly more herself. She had never put on airs of any kind with Keane; she'd never felt the need to.

A stirring began low in her stomach and developed into a restless need. She had the urge to turn into the security of his arms and be held like a lover, to *be* his lover. And why shouldn't she? He was hers alone in this ancient world that knew no others of their kind. But how long would he remain hers? Until they found their way back to their own time? Or just until one of the pretty young women of the tribe caught his fancy? The two of them had slept together in this room for over a week now, and he hadn't tried to touch her in an intimate way. Perhaps he didn't find her the least bit attractive, despite his constant flirtations and claims to the contrary. Perhaps he merely found his amusement by toying with her.

She sighed and closed her eyes. Darkness indeed makes the mind play with strange notions and disturbing needs that can more easily be ignored by daylight.

Then, as if her thoughts had been spoken aloud, Keane stirred. She tensed as his leg slid over both of hers, holding her a breathless captive. If she moved now she would be sure to wake him.

She felt him shift again, this time rising up on his elbow above her. With a hammering heart she realized he was awake, watching her as she had been watching him just a few minutes before. Not knowing what else to do, she feigned sleep. In another moment, she felt his arm gently slip across her waist. She lay still, waiting anxiously for what he planned to do next. She wondered if it had been dreams of her, or of old girlfriends, that had brought him to her side.

He moved closer, pressing his chest against her shoulder. His breath came in little puffs against her cheek and the corner of her mouth. Then his lips brushed lightly against hers. It was all she could do not to respond. She feared he would hear the hammering of her heart in the stillness of the tiny room. She was positive he would detect her pulse wildly leaping against his bare skin.

A moment later, he settled back onto his own mattress. She was disappointed, but knew that if he'd continued she would have responded to him. She would have duplicated the same mistake she'd made years ago with Frankie, whose reputation for being a playboy easily rivaled—perhaps even exceeded—Keane's. She had been foolish back then to be-lieve that she was the one Frankie had been waiting for. It had merely been something he'd told every woman he wanted to bed. She wouldn't be surprised to learn that Keane used similar tactics.

Since that disastrous first love affair, she had not allowed herself to get involved again with anyone except Edward. She felt safe with Edward. He would never break her heart the way men like Frankie and Keane were wont to do. Edward would never deceive her either, as Keane had suggested. If Edward had found another woman, he would tell her. She was almost positive of that. Most importantly, Edward's presence and his touch did not incite the dangerous flames of desire that had opened up her heart once before for heartache.

She listened to Keane shift around restlessly on his grass mattress for a while longer until finally he settled back into sleep. She didn't have such an easy time herself. The first gray light of dawn came and still she lay awake, listening to the soft patter of the rain, and to the sounds of people stirring in the apartments. They got an early start here in the dwellings. Normally, by the time the sun was up, the men were out in the fields doing as much as they could before the heat drove them back into the cool shadows of the cliffs.

She looked over at Keane's broad back, remembering the pleasing brush of his lips against hers that made her all too aware of the nights she'd spent alone. Oh, how she would like to end that loneliness, if only she dared.

Suddenly she sat up. It was time to go to work, to collect the information she wanted to collect before Ten-Moon chanted them back to their own time. Her work was all she had ever had to take her mind off her loneliness; it wouldn't fail her now.

She gave Keane's arm a vigorous shake. "Wake up. It's raining."

He came away grumbling. "It's still dark, T. D. Besides, it's been raining all night. What can we possibly do outside today? I doubt the men will even go to the fields."

"Keane," she shook him again, fearing he was going to drift back to sleep. "It's *raining*. Now the people will believe for sure that we're kachinas."

"Huh?" He squirmed around some more, pulling the turkey feather blanket up over his shoulder. "So . . . it's raining. The rain gods must have listened to Ten-Moon's prayers. That'll buy us some time. Now, unless you want to make love to me, I suggest we go back to sleep until noon."

She gave him a disgusted look that he didn't see. "You take everything so lightly. This rain isn't only the people's salvation, but ours as well. As for making love to you, you treat it as if it was no more important than sitting down to a cup of coffee. Is that all it is to you? Haven't you ever been in *love* with the person you've had intimacies with?"

He forced his eyes open and raked a hand through his hair. "That's a hell of a question to ask a man who has just gotten yanked from a deep sleep. I can't think, let alone deal with questions that require serious concentration."

"Then just go back to sleep." She tossed her covers aside. "I'm not going to waste my time sleeping when I could be collecting valuable information about the Anasazi."

Keane forced himself to a sitting position, looking for all the world like a grouchy old bear roused from hibernation. "It's just me and you in this world now, sweetheart," he said. "We need to turn to each other instead of away from each other. You might even have to marry me, whether you like it or not. It's sort of like being the last two people on the face of the earth."

"It may be a different world, and you and I might very well be the only white people on the North American continent, but I'm not that desperate yet. Why should I? You'd just lose interest in me as soon as one of those bare-breasted young native girls threw herself at you."

"What makes you think I wouldn't honor wedding vows?"

"I seriously doubt it's in your nature to be faithful. Besides, I've seen the way you were looking at them."

"Be a little more understanding of the situation." He yawned. "I'm not accustomed to going to a party full of women wearing nothing but yucca string aprons. I could have tried not to look, but, being literally surrounded, my only recourse would have been to keep my eyes shut or put on a blindfold. They might have been offended if I'd done that. Besides, you did your share of gawking at male derrieres, if I recall."

She ignored the remark, considering it invalid. She continued doggedly with her point. "I suppose if Screaming Panther offers you his daughter, you'd accept."

"And if he offers you his son?"

"Pávati is only sixteen, for heaven's sake."

"Maybe they like older women to initiate the young men into matters of such great importance."

"I've never heard of such a thing."

"I have. And you never know what the Anasazi believe in. Now, this is a hypothetical question, T. D., but tell me—what *would* you do?"

"I would try to get out of it, of course."

"But what would you say to keep from offending the head chief?"

"I would say that I was . . . that I was . . ."

"My woman?"

Tanya went to her knees, rummaged through the things they'd been given, and found the comb. His questions were getting too personal. Rapidly she tried to come up with an evasive answer. "I suppose I would, if I thought that would work. And how about you?"

"I'd say the same thing. That my loyalty was with you."

She laughed and looked derisively over her shoulder at him. "Maybe you should just go back to sleep. It's too early in the morning for me to swallow lies."

Fully awake now, he leaned forward and circled his knees

with his arms, watching her smooth the tangles from her hair. She was grateful that he had a blanket covering his lower half.

"I'm not feeding you lies, Tanya. I was actually offered a woman the other day. That snake-eyed Ocelot tried to fix me up, and in exchange, he wanted me to hand you over to him."

"What?"

"Don't worry. I didn't go along with his little scheme. I didn't think you'd want to share his lair. I wasn't wrong, was I?"

Her comb, driven by an agitated hand, snagged a tangle and made her wince. His annoying grin didn't help matters. "Of course I wouldn't want to go along with such a ludicrous arrangement. I appreciate you nipping the notion in the bud. I suppose it upset you, though, to have to turn down his offer."

"Not at all. When a man has a woman like you in his room, he isn't interested in any others."

She felt like a piece of warm bread being smeared with fresh butter and a gallon of honey. But she had never fallen for his sweet talk yet, and she wouldn't start now, regardless of the unusual circumstances they found themselves facing.

"Did he ask if I was your . . . wife?"

He seems to assume you are, but apparently that doesn't make a difference in this society. Some things never change, do they, sweetheart?"

"I don't know. Perhaps in this culture, like other Indian cultures, it's all right for a man to have more than one wife," she countered sensibly, looking for an explanation that would bring her more satisfaction than the one he'd given. "If he thought we weren't married, then maybe he was proposing a wife for you, and himself as a husband for me."

"He wasn't offering a wife. Nor was he offering to be your husband. I told you the guy was a real lowlife, didn't I? I also know that if Ten-Moon doesn't come up with that chant real soon, I'm going to have to resort to smoking that noxious tobacco they grow, or give up the habit entirely. Where are my last two cigars anyway? Have you seen them? I hope one of those gents didn't sneak in here in the night and steal what I had left."

"For a man who's lived in luxury acquired from stolen artifacts, you shouldn't hold it against them for doing a little 'time stealing' themselves."

He reached for his khaki trousers, and Tanya turned her back while he slipped them on. "I've lived a life of adventure," he said from behind her, "but never one of luxury. Call me a thief of time if you want. I won't apologize for it because I don't steal anything. I do research on valuable and legendary articles from ancient times. I find artifacts that have been hidden or buried and forgotten for centuries. They're anybody's treasure. I sell them to collectors who care a lot more about their historical significance than people who wander into a museum to browse. Nine times out of ten, the latter group usually doesn't know what they're looking at and don't really care. They're just killing an afternoon. You can turn around now."

She did, and watched him shrug his broad shoulders into his khaki shirt. His explanation certainly put a different perspective on things, but she wasn't ready to completely condone his private enterprise.

"Why did you choose this line of work?" she shifted the direction of the conversation. "Your father is one of biggest manufacturers of carriages in New England, isn't he? I've heard you're independently wealthy."

"Funny how rumors get started, isn't it? The truth is, Connecticut Carriage Company supports my parents as well as my two brothers and their families, and it does it in style. But I didn't want to be part of something I couldn't be in charge of."

"Is that the real reason? I heard you had such a yen for roaming and for landing in trouble that your father told you not to come back home until you were ready to settle down."

He shrugged. "My father and I have never seen eye to eye. He couldn't understand my restless side, or my ideas for the company. He tried to clip my wings, even to the point of choosing the proper woman for me to marry.

"My brothers are content with a job that brings them home every night to their wives so they can sit in their easy chairs and read the newspaper in front of the fireplace. When one of them does travel for the company, their wives complain because they hate spending a few nights alone.

"I'm an adventurer. I'd go crazy if every day was the same. If there comes a day when there's nothing left to discover, and I'm too old to outrun the natives, then I'll consider retiring to my rocking chair."

Tanya nodded in full agreement. She understood his craving for traveling and new exploits. It had been her life, too, and she couldn't imagine doing anything else. "When I was growing up," she said, "my father and I were seldom home—or at least it seemed that way. The house in Boston was more like a place to land occasionally, regroup, pack some different clothes. After my mother left with my two younger sisters, Nicole and Renee—"

"Your mother left?" he interrupted, his voice rising on a note of surprise. "I'd heard she'd died and that you were an only child."

"No, she didn't die. She was like your sisters-in-law, wanting her husband home every night. Dad used to ask her to go with him, but she always refused. She hated dirt, an ironic intolerance for a woman married to an archaeologist.

"I think they were in love," she continued thoughtfully. "They were just mismatched. So one day she just walked out the door. I don't even know where she went. She never kept in touch—or if she did, Dad never told me. He only mentioned once that he hoped she got along better with her new husband. I've thought about trying to find her and my sisters, but I guess I figure that if they wanted to find me, they could have a lot easier than I could have found them."

"Why didn't she take you?"

Tanya looked at a spot on the wall where some plaster was crumbling. "I really don't know. I was the oldest and the closest to my father. She probably figured I'd be one less burden for her if she left me behind. It doesn't matter."

Keane could tell it *did* matter.

"Anyway," she continued, "my father promptly packed me up, along with the rest of his baggage, and we set out for forgotten worlds just waiting to be rediscovered. That was one of the things Edward and I—" Suddenly she caught herself, realizing she was telling Keane Trevalyan more about herself than she had intended.

"What about you and Eddie?" he probed.

She might have known he wouldn't let it lie. "Oh, nothing. It's not important now."

"Then it won't hurt to talk about it. Unless talking about Eddie still upsets you after all this time."

"It's nothing. Edward and I just had some differing opinions on how children should be raised. He wanted me to stay home and take care of our future children. I wanted to pack them up and take them with me, the way my father had always done with me. I would never dream of leaving my children for months at a time. Yet, I can't imagine giving up my work as an archaeologist either."

"Eddie didn't see it that way?"

"No. He even wanted me to step down from my position at Wellesley, stay home, and make quilts or something."

"Now, there's a boring prospect." He agreed with an understanding grin. "If he comes back, will you bend to his wishes?"

Tanya had forgotten the task of combing her hair. She was remembering how things had been and looking at them honestly for possibly the first time ever. She had led herself to believe that she and Edward would work it out. Now, she wasn't so sure that was possible.

"The past is a passion for me. I can't give it up."

"Then you need a man who understands that part of you, Tanya. A man who would never ask you to change, or to give up the one thing you love doing over everything else."

That sinister something that had crouched on the edge of her mind earlier suddenly returned, startling her. She didn't know what had brought it back, possibly the talk of her past and of Edward. It all seemed to have something to do with the dream she could not remember. Was it some sort of premonition so horrible that she had blocked it from her mind? Or had the dream just been an unpleasant memory?

"Do you really think Edward is dead?" she asked quietly, still studying the peeling plaster. "Or do you think he was just too cowardly to come back and break off our engagement?" She wasn't sure if she wanted Keane's opinion on such a personal matter, but she needed it just the same.

There was a considerable silence while Keane contemplated her question. Finally he replied. "Whether Eddie is alive or not, you need to get on with your life, Tanya, and put him behind you where he belongs. It doesn't sound as if the two of you would have had a very successful marriage anyway. Your ideas were too different."

"What would you know of marriage?" she gibed, easing the solemn moment with a bright smile.

He grinned that grin that was famous for melting female hearts. "Enough to know that a man would be a damned fool to try and keep a woman like you at home, unless he intended on staying there with her."

"About as foolish as a woman trying to make you build carriages, do paperwork in an office, and read the newspaper in the evenings from an easy chair."

"I'd rather be making news than reading it, sweetheart."

"Then neither one of us is good marriage material, are we?"

"No, I guess we're just a pair of renegades. Maybe it wasn't a mistake that we ended up here together. Maybe it was the only way God could get us together."

She found it amusing that he would attribute fate to their situation. Surely he didn't believe in supernatural intervention on such inconsequential matters as romance? But there was something in his eyes that touched her intimately, as if he truly wished it was so, even if he didn't believe it.

She just laughed to cover the way those emerald eyes made her weak in the knees. "I already told you, Keane, it's too early in the morning to be fed lies."

"Then let me buy you a real breakfast down in the plaza. I know of a little table out of the rain . . ."

Twelve

The people called it a female rain because it fell softly, gently, warmly, and because it lasted for four days. "It is the sort of rain that the earth will soak up," said She Who Sees Far. "The corn will grow now, and the people will not go hungry this winter."

She was heavy with child, but the young Anasazi woman nimbly led the way over the rugged terrain from the cliffs to the canyon floor. She and Tanya had made the trek together every day to collect the precious rainwater in their big clay jars. Being an honored guest and a kachina, Tanya was not expected to do manual labor. She had been offered a young girl for a servant. Even though honored by the gesture, she had politely refused. She had never been one to sit idle, watching others work, but she also realized that if Ten-Moon couldn't get them back to their own time, she might not be able to pose as a kachina forever.

Today, however, she was very tired and would have welcomed any assistance. She attributed her weariness to the dreams that had, over the last few nights, stolen her sleep. In each one, she had felt as if someone was on the perimeter of it, watching the scenes unroll in her mind along with her. She awoke exhausted each morning. Today, a glance in the pond revealed dark circles under her eyes.

For all the rain that had fallen, it had taken only one day of sunshine to dry the sandy soil on the path. It was the same path Tanya had taken the first time she'd left the field crew and gone into the ruins alone. There was much about the path that she hadn't seen the first time, things that had been lost to time and erosion and to the growth of trees and underbrush. After having spent nearly two weeks with the Anasazi, she was now very familiar with the series of small reservoirs built on the slopes that led to the canyon bottom.

The first reservoir was just below the cliff dwellings at the front of the cave itself. The older women took the reservoirs closest to the cliff dwellings; the younger women were forced to make the longer, harder trek into the canyon bottom. Tanya and She Who Sees Far continued down the path until they came to a reservoir far down in the canyon.

Most of the reservoirs were in the shade of trees and cliffs, and the water they held was cool and fresh. The ponds measured six to eight feet in width, and many were over twenty feet in length. Most were two to three feet deep. Lined with rock and mud of blue shale, all the reservoirs had been cleaned before the rainy season to prevent the silt from collecting and minimizing the holding capacity. The rains had filled them all to overflowing, and the overflow spilled down to the next reservoir.

Tanya was fascinated by the women who balanced the huge water vessels on their heads, protected by a small round pad of yucca fiber. Every woman walked with a back as straight as a rod, and had a strong neck and flowing stride. They moved as easily with the jars as if the containers were hats attached to their hair with hairpins. Most of the women could climb ladders with the jars on top of their heads and were even able to scale the cliffs to the mesa top, keeping their hands free to navigate the toe and handholds chiseled into the sides of the cliffs. A pot was occasionally broken, but the potsherds were simply gathered up so they could be crushed and used in future pots.

Tanya, too, had started going without her boots. Today she wore a pair of yucca fiber sandals that had been given to her as a gift. She could get a better grip on the canyon paths with her sandaled feet than she could with her slick-soled boots, and she could carry the jars easier if she used her head instead of her arms.

After the water was collected, it was stored in rooms located behind the living spaces that were too small for habitation. Water had also been collected from the plaza itself. As the rain had poured down over the lip of the mesa and over the cliffs, it fell into strategically placed jars.

The only thing Tanya could see that the men had to do during the rain was to keep watchful eyes on the reservoirs. If any showed signs of breaking or leaking, the men went in haste to make repairs. Otherwise, they lounged around the plazas talking, gaming, or weaving. They might take this time to repair their farming and hunting implements.

Each person seemed to have a specialty such as making sandals, sashes, knives, tanning leather, or designing and painting pottery. One woman was particularly artistic and painted beautiful frescoes in people's rooms in exchange for other products. Most of the people were industrious and worked on their personal items during the bad weather, preparing them for future trade.

Tanya and She Who Sees Far squatted side by side at the reservoir. Using clay dippers, they filled their jars while they carried on a lively conversation. Tanya had become considerably more fluent since befriending She Who Sees Far. The young woman was more than eager to teach her new words and signs. She also had a knack for knowing what Tanya was thinking even before she said it.

"The ponds were nearly dry and now there is more water than we can collect in our jars," remarked She Who Sees Far. "We have been especially blessed by the gods, and the role you and your companions have played as intermediaries on our behalf will never be forgotten.

"The high priests and Ten-Moon are making a new dance and song that will be sung every year at this time in remembrance of what the Kachina People have done for us. They will present it to you at the time of the big feast that will be held in your honor."

Tanya had heard murmurings about another big feast that would be held in a week. She was thankful for the rain that would help the Red Sand People, but the guilt at having to deceive this young woman who had become a very dear friend was becoming a tremendous burden. It disturbed her, too, that Ten-Moon was not spending his time working on the chant that would return them to their own time. She was not overly anxious to return, but she knew that the longer they remained the greater was the possibility of their true identities becoming known. She did not think these people would take kindly to being deceived in such a grand fashion, and her life and the lives of her companions could be cut short because of it.

She Who Sees Far continued. "As our stories are told and retold around the campfire for generations to come, Woman With Eyes of Sky, He Who Laughs, and One Of Many Words will become part of our legends."

"He Who Laughs?" Tanya inquired, perplexed, wondering if she'd interpreted the woman's words correctly.

She Who Sees Far smiled. "Your man. *Tray-Val-Yawn*. It is what the people are calling him because his mouth and his eyes are always dancing with a smile and his frequent laughter brightens the day. We call him that, too, because his name is difficult for us to say. You must make him very happy; he seems to take great joy in life."

Tanya looked away, embarrassed and wishing she could take the credit. She hoped She Who Sees Far wouldn't detect the true nature of their relationship.

Keane's words about them being brought together by fate had stayed in Tanya's mind. She wondered if he truly cared for her and saw this as an opportunity to show her. Or did he believe they were merely caught in an intermission that had no beginning and no end? A middle complete unto itself that would enable him to experience the full gambit of love without worrying about the final scene?

She Who Sees Far rested her dipper on the edge of her jar and looked at Tanya. "Were you together as man and wife before you became spirit people?"

Tanya had learned a little more about kachinas from Swift Blade, who had explained that man must plod along the evolutionary Road of Life, being born and reborn into many lives and many bodies to learn the lessons that God intended for him to learn. Those who learn the lessons of life early and adhere to them rigidly are released from this cycle and sent directly to the spirit world as kachinas. Tanya, afraid she might say something that would give away her ignorance, merely replied, "We have been together for a long time."

She Who Sees Far smiled with satisfaction. "You may wonder how I acquired my name," she said. "It is not just because I can see far distances. It is because I can sometimes see far into the future. I can see things other people cannot. I see you and He Who Laughs together in another world, a future world, helping other people just as you are helping us."

The woman's prophetic ability was a gift Tanya would have marveled at under different circumstances. Fearing again that her friend would see the truth, Tanya glanced into her dark eyes for an indication of such. She saw only a deep faith that She Who Sees Far believed Tanya was truly a kachina sent from the gods.

"And where do you see *me* in the future?" came a smooth, female voice from behind them. "As the wife of a chieftain, perhaps? Or some other man of great power and influence?"

Startled by the silent approach of the intruder, both women looked up from their water-gathering task and into the glittering eyes of the young Sand Clan woman known as Snow in Summer. When She Who Sees Far did not respond immediately to the sardonic remark, Snow in Summer continued.

"If I were you, She Who Sees Far, I would be careful what I said. People might begin to think you are a witch, and that it is you causing the trouble for the people these past few years." Her lip curled derisively; her words were thick with challenge. "Unless you are speaking to a person who is a sorceress, too."

Personally affronted, but accustomed to dealing with sharp-tongued people, Tanya set her dipper aside and slowly rose to her full height, towering over the Sand Clan woman by a good six inches. Fear flashed in Snow's eyes as she realized she had made one accusation too many.

"Your actions are being watched and judged by those in the spirit world," Tanya warned. "It is not power, but regret and misery, that await a woman with a foolish tongue."

Snow in Summer lifted her chin defiantly, but the cold scrutiny of Tanya's eyes froze any further remarks on her pretty, bow-shaped lips.

Then a noise and movement in the trees along the river drew their attention and served to ease the tension that stretched tautly between the three of them.

"Look there," Snow in Summer said, regaining her composure. "Ocelot and the men return from hunting. I see they have a fine mule deer, too. Your man and the One of Many Words are also with them, kachina woman. I am surprised. I thought they would have preferred staying back in the village stringing shells with the women."

The snide remark was said just as Snow turned on her heel and darted away to join the men. The young girl behaved like the classic fool, waving and calling to the group as she ran down the hill toward them. She acted as if she expected them to be as overjoyed to see her as she was to see them.

"Is she always so pleasant?" Tanya remarked dryly.

She Who Sees Far was getting accustomed to Tanya's

sarcasm. She smiled. "Only to women she is jealous of. She is always very nice to men."

"I'll bet."

They watched as Ocelot handed his bow and quiver of arrows to Snow In Summer. The young woman seemed a bit affronted at first, then proudly lifted her head, pretending she had just been appointed as the group's new leader, instead of relegated to the rank of servant girl. Looking idiotic, she motioned the men to follow her back to the village. They did, but snickering behind her back.

Ocelot, Keane, and Swift Blade left the group and headed toward the pond where Tanya and She Who Sees Far were finishing filling their jars. The women returned their full attention to the task, pretending that they hadn't been watching the scene by the river.

Ocelot led the way. He had removed the prized corset, apparently deciding it should be used only for formal occasions. He stopped a few feet from them. His gaze, always like smoke just before fire, flickered from Tanya to She Who Sees Far and back to Tanya. She detected the flirtation on his handsome face and found she couldn't resist a peculiar stirring of feminine appreciation.

"Tanya." He gave her a slight bow, speaking her name with only a slight accent. "You should not be carrying these heavy jars. Allow me to summon a servant."

Keane had stopped next to Ocelot. He stepped past the smaller man and graced Tanya with a rakish grin. "That won't be necessary, Big Wind. I'll carry them for her. Swift Blade, you carry the pots for She Who Sees Far. She shouldn't be doing this kind of work either, being so close to giving birth."

He slipped his bow over his head and across his chest. The jar Tanya had brought to the pond today was fashioned with ropes secured at the necks, serving as handles. She Who Sees Far had suggested it, since Tanya had not yet mastered the art of balancing the jars on her head.

Ocelot curled his lips into a mocking smile at Keane. "If all kachina men do women's work, then I will be in no hurry to go to the spirit world and become a kachina."

Keane had no smile for the Bow Clan leader. Only a cold challenge gleamed in his eyes. "If a man helps his woman with small things, she will in turn help him with big things."

"And she will lose her respect for him," Ocelot quickly countered.

"There is strength in tenderness, Big Wind. Only a man of great wisdom and experience knows these secrets; a man who is well along on the Road of Life."

Ocelot offered Keane a deadly glare, then returned his attention to Tanya. "We are greatly humbled by your presence, Eyes of Sky," he said deferentially. "And we are honored by the rain you have brought to our people. Your visit here is even now being recorded in the memories of the storytellers and on the walls of the great rock so that future generations might know it as well."

"We are here by the power of Ten-Moon," Tanya replied, not liking the idea of taking full credit for the rain. "The people should never forget to honor him as well in your histories."

Ocelot bowed. "Rest assured. His name will not be forgotten. I hope you will not be leaving as soon as the feast is over?"

Tanya turned to Keane and spoke in English. "How do we tell him we might be here for the rest of our lives?"

Keane didn't care for the way Ocelot flirted with Tanya, nor the way she responded. But it was the duality in Ocelot's eyes that made him more uneasy. While the Indian suggested he would like them to stay after the feast, his eyes hinted he would be eager for them to leave.

"You bluff, sweetheart," Keane said with a grin. "And then you pray for a miracle."

Tanya turned back to Ocelot and pieced the words together with some help from Swift Blade. "We are here at the request of the people, and by the approval of the gods. Only they can decide when it will be time for us to return to our own world. There might be other things they will want us to do here before our sojourn ends."

Ocelot bowed respectfully to her. "I hope they will decide to lengthen your stay. Now, if you will excuse me. I must return to the village."

Keane was the first to speak when Ocelot was gone. "I don't think he likes old Ten-Moon anymore than he likes Screaming Panther. It would seem there are few leaders in this village whom our great Ocelot *does* like, except himself, of course."

She Who Sees Far could not understand the words spoken in English, but she clearly heard the derogatory tone and saw the derisive curl of Keane's lip. "Let me explain something to you about Ocelot of the Four Winds," she offered. "He is a man who has traveled many trade routes, seen many things, and met many people. He sometimes thinks that because of this he is more important than others of us in the village.

"I sense that what is inside him is not always good. My judgment might be hindered by the fact that I am of the Bear Clan. He is of the Bow Clan, and there are many of his kind who still carry the tainted blood brought from the Third World. He longs to rule in the place of Screaming Panther. I fear for that day to come. I would hope that the gods would intervene and not allow it to happen. It is written that the Bear Clan will always rule on this Fourth World, but who is to say that by some strange twist of fate, Ocelot might succeed in taking over?

"I am only a woman of this village and not of great importance. Still, I question things, and I fear for myself and my children and future generations. I fear because I *am* a woman and have very little power to stop certain things from happening. I do not even have the power to stop my dreams that of late have shown me the death of a great leader, although I cannot see his face."

Keane frowned. "Screaming Panther? Ten-Moon?"

"I do not know." She laid a hand to her rounded belly as if to protect the infant inside. "It could be the death of my own child, who, if a boy, would be in line for Bear Clan leadership someday." After a moment, she continued in earnest.

"The gods have sent you, the Kachina People, to save our crops and our future with the rain. If they would send you to save us, surely they would not allow us to perish once again under the corrupt leadership of the Bow Clan. Can you tell me, will you stay long enough to ensure this won't happen?"

That they would have the power to stop some deep, dark evil from taking control disquieted all three of them. This was a request for their involvement that was much more immense, dangerous, and improbable of fulfilling.

They looked to each other, each trying not to let their reaction to the request be too evident in their eyes. To turn her down, or even act reluctant to help, would not look good for them. She Who Sees Far stood stoically, waiting for their response to her question.

"How about getting us out of this one, Swift Blade," Keane said casually.

"She is right about Ocelot," Swift Blade said, his young face so serious it looked pained. "I, too, have felt his evil."

Tanya tried to curb a sudden rise in her temper. "How can you say that? He's one of the nicest men I've met. A true gentleman. He's been extremely kind to me and I think you're all over-reacting."

"Even She Who Sees Far?" Keane countered. "Unlike Swift Blade and me, she has no reason for jealousy. You're only defending him because you find him attractive."

"That isn't true!"

"Isn't it?"

"He's a handsome man, of course. Anyone can see that. But I'm not attracted to him."

Keane's eyes told enough to let her know he wasn't convinced of her denial. Tanya didn't know what to think. Was everyone else right and she wrong?

"Maybe She Who Sees Far has listened too long to the stories about the Bow Clan and has been influenced by what the others have said. Don't judge the man guilty for something he hasn't done yet." She turned to her friend. "Tell me what Ocelot has done that has made you believe he cannot be trusted?"

The young woman considered the question, looking away to the distant cliffs on the other side of the canyon as if her answers might lie there among the rocks and brush. Finally her eyes once again met Tanya's. "There are intangible reasons. Intuition. Possibly just the way he looks at me. The way he sometimes looks at others. Perhaps we don't like each other because of the rivalry between our clans.

"There is more. It is rumored that his father was born with the secret power of the Animal People, having the ability to change into whatever animal he chooses to become. Like an animal, he had the power of the Magic Eye to see in the dark. Some of us believe Ocelot was also born with these powers and uses them for his own selfish and evil purposes. There are many in the village who fear him."

It sounded too farfetched for Tanya. "What *are* his evil purposes?"

"To become leader, of course, and to destroy those who stand in his way."

"If the people suspect this, why can't they do something about it, such as banish him from the village."

"No one dares speak up without proof."

"It is all too ridiculous," Tanya said in English to Keane and Swift Blade. "A person can't change into an animal. How could anyone believe such nonsense?"

"After considering where we are, sweetheart, don't you think anything is possible?"

She Who Sees Far seemed to understand Tanya's refusal to believe by the sheer tone of her voice. "You must believe me, Tanya. You must."

"She is your friend," Swift Blade put in. "It would not be wise to let her know her request is upsetting you, Miss Darrow, or to suggest that the three of us are not in agreement. Let us talk in a calmer tone of voice, please, or she may become suspicious of us."

Tanya nodded, getting a grip on her anger. "All right, but I still say you are all being silly about Ocelot. She admits herself that she doesn't trust him because he's of the Bow Clan."

"You do not understand the history of the Bow Clan people," Swift Blade said. "It is nothing to take lightly."

"Then explain it to me," Tanya said. She was very aware of how closely She Who Sees Far watched them. Was it possible the woman who claimed to be psychic was also able to understand more of their conversation than she should?

"The Bow Clan was once the powerful and leading clan of the Third World," Swift Blade said. "Because of the clan's inherent wickedness, they corrupted that world and caused it to be destroyed. Upon emergence into the Fourth World, this world, the Bear Clan was named the leading clan. The Bow Clan was to be left behind to perish in that Third World when it was destroyed by water, but some escaped and followed the other clans into this world.

"Your friend fears that if Ocelot were to somehow become the next tribal chief, then the Bow Clan could come to dominance again in this world and ruin it the way they did the previous three worlds."

"And do you believe this?" Tanya queried.

"Yes, I do, Miss Darrow," he said without hesitation. "I believe it very much."

"Then what do we tell her? I think we'd better give her an answer real soon."

"There's only one thing we can tell her," Keane put in. "Tell her we'll stay until we are summoned back to our own world. But we cannot interfere with the plans of the Creator."

She Who Sees Far accepted the explanation, although it was not what she had hoped to hear. Releasing a sigh of resignation, she led the way back to the village.

Thirteen

Keane cursed the complete darkness of the tiny room. What he wouldn't give for a match. A match and a cigar. A match and a cigar and . . . a shot of whiskey. A steak . . .

But first things first.

On hands and knees he inched his way to the narrow, high-silled doorway. It reminded him of the door on a bird cage, minus the bars and hinge. Every rustle of clothing against the grass mattress seemed amplified to booming proportions in the small area. But Tanya slept on.

Probably too much of that wildberry "punch" Ocelot had plied her with at the feast.

God, it had been both heaven and hell sharing this room with her. Tonight especially. Her eyes had shown brilliantly with a sensual glow after they'd returned from the feast. Again, he blamed the punch. He hadn't drunk much of it himself, finding it too bitter tasting, but Tanya had surely seemed to enjoy it. Or perhaps she had been drunk on Ocelot and been oblivious to the punch. Ocelot had settled next to her and stayed there the entire evening. They'd even communicated fairly well, turning to Swift Blade only occasionally when hand signs and a few words weren't sufficient to relay their thoughts.

He hadn't seen Tanya so schoolgirl giddy in his life. He'd reminded her to behave like a kachina, or at least like she was his woman, so as not to arouse suspicion. She had merely laughed and said, "I don't see why you're getting so upset, Keane. Ocelot is charming and friendly. His intentions are completely honorable."

Yeh, about as honorable as a mountain lion stalking a fawn.

To make matters worse, Tanya had quit sleeping in her clothing several days ago. She'd started sleeping in a skimpy, low-cut leather "sack" thing that barely covered her fanny. Technically, one could probably call it a leather chemise. She'd made it herself from a couple of pieces of finely tanned white leather. It was almost as soft and supple as chamois and very thin. He guessed at least four mountain goats had sacrificed their lives for it. With the help of She Who Sees Far, Tanya had used a bone needle and leather rawhide lacing to piece it together.

Keane would never have dreamed such a primitive rag could be so sexually arousing. She'd taken to blatantly wearing it in front of him before they went to bed. He couldn't help but wonder if she wore it for him, or if she had Ocelot on her mind when she snuggled beneath her turkey feather blankets.

Suddenly his foot made contact with a clay pot, which made contact with another clay pot, which tipped over, spilling all the jewelry they'd been given by the People.

Tanya turned over and sat up. "Is that you, Keane?"

In the dark of the room he could barely see her. Only a bit of moonlight coming through the tower windows lit the room. It danced on the golden length of her hair, spilling over her shoulders and breasts. Maybe he was wrong to hurry Ten-Moon along on the chant that would take them home. If they stayed here, time might work in his favor, and eventually she would share his bed.

Or Ocelot's.

Damn reality. It was always there where Tanya was concerned. She didn't even like him. He was foolish to hold out hope that being here with her alone would somehow change her mind. He had the Turquoise Sun and soon he'd have the vase and mirror. A bundle of money was the most he could hope to get out of this adventure. It didn't look as if love was in the stars.

"It's just me, sweetheart," he whispered, watching her lift a slender arm and brush her hair back from her face. "I'm just going out to visit Mother Nature. Go on back to sleep."

She mumbled something and then groggily burrowed back down onto her grass mattress. Hopefully, she wouldn't remember any of it by morning.

He made it through Swift Blade's quarters with no incident. The Hopi was as lifeless as the rock that surrounded him. Pávati wasn't there tonight. He had night watch on the mesa.

In the corridor, pebbles crunched beneath his boots as Keane crept along like a thief in the night. A few dogs, lounging on the plaza, lifted their heads suspiciously as he passed. Only one growled, and none barked or attempted to bar his way. The Sacred Kiva was on the far end of the complex. He stayed to the shadows, taking the dark corridors that wound back to the kiva. Once there, he wished for a match again, but had to rely solely on his night vision and that piece of moon. He momentarily wished for the Magic Eye that She Who Sees Far had talked about. It would come in handy for sneaking around at night.

The kivas were normally occupied at night by bachelors, old men, or married men who were on the outs with their wives. Since their arrival, the two kivas that connected to the underground cavern had become sacred ground, and the only people who went in them now were the medicine men and the high priests. But as Keane started down the kiva ladder, he heard a low intoning coming from the smaller, inner kiva. He stopped and listened. It was a familiar sound, a familiar voice. Ten-Moon was down there, practicing the chant that would supposedly take them back to their own time.

Keane hesitated, not knowing what to do. The old man

would question his reason for wanting to reenter the cavern, and he couldn't tell him. He could go talk to the old man, though. He wanted to know how the chant was coming and when it would be ready. On the other hand, perhaps it wouldn't be a good idea to disrupt a *túhikya* when he was deep in concentration, especially an old *túhikya* who might have a fragile memory.

He was half in, half out of the kiva, pondering his choices, when a horrific scream from above him shattered the stillness. He looked up in time to see a human body, dark against the moonlit sky, fall from the cliffs into the rocks and brush below. Almost instantaneously, dogs began barking. Then confused people rushed from their rooms carrying hastily lit torches, shouting questions, and running around in confusion. Keane leaped from the kiva ladder and started across the plaza toward the brush where he'd seen the body disappear.

"Over here!" he shouted. Even though he knew they couldn't understand the words, they could understand the urgency in his voice and the motioning of his hands for them to follow him.

He slid down the rocky, brushy incline on his heels, knowing in his heart that no man could have survived such a fall. A few minutes later he spotted the broken form, face up on a long slab of rock. Blood flowed darkly from the victim's mouth, which was frozen in a scream of terror. His eyes stared sightlessly at the starlit sky.

Keane advanced on the body, followed closely by the other villagers. A murmur of new shock rolled through the crowd when they recognized sixteen-year-old Pávati, the chief's son. Keane knelt next to the youth and felt for a pulse. Finding none, he dismally sat back onto his heels.

The boy's mother shoved her way through the crowd, screaming, crying. She gathered her son in her arms, trying desperately to revive his broken body and refusing to believe he was dead. Screaming Panther knelt next to her in silent shock. The look on his face suggested that he thought it might all be part of a bad dream, from which he would soon awaken.

Swift Blade, Tanya, and She Who Sees Far joined Keane. Others continued to come from their rooms. The young men guarding the crops made the treacherous night trek down from the mesa. Screaming Panther lifted his son's limp body into his powerful arms and pushed his way through the crowd. Almost everyone followed him, but questions began from those who were left behind. The older men turned to the young men who had been on the mesa with Pávati, wanting to know what the boy had been doing so close to the edge of the cliff.

A young man named Sakngöisi was the first with an explanation. "We were all at our posts, but Pávati had been acting strangely all night. I think he might have gotten into some bad mushrooms, for he was having delusions. He kept saying he could fly like the eagle. We laughed at him and told him to go to sleep. We do not know what he did after that, but maybe he was trying to prove he could fly."

Keane listened to Swift Blade's translation of the story with a peculiar feeling building inside him. For some inexplicable reason, he didn't believe Sakngöisi, and he debated whether to speak up. He opted for minding his own business, although something about this entire scene didn't feel right.

Ocelot, whom no one had seen until that moment, stepped from the shadows into the light of the torches. He leaned indolently against the very boulder that had stopped the boy's fall and was now stained with his blood. The trader folded his arms across his chest, affecting a look of bored arrogance. "Does an eagle scream when it soars?" he queried. "Or when it dives? If Pávati had believed he was an eagle, wouldn't he have soared into the air quietly, arms outstretched, floating on the wind currents? Free."

Sakngöisi's face visibly paled beneath the red glow from

the many torches. His black eyes darted nervously with sudden fear. "I . . . I don't know. I was watching for beasts that would destroy the crops. I didn't really see anything. Maybe someone down here saw something."

"Who reached the body first?" Ocelot questioned the crowd.

The men looked around, trying to remember. Finally all eyes came to rest on Keane. A middle-aged man said, "Trevalyan was here when we came out. He knew where Pávati had fallen."

"Did you see him fall, Trevalyan?" Broken Spear, the Hunt Chief, inquired.

A faint smile of gloating satisfaction touched Ocelot's lips and he lifted obsidian-black eyes to Keane. "Yes, tell us, Trevalyan. Did the eagle soar, or did he dive?"

Keane had the uneasy feeling that no matter what he answered, Ocelot would play with it the way one would play with a cotton cord. Twisting it around and around until it eventually becomes so hopelessly tangled that no one could return it to its original shape.

In the black depths of Ocelot's eyes, Keane saw the confidence of someone who is accustomed to getting what he wants by the use of intimidation. But Keane wasn't afraid of him. "I heard a scream and looked up in time to see the boy falling from the cave's overhang," he said. "I didn't get the impression it was something he wanted to do."

"Perhaps you'd care to tell us what you were doing so far from the Tower House." Ocelot's eyes bore deeper, even though his tone remained unaccusatory. "This is an unproductive time of the night for anyone to be out, except thieves, hungry animals . . . and witches."

A heavy silence fell over the remaining group of men. Ocelot was clearly trying to destroy Keane's credibility by placing suspicion on him. Everyone waited to see what his reaction would be.

Keane brandished his best poker face, making it impossible for Ocelot or anyone else to suspect that the comment had brought anything other than amusement. "Accusing a man of being a witch could be costly, Big Wind. Unless the accuser is a witch himself."

Hatred flickered over Ocelot's eyes like a wave of quiet sheet lightning across a distant, stormy sky. Keane wondered if anyone else had detected it, for it had lasted only a split second. He knew they were weighing the possibility that Ocelot, too, might not be who he claimed. Doubt was exactly what Keane had hoped to achieve by the remark.

Before the trader could reply, Ten-Moon shoved his way through the knot of men. "You are playing with fire, Ocelot. Do you not know that your words reach back into the realm whence Trevalyan came? You will pay for your lack of faith."

"There is nothing wrong with questioning the truthfulness of something, Old Man. It is not wise to be gullible. It is the way a man dies."

"Perhaps it was the way Pávati died," Keane added. "Perhaps he was too trusting of someone he'd considered a friend."

"Are you saying he was thrown from the cliff?" Ten-Moon put in. From the look in his eyes, he had already deduced the same thing. Keane turned to Sakngöisi. "The only ones who could possibly know are those who were on the mesa."

Sakngöisi, put on the spot again, stuck to his original story. "I did not see it happen. All I know is what Pávati was saying and how he was acting. His mind was not his own. I think a witch got inside it and was telling him what to do. Ask the others their opinion."

The other young men also denied seeing anything. Getting nowhere, the group finally broke up and started the climb back to the dwellings or to their posts on the mesa. Keane, Swift Blade, Tanya, Ten-Moon, and She Who Sees Far were among the last to leave. The pregnant woman's eyes looked hollow and haunted. "My vision was of Pávati's death. I realize that now. He would have been a future and wise leader of the Bear Clan. This is indeed the work of the same witch that has brought the other misfortunes to our people."

"What is she talking about?" Ten-Moon's old eyes crinkled suspiciously again.

Tanya explained the vision. When she was finished, Ten-Moon considered She Who Sees Far with new interest. "Why did you not come to me with this vision, woman? Perhaps Pávati's death could have been prevented."

"Would you have listened to *me*—a woman?" she replied curtly. "You and the other priests have never wanted to consider that a woman might have the seeing gift. But my mother had it. She saw it in me, too, so she gave me the name I carry as an adult. You have all thought she named me as she did because I could see across great distances, but I can see beyond even the horizons into what is to come."

Ten-Moon grunted. "We will talk later about your gift. There is nothing we can do now to change the boy's death."

"The Kachina People could put the spirit back into his body."

Ten-Moon's bushy brows shot up. He glanced nervously at the time-travelers, not knowing what to say. Keane immediately rescued him from the touchy situation and the impossible request. "I am sorry, She Who Sees Far," he said, "but we Kachina People are not granted to alter the course that the Creator has already set down. Pávati's death seems senseless, I know, but there are reasons for all things that happen."

Ten-Moon, pleased by the answer, led the way back to the dwellings. By the time they reached the first terrace the plazas were empty. Everyone had returned to their rooms to either grieve or to discuss the tragedy and its far-reaching effects. Pávati had not been guaranteed as the next leader of the Bear Clan, but, as Screaming Panther's son, he had been favored for the position. Now the people would be forced to consider others for future leadership.

As soon as She Who Sees Far had returned to her quarters, Ten-Moon grasped Keane's arm in a talonlike grip. "We must be careful, Trevalyan. Ocelot is not to be trusted. His mother is of the Spider Clan; his father the Bow. It is a bad combination. In the past, both clans have abused their powers and have since been stripped of their leadership rights, but there are those who would try to take the power back. It is up to the rest of us to see that it never happens. If the Bow Clan were to cause the people to lose faith in the Bear Clan, and to wrest the leadership from them, then I fear this Fourth World could be destroyed just as the three before it were destroyed. Unleashed to do as they please, there would be no end to the evil the Bow Clan can create."

"Thank you for the warning. I'll be careful not to turn my back on Ocelot. Can you tell us how the chant is coming?"

The sudden change in topic caught the old medicine chief by surprise. A sheepish smile eased onto his old lips. He shrugged bony shoulders. "Other matters have kept me busy, but I was working on the chant tonight when you came to the Sacred Kiva. I hope to have it ready soon."

"You knew I was there?" Keane's brows shot together. The old man's knowledge was unsettling.

"I sensed your presence, yes. You wanted to come into the kiva, but you didn't want to disturb me. Anyway, I have a little more to do and then we will try it."

"Can you guarantee the results?" Tanya asked worriedly.

The old man fidgeted and spoke evasively. "You must understand that many factors could be involved; the time of the year, the position of the moon, the sun, the planets. It could be that the opening in the veil of time may never come again in our lifetime." Seeing their glum expressions, he hastened to amend his remark. "But do not give up hope. I will keep trying."

"And if you send us farther back in time, or farther forward in the future?"

"There is no way of knowing if that will happen," he admitted. "I can only ask for the gods' guidance."

"Well, you'd better hurry," Keane replied. "If Ocelot gets these people to thinking I'm a witch, he might convince them you are, too."

Ten-Moon's eyes twinkled. "The only difference between a *túhikya* and a *powáqa* is how each chooses to use his powers, Trevalyan. Now, daylight will be here much too soon. I must take advantage of the stillness of the night so my old ears can hear the words of the gods."

He hurried back to the Sacred Kiva on skinny, bowed legs.

Watching his departure, Keane hooked his thumbs in his back pockets and shook his head. "I don't know about the rest of you, but I get the awful feeling that old man doesn't have the slightest idea what he's doing."

Tanya had barely stepped over the threshold into their quarters when she took a stance with her hands on her hips. Keane ducked into the small room and was hit with the full impact of her unexpected anger.

"Just what were you doing at the Sacred Kiva in the middle of the night, Keane Trevalyan?" she demanded. "And I find it interesting that Ten-Moon didn't ask the same question. Did he already know why you were there? Was he covering for you? What were you going to do? Have him try to sing you back home—minus me and Swift Blade?"

Keane took her outburst in stride and stepped past her. Settling on his mattress, he propped himself up on one elbow. It was amazing how good his night vision was getting since he'd been here. He supposed it had something to do with not having any matches.

He looked up at her long, lovely legs and grinned. For the hundredth time in a week his loins tightened with desire and need. "Leaving you behind is the last thing I'd ever do, sweetheart. Why, it would be the same as turning you over to that oversized kitty cat out there, and I don't intend on doing that either."

"Kitty cat?"

"Ocelot." He reached up and took her hand, holding it tightly because he anticipated she'd try to pull away. She did, but there wasn't much force behind the attempt. "Come and sit down, and I'll tell you what I was doing out there."

Curiosity got the best of her, and she curled up next to him with those gorgeous legs tucked beneath her.

"All right," she said. "Let's hear it."

His gaze slid over her little animal hide getup. She seemed completely unaware how she tortured him when she dressed like that.

"Honey, I told you where I was going. Don't you remember?"

Her eyes narrowed with suspicion. It was in her voice, too. "No, I don't remember."

"Well, I figured that wildberry punch had gone to your head. I guess I was right."

"What are you talking about?"

"It was fermented, sweetheart. Without going into too much detail, Ocelot got you just a teeny bit drunk."

Irritation thinned her lips and flashed across her eyes. She rose to her knees as if the added height would give her an advantage. "Oh, you're so full of bull, it's a wonder your eyes are still green."

He chuckled. "I'm flattered that you noticed their color. But what do you say we just go to sleep? I've noticed these people get up with the turkeys around here."

He rolled to his back and closed his eyes. She laid a

hand on his shoulder and shook him. "Not so quick, sugar-plum. You never did say why you were over to the Sacred Kiva in the middle of the night."

He groaned and opened his eyes again. Her blond hair was hanging down, tickling his bare chest. He slid his hand over hers where it was still resting on his shoulder, and, before she could react, he drew it to his lips. She allowed the kiss for just a second, then she yanked her hand away as if it had been burned.

"You'd try to sweet talk your grandmother out of her last dollar, wouldn't you?"

"You don't know my grandmother." He grinned again. "She's a clever old gal, and the only one in the family with any spirit of adventure. She would like you immensely. You're a lot alike. She says and does what she pleases, too. She would have loved being here with us."

"Keane, you're evading again."

"Honey, I only went to visit Mother Nature. Honest."

Her lips pursed in growing aggravation. "And you had to go clear to the other side of the village to do that? Why do you persist on treating me like a fool? Other than trying to get back to your own time, there's only one other reason for you to go to the Sacred Kiva in the middle of the night. You were going to steal the vase and mirror, weren't you?"

He tried his best to look flabbergasted. "The thought never crossed my mind, T. D. What would I do with either one of them in this place anyway? Now, if I could get back to New York . . ."

"You could keep someone else from finding them until you get out of here."

"You honestly believe I'm without scruples, don't you?"

"I don't believe it. I *know* it."

"Well, you're not as pristine as you'd like everyone to believe, sweetheart. Give Ocelot a few more feasts and a few more glasses of wildberry punch, and you'll be warming his blankets."

If looks could kill, he would have resembled a dart board filled with daggers. "How dare you," she huffed. "You of all people to even consider judging what I might do in my personal life. And I never said I was pristine. If you thought that, it was your own misconception. I do what I want, suffer any consequences, and apologize to no one."

She whirled and was about to escape into Swift Blade's quarters when Keane caught her around the waist. She turned into his arms in an attempt to push him away.

"What have you ever done that could possibly cause you to suffer consequences? You've lived by the book your entire life."

"I don't have to explain anything to you. For your information, I have a right to warm anybody's blankets I choose to," she insisted, not wanting to tell him about that reckless, brief affair she'd had years ago with Frankie. Although she suspected he had probably already put the pieces together. "You're only jealous because I refuse to warm *yours!*"

The struggle between them turned into both a physical and a verbal wrestling match with neither giving in to the other.

"Why should I be jealous?" Keane countered. "I could have any woman in this place."

"You conceited bastard."

"I'm not conceited."

"At least you're half-honest."

"You're right about that, sweetheart."

"Let me go."

"So you can get into trouble with that snake? You're about as dumb as Eve in the Garden of Eden if you let yourself fall for his smooth talk."

"What makes his smooth talk any different than yours?"

She pushed. He held tight. She pushed again. Suddenly his heel landed on the edge of a large metate and he lost his balance. They both fell backwards onto his grass mattress with Keane breaking Tanya's fall.

They were startled to find themselves in a very compromising position, but neither made a move to rectify it. The soft imprint of Tanya's breasts pressing into Keane's chest subdued him. The intense blue of her eyes mesmerized. He was positive she would come to her senses any second. And he didn't want that to happen. Gently, he rolled her to her side, where he could more effectively imprison her in his embrace. To his dismay, she didn't have any more nasty things to say to him. She didn't even try to get away. But she did watch him warily in the semidarkness, waiting for his next move.

His gaze touched her silent mouth; in the next instant his lips did, too. His first real kiss lasted only a moment, then he drew away from that touch of sweet pleasure, afraid that to move too swiftly would seal her mind against him forever.

The fleeting taste of honeyed ecstasy was not enough. Desire rampaged throughout his entire body. "God," he murmured. "I wish I had a match."

She was a long moment before responding, as if she'd been submerged in a warm tub of water that she didn't want to step out of. "Why?" she whispered. "Why do you want a match?"

"So I can see you better, sweetheart. You're the most beautiful woman I've ever known."

He kissed her again. And again, she did nothing to stop him. Her compliance caused a terrible wildfire to burst into a rampaging fury inside him. The flames shot higher, threatening to engulf him when she slipped her hands and arms free of his embrace and moved her fingers up his bare arms to his shoulders. He had yearned for this moment for years. Fantasized about it in waking hours. Dreamed about it in his sleep. And it was everything he had hoped it would be.

He didn't know if he believed in fate, but he did believe in magic. They had been brought here by an old wizard whose magic had made it possible for him to finally hold

Tanya Darrow in his arms. But how long would the magic last? Forever? Or just for a moment?

Did Tanya feel the magic, too?

Difficult as it was, he doused the fire of his blazing passion. Sighing raggedly, he rolled away from her and sat up. He trailed a finger along her cheek and tucked a strand of golden hair behind her ear. He kissed her one last time. Her lips parted fully beneath his, in open temptation. But he moved away from them, from her, until a distance was between them again. Tanya was not a one-night woman, and he didn't want her to be. It was time to stop while he still could.

"Best get some sleep, sweetheart," he whispered. "There will always be tomorrow."

He turned to his side, away from her, and heard her getting settled onto her own mattress. He wondered if she was now as restless as he was. Was she as disappointed that he had brought it to an end? Maybe he shouldn't have. Maybe he should have taken it as far as she would have allowed.

Minutes dragged by. He sensed her wakefulness and the thoughts churning through her mind just as they were churning through his. So much had happened tonight. Changes had taken place that could alter everything about what tomorrow might bring. He knew her mind was going full circle over everything that had happened from Pávati's mysterious death to the passion that had erupted between them.

If Pávati had been pushed over the ledge, then why? Who would have wanted to kill the chief's son? Were there indeed evil forces at work inside this village, or just a lot of paranoid minds? Was there really someone who didn't want the chief's son becoming the next leader of the village? Or was it just coincidental that he was Screaming Panther's son? Perhaps his death had nothing to do with the Bear Clan, the Bow Clan, and the future security of the Red Sand People in this Fourth World.

And maybe Tanya's passion went no deeper than need and loneliness.

It must have been twenty minutes before Tanya's whisper once again reached him in the darkness. This time there was no anger in it, as there had been earlier. No demanding tone. It was just a soft, curious question. "You never did say what you were doing at the Sacred Kiva."

He'd nearly forgotten the question that had started their argument in the first place and that had led to the moment of intimacy. "I was going to find Ten-Moon and ask him how the chant was coming."

"You could have done that during the day."

"The old man sleeps all day and chants all night."

Tanya said no more. Keane sensed she still didn't believe him entirely, but she didn't press the point. He was glad because he intended on trying again to get into the cavern to hide the vase and mirror. He would have to be extremely careful to keep Tanya from finding out, though. If she did, he would lose what little ground he had gained with her tonight. On the other hand, he wasn't so certain the vase and mirror were worth that risk.

Fourteen

In the hour after midnight, the only sounds that came to Ocelot's ears were the occasional creaking and groaning of the rock overhead, or the settling of someone's sandstone dwelling. Even Ten-Moon had ceased his prayers. The chanting had been little more than a murmur, a sound that the others in the cave could not hear. But Ocelot's mind was capable of reaching out across the distance, beyond the confines of his inner self. He could hear even the smallest disturbance, could feel the energy of any power he chose to focus upon. What he had not been able to detect were the exact words of the old man's earnest request to the gods. He could hear only the tone and rhythm, which sounded like his usual plea for rain. Ten-Moon had been in the Sacred Kiva for days, coming out only to eat and relieve himself in the bushes. If the old fool's prayers were answered again, the corn would very likely be washed away. He was losing his mind, probably. That didn't trouble Ocelot. The old man had to die anyway—and soon—if Ocelot was to have any success with his plan.

He took more of the Sacred Datura and waited for the glowing effect of its magic that would aid his supernatural powers. He tossed some dry sticks onto the fire and watched the sparks lift the darkness. Here in this small, secluded cave not far from the main dwellings, he was sure no one would see his fire. There were no human habitats across the canyon. Neither those people from the main village nor the young idiots tending the corn fields would be able to see him. He'd found this cave when he'd been a boy of nine. He'd come here ever since to be alone and to allow his mind to work its psychic powers.

Carefully he gathered the single strand of golden hair he had so cleverly acquired from Tanya's head the night of the honorary feast. He laid it across his left palm and closed his fingers around it. In the other hand, he cradled the cup she had drunk from. Lifting it to his own lips, he tasted the essence of her that still lingered on the clay. Her aura was strong in these two items. It would be easy to slip into her dreams tonight. Easier than before.

She could see nothing. She could only feel. And she felt his warmth in the darkness. He moved next to her, molding his naked length to hers, slipping his arms around her to hold her closer. She felt the rough pads of his fingertips move gently over her skin, caressing the curve of her waist, her hip. Then they moved back up, brushing over the patch of hair between her legs and settling finally on the flat of her stomach.

I love you, Tanya.

And I love you. I have always loved you, but I never knew you. Never knew you at all until this moment.

She felt his warm breath against her cheek, against the corner of her lips. His hand glided up to cup a breast, then move to the other. Her need for him pulsed throughout her body, pounding incessantly like drumbeats in the distance. She'd heard that primitive rhythm somewhere before, but she couldn't remember the time, the place. All she knew was that the beat matched the beat hidden too long now in her soul.

She lifted her arms to him. Her legs . . .

His kiss urgently parted her lips; his tongue stroked her senses; his fingers plucked gently at the bud of her woman-

*hood and the pulse of her being. Then he was inside her,
moving and filling her with his presence, his hardness, his
power.*

*Oh, my love. I have waited so long. So very long. I was
waiting for you even before time began.*

*Yes, Tanya. And I, too, have waited for you since the
beginning of creation. So very long.*

*She cursed the darkness. She wanted to gaze at his hand-
some face, see his expression as he made love to her. She
had to see his face. Had to. But what was this weight that
pressed her eyelids down? Damn the darkness! Then at last
her eyes opened. Thank God! At last she could see . . .*

The muffled scream brought Keane out of his sleep as
surely as if he'd been shot from a cannon. It took only a
second for him to get his bearings and realize the scream
had come from Tanya. He could barely see her in the darkness, just enough to tell that she was sitting up, breathing
as if she'd been fleeing from a hungry mountain lion.

He left his pallet and would have pulled her into his arms,
but she gasped and backed herself up against the wall, getting as faraway from him as the room would allow.

"My God, Tanya. It's just me—Keane. I'm not going to
hurt you. What's wrong?"

She stifled a wrenching sob. When he offered his arms
again, she fell into them as if groping for a lifeline. He
smoothed her hair back and saw no tears on her lovely face,
only terror.

He half expected Swift Blade to lift the trapdoor and ask
what was going on, but the Hopi was quickly acquiring a
reputation for sleeping like the dead. Only snoring could
be heard from the room below.

Keane worriedly stroked Tanya's cheek. Her breathing
was still ragged; her pulse thumped violently where his
hand rested along the heated column of her neck. "Did you

have another dream?" he asked tenderly, lifting her chin with the tip of his finger. She nodded, but said nothing.

Gradually her breathing returned to normal, but she made no move to leave Keane's protective embrace. She burrowed her face into the curve of his neck, eliciting a medley of emotions ranging from desire and pleasure to protectiveness.

He ran a hand up her backbone, over the soft leather chemise. "Want to talk about it, sweetheart?" he whispered against her ear. "It'll make it seem less real."

She only held him tighter.

"It's okay," he assured her. "I told you I'd protect you and I will, even if it's only from nightmares. You've been having a lot of those lately, haven't you?"

Tanya nodded and closed her eyes, but opened them just as quickly when the ghoulish image of her dream leaped back out at her again from the depths of her own mind. She took a deep breath, hoping to calm the pounding of her heart and ease her frightened nerves.

"It was so real, Keane."

"Can you talk about it?"

She would have left his arms if it hadn't been for the darkness still smothering her. How could she be certain she wasn't still being watched? Listened to? Spied on? And she couldn't tell Keane she'd dreamed of making love to him. Nor could she speak of what she'd seen when she'd opened her eyes in the dream. She'd expected to see Keane's sultry and seductive gaze. Instead, she'd been terrified by inhuman eyes gleaming at her from a bed of unfathomable blackness. Yellow eyes, like those of a mountain lion.

But the catalyst that had brought her awake screaming had been the evil intent behind those eyes, and the powerful feeling of fear they had evoked. They had given her the sensation that she was being sexually and mentally violated by whatever beast had been behind those eyes. A beast of supernatural powers that had not only intruded into her body, but into her mind as well, feeding on her thoughts, her fears, her dreams, her past and all the experiences that went with it. Consuming her, until no trace remained.

"It was nothing really," she replied at last. "Just a silly nightmare."

His initial silence suggested skepticism. His words finally verified it. "Well . . . all right, sweetheart. I guess if you don't want to talk—and if you don't want to make love— then the only thing left to do is to go back to sleep."

For as wonderful as the dream of making love to him had been, Tanya was too close to the terrible metamorphosis that the dream had taken to be able to give into physical passions and hidden desires. When she said nothing, he released her. She thought it was with the same reluctance that she herself felt. He was about to return to his own mat when she caught his hand.

"Keane?"

"Yes?"

She didn't think she had misread the hopefulness in his one word, and because of it she felt foolish and humbled. But fear drove her on. "Can I . . . sleep with you? Not to . . . you know. I'm just . . . I don't know . . . it seemed so real . . . I'm still just so . . ."

"Frightened?"

"Yes."

There was another moment of hesitation, and she feared she'd overstepped her bounds. After all, a woman didn't ask to sleep with a man unless she intended to make love to him. But finally he replied, in a subdued and rather dubious voice, "All right, Tanya. At least it's not me you're frightened of."

He turned to his side, and she curled up next to him with her back against his chest, her buttocks molded to his loins, her bare legs against his bare legs. The sensations of his heat and his strength were even more vivid than they had been in her dream.

"You really know how to test a man's willpower, T. D.," he murmured to her back.

"I'm sorry, Keane. If you'd rather not, I won't—"

"No," he said hastily, and reflexively pulled her closer. "I can handle it. Now, just sleep. I'll take the night watch, and I promise no bogeyman will get you. But I won't vouch for myself."

She breathed a sigh of relief and stared into the darkness. It was still frightening out there beyond where she lay curled in Keane's protective embrace. She felt like a child afraid to hang an arm or leg over the edge of the bed for fear a flesh-eating monster laid in wait beneath it. But after what seemed a long while she closed her eyes and drifted back to sleep. And the yellow cat eyes did not reappear.

Ocelot came out of his trance with a start and felt his loins throbbing and his seed on the verge of spilling out onto the ground. How easily he had put himself in Treval-yan's place. If only the woman hadn't opened her eyes and saw his lust, his insatiable hunger for dominion over every part of her.

She had left him aching, the witch. Yes, she was certainly a witch. She had to be to have had such power over him, to consume his every thought since he'd walked into the village that first night and seen her. He had slipped into her dreams tonight to gain access to her thoughts and to acquire knowledge that would tell him her true identity—for he did not believe she and the others were kachinas. But he had not succeeded in his intent. She had skillfully pulled him into her erotic dream, causing him to succumb to his own lust. That had never happened with any of his previous subjects. Now, he feared she might be a great wizard who had sensed his presence and had seduced him intentionally to prove her superiority, or to expose *his* identity.

She had not stopped his intrusion the previous times he

had gone into her mind. If she were indeed a wizard, she had allowed him to glimpse a man named Edward who had gone away from her and never returned; an older man who seemed to always be by her side; and scores of other faces, peculiar places, and wondrous sights that surpassed even those he'd seen in the great southern cities. What he had not been able to do, however, was to see her emotions and her inner thoughts, but only frustrating images that told him nothing. He feared that even these things she had allowed him to see were not real, but figments of her imagination to confuse him and weaken his power, which they had.

The peculiar images he had seen in her mind had him more convinced than ever that she was not a kachina, but one of Ten-Moon's witches called up from the underworld of demons. What other creature besides a demon could possibly ride the backs of huge, hairy beasts and have power over them, as he had seen her and others doing in her dream-thoughts.

Ten-Moon and some of the others did not like him nor trust him, and never had. They were rightly suspicious, for he was their enemy and always had been, even before the emergence into the Fourth World. His father's people, the Bow Clan, were depending on him to lead the rebellion. He would have to do away with those who stood in his way. He'd started with the easiest obstacle first: the boy Pávati. For years, the boy had rebelled against his father, and Ocelot had hoped to deepen that widening gap between them. It would have been a great coup indeed to have one of the Bear Clan, even a possible future leader, turn away from his own clan. In the end, the boy had matured and had come to show too much resistance to the *peyotl* and to the power of suggestion. He had known far too much as well. It would have only been a matter of time before he had gone to his father and shared his knowledge.

Pávati's death had served another, greater purpose. Screaming Panther would grieve now, and the grief would weaken his body's defenses, his mind's alertness. It would be easy to inflict the ghost sickness on him. In his depressed state, it was unlikely any *túhikya* could save him, not even old Ten-Moon.

Ten-Moon himself would be very easy to eliminate. No one would question finding his body one morning in his kiva. They'd been expecting him to die for years now, and the cause of his death would be readily accredited to old age.

He would deal with Screaming Panther and Ten-Moon eventually, but first he had to eliminate the white man and woman in a manner that would not draw suspicion. He feared that even though he had disguised himself in the woman's dream, she might be clever enough and powerful enough to recognize him when daylight came, if she had counter-read his mind in the moment of his sexual weakness. Trevalyan, too, seemed highly suspicious of him.

Angrily he stood up and paced back and forth in the cave's small confines. It didn't matter who the three intruders were. They were interfering with his plans and gaining the trust and adoration of the people so that they were paying less attention to him. Villagers were now openly looking at him warily, considering the accusation by Trevalyan that he might be a witch. If Trevalyan hadn't been there at the time of Pávati's death, nosing around the village in the middle of the night, no one would have had reason to question the cause of the boy's death as anything but his own desire to die.

The couple's powers were strong and would be hard to penetrate. He needed to separate the two of them, to drive a wedge between them and weaken the force they generated. He could lead the people away from this primitive lifestyle, and be their powerful and rich ruler. He could take armies south to conquer those great cities and the tremendous wealth that awaited him there. All he had to do was convince the people to give up the archaic ways that centered

4 FREE BOOKS

These books worth almost $20, are yours without cost or obligation
when you fill out and mail this certificate.
*(If the certificate is missing below, write to: Zebra Home Subscription Service, Inc.,
120 Brighton Road, P.O. Box 5214, Clifton, New Jersey 07015-5214)*

Complete and mail this card to receive 4 Free books!

YES! Please send me 4 Zebra Lovegram Historical Romances without cost or obligation. I understand that each month thereafter I will be able to preview 4 new Zebra Lovegram Historical Romances FREE for 10 days. Then if I decide to keep them, I will pay the money-saving preferred publisher's price of just $4.00 each...a total of $16. That's almost $4 less than the regular publisher's price, and there is never any additional charge for shipping and handling. I may return any shipment within 10 days and owe nothing, and I may cancel this subscription at any time. The 4 FREE books will be mine to keep in any case.

Name _____

Address _____ Apt. _____

City _____ State _____ Zip _____

Telephone ( ) _____

Signature _____ LF0197
(If under 18, parent or guardian must sign.)

A $19.96
value....
absolutely
FREE
with no
obligation to
buy anything,
ever!

ZEBRA HOME SUBSCRIPTION SERVICE, INC.

120 BRIGHTON ROAD

P.O. BOX 5214

CLIFTON, NEW JERSEY 07015-5214

on the Emergence and the migration, and make the young people restless and unhappy enough with their lives so that they would rebel against the Old Ones and follow him to glory.

But they must not turn from him to give their devotion to the interlopers, whom they believed to be messengers of the gods.

He laid back down. His loins still throbbed. His shaft ached at the memory of being inside that golden-haired witch, even if only vicariously. He reached down and encircled it with his hand. A few strokes. That's all it would take to ease the pain. Next time, he would be stronger. Next time, she would not control him, nor hide her thoughts so cleverly.

Tanya wouldn't have believed it if she hadn't seen it with her own eyes. Keane Trevalyan was working. He was working so hard in fact that the sweat poured in rivulets from his naked torso and stained the waistband of his khaki pants. The khaki-colored shirt fluttered nearby on the limb of a dead juniper tree. Next to it on the ground were his scuffed brown boots with his socks haphazardly draped over their tops, baking in the heat. He'd retained his hat as protection from the midday sun. The other men had taken a break and stretched out in the shade of junipers and pinyons to sleep until things cooled off.

Surprised by the sight of him toiling for the benefit of someone else, Tanya wound her way through the cornstalks to his side. When he saw her, he straightened and leaned on his hoe until she stopped a few feet from him.

"I'm glad you came when you did," he said. "I've been thinking, and I finally figured out the answer to that mystery of yours."

"Are you sure you haven't gotten too much sun?" She

eyed him skeptically. "I don't know what mystery you're talking about."

"The mystery of what happened to the Anasazi. I know now why they left here and never came back. I also know where they went. It had nothing whatsoever to do with a migration plan."

Normally finding missing puzzle pieces was enough to set her heart to fluttering, but something about his insouciance put Tanya immediately on guard. "I'm listening."

He lifted his hat long enough to wipe the sweat from his brow with the bandana dangling from his back pocket. He leaned a little heavier on the hoe and looked out across the mesa with serious contemplation settling in his eyes.

"It's simple really," he finally said. "The Anasazi just got plumb tired of hoeing this damned corn in this horrific heat, so they revolted, packed their bags, and went to California."

Tanya's lips twisted into an annoyed curve. "I might have known you hadn't worked long enough to sweat out any of the nonsense that's been backed up in your brain for years. Why are you out here anyway?"

"Because I love to work."

Tanya bent over and began rolling up her pant legs. Keane watched her with amused interest. "So you're going to find yourself a sharp rock and a stick, tie them together with a piece of leather, and help me hoe?"

She straightened. "No. I just don't want my pant legs to get soiled. The bull is getting deeper by the second around here. How about telling the truth. You know you can do that with me and it won't make me think any less of you."

His lips curled derisively. "No, I don't suppose you could possibly think any less of me." At her impish grin, he conceded. "Actually I was out here for several reasons, T. D. One, because I was bored with looking at all those barebreasted women down in the village. Two, I was trying to figure out a way to fix up a corn whiskey still. Three, because there seems to be a group of lazy jackals who do nothing but sit in the kivas all day and gamble when everybody else is up here working their fingers to the bone. And four, me and Swift Blade are up here eavesdropping to see if we can pick up a clue as to why Pávati thought he was an eagle."

Tanya believed the last reason and glanced across the cornfield to where Swift Blade was resting and talking to some of the other young men in the shade of some pinyons. He blended in so well that he could have been of this time, this people.

"Can you understand much of what they say yet?"

"It's not a good sign probably, but I'm even beginning to think in ancient Hopi. Plus, I've been writing words down over there on the ground when I hear them. I figure when Swift Blade wanders over here again he can tell me what they mean."

Tanya glanced in the direction he had pointed and saw a patch of earth that had been cleared of all foliage. On it were strange words, broken into syllables and written according to the way they sounded in English.

"How are they reacting to having a kachina up here working alongside them?"

He repositioned his hoe and leaned on it again, squinting his eyes against the glare of the sun. "They seem honored. I think they respect me more for it."

"The women are the same way. They appreciate the fact that I work alongside them."

Tanya had been watching a stream of sweat trickle down the side of Keane's face from beneath his hat. On impulse, she pulled her bandana from her back pocket. She was just about to wipe the sweat away when her hand halted a few inches from his face. Shocked by her own boldness, she realized she was getting so accustomed to being around him that she had almost touched him without giving it a second thought. He realized it, too. The twinkle of amusement in his eyes shifted immediately to a smoldering glow.

"Go ahead, Tanya," he said softly. "I won't mind."

Embarrassed now, she shoved the bandana into his hand and started to turn away. He caught her wrist and drew her toward him until her breasts brushed his naked chest. The heat from his body seemed to pour over her, scalding her with its intensity. His gaze snared her lips, slipped to the open vee of her shirt, and then drifted back up to her eyes.

"I've missed not holding you the last few nights, Tanya. You spoiled me that once."

She knew she should escape his embrace. All she could do was cling to his muscled biceps to help support legs that had suddenly turned to mush. She cursed herself for being as foolish as she always vowed she would never be. Where was her strength? Her willpower? Her fortitude? Her common sense?

Admittedly, she had truly missed not having his arms around her. For the first two nights after the nightmare, she had been afraid to sleep, afraid she might see those eyes again. She had dreaded encountering that unknown presence that lingered on the edge of her dreams in much the same way as a wolf lingers on the edge of a forest in order to see but not be seen. She had even considered pretending to have another nightmare so she could use it as an excuse to seek out the security of Keane's arms. But there was more awaiting her in his arms than security. In the end, her fear of intimacy proved greater than her fear of the dreams.

"I haven't had any more dreams," she said softly, glancing away from his steady perusal. "At least none I could remember by morning."

"Then I wish you would," he replied just as softly but very suggestively. "And have them of something pleasant, like making love to me. A lot can be said for the power of suggestion."

He stepped closer. Her breasts no longer just brushed his

chest, but were pressed firmly against it. The bulge at his loins molded provocatively against her lower stomach. She made no objection when his hand slid around to the back of her head and his fingers tunneled into the length of her hair.

Their eyes met in a moment of silent questioning and unspoken desires that both knew had been held inside too long. Without warning, that fire burst into flame. In the next instant, Tanya was in his arms being consumed by the splendorous agony of wanting him. Their lips met, tossing the sparks higher, driving the two of them deeper into their tumultuous need. He pulled her hips closer to his, feeding the hunger that raged through her.

Torn between what her body cried out for, and what her pride simultaneously refused, Tanya finally found the strength to push him away. "This is insane, Keane. Stop it."

He caught her arm just as she turned to run, and he pulled her back into his embrace. "Why is it insane?"

"It just is." She struggled against the desire to take everything he had to offer and give fully of herself in return. "Keane, please. It would be a mistake for you and I to become involved."

His lips brushed hers again, then set out to roam her cheek and jaw. "I don't agree."

"I have Edward to think of. He trusts me." She pushed at him again, but the attempt was weak and ineffectual. His kisses continued across her eyelids, her forehead, the tip of her nose. All she could concentrate on was the rush of need flooding over her body, dulling her mind, but certainly not her senses.

"In case you hadn't noticed, sweetheart, Edward doesn't exist anymore. It's just you and me in this Fourth World of the Anasazi."

She tilted her head back, willingly exposing more of her throat to his kisses. "But . . . that's what I came to . . . tell you. Ten-Moon is going to . . . chant us back. Tonight. Midnight. The Sacred Kiva."

"A hundred medicine chiefs combined aren't going to be able to get us out of this world."

Tanya released a deep sigh of defeat. She wasn't sure if she felt that way because of the hopelessness of their situation, or because she didn't have the strength to fight Keane's lovemaking. Whichever it was, it was easier to allow her mind to sink into the delicious touch of his lips. Like wildfire rushing through dry prairie grass, his kisses left a smoldering trail in their wake. He pulled the collar of her shirt aside, exposing the base of her throat to even more of his ardent caresses. She dug her fingers into his biceps to push him away, but found herself only holding him tighter. Deep inside, a throbbing began that urged her to move closer to him. She hadn't felt this driving force with Edward, only Frankie. And she must never forget Frankie and what he did to her.

It was another full minute before she managed to muster another protest. She opened her eyes to cornstalks, the sun, and the bright face of reality. "You must stop, Keane. The men could be watching us. What will they think?"

"That I love you." The words brushed the sensitive skin at the base of her throat. "Because I do."

He was lying, of course, just as Frankie had lied. Somehow it didn't matter. She even loved him at the moment.

He tugged harder on her shirt collar to gain better access to her throat. The top button popped free, vanishing in the dirt at their feet. His efforts succeeded in exposing her collarbone and one shoulder, which he promptly branded with more kisses. She began wishing for a bed, shade, and soft sheets.

She mustered every ounce of her fortitude and pushed at his chest until she had him at arm's length. "You don't need to ply me with false words of love, Keane," she said gently but firmly. "I'm not going to believe you anyway."

The distance helped to sober them both. The male chuckles that reached their ears did the rest. Tanya glanced toward the pinyons and saw that their antics had, indeed, captured the attention of all the young men who weren't sleeping. She looked away embarrassed, self-consciously pushing a strand of hair behind her ear.

Keane only grinned at his audience and picked up the primitive hoe he'd dropped in the moment of passion. Nonchalantly, he returned to chopping weeds. "That's what I like about you, sweetheart," he said sardonically. "You have such interesting preconceived notions of who and what I am."

"What are you talking about?" She glanced over his shoulder and saw that the young men, having decided the action between them was over, had returned to their discussion with Swift Blade.

"I say I love you, and you say you aren't going to believe me. That's what I'm talking about, Tanya. How can you be so sure I don't mean it?"

"I'm gauging my response based on your reputation with women."

"Why don't you drop all the crap about my reputation." His tone took on a sudden uncharacteristic edge of irritation. "For just once in your life, why don't you do your own thinking where I'm concerned, Tanya. I've never done anything to hurt you. I'm certainly not guilty of stringing you along through a four-year courtship, a year of engagement, and then running off to disappear in the jungles of Central America for another two years. You've wasted seven years on that stupid Englishman. How many more years are you going to waste before you get on with your life?"

He was hoeing with a vengeance now. The sweat rose to a sheen on his chest, dampening the patch of black hair and twisting it into curls. It collected on his tight stomach muscles and rolled down toward his pants' waistband.

"What does Eddie do anyway that makes you so sure

he's in love with you? You already said you don't really see eye to eye on things. Did it ever occur to you that he's just using your status at the college and your father's position to aid his own advancement?"

"That's absurd. You don't even know Edward or you wouldn't say such a thing."

"Have you been in the field with him?"

"No."

"I didn't think so."

"What's that supposed to mean?"

"It just means that you might be surprised by the Eddie Chatham you see out in the field. I know him better than you think I do."

He had her so angry she could barely keep her feet on the ground. She clenched her fists at her sides, making a tremendous and concentrated effort not to put both of them right in the middle of his handsome jaw. He didn't know what he was talking about. Edward would never do such an underhanded thing as to use her and her father. Keane was only trying to cast doubts, and she refused to listen.

"I know he loves me. Why else would he ask me to marry him?"

"And you must love him, or why else would you have consented?"

"That's absolutely right."

"You'd best find a place out of the heat, Tanya. Maybe a nice cool kiva where you can safely hide from yourself and your emotions and everything in this world that means something."

She stared at him, and at the muscles bulging in his arms and chest with each hack of the hoe. She didn't fully understand what had happened between them and why. Still, it was no reason for him to attack her and Edward.

"What are you insinuating?"

He didn't look up. "I was insinuating that you don't have the slightest idea what love is."

Sparks of anger flew sky-high. "How would you know what I know about love, Keane Trevalyan? Just because I don't love *you* doesn't mean I've never loved a man! I didn't come up here to discuss my private life with you. You can meet with the rest of us in the kiva at midnight if you want to. Personally, I don't give a damn if you miss the next train out of here."

"That doesn't surprise me," he replied flippantly, then called after her hastily retreating figure. "And tell that old fool of a *túhikya* that if he can get me back to Colorado tonight he can have my last cigar. He can have my hat, too!"

Fifteen

The fire in the center of the Sacred Kiva cast ghostly shadows on the sandstone walls. Despite its warmth, Tanya shivered. The old man's supernatural power was strong tonight, as was the cloud of smoke from the noxious tobacco he'd been smoking before their arrival. His eyes looked glazed and distant. Swift Blade said it was because he had used Sacred Datura to aid in his journey to the spirit world.

In his hand, he held his medicine bundle. It was a leather pouch containing small objects such as spear points, pretty stones, feathers, bits of bone or wood. These simple items held some special significance in his life and were, therefore, imbued with an extraordinary power. The pouch would most certainly contain a bone whistle. According to Swift Blade, every *túhikya* used one to summon good spirits, to repel evil ones, and to help him settle into the frame of mind necessary to conduct any given ceremony.

Standing upright on the kiva's dirt floor, symbolic of man's connection to the earth, were the omnipresent *páhos,* a required element in all kiva ceremonies. The prayer feathers Ten-Moon used were the simplest kind, consisting entirely of down feathers from the eagle. A string of native cotton was attached to the base of each one.

The legend goes that at the Emergence into the Fourth World, the people met a great eagle who would not give them permission to occupy his land until they passed several tests which he himself conducted. After they had completed the tests, he told them that because they had proven themselves so worthy, he would allow them to use his feathers whenever they wanted to send messages to the Creator. "Only I have power over the space above," the Eagle said. "Only I can deliver your prayers."

With an ancient brown hand that resembled the twisted branch of a pinyon, Ten-Moon motioned for the trio to join him near the fire. He approved of the bundles each had brought. "The Red Sand People will be honored that you are taking some of their gifts. It is unfortunate that you cannot take them all."

"That was my opinion exactly," Keane replied, giving the old man his most congenial smile.

Tanya settled next to Keane. "Aren't you going to tell him that you picked everything that would bring big money on the black market? And that you plan to sell even that obsidian knife he gave you?"

Keane's smile never faltered because her question was spoken in English. "There's no need for that, T. D. What he doesn't know won't hurt him."

"All you think about is money. What about history? Or even sentimental value?"

"The stuff in this bag represents my livelihood for the next few years, T. D. Or maybe the rest of my life, if I'm real lucky at the bargaining table."

"There's no hope of you ever changing, is there?"

His gaze penetrated hers. His humor seemed to falter. "Well now, if I'd had a pretty native girl giving me a special gift the way Ocelot did to you, then maybe I'd have something to cherish. Something no amount of money could buy."

He had said it casually enough, but Tanya was struck with the realization that, when it all boiled away, Keane Trevalyan was a man very much alone. Furthermore, he was more than aware of it. She suddenly felt very guilty for the many years she had assumed he was a man without emotional needs.

She glanced at the bag in her own hand. The first thing she'd put in it was the doll Ocelot had given her. The rest of the decisions had been tougher. She had wanted to bring some of the better pottery, but had had to settle for the smaller pieces that would be easier to carry. The things she'd selected would be her only proof of where she'd been. But who would believe her except her father?

She felt humbled. She also felt like a thief in the night with her bundle of booty slung over her back. No, not a thief in the night, but rather, a thief of time. Keane might be taking things that would ensure the most money, but she was taking things that would ensure the most prestige and acclaim. Was her cause any more honorable than his?

Keane and Swift Blade weren't so confident that Ten-Moon would be completely successful, so they'd brought along some bows and arrows, too. "You never know what time period that old man will dump us out in," Keane had said. "No telling what we might be facing."

"Try to be more optimistic about his abilities, would you," Tanya had admonished. But secretly she was scared to death.

Swift Blade had brought a few things, but only to prove to his relatives and the high priests on Black Mesa that he had indeed gone back in time.

She watched the old man now and thought she recognized uncertainty in his jerky movements. Maybe Keane was right. Maybe he didn't have the slightest idea what he was doing. He had made a terrible mistake by bringing them here. Would he make an even worse one in attempting to send them back?

Finally satisfied that he had everything in order, Ten-Moon turned to them with a near-toothless smile that made him look borderline addled. "I think you should all go back into the tunnel and to the cavern you say is on the other side. When you do this, we should be ready to proceed. Since I do not have the strength of the other priests with me tonight, it would be best if all of you would focus on the chant, let your minds go into it and become one with it. Do you understand?"

Swift Blade translated his instructions so Keane and Tanya would not miss or misunderstand a word.

"There is one more thing I would like to say before we begin," Ten-Moon added. "Someday I might find the right moment to tell my people that you were not kachinas, but that you were people of the future. If I should tell them this, I would also like to be able to tell them what lies on the other side of tomorrow."

The three exchanged dubious glances and debated if they should tell him anything. Finally Keane said to Swift Blade, "Tell him what would please him to hear about his people."

Swift Blade looked deeply into the old man's eyes. Age had made them rheumy, but it had also given them patience and wisdom and a childlike faith. The young Hopi cleared his throat. "Some of the clans left here, as you know," he said. "They followed their star and completed their migrations, as it was intended for them to do. I cannot tell you where they eventually settled, because it would not be wise of me to interfere with the course set down by the Creator."

"And those who did not complete their migrations?"

"They were lost, swallowed up by time and other people who came from across the great eastern water we call the Atlantic Ocean."

"Atlantic Ocean." Ten-Moon rolled the name across his tongue so he would not forget it. Then he said, "How many circles has Father Sun taken around Mother Earth from my time to yours?"

"We do not know for sure, but we think about six or seven hundred."

"Ah, many generations."

"Yes, many generations."

"What is it like on the future world? I can tell by your clothing that some things have changed. Tell me, has the face of Mother Earth herself changed, or the color of Father Sky? Do the animals that roam here now still exist in your time?"

"Mother Earth has withstood time well. But there are many, many more people, and they have caused most of the changes. They are people of all the four colors; red, black, yellow, white."

"And they get along?" The old man was clearly amazed.

Swift Blade smiled. "Sometimes. In some places."

Ten-Moon's tone lowered, taking on a note of anxiety. "And are the Red Sand People the leaders of all these others?"

Swift Blade looked directly into the old eyes. There would be no deceiving him. "No, but we have retained our dignity."

Ten-Moon nodded, as if he had expected as much. "That we were not lost entirely is a comfort."

"What will you tell the people about our abrupt departure?" Tanya asked.

"I will tell them that the gods summoned you back, having completed your work here."

"And if they don't accept it?" Swift Blade put in, worried about the ramifications of the old man's magic conducted in secrecy and without council from the other priests and clan leaders.

Ten-Moon merely shrugged his bony old shoulders. "What can they do? Send me away from the village for being a *powáqa?* I am an old man and ready to die anyway."

Yes, that's what they were all afraid of.

"Let's get started then," Keane said, gathering up the bundles he'd set on the ground. "The witching hour is waning."

"Yes," agreed Ten-Moon. "It is time to begin."

Considering the lantern a sacred fire item, Ten-Moon had

left it in the tunnel. They lit it now to guide their way into the cavern. Once there, Keane's first glance assured him that the vase and obsidian mirror were still safe. He wasn't sure how he would get his hands on them, but he was positive he could think of some way to get to them before Tanya carted them off.

He suspected that when they got back, she would pretend nothing had ever happened between the two of them. The thought brought an unexpected heaviness to his heart. Still, there was little he could do about it. He had to accept the fact that no matter what time they happened to be in, Tanya Darrow did not like him. She might like his kisses, and eventually even like his lovemaking, but she would never like *him*. The only good thing about leaving was that he'd be getting her away from that snake-faced Ocelot.

From the tunnel, they heard Ten-Moon's chanting begin, distant and faint. "In order to keep our departure a secret, he sings quietly," Swift Blade explained nervously. "We should sit in a circle with the lantern in the middle, like a fire. We will close our eyes and focus on Ten-Moon's words as he said we should. We must put ourselves into what he is singing."

"You don't look too enthusiastic about this," Keane teased the younger man.

Swift Blade's attempt at looking positive faded entirely when put under fire. "I'm not," he admitted. "How can one go back to the future when one does not know how he got into the past in the first place?"

"I guess we have no choice but to give it a try and suffer the consequences later."

"It is those consequences that have me worried," Swift Blade replied. "But we must try not to be skeptical of Ten-Moon's ability. If we do not believe, then he will surely fail. He needs the strength and confidence of our minds in order to make this work."

Tanya and Keane settled into position as Swift Blade instructed. Tanya easily drifted back into the monotonous intoning of the chant's words and rhythm. It sounded exactly the same as the original chant that had pulled them over to this side. After a few minutes, though, she realized her mind was restless, discontented. Soon it wandered away entirely from the chant and into its own realm of thought.

She found herself regretting that she would have to leave behind the little room she shared with Keane. Back home, they would go their separate ways again as if nothing had happened. Keane would find another woman—*women*. And she would settle back into the mundane routine of teaching at the university, going on summer digs, and waiting for a man she no longer felt sure of. A man who might never return.

Keane had rekindled her longing for desire and passion, and the deeper need to have a more soulful connection with a mate. She was positive these were things she would never have with Edward. She was beginning to think that she and Keane were more alike than they were different.

Keane shifted, as if he'd heard her thoughts. The movement brought his knee in contact with hers, but she didn't move away and neither did he. That contiguity became the focal point of her awareness. She began drifting into the memory of his kisses, the gentle touch of his hand caressing her body, his arms around her in the night protecting her from nightmares and from the evil eyes of her imagination. If they went back home, all that would end. Their relationship would return to what it had been before.

She didn't know how long her thoughts churned. Minutes, maybe hours. She was surprised when she was drawn out of a near-stupor by a hand on her shoulder, gently shaking her.

"Wake up, sweetheart. I think Ten-Moon has finished his chant. Let's go see if it worked."

Tanya's eyes came open with difficulty for she had drifted into a pleasant and private world of thoughts, emotions, and sensations. All was silent now in the cavern, except the distant drip of water on rock. They left their bundles where they lay and followed Swift Blade back into the tunnel. Tanya's heart raced with fear and anticipation. But above all, reluctance. She wasn't ready for her time with Keane to end. There were things too unsettled between them.

Upon emergence into the Sacred Kiva the first thing they saw was the dying fire in the center. Only embers remained, leaving the kiva dark. At the edge of the lantern's circle of light, they saw an outstretched hand and gnarled fingers curled loosely around a *páho*. Swift Blade took a step closer with the lantern. The old man was stretched out on his back with his eyes closed and his mouth gaping open.

Tanya's heart leaped to her throat. "My God, is he dead?"

At the sound of her voice, the skinny body jerked and a long snore thundered through the large nose and into the silent kiva. Ten-Moon came awake, blinking away his sleep in utter confusion.

"You are still here! But it cannot be!"

Keane lowered himself to his haunches and scrutinized the old man's stricken face. "Swift Blade, tell him we're still here because he sang himself to sleep."

It was the young Hopi's turn to look stricken. "I cannot tell him that, Keane. It would be a most disrespectful thing to say to a man of his age and a man who possesses his power."

Keane shrugged. "Well, his power was impressive the first time around. I can't say as much for it the second."

Ten-Moon forced his rickety legs to bend at the knee while he leaned forward and tossed more sticks onto the embers, and then breathed life into them. In a moment, new flames burst forth from the center of the fire pit.

He was fully awake now, but his old eyes were still watery and bloodshot from a combination of smoke, lack of sleep, age, and possibly even the Sacred Datura. "Your thoughts were not on going back to your own time." He looked accusingly at Tanya and Keane, as if they were young children who had not minded their elders. "I sensed neither of you truly wanted to leave here. Before we try this again, you must decide what it is you want to do. Without the power of the other priests, you must put your supernatural powers with mine so that we will be successful."

"But we're not gods," Tanya reminded him. "We are only people of the future and we have no supernatural powers."

His eyes bored into hers. "Have the Future People lost all their powers? If they have, then I certainly do not want to see your world.

"We will not attempt this again tonight." He began clearing up the objects pertinent to the ritual. "Daylight will be here much too soon and I am very weary. We will try again as soon as I feel rejuvenated. Perhaps during the waxing moon, because the moon was in that position when you arrived."

Keane's lip curled derisively. "Since you're sending us forward in time, maybe you should reverse things and wait for the waning moon."

The old man's brows lifted as if it was a very good idea that hadn't occurred to him. "Yes, yes," he began to mumble. "Perhaps the waning moon would be the better one . . ."

"He doesn't have the slightest idea what he's doing," Keane said, rolling his eyes skyward. "What difference could it possibly make?"

"I can't tell him that," Swift Blade said. "It would be—"

Keane held up a hand. "I know—disrespectful. Never mind. Let's get back to our rooms. Spending too much time in this squatty kiva is putting holes in the knees of my pants. And, since they're a precious commodity around here, I'd like to make them last as long as possible."

They left the old man staring into the fire with a distant and dazed look on his face. He was still trying to figure out why the chant hadn't worked . . . besides the fact that he had fallen asleep in the middle of it.

Outside, the night torches were burning low; daylight would be upon them soon.

"I think I'll take a walk down to the river," Keane announced. "I'm too wound up to sleep."

"I'm going back to bed," Swift Blade countered with a yawn, not looking too disappointed in the outcome of the chant.

"Tanya? What about you?"

Tanya saw in the depths of Keane's eyes, the anticipation that her response would be positive. She received the distinct impression from the sultry glow therein that he wanted to be alone with her. Should she listen to her common sense, her better judgment? Or should she allow him to lead her into a ring of fire where one wrong move could burn her forever?

"I doubt I could sleep right now," she heard herself say. He held out his hand. "Then take a walk with me."

Her fingers touched his. "A walk sounds good."

They took the well-worn path down through the trees. At the edge of the talus slope, Keane jumped down first, then turned to assist Tanya. He fully expected her to sidestep his outstretched arms, but she surprised him by placing her hands on his shoulders. He circled her waist, just as she leaped from the edge. As her feet touched ground, her body slid the length of his. He held onto her for possibly a moment too long, but he found himself transfixed by her laughing eyes and the softness of her breasts. Her lips, too, were much too close and tantalizing in the moonlight.

He would have kissed her then, but she must have recognized the desire in his eyes. Suddenly she glanced nervously over her shoulder. In the next instant, she had taken his hand and was leading the way down the darkened trail through the trees. If he wasn't mistaken, she seemed in a terrible hurry to lead him away from the ruins. She glanced over her shoulder several times until the torchlights could no longer illuminate their departure.

On the canyon bottom, sometime later, she released his hand and moved upriver. She didn't stop until she had reached a heavy stand of brush and moved into the seclusion it offered. He settled next to her on the soft grass. They remained silent for several minutes, just watching the dark band of water barely discernible in the predawn hour. The canyon walls formed a black platform for the star-filled sky.

"It's beautiful, isn't it?" she whispered. "When I first saw this place, I had the strange feeling of *déjà vu*. I was touched with an array of peculiar emotions. One was a very disquieting feeling. I seemed to sense danger, although I couldn't pinpoint what it was or where it was coming from. But there was also a comforting feeling, as if I had come home."

"Maybe you *had* been here before, in a peculiar sort of way," Keane replied with a mysterious hint to the tone.

Her eyes glittered with curiosity. "What do you mean?"

"Maybe you felt *déjà vu* because you *had* been here before. Right Now. It's like being caught in a circle of time. If you're here now, then you were here before you rode out of Durango with the field crew. Maybe you came here on the expedition because you were drawn back, possibly searching for something you had left behind from this time that we're in now. Or maybe you were called back because you left something undone. Was that why you weren't concentrating on Ten-Moon's chant? Because you knew you had left unfinished business and weren't ready to leave?"

"That's an interesting theory, but a farfetched concept," she said with a smile. "I'm here now because I went on the expedition, not vice versa."

"*Being* here is a farfetched concept." He picked up a stone and skipped it across the water. "And why were you so anxious to get away from the village a little while ago?

You acted as if you were afraid someone would see you kissing me. You did up on the mesa, too. Was it me you just didn't want to be seen with, or is it something else?"

Tanya found her own stone and rolled it between her fingers while she stared into the vast stillness surrounding them. Finally she began walking; he fell into step beside her.

"It has nothing to do with you, Keane. But in the dreams I've been having, I feel as if I'm being watched. Then when I open my eyes, in the dream, there *are* eyes watching me. Just eyes, gleaming from a bed of complete blackness."

"Eyes? Whose eyes?"

"No ones. They belonged to a creature—a cat. And yet there was something very human and very sinister about them."

A chill sneaked down Keane's spine and made him glance behind them, too, half expecting to see someone watching them from the shadows. Tanya's dream foreboded ill, and he didn't like it. Suddenly he began tossing the pebbles into the river with all the force he could muster.

"What's wrong?" Tanya asked from behind him. "I don't know that I've ever seen you so upset."

He tossed another rock, this time so hard it sailed clear across the water to the other side. "Am I upset?"

"I would say so."

He tossed the last rock across the water and then shoved his hands into his back pockets. "If I tell you what's on my mind, you won't believe me, and then you'll be the one who's upset. You'll probably even tell me to go find Pávati's diving board and give it a try."

Tanya was mildly surprised by this side of Keane Trevalyan. He usually took everything not only in stride, but with a grain of salt. She was seeing all sides to him since they'd been forced to live together, and his playboy image was no longer the prevalent one. As a matter of fact, that image was fading rapidly.

He took a position against a huge sandstone boulder. Folding his arms over his chest, he stared into the predawn darkness.

"Why did the thing about the eyes upset you so much, Keane?"

He smiled wryly. "I could use a cigar. If we end up having to stay here, I'll have to start my own cigar factory."

"Quit trying to evade the question."

He contemplated her seriously. "You've always seen right through me, haven't you, Tanya? Do you suppose that's because we're kindred spirits? Two people so totally different in so many ways and yet so completely alike in others. I mean, we can practically read each other's minds."

Tanya smiled, finding that amusing. "I'm afraid I can't read yours right now."

His eyes probed hers for another moment; his were dead serious. "Ocelots are cats, Tanya. Think about it."

Her brow furrowed. He continued.

"I'll stake everything I own that it was Ocelot you sensed watching you, even in your dreams. I've seen him watching you when you've been working in the plaza, and you've probably sensed it yourself. He's infatuated with you, T. D., and it scares the hell out of me."

The conviction in his eyes sent a chill down Tanya's spine. How could he have known that she had sensed being watched while she was in the plaza? And the eyes in the dream *had* been those of some kind of cat. But it irritated her that Keane was so quick to blame Ocelot for something that connoted evil—evil aimed toward her. She refused to believe such nonsense. Ocelot had been nothing but kind and chivalrous toward her.

It was her turn to pace the sandy loam by the river. "You just don't like Ocelot for some reason, and you're trying to turn me away from him by frightening me. Well, it won't work."

Keane grabbed both her arms and brought her to a halt

in front of him, forcing her to look at him. "No, I don't like him, and I *am* afraid for you. I'm not making this up—I've *seen* him watching you."

"But in my dreams? He couldn't do that."

He released her and ran a frustrated hand through his hair. "How should I understand that anymore than you do? How can we explain traveling through time? There's magic in this place—both good and bad magic. If Ten-Moon can capture us on the strains of a song and pull us back hundreds of years in time, then I would imagine Ocelot could get into your dreams relatively easy. Maybe he's the damned witch that's been wreaking havoc on the village. For all we know, that obsidian mirror that supposedly belongs to Great Bear of the Night Sky might really work, too."

"And how do we know this isn't *all* a bad dream?"

"We're honestly here, Tanya, in a mystical place where nothing is impossible. Nothing. You need to accept that if you ever plan on coming out of here alive."

"I've always known you were capable of a lot of stupid things, Keane, but you've really jumped over the edge this time. The eyes I saw in my dream might have been those of a cat, but they did not belong to Ocelot. I've never been more sure of anything in my life."

She started to run away, but he caught her arm again.

"You're being so blind that if I didn't know any better I'd think you'd fallen in love with him."

She tossed her head back defiantly and met his flashing green eyes. "If you didn't know better? What does that mean? You suggested once before that I was incapable of loving anyone. Well, let me tell you something. If anyone is incapable of that particular emotion, it's you! You criticize my relationships with both Frankie and Edward. Now you're trying to frighten me away from Ocelot. You're the one with the problem, Keane Trevalyan! Not me!"

She wrenched herself free of his grip and sprinted down the riverbank back to the cliff dwellings, running as swiftly as the darkness would allow. But he could run faster, and she heard him right on her heels.

"Damn it, Tanya. Come back! We need to talk."

She pushed herself until her lungs burned and her heart hammered unmercifully against her chest wall. Her hair streamed behind her like a golden flag, occasionally whipping around into her face to block her vision. She dove into a grove of aspens and underbrush and immediately saw her mistake. The branches slapped at her face, slowing her down, and the brambles tangled around her feet. She could barely see now for the tears that inhibited her progress. Then something caught her foot and she felt herself falling. There was absolutely no way she could escape her pursuer now.

Sixteen

"Who are you running from, Tanya? Me or yourself?"

She tried to get up, but the brambles that had felled her were still wrapped around her ankle. In the semidarkness, she could only fumble blindly in an attempt to free herself while wiping proud tears from her eyes. "I would appreciate it if you would keep your nose out of my private life."

Keane lowered himself next to her to assist with the brambles. "That's a little hard to do when we share quarters."

She pushed his hands aside and tried again to free herself. "With Pávati dead there's no reason why you can't move into Swift Blade's room."

Keane was getting as frustrated with her as he was with the brambles. All he wanted to do was make love to her. Did the woman always have to be so contentious?

He pushed her hands aside and tried turning her foot to various positions to see if it would slip free of the bramble. "I suppose you think good old Edward would have thought of that immediately; him being such a gentleman and all."

"He *was* a gentleman, and I'm tired of you insinuating otherwise. Our courtship and engagement might have been long, but Edward wants to get better situated financially before we marry. He wouldn't use me, and he wouldn't betray my trust while he's out in the field."

Keane sat back on his heels and removed his knife from its scabbard. "Do you honestly believe he's been faithful to you all these years? *If* he's alive, do you think he's being faithful to you right now?"

"Why are you trying to put doubts in my mind? Be careful what you cut with that Bowie."

Keane kept his eyes on the brambles. "I know how to handle a Bowie, and I'm not trying to put doubts in your mind. Maybe I'm just trying to make you see the truth. Sometimes a person thinks he knows another person and comes to find out he doesn't know that person at all. Didn't you ever wonder why Edward doesn't want you with him on the digs? Or why he wants you to stay home and be the perfect wife and mother after you're married, instead of taking you with him?"

Tanya's eyes were glued to the knife, sawing dangerously close to her leg. "No, all that stuff didn't occur to me because I trust him."

"A man in love would want his wife along, if at all possible," Keane continued. "And especially if she actually *wanted* to go with him. Nights are lonely out in the field, as you well know. If you were my wife, I'd want you with me."

"That's amusing."

"What is?"

"You with a wife."

"Laugh if you like, T. D., but I'd bet every piece of pottery in this village that Eddie only wants to marry you so he'll have somebody to wash his dirty socks when he comes back from digs. He doesn't strike me as the real settling type."

"And you ought to recognize that type?" Tanya gave him a shove and he fell backwards, cursing, onto a pile of prickly pear cactus. His knife slid under the bramble and vanished in the darkness.

"Damn it, Tanya. Why'd you do that?"

"Because I'm getting tired of you constantly saying mean things about Edward just to hurt me."

Keane didn't know how to get off the cactus without inflicting more pain on himself. The situation was escalating into one that was putting him in about the foulest mood he could ever recall having been in. Or maybe it was just Tanya. She had a way of turning his guts inside out and his mind upside down.

"To set the record straight, sweetheart," he said, gingerly picking himself up off the cactus. "I wasn't trying to hurt you. I was trying to shine some light in your eyes. Just for a minute, think seriously about your relationship with Eddie. What does he *really* want? What do *you* really want?"

Again Tanya attempted to free her foot from the tangle of undergrowth, going at it now as if it were a matter of life or death. It wasn't the tangle she was so anxious to be away from, but her nemesis, dear old Keane Trevalyan, always hanging around in her life like the proverbial albatross around the neck. Why, she couldn't even get away from him in the thirteenth century!

"I already told you," she snapped. "He wants a wife, children, a home, respectability in the community."

Keane struggled to his knees, plucking cactus thorns out of the seat of his pants. "Ah, that last one is the clincher, sweetheart. And you can give him that without a doubt."

"He wouldn't use me."

"How do you know?"

"Because I do." She looked away quickly and put her mind on disengaging her foot from nature's trap.

Keane leaned back on his heels, giving her a disgusted appraisal. "I get it. Just before he left, he told you how much he loved you and made you a bunch of pretty promises and said he wanted to have something to remember you by. And you gave it to him, didn't you?"

"No!"

"Well, maybe you should have," he muttered. Then, "Was he your first?"

She wasn't ready to tell him about her tumultuous love

affair with Frankie Locke. Nor was it any of his business that she had done nothing more than hold hands and exchange a few kisses with Edward.

"That's none of your business, Keane, any more than it's my business to know with whom you've been intimate! I doubt you would even remember the names of most of them. Let alone your first."

Keane was up on his hands and knees now, lifting brambles in search of his knife. "As a matter of fact, I remember the first one very well. I sincerely doubt I'll ever forget her."

Jealousy leaped up from Tanya's heart and stuck like dry cornmeal in her throat, threatening to choke her. She forgot about the bramble and found herself meekly asking, "Who was she?"

Keane found his Bowie and returned to slicing away the green, tough branches of the tenacious bush. "She was a beautiful brunette named Honoria. She lived on a lonely ranch outside of Denver. She took me in and gave me a job when I was eighteen and hungry. I was hungry in about every way a man can be at that age. She was twenty-five and her husband was away, working, and she had a few hungers of her own. Anyway, I fell in love. She didn't. But I guess she was fond of me, because there were tears in her eyes when I left.

"What is important is that you don't have to be honor-bound to Eddie. Sometimes the first one isn't the right one, no matter how much we'd like for it to be."

She wondered what he would think if he knew about Frankie. Would he lose respect for her? Think she was loose? Or maybe he already did know. If so, he didn't seem to hold it against her, as some men might.

"And why did you leave this gorgeous brunette?" she asked flippantly, hoping to hide that inexplicable stab of jealousy.

He shrugged indifferently. "Her husband came back."

"Why did you, the son of a wealthy carriage manufacturer, need to turn to a stranger in Denver for help?"

"That's a part of my life that's over and done and behind me. No point in dredging it up. Let's just say I was a kid who had bit off more than he could chew, and found out the hard way that the world away from home wasn't all fun and games."

"I get it. It's okay to probe into my past, but yours is sacred. Well, why don't you just leave me alone and go sleep with Swift Blade, because you're not going to share my quarters tonight!"

She shoved again and he landed in the cactus again. When he finally got to his knees the second time, he thrust his hunting knife into its scabbard and stood up. "I'll sleep with the turkeys first, sweetheart. No offense to Swift Blade—he's a nice young man—but he isn't my type." He shot her one last angry look, then started back to the village.

She twisted her foot again and it came free. Scrambling to her feet, she started after him. "Just where do you think you're going?" she demanded.

He didn't even slow his pace, just hollered over his shoulder. "To find the turkeys. What else?"

Ocelot couldn't see the witch. She wasn't in her quarters, nor was Trevalyan. Angrily he paced his little cave. Where could they be? What evil were they concocting against him? Or had she used her great power to prevent his mind from finding hers? He was positive now that the two of them hadn't come to bring rain. That had only been a ruse. No, Ten-Moon and the other priests and clan leaders had summoned them to use their influence and all their powers to keep him, Ocelot of the Four Winds, from leading the Bow Clan to a mighty victory over the Bear Clan.

Fighting a growing rage, he left the cave and scaled the canyon wall, coming out on top of the dark mesa. Like his namesake, he could see well in the dark, and he slunk past the cornfields and the young men who were, as he'd expected, snoring when they should have been guarding the village and the crops in this crucial hour before dawn. The hour when an enemy, if he was inclined, would choose to attack.

He found the familiar trail to the village below and easily descended it in the darkness. Drawing his knife, he went directly to the Sacred Kiva. He was going to find that secret passage to the underworld—or prove it did not exist. And if the old *túhikya* was in there, he would kill him. He was running out of time, and he had already run out of patience. He wanted answers and he needed them quickly—before dawn.

The outer kiva was empty, and he heard no sound from the inner kiva. Not a snore, nor the faintest murmur of a chant. He crawled through the tunnel, knife still drawn. But the inner kiva was empty, too, except for a few coals from a recent fire. Gauging by his previous activities, the old man had probably been here most of the night. Chances were good that he had gone to his clan kiva and would not return here until night fell again.

Gathering a torch from off the kiva's stone seating bench, Ocelot thrust it into the fire until the tip burst into flame. He feared very little, for he was a man confident in his own powers. But as he gazed into the small tunnel that led to the center of the earth from whence the Kachina People were said to have emerged, he felt a degree of trepidation. What if the gods were there, just on the other side, waiting to strike him down for entering onto sacred ground?

He moved closer and listened while peering down the tunnel's dark length. The torch's light was quickly swallowed by a bend in the tunnel, but it caught on a strange contraption sitting near the entrance. The upper portion of the object was protected behind a hard, clear substance that he could see right through, and which appeared very fragile, like the first ice that formed on the ponds just before the snows came. The base of the object was of a shiny, smooth metal similar to some he'd seen in the southern cities. It was like the gold breast plate, heated and flattened, but much thicker, and of gray color.

Not knowing what it was for and what powers it might hold, he resisted the temptation to touch it. There was always the possibility that a curse had been placed on it by the Kachina People, and to do so would bring instant death.

At last he conjured the courage to enter the tunnel. Slowly he crawled after the lighted torch he held extended in front of him. A few minutes later, he emerged into a huge cavern. He questioned the wisdom of interloping in this awesome and sacred realm, where stone daggers of peculiar colors grew down from the ceiling and sprang up through the floor. A place where silence was so absolute that the thumping of his heart echoed back to him.

When he found the black vase and obsidian mirror, centered on an altar of stone, there was no doubt in his mind that the mirror was the magical one belonging to the Great Bear of the Night Sky. At the base of the altar were the gifts the Red Sand People had given to the Kachina People, who in turn had brought them here as offerings to the Great Bear. It was likely the Bear would come for them soon, and Ocelot knew he must not be here when he did. Yet, the mirror had caught his reflection, and the Great Bear had probably already seen him here, trespassing. Perhaps the Great Bear had seen everything he'd done, as it was said he could do. Maybe he knew, too, every thought that crossed Ocelot's mind.

There was immense power in the mirror. The legend of its existence had traveled all the way to the southern cities and become a part of their legends as well. The legend said it was kept in a cave in the north, but no one had ever found it—until now.

He feared the power pulsating in it. The power that,

through it, the Great Bear must have extended to Trevalyan, Tanya, and their interpreter. The trio were indeed more than witches; they were sent by the Great Bear at the request of Ten-Moon to see that Ocelot and his followers failed in their quest.

Panic swelled inside him until he found it hard to breath. All this power was at work against him. He would never succeed with his plan now unless that power was broken. And the only way that he could see to do that was to break the mirror.

Throwing aside the consequences of such harsh and desperate action, he lifted the mirror from the vase and held it in his hands, the reflecting piece facing away from him. With one mighty dash, he struck its face against a large rock and watched the heart of it fall to the rock floor in three separate pieces. Satisfied that he would now have no interference from the only power that was greater than his own, he hurried from the cavern, looking back only once.

Keane had barely fallen asleep in the grass by the river when screaming jolted him awake. Not sure if it was part of a dream, he tried to make sense of where he was and of the bloodcurdling cries of women and children and the frantic shouts of men. Dawn barely touched the eastern horizon, turning the canyon walls blood red. He was alone. Tanya was up there with the People.

He shot from the seclusion of the willows. His feet pounded down the edge of the shallow river. The screams grew louder; the shouts closer. A glance at the village and the mesa above confirmed that the Red Sand People were under siege.

The trail had never seemed so long nor so steep, and his leg muscles burned fiercely before he was halfway there. Trees slapped him in the face, stinging and cutting him. He reached the talus slope and scrambled across it, his boots slipping on the rock. He could see the young men on the mesa in hand-to-hand combat with the enemy. They'd been asleep at this hour and caught off guard.

In the shadows of the rock overhang, enemy warriors with ghoulishly painted faces and bodies scaled the ladders leading to the people's rooms. Their knives and spears caught their victims unprepared. Women fled into the canyon with screaming children in tow. A few were cut down by enemy spears.

Keane searched the mêlée for yellow hair, but in the coming light he did not see Tanya. Had she returned to their room last night? Why hadn't he waited to see where she'd gone? Could she, too, have preferred the solitude of the river after their argument?

Pulling his knife from its scabbard, he dove into the battle, dodging whoever and whatever blocked his single-minded intent. Thoughts of Swift Blade and Ten-Moon flashed across his mind, but he had to find Tanya first.

A grisly war shout made him look up just in time to see a knife-wielding Indian hurtling down on him from one of the sandstone ledges. He leaped backward, but the man's weight drove him down and into an immediate struggle. Keane's knife blade was swift and caught the attacker in the chest. The enemy froze in stunned shock as he stared at the hilt protruding from his heart. Then the life went out of his eyes and he slumped over Keane's arm. Keane pulled the knife free and ran on toward the Tower House, frustrated by the fight that had taken precious minutes.

He saw Tanya then. An Indian with his face in hideous paint had her by the arm and was pulling her across the plaza toward the serpentine trail that led down into the canyon. He cut through the trees as fast as his feet would carry him and waited for them near the trail's third switchback. Hiding behind a tree, he positioned himself on a big rock. When the Indian was directly below him, he leaped. The force of contact sent Tanya sprawling backward and threw himself and the enemy off the trail and down the hill into some brush. The Indian landed facedown with Keane on top of him. He had the advantage of weight and surprise. He grabbed the Indian by his long hair and was bringing the Bowie to his throat when Tanya screamed.

"Keane! It's Ocelot!"

That second of hesitation was all it took for Keane to falter over the murderous deed he'd been about to commit. It didn't make him want to kill the man any less—maybe more, knowing who he was. He maintained the position of the knife, deathly close to the trader's jugular. And he found satisfaction in doing so.

Tanya hurried down the hill, sliding on her heels. "He was only trying to get me out of there to keep me from being captured by the enemy."

For the first time, Keane saw the primitive knife clutched in Ocelot's hand. "Drop the weapon, Ocelot."

"What are you talking about? I'm your friend."

"You'll never be that. Now, just do it. And toss it out of reach!" He pressed the Bowie harder against the pliant skin, drawing a sliver of blood. Reluctantly, Ocelot tossed the knife into the brush. Just as reluctantly, Keane let him up.

"I'll take over from here," he said. "You go back up and try saving some of your other people. Tanya will stay with me."

Ocelot touched the skin on his neck and, when his fingers came away, they were tinged with blood. "You are crazy," he said, his black eyes cold and unforgiving. "You do not act the way a kachina should act."

"Then you don't know much about kachinas, do you?" Keane's lip curled with the contempt he felt for the man. "You might try explaining why you've got all that paint on your face. I mistook you for one of the enemy. But then, I'm not so sure you're not."

"I was performing a prayer ritual for Pávati," Ocelot replied indignantly. "But you should know that. You should recognize the lines on my face are not those of a man going into battle."

Keane realized he'd just made Ocelot even more suspicious of who he really was, but he offered no further explanations. He took Tanya by the arm and started back up the path. "I think you'd be wise to get back to your people, Ocelot. They might need you."

Ocelot looked up the hill toward the village. "I believe the fighting is over. The enemy has fled."

There was only crying now. The screaming and shouting had stopped, but the three of them hadn't noticed it during their own private battle. In contrast to the blood spilled on the red rock and the green mesa, the first rays of the morning sun topped the horizon and sent golden streamers of light down the center of the canyon. It glistened off the river as it played hide-and-seek with the trees lining the crooked banks.

"Why did they leave so suddenly?" Tanya asked.

"They did not come to conquer," Ocelot replied. "Only to weaken. To torment. To steal."

"Will they be back?"

"It will depend on how well our people defended themselves. If we proved ourselves to be weak, they will return. If strong, they may get reinforcements or decide to attack another, smaller village. Now, as you said, I must go back."

Keane and Tanya followed, anxious to see who had survived and who had not. They found Swift Blade alive. He'd been up on the mesa and had been in the thick of the battle. He had some knife wounds crisscrossing his brown torso, but it appeared that none were life-threatening. Ten-Moon tottered out of his small apartment, not having been found by any of the raiders. It was a good thing, too, for they knew the old man would have been no match for a young adversary. She Who Sees Far appeared fine, but frightened. Screaming Panther had a gash on his arm made by a spear and it was bleeding quite heavily, but his wife was already attending to it.

There were a few who had been killed, but none of the women had been stolen, nor the children. Ocelot conducted the removal of the enemies' bodies and had his followers take them down into the canyon where they would be burned. He whisked them away so quickly, there was barely a chance to look at them.

A young boy named Kacha Hónaw, White Bear, about four years old, took a position in front of Keane. Silent tears ran down his brown face and blood trickled the length of his chubby arm. He did not wail the way an injured child will usually do, but his black eyes were nonetheless overflowing with pain and fear.

Keane drew the boy onto his knee, spoke to him, and gently applied to the wound some of the healing poultice which the women were busily making. He asked the boy how he had come to be injured and learned that the child had caught a warrior's blade while trying to protect his younger brother. The two-year-old was fine and stood silently next to his brother, wearing a grim expression.

After the children saw Kacha Hónaw bravely sitting on Keane's knee, they lined up to receive similar treatment for their own small cuts and bruises. Some just wanted to be held by the man whom they knew now as He Who Laughs. Tanya noticed that Keane had a way with children and soon had them all smiling, forgetting the trauma of the early morning. Even after they were treated, they remained nearby until their mothers led them away.

The sun had been up for two hours before all the injured had been attended to. The only wounds left to be treated were those on Keane's face, the scratches and cuts he'd received from running through the brush and trees.

There was still some poultice in the bowl that Tanya held on her lap. Taking a bit on the ends of her fingertips, she placed some on his cheek. Instantly he pulled away and stood up.

His eyes bit into her, as did his words. "Save it for Ocelot. Knife cuts to the throat are more likely to take infection."

He stalked off once again, going directly to their quarters. Tanya felt as if she'd been slapped. What had gotten into him? Why he was behaving so out of character? Where was the fun-loving Keane Trevalyan that always had a smile and a wisecrack? Well, if he thought he could put her off a second time by running away, he was dead wrong. This time she knew where to find him.

Seventeen

Tanya took the ladder to their second-story room and found Keane busily placing blankets and pottery in the center of a piece of cloth. She stepped from the last rung onto the stone floor and waited with her hands on her hips for him to acknowledge her presence. He didn't.

Finally she forced the issue. "What exactly is it you're doing, Keane?"

He still refused to look at her. "I'm leaving, of course. Isn't it the custom here that when people marry, the man moves in with the woman?"

Tanya suddenly felt as cold as if she'd been doused with a bucket of ice water. He was getting married? To whom? He had paid virtually no attention to any woman here except for herself.

She lifted her head proudly, pretending she could care less that he'd found another woman. After all, she should have expected that of Keane Trevalyan.

"That must be one of the best kept secrets in the village. Who's the lucky woman? Or should I say, *unlucky* woman?"

He gave her a look that bordered on surprise and confusion. "It has nothing to do with me, Tanya, so don't try to act the innocent and turn the tables here. I finally put two and two together. Actually, it hit me broadside while I was down there patching up cuts and scrapes. I honestly believed the story about Ocelot trying to get you away before you were abducted. Then I realized that he'd been here with you all night. The minute I was out of the way, you invited him in. I expect you'll want to get married next. So, obviously, it's time for this old bachelor to find another place to toss his bedroll."

Tanya was flabbergasted by his ridiculous accusation. "I think you've been consuming some hallucinogenic plant, Keane. Even if I *had* invited Ocelot to my room—which I didn't—it's not for you to be making judgments one way or the other about what I do in my personal life. I followed you up here to try and make amends, but now you can just go as faraway as you please. Maybe two or three hundred years in either direction."

Cursing herself for having had a moment's weakness toward him, she stepped back onto the ladder, wanting to get as far away from him as she possibly could. She had only put one rung behind her when he caught her arm.

"Am I right about Ocelot, Tanya? Just tell me the truth."

"The truth? Now isn't that a switch for you?"

She pulled her arm free and completed her exit without any more interference from him. She left the Tower House and hurried through the corridors and into the shadows. Here she could hide the inexplicable pain and humiliation from any curious onlookers. She wanted to cry, but she fought the urge until her head and throat hurt from the effort. At last, in a vacant little cubbyhole between rooms, she hid next to some water jars and let the tears flow.

Never in her adult life would she have ever dreamed that Keane Trevalyan, of all men, could make her heart hurt so badly and send her mind into such a maze of confusing and conflicting emotions. The worst of it was that she didn't even know why. But she stayed in her cubbyhole for a long time with her back against the cool stones and her knees drawn up to her chest. She thought about Keane and what he'd said, and how he'd been acting recently. She tried to make sense of it, to rationalize his behavior, to blame it on the strange journey back in time. In the end, all she knew for certain was that she had seen pain slipping through the anger in his eyes, and she wondered if he was hurting right now in the same way that she was.

There was a barrier between them, and she had put it there herself to protect her heart. To remove it now would mean to surrender herself entirely—heart, soul, body, and mind. She couldn't take the chance of being hurt again in the way Frankie had hurt her. There was no pain worse than the pain of a heart deceived.

Keane found sanctuary in the Sacred Kiva. Ten-Moon had been there recently, for embers still glowed in the fire pit. It would be no problem for him to reenter the tunnel and go into the cavern to reassure himself that the vase and mirror were still there. Besides, action of any sort might help take the sting out of knowing that Tanya could not be convinced that he wasn't a worthless bum. He needed sleep, but he was sure it wouldn't come with all the pain so fresh on his mind and heavy on his heart.

He touched a dry twig to the embers and used the small flame to light the lantern. Quickly he made his way into the tunnel. For a moment, when his feet touched the rock floor of the cavern and the lantern light reached out in a circle surrounding him, he feared that the strange but powerful force that had brought them here might return and take him to another place, another time faraway from Tanya. He was suddenly reluctant to take another step. He didn't fully understand the feelings he had for her, but he knew how much he had always looked forward to events where she would be present.

Since they'd been here, sharing a room in this Indian village, those feelings had deepened. He looked forward to each moment he could be near her, settle his eyes on her, touch her. The feelings were growing stronger, and the fact that she had kicked him out of the room, essentially out of her life, hurt in a way he could barely describe.

His family and older brothers had never had time for him and basically ignored him, letting him run wild and then chastising him for it. Despite their disregard for him, and the fact that he'd always been alone, he could never recall having been lonely. That particular emotion had never been a part of who he was. He had taken life by the horns, refusing to sit idle and watch life pass him by. He'd watched for opportunities and adventures. If misfortune chanced upon him, he had always found a way to turn it into opportunity.

When he'd found himself stranded in this world of the Anasazi, he'd maintained the optimistic notion that Tanya at last had no place to run, no one to turn to but him. In his dreams, he had always envisioned that she would come into his arms with love in her eyes. Unfortunately, he now had to accept, once and for all, that her feelings for him could not be manipulated in the way other things in his life had been.

He advanced across the large stone room toward the vase and mirror. The light finally reached it a few moments before he did. But suddenly his stride faltered and he stopped dead in his tracks. The obsidian mirror was gone!

Frantically, he glanced around. It was nowhere to be seen. Someone had been here and stolen it. But who? Ten-Moon? Had that old geezer taken it in hopes of gaining power from it? Or maybe Tanya had taken it to keep him from having it.

"Damn it."

The words echoed in the cavern, circling around him several times before fading away. Angry strides took him the last few steps to the empty vase. He ran a finger along its smooth, black surface, wondering again about the peculiar material he had never seen before, a material that made him think it had come from the future, even beyond his own time. At least the vase hadn't been taken. He would hide it, and then if he ever got back to his own time, he would be able to find it.

As he turned to scout out a secret receptacle, the toe of his boot caught something on the stone floor. The object was sent skidding in front of him until it was halted by one of the many stalagmites in the cavern. Narrowing his gaze on the object hidden in the shadows, he knelt to inspect it closer and quickly identified it as a piece of the mirror.

At once relieved that the mirror hadn't been stolen, he was simultaneously infuriated to think that someone had come in here, probably nosing around, and had carelessly broken it. He picked the fragment up and rolled it over in his fingers, mindful of the sharp edges that could slice skin as easily as his Bowie.

A niggling notion began working on his brain as he examined the fragment. Soon he decided that there was something more perplexing about finding the mirror broken than if he'd found it stolen. What if someone hadn't been careless? What if someone had broken the mirror intentionally? If they had, then why leave part of it behind? Why not destroy it and all evidence of its existence and of their dastardly deed?

The notion that evil intent had been behind the destruction of the mirror wouldn't leave his head. Tanya and Swift Blade would not have been so careless or so evil. They hadn't told Ten-Moon about the mirror, but even if he'd come into the cavern and found it, he would not have destroyed it. No, the three of them would have handled it with religious reverence. Tanya for its historical qualities; Ten-Moon for its mystical power; Swift Blade for both reasons. Who, then, would have done such a thing?

Keane searched the floor and found the other two pieces. He slid them together, using the floor as a table, and saw that they fit perfectly. He was startled to feel heat emanating from the stones, and a peculiar throbbing, like some sort of energy flowing through them. Feeling as if his flesh was about to be singed, he removed his hands from the broken obsidian.

Another inspection uncovered the handle and the back of the mirror, which was still all in one piece. Gingerly, he lifted it out of the crevice between two rocks where it had fallen and returned the pieces of the broken obsidian to their proper place. The pieces could be glued in place. Even though it was damaged, he could find a buyer in New York and sell it for a fortune, especially with the legend of the Great Bear that was linked to it. It was possible it might bring more money than the Turquoise Sun. With the proceeds from both of them he wouldn't have to worry about money for years. He could even pay the remainder of what he owed on his Connecticut estate.

He found a hiding place behind the stone table for both the vase and the broken mirror. Returning to the Sacred Kiva, he decided to find Swift Blade and see whether he knew if anyone had been to the cavern.

He had no sooner squirmed from the cavern tunnel and doused the lantern, when a scraping noise drew his attention to the short, outer tunnel between the two kivas. Having no place to run, nor the time to do so, he watched gnarled hands, brown wrinkled arms, and a gray head of scraggly hair emerge from the tunnel and into the Sacred Kiva. When Ten-Moon got his old body straightened out, his eyes ovaled in surprise at seeing Keane standing there in the near-darkness.

Expecting to find the Sacred Kiva empty, as he had on every other occasion, the medicine man eyed Keane with a certain degree of suspicion that also took in the satchel of belongings dropped carelessly not far from where he stood. At first he said nothing, but went to the fire pit and placed dry twigs and small sticks on the dying embers until the fire was self-sustaining.

"Are you here because you are anxious for me to try the chant again?"

"I was waiting to talk to you. To find out how things were progressing." He saw the old man's attention drift to the satchel and felt an explanation was in order. "I was also bringing a few more things I didn't get the first time."

Ten-Moon nodded but his eyes swam with skepticism. "I am more inclined, my friend, to think that your yellow-haired woman has made you leave your dwelling place. A little argument perhaps?"

So the old man couldn't be fooled? Somehow that didn't surprise Keane, but pride held his tongue. He did not care to discuss what had caused him so much inner pain. "I came here because I needed to be alone after the raid. To rest. I hadn't had much rest from last night."

"Ah, yes," Ten-Moon replied ruefully, having been reminded of his failure. "I had hoped to be more successful, but I felt that there were forces working against me. Neither you nor Tanya seemed to be focusing on leaving. If anything, I had the feeling that neither of you were ready to go. Perhaps one of you isn't feeling well. Perhaps that is what keeps your minds from focusing. There are *powáqas* at work all the time. It could be that one is interfering with your concentration. You do not look as if you feel too good right now."

"I'm fine," Keane quickly denied, lest the old man see the truth. "I'm just tired, as I said."

Ten-Moon reached across the fire and circled Keane's arm in an iron grip. "Come and sit by the fire, my son. I will tell you what is troubling you."

"Nothing is troubling me."

Ten-Moon ignored him, insisting that he sit down next to him. Keane finally settled cross-legged just to relieve his arm of the bruising, talonlike fingers. Satisfied, Ten-Moon released him completely and knelt in front of him, sitting back on his heels as he usually did. He lifted his withered arms, skin sagging, and placed his hands on Keane's head. After a moment, he moved his hands to a spot above Keane's eyes, then his throat, his chest, and at last his belly. Between each new position he closed his eyes for several minutes as if listening. At last, he lowered his hands and looked at Keane with clear compassion.

"What was that all about?" Keane asked nervously, feeling unusually exposed.

The old man's dry, brown lips curved into a snaggle-toothed, sagacious smile. "I can feel the vibrations from your body's life force centers," he explained. "Like the earth, man was made with a central stalk from which everything in his body originates. It is like the trunk of a tree; the stalk of a corn plant; like the main river and its tributaries; like the axis buried deep in the center of Mother Earth. Man was given a backbone and all parts of him flow out away from it. Along the backbone, the life force centers send out messages, like echoes, of what is going on in the body. It is like the vibrations that come from the center of the earth and move outward to shake the ground we stand upon. As a *túhikya,* I can touch these centers and feel the echoes that tell me where your sickness lies."

"But I'm not sick."

Ten-Moon's smile remained confident, wise. A mischievous twinkle started like the flame of a tiny fire in each of his eyes. "But you are, my young friend. You are sick in the heart. Not in the sense of those with Two Hearts—evil hearts. No, that is not the sickness that is yours. I had thought that perhaps a *powáqa* had cast a spell over you, but I can see that the only spell that has been cast over your heart is that of love."

The old man turned away then and went back to preparing his fetishes for the chant that he would be working on again tonight. Keane's gaze followed his slow, meticulous movements. Could Ten-Moon actually read the signals of the body, or was this love inside him for Tanya so blatant that any fool could see it?

"That is why you're here, isn't it?" Ten-Moon continued. "Tanya has kicked you out of your dwelling place."

Keane finally assented. "We had a little argument."

"Ah. Little arguments are the worst kind, because they grow into big arguments. I would suggest that you go back to her and apologize."

"But I didn't do anything to apologize for."

Ten-Moon shrugged. "Perhaps no more than she did, but are you not the man and therefore the stronger?"

He pinned Keane with wizened eyes. Keane didn't know if he fully agreed with the old man, for he knew just how strong Tanya Darrow was. He knew she could hold her own beside any man. But the medicine man was of the culture that believed women were the weaker sex, so finally Keane gave a reluctant nod, knowing it would be futile and disrespectful to argue.

"Then you should be the one to take on the responsibility of getting the matter settled," Ten-Moon said. "Be the first to say you are sorry."

"But I didn't do anything," Keane insisted stubbornly.

"So you have said. I say you must have done something or you would not have made her so angry that she kicked you out." He placed his hand on top of Keane's head again. "When you were born there was a soft spot in the top of your head. It is the first and most important force center of the body. We call it *kópavi,* the open door. Through this door you receive your life, and through it you communicate with the Creator.

"Beneath the *kópavi* is the second most important force center, the brain. This enables you to do your own thinking. You will think about what you do here on earth, both your actions and the work that you accomplish. Those who are wise will learn over the course of their life that what they think and do should agree with what the Creator wants them to think and do.

"So you see, in essence the brain is carrying out the plan of the Creator. A wise man will ask himself many questions, and he will look at himself as if his face is reflected in a pool at all times. Now, I suggest you go and talk to Tanya. For her heart is breaking also."

"How do you know this?"

Ten-Moon shrugged and twisted his eagle feathers around in his gnarled fingers. "One never knows what a woman is thinking. Emotions run as hot as fire in their veins—or as cold as ice. But we men can always hope that their thoughts are favorable towards us, and that the blood in their veins is hot."

Keane wondered if the old man's "wisdom" was really just an excuse to get him out of the kiva. Nevertheless, he left. He didn't go directly to their quarters, but sat outside the kiva in the afternoon sun until the searing orb had vanished below the western rim of the canyon. Only then did he make his way to the Tower House, realizing as he went that he had not the slightest idea what he would say to Tanya.

He found her asleep in the coolness of their room. Not wanting to wake her, he started back down the ladder, but his boot scraped on one of the rungs and the noise brought her awake. She sat up, pushing the lengths of blond hair back over her shoulders.

"Keane. Is something wrong?"

Her voice was soft and melodic, her sleepy movements clearly of a self-conscious nature. He sensed it embarrassed her to be found asleep with her hair a gorgeous tangle that she, being a woman, would undoubtedly think was a mess. Even now, barely awake, she was automatically trying to smooth it.

If this was a woman whose heart was breaking, then Ten-Moon was not a very wise man after all. If she felt as lost as he felt, as lonely, wouldn't she have red eyes from crying? Wouldn't she be lying awake, sad and lonely, not sleeping like an angel with an uncluttered mind? He sensed she had dismissed him and their argument as soon as he'd left the premises.

All the wisdom Ten-Moon had imparted seemed no more relevant than a fairy tale when put in the face of actual confrontation. What was the use in trying to explain any of what he felt? Tanya didn't like him and she never would.

"I just wanted to tell you I'm sorry for what I said about you and Ocelot. You have a right to do whatever you choose, with whomever you choose."

He took another rung down on the ladder when her words stopped him a second time. She seemed to be fully awake now with her eyes clear and shining and focused on his in a very serious way. "I think it would be wise if you moved back in, Keane," she said. "I mean, the Anasazi might lose faith in us being kachinas if we start behaving as erratic as human beings."

He found himself lost in the blue of eyes that rivaled the color of the summer sky. He searched their depths for the things he wanted to see there. "You're right. They might start getting suspicious. How can we bring order to their lives if our own are filled with discord?"

"Then you'll bring your things back?"

It was a moment more before he spoke. He hesitated this time because he knew how hard it was going to be to go on sharing this room with her in the capacity they had been sharing it. Didn't she know the hell he was going through being so close to her every night and wanting to make love to her, but not being able to?

Still, she was wise to protect her heart, her future, and her reputation. He just couldn't understand why she had risked it all on Frankie Locke and Eddie Chatham, when she wouldn't risk it on him. Why did she have to be so determined not to give him a chance? Or was she? Maybe she was giving him that chance right now.

"I'll get my things. They're in the Sacred Kiva."

He was about to leave when emotion suddenly gripped him and pulled him back up the ladder. He stepped out into the room and stood just feet from her, his eyes locked with hers. All the pain and anxiety he'd been feeling welled up in his chest. He crossed the short distance separating them and pulled her into his arms, burying his face in her hair. To his surprise, she returned the embrace and held him just as fiercely, as if she had missed him the way he'd missed her.

"I wanted to kill Ocelot," he said gruffly. "But only because I thought he was going to hurt you, Tanya. I said I would protect you when we came to this place, and I'll stand by my word. I'll be here until you tell me to go, until you find another who can do the job better. You *will* tell me when that happens, won't you? You won't make me guess?"

A great warmth, like a golden strand of sunlight, showered down over him and held him secure for a minute.

"I'm grateful for your concern for me, Keane," she said against his chest. "Believe me when I say that Ocelot did *not* spend the night here. I was entirely alone."

"As I was."

Her lips grazed his neck and the curve of his jaw. Her touch electrified him, weakened him in a glorious way. "I don't want to be alone again tonight," she whispered. "Please, Keane, let's finish what we have started so many times. Make love to me."

Her scattered, heated kisses brought the blood pumping erratically in his veins. "Are you sure, Tanya? There can be no going back."

Almost urgently she drew him down with her onto his mattress of grass. "Is that a promise, Keane Trevalyan?"

He cradled her in his arms and brushed another kiss across her lips. "Yes, Miss Tanya Darrow. That is, most certainly, a promise."

Eighteen

Tanya suppressed the painful lessons she'd learned so long ago, and she fell, a wiser fool, into the silver splendor of Keane's touch and his kisses. She fell even more eagerly than she had once fallen into the lies of Frankie Locke. The reason was simple: an adventurous, gambling heart ultimately believed in promises and hope, the two things that were often all that remains at the end of a long road.

Ardent, but beautifully gentle, Keane laid her back, stretching his long, lean frame over her softer curves and molding his body to hers in the way intended by the Creator. The rough pads of his fingertips moved tenderly along the lines and angles of her face, insinuating a degree of wonder. It was reflected in a similar spark of awe which swayed like a candle flame in the depth of his green eyes.

She felt the focus of that flame as it ignited charred memories of desire, sweeping them both into an all-consuming blaze. Keane's caressing fingers slid along her neck, awakening needs that, like deciduous trees in winter, had lain too long in shades of gray. His lips followed the tiny paths created by his fingers and swiftly and deftly erased any doubts that might have lingered in her mind.

His were strong lips that scattered sure kisses. His were hands that knew where to touch and how. She closed her eyes to revel in the mastery of his lovemaking, to memorize forever each nuance of sensation, to succumb to the powerful crescendo building inside her. His hands sank into her hair, his faint moan of pleasure was swallowed by her own as he abandoned his roaming and tasting of her flesh to claim her lips more fervently than before. She parted her lips and he filled the hungry emptiness with the swift thrust and dart of his hot tongue.

The primitive dance of bodies began in earnest. Hips moved against hips, lifting, swaying in time to the rhythm of rapture. Clothing was removed and cast aside onto the warm stone floor. His brawny, hair-covered chest settled onto the soft fullness of her breasts. His erection shuddered in eager anticipation against the soft, wet folds of her womanhood.

She would have taken him then, but he eased down her length, twining his fingers with hers as he did, all the while scorching a trail of love and lust from her collarbone to the flat tautness of her stomach. His kisses found her jutting hip bones, the sensitive flesh at the sides of her slender waistline, the rounded curve of velvet-smooth buttocks, and retraced a path to her aching breasts. He released her hands and cupped her breasts tenderly, suckling the pert peaks, curling his tongue around and over first one and then the other until she tossed her head on the grass mattress, gripping his shoulders and writhing in a sweet mixture of agony and ecstasy.

They were together at last. Nothing else mattered. All was forgotten; the past, the present, the future. Only the moment existed, hanging suspended in time as if it might miraculously go on forever. Of course it couldn't, and at last Tanya whispered, "I need you, Keane."

He settled back into her arms, his eyes meeting with hers in passionate understanding of her needs and a willingness to comply. "Sweetheart."

The one word, spoken in a husky, delicious whisper, said all she needed to hear. She lifted her legs and took him deeply inside. They moved as if they'd done this dance together before. Rising and falling like the high and low chords of an ancient and magical chant, they moved.

Dreams were fulfilled in the constant sureness of reality. Gone were ghostly feelings and images that could not be grasped in the world of dreams, where pleasure always vanishes in the first second of awakening.

Their thrusts were strong and perfectly matched. They cried out in simultaneous fulfillment, forgetting the presence of the world and the village surrounding them. This was a joyous song they would sing, loud and clear; a triumphant song that would not be denied.

This melding of hearts and bodies went on, time and again, into the night until darkness and exhaustion found them quietly resting in each other's embrace. All worlds beyond, wherever they might exist, were inconsequential. They were two people who had at last, and after a very long journey of time and years, found their own world, their own time. More importantly, they had found each other.

There was no knowing the hour that Tanya finally fell asleep in Keane's arms with a satisfied lift to her lips and a relaxed contentment to her lithe body. When darkness had fallen, they had lit a small torch, and now Keane studied her elegant features in its golden, flickering glow. He rested a hand on her flat stomach, wondering if his child might be growing there already. Just the thought made his heartbeat quicken with a deeper love than he'd felt before. He would like nothing better than for them to share a child, but would she feel the same way? When morning came, would she regret the bond they'd made tonight in wild abandon? Would she decide she'd been foolish for forgetting that he was, as those in archaeology circles termed it, a thief of time? A plunderer of history whom she had previously had no respect for?

Being reminded of the things that had kept them apart, and knowing that their lovemaking hadn't changed who or what either of them were, Keane thought of the Turquoise

Sun he'd hidden in a leather pouch beneath his grass mattress. The entire village knew about the gaming confrontation with Ocelot, what they'd both gambled, and how much Keane had risked but had ultimately won. As he'd told Tanya earlier, his prowess in the game had put him in an even higher position of honor and respect among the people. He was as daring as any warrior, for in this society great regard was given to men who could risk all and come out victorious. He also knew, however, that the necklace would be an enticing lure for many men. He hadn't checked on it since he'd hidden it, and he wanted to make sure it hadn't been found, or stolen in the raid. Or that Ocelot hadn't returned to the room in their absence and stolen it back. He would put nothing past the trader.

Carefully he lowered Tanya back to the fur-covered pillow and covered her with a cotton blanket. She stirred only slightly. He reached under the edge of the mattress until his fingers closed around the rough leather pouch. He drew it from its hiding place, relieved that it was still in his possession.

Loosening the rawhide strings, he tipped the pouch. The necklace fell out onto the mattress, making a metallic clink. As quietly as possible he fanned it into the shape of its namesake. It gleamed richly in the glow of the torch. Nothing he had ever seen could compare to its beauty, its elegance. It had been his intention to take it to the cavern and hide it with the vase and mirror. Now, ambivalence began to gnaw at his gut. He began to feel as if he was being torn apart from the inside out. The only purpose the necklace would serve in this world was to exemplify wealth, or possibly power. Unlike Ocelot, he would never be vain enough to wear it. It was too beautiful to adorn a man's neck, even though it had. Realistically, it should warm the neck of a creature whose beauty would compliment its own.

Gathering the necklace in one hand, Keane knew it was

time to gamble it again, but this time not for more treasures, nor money, but for love.

In the faint torchlight from outside, he carefully removed his Bowie from its scabbard and, using the very tip, scratched the initials TD vertically on one side of the bar clasp. On the other side of the clasp, he scratched his own initials. Now, when the clasp was joined, the initials would be locked together.

He eased back down next to Tanya and dropped a kiss on her shoulder, then a few more on her neck and ear. She stirred and was rolled to her side, facing him. Nestling against him, she was as warm and soft and naked as love itself.

It was all he could do to control his passions long enough to do what he had set out to do. Tanya Darrow was not likely to believe mere words—at least not *his* words—so he would have to prove his love to her, and this was the only way he knew to do it.

"Tanya," he murmured against her lips, touching them with short little kisses as he spoke. "Wake up, sweetheart. There's something I want to tell you."

A faint moan of objection slipped from her throat as she tried to hold onto the contentment of sleep. Gradually his kisses worked their magic. She moved closer, in a sexual way, pressing her loins to his. Bolder now than she'd been initially, she slid her hand provocatively up his thigh and encircled his rigid manhood, caressing it in a delightfully maddening way. He knew he could not take much more, and he moved her hands to a safer place until he completed what he had set out to do.

"Not just yet, Tanya," he whispered. "There's something I want to show you first."

She reluctantly opened her eyes, as if to do so might destroy a wondrous dream in which she'd been traveling. She lifted her face to his and he kissed her, finding himself too easily hypnotized by the magic of her. It was torture to pull himself away.

"Sweetheart, I have something I want to show you. Come on, sit up for just a few minutes."

She was awake now, her interest thoroughly piqued. She smiled sleepily, sexily. "What could be so important that it can't wait until morning, Keane?"

"Just close your eyes."

Her smile turned to a devilish grin. "You just told me to open my eyes. Make up your mind."

He responded easily to her bantering mood, glad that their intimacy hadn't destroyed that particular part of their relationship. "Just do as I say, sweetheart. *Trust* me."

Her laughter trilled gaily into the room. "Trust you? I think I must be dreaming."

"You'll have to trust me if you want to know what I'm up to."

Tanya sat up, modestly covering herself with the blanket. Keane was always up to no good, but his persistence and seriousness truly baited her curiosity. "All right," she teased. "I don't know why you'd wake me up just to tell me to close my eyes, but I'm closing them. And this had better be good. I don't like being woke up when I'm having such pleasant dreams."

"Are you sure your eyes are closed?"

She opened one just a crack. "Yes, I'm sure."

"You're peeking, Tanya."

She grinned. "I wouldn't do such a thing."

Keane waited until long lashes fluttered down tightly over her eyes. He took a position behind her, gathered the length of her hair, and draped it all over one bare shoulder.

Tanya heard the faint clink of metal against metal, then felt Keane's arms come around her from behind. Startled by the weight of something cool settling just above her breasts, her eyes popped open to feast upon the gleaming pageantry of the Turquoise Sun. She stifled a gasp of sheer dismay and automatically spread her hand over the fanning "rays" of the necklace.

"What's this all about, Keane?"

He kissed the curve of her neck and whispered, "I want you to have the Sun, Tanya. If I could give you the real one, I would."

The gesture left her so completely perplexed, she could barely find words. "But it means so much to you, Keane. I couldn't possibly—"

He lifted a finger to her lips, silencing any further refusal. "It doesn't mean nearly as much to me as you do, Tanya. The necklace is a token of my love for you. With it, I'm asking you to be my wife. It's the ring of gold and diamonds I don't have, but it's yours, whether you should say yes or no."

Words completely fled her mind. Was this another dream so vivid it could be real? She lifted her eyes from the necklace to his waiting gaze. He had professed his love and now she saw it gleaming brightly in his eyes. But was it true, lasting love? Keane Trevalyan was not a man she had ever envisioned as losing his heart to anyone. And surely not to her.

He waited patiently for her answer. She saw his hope and felt the nervous tension trickling through his body and down to the tips of his fingers entwined with hers. Did dreams come true in this mystical world of the Red Sand People? Was love sought actually found?

She had loved Keane Trevalyan for years, although she had never admitted it to herself before tonight. Joy soared inside her. It didn't matter if they ever found the other side of tomorrow. They had a life here together. She wondered if the Creator had intended for them to come here all along, so that they might finally discover the full extent of their love for each other, and so they could put aside everything that had ever stood between them.

"Yes, I'll be your wife," she heard herself saying.

In the next instant she was in his arms and making love to him all over again. This time it was with a wonder that surpassed even the first time. She knew things would only get better between them now.

"It's not much farther now, sweetheart. You're going to love this place. Trust me."

Keane led the way along the path, holding onto Tanya's hand. In his other hand he carried a satchel containing their picnic lunch; pieces of roasted turkey, corn cakes, and berries. It wasn't much, but they were getting used to the simple fare eaten by the people of the mesa. He carried the goatskin water bag by a strap over his shoulder, and Tanya carried a cotton blanket for them to sit on.

They wound their way through the trees, dodging aspen and juniper branches, wading through brush and climbing over rocks. Tanya caught her foot on a fallen branch and stumbled, laughing at her clumsiness. "How did you find this place? It doesn't look like a rabbit could get through this brush."

"On that night we had the argument, I took off walking and this is where I ended up."

She felt his hand tighten around hers as if he wouldn't let anything come between them again, least of all old arguments. Tanya could not remember a time when she'd felt such warmth and closeness from the simple act of holding hands.

A clearing opened before them. Small and completely secluded, it was perhaps only twice the size of their quarters. Its center was covered with lush grass that seemed unaffected by the scant rainfall. Together they spread the blanket in the very center of the secret hideaway. While Keane untied the cotton cord that held their lunch satchel together, Tanya leaned back on her elbows on the blanket and drank of the patch of blue sky visible above the tree-tops.

"It's beautiful here, Keane. Almost like a world within a world."

He grinned and fed her a berry; the juice stained his fingers and he licked it off. "I'm glad you like it, sweetheart," he said. "I thought you would."

There was a way he said sweetheart now that was different than the way he used to say it. He still teased her and flirted with her. They still bantered and even disagreed on things, but when he said that word it sounded softer, sexier. It brought a tight, pleasant curl to the pit of her stomach, reminding her of the intimacies that made them man and wife by the unwritten laws of this primitive society. When he called her sweetheart, she felt truly loved. And what the word didn't say, his green eyes did. Since they'd committed themselves to each other, she could look into his eyes and feel wrapped in the wonder of his love.

She picked up a berry and fed him, as he had her, then she chased the offering with a kiss. He leaned into her, nuzzling her neck. "Perhaps we should eat first," she whispered.

Keane didn't know what he wanted the most, food or more of her lovemaking. She was the only woman to ever completely satisfy his physical need and fill that empty spot in his heart. He had never committed himself to a future with just one woman, because he'd never found the right woman until now.

He moved closer and gently cupped Tanya's breast in his palm. It was soft and full beneath a gray leather vest cut from the velvety skins of rabbit hide. Leather lacing held it together in the front and at the sides. Fringe decorated the bottom and armholes. He liked her feminine curves unprotected by confining whalebone and intricate metal fasteners, and was grateful that she no longer wore her riding corset.

"M-m-m-," he murmured. "I don't know what I want first. Food or love."

Neither did Tanya, but if one measured degrees of hunger, she could safely say her appetite for Keane Trevalyan was greater than her appetite for cold turkey and corn cakes.

It seemed an effort, but he pulled himself away from her lips and sat up, rising to his knees. He pulled her up next to him, until they faced each other, their thighs touching. His gaze, alluring and scorching, settled on her intently and never shifted. He lifted her hand to his lips, feathering kisses across her fingertips. The withholding of that sweet possession made it all the sweeter when it came at last.

He loosened the rawhide laces on her vest and slid the garment off her shoulders, down her arms, and over her wrists. She wore the Turquoise Sun and he removed it, too. His clothing followed.

He turned to his back and lifted her over him. His mouth found her breasts and her hands sought out his tight, throbbing shaft before she took it inside her. Soon their bodies undulated in a rhythm as steady and sure as the beat of an ancient Indian rain chant. Urgency built inside her. She arched her back as his thrusts became harder, faster. The sheen on her skin was not caused by the heat of the sun overhead, but by the fire within. She flung her head back, her eyes closing to the tumultuous waves of rapture rolling through her. Soft moans of pleasure escaped her lips. She rose to the height of passion, seemingly swirling into the heat of Father Sun himself. She met Keane's powerful strokes and joined him in the exquisite journey of ecstasy and fulfillment.

Time was a lost and forgotten factor in their hideaway. At last they lay sated in each other's arms. The sun had moved to a new position, placing them in sun-dappled shade. Keane pulled Tanya closer and draped a leg over hers, effectively preventing her from fleeing, although she had no inclination to.

She stroked his cheek, ran kisses along the underside of his jaw, and found satisfaction in his smile. "I guess we should think about getting some nourishment if we plan to continue such vigorous exercise."

They slipped back into their clothes and sat in silent closeness while they ate. Keane chewed on a corn cake and said, "We're going to have to help these people expand their diet and their mode of cooking."

"How? They have no domestic animals and limited vegetables to bring variety into their diets."

"Well, I've been thinking about making a whiskey still. That would perk things up a bit."

She laughed. "Isn't it just like you to bring corruption to the thirteenth century?"

"It can hardly be compared to the hallucinogenic plants they use freely."

"That's true, but someone would probably kill you for the recipe."

He lifted a brow, considering that possibility. "It would become a high demand item, I'm sure."

The sparkle faded from Tanya's eyes and she looked up into the sky. To Keane, it seemed she was searching for answers out there beyond the mesa, beyond the sun, beyond time.

"What will we do if Ten-Moon can't get us back?" Her voice took on a worried edge.

Keane focused his thoughts closer to home. "We'll live, Tanya. That's all we can do. We'll raise our children and do the best we can. We'll adjust." He took her hand in his. "We have each other. That's all that matters."

She managed a smile, secretly wishing it was all that simple. "They won't always believe we're kachinas."

"I know."

"Then what?"

"We can only hope Ten-Moon will be able to explain it to them and make them understand. Perhaps he'll be able to make them realize that by bringing Future People here, he has accomplished something even greater than bringing kachinas. Maybe we can save ourselves by showing them new methods of doing things."

"Wouldn't that change history?"

He shrugged. "We can't worry about that." He pulled her into his arms again, smoothing her hair back from her face and kissing her lips gently. "Our lives are together now, Tanya. Wherever that might be. I told you I would protect you, and I will. No matter what it takes—even if it means we have to leave here and live alone."

"Start our own little tribe in California?" she gibed.

"Maybe. It doesn't matter, just as long as we're together."

"You have seemed very happy these last few days, my friend," She Who Sees Far said with a sly, knowing smile. "Can the contentment on your face be credited to something your man has been doing differently in your room at night? I cannot imagine a gift, even one as magnificent as the necklace, bringing such a glow to your face."

Tanya followed the pregnant woman along the winding trail through the pinyons. Yards ahead, young Snow in Summer led the way in their search for the plants that could be used for food, medicines, and dyes. She seemed intent on finding the best plants for her basket, leaving the poor quality for them. She made the chore into a contest. Intent on being the winner, she had paid very little attention to the two of them or their conversations.

Tanya was glad the young girl was not present. There was something about her she didn't like, and she wouldn't have wanted to discuss personal matters in her presence. She lifted her gaze to the mischievous black eyes of her friend.

"Am I correct in my assumption?" the young woman prodded.

Tanya supposed it was fairly obvious—the change in herself and Keane and the way they'd behaved towards each other. They were closer now, in every way, and they had seldom been apart these past two weeks. Under the circumstances, they hadn't been able to announce their marriage. Because they were sharing a room, everyone already assumed they were married. In this society no special marriage ceremony was performed, only a formal announcement followed by the couple moving in together. In their hearts they *were* man and wife. At the mere thought of the intimacies they'd shared and the soft words of love spoken in the privacy of their room, heat crept up into Tanya's face. She turned away, busily looking for plants and hoping that She Who Sees Far wouldn't notice.

"He's been most agreeable," she managed as casually as she could.

She Who Sees Far saw through the ruse. Her delighted laughter spilled out into the trees. "Yes, I would say so if the color on your cheeks is any indication. He is a most handsome man, and one that would make any woman's blood race. Even that of a kachina woman who could have any pleasure on this earth that she might desire. However, I think there will be one who is very disappointed in the solidity of your relationship."

Tanya's hand halted over a juniper branch. "Oh? And who is that?"

"Ocelot, of course. I have seen him watching you on many occasions. He is very fascinated by you."

Tanya didn't like hearing that yet another person had noticed the Indian watching her. But being fascinated and having evil intentions—as Keane had suggested—were two different things. She returned to the juniper branch and broke off a twig, pretending she was indifferent to Ocelot's interest.

"Tell me, why hasn't he married? I would think he's quite eligible."

She Who Sees Far lifted her square shoulders in the semblance of a shrug. "There have been many women who would have gladly become his wife, but Ocelot seems uninterested in any woman of this village—at least on a permanent basis. There have been rumors of women to the south, in the cities there. The men do not say much in front of the women about such masculine matters, and the women can only sit around their campfires and conjecture."

Tanya chuckled. "Where I'm from we call that gossiping."

She Who Sees Far tilted her head contemplatively and rolled the new word over her tongue. "Goss-ip-ing? It is a funny word, as many of your words are."

"No funnier than yours," Tanya returned with a grin.

She Who Sees Far laughed delightedly. "I think we have lost Snow In Summer, or she has lost us. But as much as I would like to lose her forever, I was sent out as her guardian."

"She needs a guardian—at her age?"

"She is a minx, my kachina friend. Her mother dares not let her go out too far from the village without a chaperon. But she eludes anyone she is sent with. I would not be surprised at all if she has made arrangements to meet a man out here, so we must hurry and find her before I get into trouble with her mother."

They had only gone a few yards up the steep hill when She Who Sees Far suddenly gasped and clutched her protruding brown belly, doubling over in pain. Tanya was at her side in an instant, taking her by the arm and forcing her to lie down in the shade of a pinyon.

"Is it your time? Should I get your husband?"

She Who Sees Far took a deep breath and managed a weak smile, but she couldn't completely conceal a hint of fear in her eyes. "I am due. Perhaps today will be the day. Let me just lie here for a moment."

"Have you had these pains before?"

The young woman nodded. "Yes, but not as bad. My mother and my grandmother tell me this tightening in my stomach is normal. That my body is preparing itself for the birth of my child."

The pain continued for several minutes. "I think I should go for help," Tanya said, pain creasing her brow. "I'll see if I can catch Snow In Summer and send her for help. I'll stay here with you myself."

"Have you brought babies into this world?"

Tanya shook her head regretfully. "No. I've never been called upon to do so, but don't worry. Everything will be fine."

She Who Sees Far's attempt to smile was lost. She looked into the infinite sky. "I had another dream. It is one I cannot interpret at all. I only know it leaves me empty when I awake. It is as if I have lost something, but I do not know what it is, only that it is something I will never get back." Her eyes locked with Tanya's, searching for answers and comfort. "I fear for my child, Tanya. Can you tell me, as one who is sent by the gods and as one who has seen many worlds and many people, do you see my child in the future?"

The young woman was tightly gripping Tanya's hand now. Through the physical connection, Tanya could feel the severity of the contractions. Surely She Who Sees Far wasn't having a premonition of the death of her own child?

She placed a hand to the younger woman's forehead. "You must not worry. Lie very still. I'll run ahead and find Snow In Summer. She's swift and knows the trails well. She'll bring your husband and some others who can carry you back to the village."

She Who Sees Far nodded as another contraction gripped her. Tanya, giving her one last worried glance, ran up the trail through the trees, seeing no sign. Tanya paused on the crest of a small knoll to catch her breath and visually search the terrain again. All she could see were trees, red rock, and heat waves. All she could hear was the continual buzz of insects in the still air and the frightened thumping of her tired heart.

"Damn it, Snow In Summer," she muttered. "This is a fine time for you to run off. I would have been as well off to return to the village myself."

She set off again, trotting over the knoll and into a shaded wash through which ran a small stream. Not far below, she saw a flash of movement in the trees and recognized the girl. She would have called out, but didn't want to give Snow the opportunity to elude her again. Besides, her lungs were burning so badly she doubted she could do more than croak. The foliage along the stream was thicker and she had to slowly pick her way through it. Within fifty feet of Snow, she heard the girl talking to someone. Tanya saw a man then, resting on his haunches near a tree. A bow and quiver of arrows were slung over his naked torso. The shadows hid most of him, but as Snow approached him, he stood up and was made clearly visible in the midday sunlight.

Tanya released a sigh of relief when she saw the man was Keane. He could help her with She Who Sees Far. She was about to run to him, to call out his name, when suddenly her throat constricted and strangled the words. She faded back into the shadow of a large pinyon, unable to hear what Snow was saying, nor what Keane replied. All she could do was watch, and she saw the way Snow sidled up to him, her hips swaying. She saw the way he smiled in return just moments before the Anasazi woman placed her arms around his neck and pressed her lush, nearly naked body down the length of his. But when Keane's hands curled around Snow's slender waist, Tanya could watch no more. She turned on her heel and fled back through the trees, running blindly through a blur of tears.

Nineteen

Tree branches slapped at Tanya's face and tore at her hair and clothes. Unmindful of anything but the pain in her heart, she ran on until she stumbled back onto the path and fell to her hands and knees, skidding in the loose rocks at the path's edge. Beads of blood sprang to the scrapes and gouges on her palms, but she leaped up and ran on. She'd barely gone another ten feet when Keane caught her arm and she found herself being jerked around to face him. Through a flood of blinding tears, she fought him with her last ounce of strength.

"Let me go! I should have known you couldn't be faithful."

"Stop fighting me, Tanya. What you saw is not what you think you saw."

She tried to wrench free of his iron grip, refusing to look at his lying eyes. "I don't have time to listen to your excuses! She Who Sees Far is going into labor, and I have to find someone who can help me."

Keane's brows shot together. "Where is she?"

"Just over this hill."

Keane grabbed her hand and started down the path, moving as swiftly as the terrain would allow and giving her no choice but to follow. She Who Sees Far wasn't where Tanya had left her. They finally spotted her a hundred feet farther up the trail, sitting against the trunk of a pinyon with eyes closed against another wave of pain. Upon reaching her, they dropped to their knees.

"She Who Sees Far," Tanya said, laying a hand to her friend's brown arm. "Are you all right? I found Keane. We'll get you back to the village."

The pregnant woman's eyelids fluttered open and she looked at them through pain-glazed eyes. She managed a weak smile. "I tried to walk a little way, but I . . . couldn't."

"I'll carry you back to the village," Keane offered, his eyes and tone as anxious as Tanya's.

She Who Sees Far nodded gratefully. He gently gathered her up and she put her arms around his neck. Tanya collected the baskets and followed, once again feeling a stab of jealousy at the sight of another woman's bare breasts pressed against Keane's naked chest. Even pregnant, She Who Sees Far was small and light, and Keane carried her with no difficulty. He stopped only a few times when her pains came hard and strong.

The climb up the canyon path and over the talus slope was the worst and the steepest. As soon as they reached the level ground of the plaza, Keane called for assistance and everyone within earshot came running. In no time, someone had summoned Yellow Bear. He carried his wife to her room and left her in the capable hands of her mother, grandmothers, and a bevy of aunts, sisters, and cousins.

Tanya and Keane retired to the plaza and lost themselves in a congregation of men and women who would now try to keep busy while awaiting the birth of the child. It was always a great occasion among the Red Sand People, for each new life was greatly revered.

But the hours dragged by, and the screams that were occasionally heard coming from She Who Sees Far's quarters became weaker and weaker. The people knew that a first baby took its time coming into the world. They were cheerful at first and unconcerned about the lengthy delay. They spoke of the crops and how the rain had saved them. But others muttered in the background that if the Kachina People didn't bring more rain, it would all be for naught.

Around midnight, She Who Sees Far's mother, named Masavehma, or Butterfly Wings Painted, sent for Ten-Moon and his apprentice, Long Scar. Soon their chanting began. The people's light mood vanished. Conversations became more subdued, and they could be heard discussing the fact that it was not common to bring a medicine man into a birthing unless the delivery was not going well.

Tanya began pacing the plaza. Several times, Keane convinced her to sit down, assuring her that everything would be all right. But he knew she didn't believe that any more than she believed his confrontation with Snow In Summer had been purely accidental. He wanted nothing more than to explain it to her, but she was in no mood to listen. The child's birth was a convenient distraction from facing the inevitable discussion that was sure to come.

The fires in the plaza were built up as the night chill slipped in. They had to be replenished many times. Most of the people ran out of things to talk about and finally retired to their beds. Some believed that the baby, and maybe the mother, too, would not live through the ordeal. Tanya thought of the dream She Who Sees Far had shared with her, and she hoped it hadn't been a premonition.

At one or two o'clock in the morning, Tanya fell asleep curled up next to one of the fires in the plaza. Keane leaned against a stone wall a few feet away and kept watch over her. He hadn't seen Ocelot during the entire ordeal, but he didn't want the man anywhere near Tanya after what she'd told him of the dreams. Even as he watched her sleeping, seemingly so peaceful, he wondered if the Indian was somewhere right now, worming his way into her mind, stealing her thoughts, interloping on the private territory of her dreams. He wondered, too, if he himself might be a part of her dreams. If he was, his position there tonight would surely not be a good one.

Just as the sun's first rays streaked up from the gray horizon, a wrenching scream jerked everyone from sleep and jarred the turkeys on their roosts. It was followed closely by the objectionable wail of a baby and Long Scar striding onto the plaza to announce that both mother and girl child had lived through the ordeal.

Tanya came to her feet. She was so relieved she nearly forgot what had transpired between her and Keane. She was about to throw her arms around him when she caught herself, as well as the smile that had flashed across her face for an instant. Her back immediately stiffened, her chin rose a fraction higher.

"I'm going to see how she's doing."

Keane raked a hand through his hair. "I'm sure she's fine, Tanya, and probably very tired. But you and I need to talk. The sooner the better."

"There's nothing to talk about," she replied stubbornly. "You can remove your things from the room."

"I'm not leaving our quarters again," he said, pinning her with an unwavering gaze. "If you'd like to take the time to hear me out, fine. If you're determined not to, then I guess you'll have to be the one to leave."

"That's not the custom here. The house is the woman's. If there's a disagreement, the man leaves."

"The customs of the Red Sand People are not mine. I abide by my own feelings, my own rules. I know one thing for certain, Tanya. We can't keep letting other people come between us. We've got to trust each other and the love we've shared."

People began coming from their rooms and gathering on the plaza to face the new day. Women proceeded with the morning ritual of building up fires for cooking. If they noticed Keane and Tanya's uncongenial exchange, they pretended not to.

"This is no time to talk about your affair with Snow In Summer," Tanya said. "Nor is it the place."

"Then when is a good time? A good place? You tell me, Tanya. It matters very little anyway. They can't understand us and they're too excited about the new baby to pay us much mind."

"You were waiting for Snow In Summer, weren't you? She left us and went directly to where you were. You opened your arms to her and she rushed in. How many other times have the two of you had secret meetings since you professed your love to me and made me your wife?"

She watched his eyes closely; his gaze never wavered. She saw nothing duplicitous there. "I wasn't waiting for her. I was waiting for a two-point buck that Swift Blade was supposed to chase down the canyon toward me so I could try and kill it. Ocelot is heading up a trading expedition tomorrow to some villages about a hundred miles west of here. I wanted to make sure my gear didn't need any adjustments before we set out. You never know when you'll run into enemy tribes."

The news of the expedition surprised and upset her. How long had he been planning on going? It would mean he would be leaving her alone in the village. Wasn't he concerned for her safety?

Refusing to let him see how his decision had hurt her, she said, "Apparently I was the only one you didn't inform of your plans. Snow In Summer seemed to be fully aware that you would be in the canyon to check out your gear."

He tried to curb his temper. "I didn't tell you because I only learned about the expedition this morning. Ocelot always heads an expedition in that area after he's come back from the southern cities. I went looking for you, but word was you had gone out early to look for medicinal plants. The last thing I expected to see in the canyon was Snow in Summer."

"Yes, isn't that the last thing anyone would expect to see," she replied facetiously.

He shifted his weight to the other leg, leaning on it heavily as he grew increasingly impatient with her accusations and refusal to believe him. "Snow In Summer does her hunting without a bow and arrow. Or hadn't you noticed that? Talk among the men is that she never misses an opportunity."

"Were you her opportunity of the day?"

"Apparently so."

"You didn't seem to mind. You wasted no time putting your arms around her."

"I didn't have my arms around her. I had my hands on the safest place I could find—her waist. I was trying to set her away from me without insulting her. She is the oldest daughter of the leader of the Sand Clan, keepers of the soil since the beginning of time. Must I remind you that our position here is tenuous at best? One wrong move and we could end up dead. I didn't think it would be wise to get on the bad side of such a duplicitous vixen as Snow In Summer."

His explanation sounded plausible, but men like him and Frankie were born lying, and doing it smoothly. She'd believed a rogue's lies before. How could she have been so gullible as to believe them a second time? "Seeing you with her made me accept something I had tried to overlook before," she said wearily. "You don't love me. Nor do you consider our marriage valid. You're merely taking advantage of a situation, as you've always done. I doubt you'll ever be able to love just one woman."

His eyes narrowed as he mounted his rebuttal. "You're going to believe that—after all we've shared?"

"You give me no choice."

"I'm beginning to think you're just looking for a way to turn me away, Tanya, as you've always done. You accuse me of having a love affair with a girl that's still a child.

Now I'm beginning to wonder if it's me that *you* want. Maybe you've had second thoughts and want Ocelot after all. In the two weeks since we've been together as man and wife, you've never truly given yourself to me. You always hold some part of yourself back, a part I can't seem to reach. I'm beginning to wonder if any man can reach it. Eddie probably never reached it either and that's why he didn't bother to come back."

Tanya had expected an argument. She had not expected a personal attack that cut to the quick. She struggled to keep tears at bay, not wanting Keane to know how his words had hurt her. Like any woman, she enjoyed attention from a handsome man, but Ocelot meant nothing to her. She wanted to believe Keane, but the image of Snow in his arms, and the smile he'd given the young girl, still flashed too painfully across her mind. She'd seen that rakish smile on his face many times in the past with other women he'd flirted with, and she'd seen it all night in her dreams. Now her heart felt battered and bruised. She wondered if she would ever trust a man again.

Suddenly the weight of the necklace felt like a ball and chain. It was of virtually no use to Keane in this world of the Anasazi. That had to be why he had so willingly given it to her. If they'd been in their own time, he would have sold it to the highest bidder. She wanted to rip it off and fling it in his face. But she couldn't, not here in front of the Red Sand People.

What she did do was to end the fruitless conversation. She left him standing in the plaza and went to see her friend.

From the cool shadows of the dwellings, Ocelot looked down on the scene and smiled. He spoke to the young woman standing next to him. "The kachinas' weakness is love, like any mortal human being. I would have thought they would be beyond such base emotions."

Snow In Summer lifted a shoulder in a motion that was half-indifferent, half-provocative. She was more interested in Ocelot than the white strangers. "Perhaps being in the human form forces them to suffer and rejoice just as humans do."

"Or perhaps they are not kachinas at all," he suggested softly.

"Perhaps. But one way or the other, I was very successful, wasn't I?"

"We were very successful. You would not have known Trevalyan was going to be there had I not informed you. Now that they are separated, the rest will be easy, and we will find out who they really are."

Losing interest in the estranged couple, Snow In Summer turned to Ocelot, pressing the points of her high breasts into his naked chest and blatantly swishing her yucca string apron against the leather breechcloth he wore. She slid a hand up his arm. "It's done. Let's return to our place by the river. I hunger for you again."

Me and every other man, he thought disdainfully. His gaze clipped her and lifted again to watch Tanya depart from the plaza. The one with eyes of sky was the one who haunted his thoughts. The one he must destroy before she destroyed him. She was the female he wanted to feel himself inside of, not this little whore whom he'd had more times than he could count or care to remember.

He stepped past Snow. "I am unable to get away right now. There are others I need to talk to about the plan. You must get ready if you are to do your part."

He strode away, leaving her angry. Snow In Summer was not accustomed to being rebuffed, and it was something she was not likely to forget. Ocelot's stupid plans to destroy the Kachina People did not interest her. It suited her more to warn Trevalyan that his life was in danger. Her reward for such a favor would surely be great. Just thinking of him between her legs made her loins begin to throb with anticipation. Ocelot might be surprised to learn that she had a few plans of her own.

Like all the rooms in the village complex, the room that She Who Sees Far shared with her husband, Yellow Bear, was small. But it was a very beautiful room that stood out from the others. She Who Sees Far enjoyed color and incorporated it in everything she created. Groups of handpainted wildflowers decorated the freshly plastered walls. Real wildflowers filled tiny clay vases that brightened the room's corners. Even the baby's cradle board was artistically enhanced with painted images of squirrels, rabbits, and other baby animals. She Who Sees Far's love of color was also evident in the cotton blankets and pillows woven with vividly hued yarns.

The young mother lay amid this color on a bed of soft furs in muted tones of gray, tan, and black. Only a light cotton blanket covered her and the baby. The infant, with a mop of unruly black hair, suckled contentedly at her mother's breast. The young mother gazed at her child fondly and stroked the downy hair. She was exhausted, but happy and content.

Tanya was their first visitor. Yellow Bear had not even been allowed to enter the room yet.

Masavehma approached Tanya. Bowing respectfully, she said, "It is my daughter's wish that you give a name to the baby girl. It is the custom that those closest to her do so. The name that is the strongest and stands out from the others will be the one that will follow her through her life.

"And, because you are a messenger of the Creator," Masavehma continued, "my daughter asks that you conduct the Blessing Ceremony that will protect her child from witches and other evil influences."

Tanya easily consented to the giving of a name, but had no idea what the Blessing Ceremony was or how to perform it. Knowing she could not refuse, however, she said she would be greatly honored.

Masavehma was very pleased and bustled about, pouring water in a low, shallow bowl. Another woman collected juniper ashes from the cold fire. While they busied themselves, Tanya took a minute to kneel next to She Who Sees Far's pallet. The young woman smiled weakly and thanked her for agreeing to conduct the first ceremony.

"My mother will bathe the baby, and then you will be able to proceed."

Tanya wanted nothing better than to ask her friend what the ritual entailed, but to show ignorance would be the same as shouting out to them that she was an impostor. She would ask Swift Blade as soon as she spoke with her friend for a minute. "Your labor was very long," she said. "Are you going to be all right?"

She Who Sees Far smiled. "I believe so. Would you like to hold my child?"

Tanya's eyes lit up. "I would love to."

She Who Sees Far carefully transferred the baby to Tanya's inexperienced arms. "You have not held many babies," she observed.

"No. I have not been called upon to do so."

"Perhaps if you stay with the people, the gods will one day give you a child of your own."

Tanya lovingly stroked the baby's tuft of silky soft hair and felt the flutter of yearning in her heart to hold a child of her own. She momentarily forgot about the discord between her and Keane. "It could be that a child grows inside me even as we speak."

"I hope it is so," She Who Sees Far said with her eyes aglitter with hope.

"Your mother has requested I give your baby a name."

"Yes, I would very much like to hear what you will call my baby girl."

From the expectant look in her friend's eyes, Tanya realized that She Who Sees Far expected her to offer a name immediately. Having no experience on such matters, and with absolutely no forethought, her mind frantically searched for a name worthy of her best friend's child.

"Perhaps I should think about it for a while."

"No. The best names are those that come quickly. You are a friend who is very wise, who has seen much, and who has been many places. Give her a strong name that will carry her through life."

Tanya rapidly considered the people she had encountered in her life. Some of their names she knew the meaning of, others she didn't, but none fit this Anasazi child. As names and places darted through her mind, she placed a hand over her heart to calm its frantic race and felt the Turquoise Sun beneath her shirt.

"What could be stronger than the sun?" she asked of herself and her friend. "Except perhaps Mother Earth."

"But Mother Earth is nothing without the sun," She Who Sees Far countered. "Like women who need a man to plant life inside their bodies, Mother Earth needs the light of the sun before life can spring from her soil. I want my daughter to be able to stand alone if she must, to be strong in the changing world that lies ahead of her. I want her to be a leader among women. A leader among men."

Tanya had the uneasy feeling again that She Who Sees Far was indeed seeing into the future, her own and that of her daughter. "I will call her Kira," Tanya said at last. "It is a name that originated among a people who were known as Persians. It means 'sun.' I give it to your daughter, for her life will be as bright as her namesake."

"Where are these people now?"

"Here on this earth, as you are. But faraway. Faraway yond land and time."

She Who Sees Far looked across the tiny room as if she could see the distant place in her mind. She rolled the name over on her tongue, testing its sound. Finally she gave her nod of approval. "It is good. It fits her. Kira."

Masavehma came to take the baby then and prepare her for the Blessing Ceremony. She Who Sees Far fell asleep and Tanya slipped from the room, promising to be right back. She found Swift Blade, pulled him away from the others, and asked him to hastily explain to her what was expected of her for the Blessing Ceremony.

"After the child is bathed," he said, "juniper ashes are prepared by one of the aunts. You will rub the ashes on the child's body and this will protect it from witches that might wish to bring it harm."

Tanya, not fully satisfied with the answer, returned to the room just as Masavehma completed the bathing and handed the naked infant to her. Tanya cradled the child again and feigned confidence she did not feel. She seated herself next to the bowl of ashes prepared by the aunts. The women relatives gathered around, waiting and watching with soft smiles on their faces. She Who Sees Far was awakened so she might take part in the ceremony. The wide-eyed baby stared up at Tanya with curious, fascinated eyes that were completely free of fear. She seemed to know that something special was about to take place.

Swift Blade hadn't told Tanya if words had to be spoken, and he couldn't tell her exactly how the ritual was done either, since a man had never witnessed it nor conducted it. Tanya dipped her fingers in the bowl of ashes. As soft as any powder, they were neither warm nor cold against the skin. The Red Sand People might believe that the ashes kept the witches and their spells away, but Tanya was more inclined to believe the success in the ritual could be attributed to medicinal qualities rather than supernatural powers.

Tenderly she wiped a strip of ash across the infant's forehead and just as tenderly rubbed it into the soft skin. She followed this procedure, covering the baby's nose, chin, and cheeks. She spoke to the baby as she did, and she also spoke to God, asking Him to protect the infant. She spoke in English so that the women would not understand her and question the way she performed the ceremony.

After the ash covered the baby's entire body, Masavehma, wearing a large, pleased smile, took her from Tanya's arms. Tanya glanced at the aunts and grandmothers and found that they, too, seemed pleased with what she'd done.

The baby was then placed on a bed of warm sand, which had been covered with a soft chamois cloth. One of the grandmothers placed an ear of blue corn beside her. Fully mature, it had come from last year's crop. It was also perfect in shape and length, and contained full kernels in straight, even rows.

After both baby and mother had fallen back to sleep, the women left the room. Tanya lingered, giving the infant one last look, one last touch. Again, she was overcome by a powerful emotion. A cavern opened up inside her, seemingly as huge as the one they had emerged from, and she knew just how empty her life had been. She'd filled it with field trips, with teaching, with busy-body projects, and with interests in ancient worlds and bygone eras. But she knew now that those things were not enough.

"Why does my baby bring you sadness, Tanya? You do not sense something wrong with her, do you?"

Tanya hastily wiped away the tears that had appeared in her eyes when meeting her friend's worried, tired gaze. She left the sleeping baby and sat next to She Who Sees Far, taking her hand and squeezing it gently. She forced a smile, not wanting her friend to worry needlessly, although she had good cause. The infant mortality rate was high among the Anasazi. In just the short time she'd been here, two other children had died. One at birth, and one that had not seen a year of life.

"Your baby is fine," she assured her friend. "Her beauty is so great it brings tears of joy to my eyes."

Her qualms were not eased. She Who Sees Far searched the depths of Tanya's soul and, after a moment of contemplation, said, "Something troubles you, my kachina friend. I sense you feel very alone. Where has the joy gone that He Who Laughs gave to you only yesterday?"

Tanya's smile wavered only slightly. "It's nothing. You should sleep now." She tried to ease her hand from her friend's, but the younger woman's grip tightened.

"It is He Who Laughs, is it not?"

Tanya looked away, too quickly realizing the evasive action had given her friend the answer she wanted. She Who Sees Far waited patiently for her to have it out. At last she sighed and said, "When I was going to find Snow In Summer . . . I found them . . . together." She felt the stinging heat of yet more tears seeping onto her eyelashes. She focused on the frescoes to avoid her friend's steady gaze.

She Who Sees Far did not reply immediately, but Tanya felt the slight flexing of her fingers around her hand. She didn't want sympathy. She didn't want her friend to know that she, a kachina, could not even hold her own man. She took a deep breath and willed the tears to stop, wiping away those that shimmered on her eyelashes.

She Who Sees Far's eyes filled with compassion and understanding. "And what does he say about this?"

Tanya related Keane's explanation then stood up, too restless to sit.

"Why don't you believe him?"

If Tanya told her friend anything, she would have to tell her the truth, and that could jeopardize the lives of all three of them. "I can't give you the answer to that, my friend. You see, there's much about me you don't know and can never know, nor understand. There's much more I'm not at liberty to tell. It's about the world where I come from. All I can tell you is that there are many things about your world and mine that are the same. People still go through the same trials of survival and love, of joy and heartache, of hope and disappointment."

Perplexed, She Who Sees Far scrutinized her. "Tell me again, my kachina friend, in the language of the Red Sand People—if you can."

Tanya wiped at her eyes again, realizing she had given her entire diatribe in English. She tried again, this time using a combination of sign, English, and the ancient Hopi words she knew of her friend's language. "It is something between Keane and me. It will not effect the reason the Creator has put us here among your people."

"Was he kissing her?" She Who Sees Far prodded.

Tanya had never felt more miserable. "No."

"And did you wait to hear what he said to Snow in Summer? What happened after that first moment?"

Tanya's eyes snapped, as did her response. "I didn't need to."

She Who Sees Far took Tanya's hand again, gently pulling her back down to her side on the pallet. "Some things are not always what they seem, my friend," she said in a way that seemed much too wise for someone so young. "I know Snow in Summer. She is a wanton young girl with a bad reputation. It could be that your man deserves more trust than you are giving. He always looks at you with love in his eyes. I have never seen him near Snow in Summer, nor have I seen his eyes lusting after her. Like many others in this village, I would notice such a thing. Perhaps what you saw is not what you think you saw at all."

"That is what Keane said, but even if Snow had been the one to make the advance, Keane did not refuse it," she continued adamantly.

"He told you why he did not refuse. He was very wise not to make her angry with him. I would not be surprised at all to learn that she's a witch, and perhaps He Who Laughs already knows this."

Tanya took a deep breath, forcing herself to be calm, but she no longer wanted to discuss the matter. Touching her friend's shoulder, she said, "You're still not feeling well. I think you should sleep now so you'll be strong for your baby when she wakes and needs you."

"It's your heart I'm more worried about, Eyes of Sky. I do not like to see it breaking. I think you should go out and talk to He Who Laughs before the feelings harden and cannot be altered."

Tanya wished she could, but her heart was still too raw with pain and distrust. Maybe time would tell her what to do. For now, she squeezed her friend's hand and moved to the door. "Everything will work out for the best."

She Who Sees Far seemed to know even then that Tanya was not going to follow her advice. "I am afraid it will only turn out for the best if you look into his soul and into your own as well. When you do, trust in what you see there, Tanya Darrow, for what you see will be the truth."

Twenty

In a world as large as this one, there was no legitimate reason why Keane couldn't find some place to go other than their room. Tanya returned from visiting She Who Sees Far to find him sitting in the coolness of their room with Swift Blade. The two were working on new arrows for their quivers, and discussing the quality and shape of the feathers that would make the arrows fly the swiftest and truest.

Because Keane and Swift Blade had proven their prowess at hunting, they had readily been relieved of field duties on the mesa and had been accepted into the Hunt Society. They went out nearly every day in search of game for the tribe. Keane was beginning to look more like a native with each passing day. He seldom wore a shirt now. His skin grew steadily darker and his hair progressively longer. He still wore his hat, although at the moment it was tossed aside.

Swift Blade looked up from his arrow and grinned at Tanya. "The ceremony must have gone well. I see you're still alive. How is She Who Sees Far and the baby doing?"

Tanya noticed Keane barely gave her a second glance, focusing all his attention on the turkey feather he was trimming for the arrow shaftment. She moved to the opposite side of the room and settled on her grass mattress. "They're both fine. I muddled my way through the ceremony. If I did it differently than the way it is normally done, no one seemed displeased or suspicious."

"You'd best get some sleep," Keane said, with no humor

in his voice. "Ten-Moon intends on trying the chant again tonight."

"Isn't he tired after last night?"

Keane shrugged. "Apparently he's getting some rest this afternoon." He stood up. "Come on, Swift Blade. Let's get out of here so she can rest."

Tanya sensed he couldn't wait to be out of her presence. The tension in the air was as tight as their bowstrings. "And what about the two of you? Don't you need to rest?"

"I think I'll go down to the river," Keane said. "It's cooler down there."

Swift Blade followed Keane outside. From the window, Tanya watched Keane head to the river. Was he going to meet Snow In Summer? If he hadn't been meeting her before, would he start now? Had Tanya driven him right into the arms of the other woman?

All she knew for certain was that the weight pressing against her heart could not be blamed entirely on the Turquoise Sun.

Ten-Moon chanted until dawn. But, once again, when they emerged from the cavern into the Sacred Kiva, nothing had changed. The old *túhikya* sat back on his calloused heels and looked at them through very tired eyes which reflected his frustration at having failed a second time.

"I am sorry, my friends," he said. "I do not understand why my song brought you here, but will not take you back. I must seek more guidance from the Creator, listen to what he has to tell me in the signs that he gives. I am beginning to think that it was his wish that you come to this world, and it is his wish that you stay among us. It could be that you have a special mission here; one you are unaware of." He shrugged his bony old shoulders. "It could be, too, that my power is simply not what it once was."

"Perhaps you need only to rest," Swift Blade suggested.

"You used a great deal of your strength last night to bring the infant into the world."

The old man nodded, looking at the earthen floor and at his *páhos* and sacred cornmeal. "This is true, but I feel a very powerful force of evil in our village. It seems to be growing even stronger with each passing day. I have discussed this with Long Scar. We are trying to battle it, but I am afraid of what a legion of witches can do. If they gain too much power, the people will expect you, the Kachina People, to oppose it. And of course you can't."

"Then you still have no idea who any of the witches are?" Keane leaned forward, his green eyes intent and as razor sharp as the arrowheads he had fashioned earlier in the day. It troubled Tanya in a way to see that the Keane Trevalyan she had always known, and who had come to this place and shared a room with her these many weeks, was changing into a man she didn't know. Gone was the jesting, the teasing, the lighthearted attitude he had always held toward the world. Appearing was an intense man whose sole purpose was shifting towards survival and war.

Ten-Moon shook his head, the iron gray hair swished back and forth across his skinny chest and shoulders. "The leader has surrounded himself with evil, camouflaging his identity."

"What do you mean?" Tanya queried nervously.

"He has many followers. Their power combined keeps me and Long Scar from finding its source." He sighed, then placed a hand on each of theirs in turn. "The sun rises. Go back to your rooms and rest. We will try again in a few days."

"It will have to wait," Keane said. "I'm going on the trading expedition that's leaving in the morning. Ocelot plans to be gone several weeks. Swift Blade is staying behind to be with Tanya should she need his help with anything."

The weight against Tanya's heart increased, as if laid there by a shadow of foreboding. What if Keane didn't return? Should she care that an abyss too wide to cross yawned between them?

Ten-Moon nodded. "I had forgotten about the expedition." He stared at his *páhos* as if greatly disturbed by the timing of the trading expedition.

Sensing he had dismissed them, Tanya and Swift Blade led the way to the outer kiva. Keane, waiting his turn, felt Ten-Moon's gnarled hand touch as lightly as that of a ghost upon his arm. "Stay and talk with me awhile, Trevalyan," he whispered in his gravelly voice. "I wish to speak to you alone."

Keane glanced hesitantly into the tunnel. He really wanted to spend some time with Tanya. Try to make amends. But the old man waited, so he called after his companions and told them to go on without him.

Ten-Moon motioned for Keane to settle across the dying fire from him. It was several minutes before he began to speak in a slow, story-telling voice, embellishing every word with hand signs so Keane could better understand.

"When the clans were to leave the Third World," he said, "they hoped to sneak away in the night so that the Bow Clan—the ones who had brought the evil to the Third World—would not follow them into the Fourth World. But the Bow Clan somehow survived the flood. They came here not long after the other clans and immediately set out to find them. At the city of Hopaqa, the chief's wife gave birth to twin daughters. After the daughters grew into women, the one gathered a large band and they separated and formed a new branch of the clan that they called the Arrowshaft Clan."

The old man took a moment of rest and continued, but with a voice that seemed weaker with each new sentence.

"The Arrowshaft Clan has always faced trouble in their migrations. This is because they do not have with them the *mongkos,* the power sticks that the Bow Clan had kept when they came to this world. *Mongkos* are the divine symbol of spiritual supremacy and power. Therefore, when the Arrowshaft Clan sets up their altar to pray to Sáviki, their deity and the Guardian of the Water Flow, they find themselves powerless."

He stared into the fire. For a moment he seemed to regress in both spirit and mind to another time, another place. Keane sensed he had finished his story, but its relevance to him or the present, escaped him.

"You must explain to me further, Ten-Moon," he said. "I do not understand the significance of what you have told me."

Ten-Moon lifted his eyes to Keane's. "I feel many interferences when my mind reaches out into the spirit world beyond us. And I feel the evil forces working against me, possibly against you. Because I am conducting this chant without the aid of the high priests, my power is weakened. Perhaps, like the Arrowshaft Clan, I have no power.

"It is this way, Trevalyan. I do not have a good feeling about you going on the expedition. Your heart is not good, and a man whose heart is not good cannot think as well as he normally would. His senses can be dulled. This disharmony in your soul comes from the discord between you and Tanya. As I said before, I need the two of you to help me, for I cannot succeed alone. You must settle your differences or I will be forced to call in the other clan chiefs and high priests. To do so would mean telling them the truth about you and your companions, and there is no way of knowing how that will be received, by either them or the people. There is no way of knowing the danger such drastic action might put you and your companions in."

Keane met his wise, old eyes. "I fear that Tanya and I will never be in harmony."

"Yes, I am beginning to think so, too. Tonight, during the chant, it seemed you both were calling out for each ;r, but your thoughts were like echoed words falling in separate canyons. The chasm I felt between you is greater than even the one I felt before. Whatever it is that is pushing you apart, must be removed from your lives. You must be together in mind when we conduct the chant again. You must *want* to return to your time, and until you truly do, my efforts are like snow in the river."

Keane came to his knees, wanting to rise to his full height but the small kiva wouldn't allow it. All he could think of now was leaving, and leaving swiftly, but he lingered out of respect for the old man. "She accuses me of being unfaithful with Snow In Summer—a young girl half my age. She refuses to believe me when I tell her it isn't true. Our relationship is hopeless, Ten-Moon. It was hopeless in the world we came from, and it is hopeless here. She sees me through eyes clouded by misconceptions. She doesn't like who she thinks I am."

The old man's head began to nod in slow understanding. "I can understand why you want to go on this journey, Trevalyan. But heed my advice and be careful. I do not like to see Tanya here alone without you. I would protect her myself, but I am an old man and no longer strong enough to be a good warrior."

"She has done well without me for many years. She has made it clear she doesn't need me, or want me."

"A person's actions and his heart seldom play the same instruments. One chooses a flute; the other a drum. It is this way for both men and women. It is something you should remember. Now, I've detained you too long. If you are determined to go, you must hurry. Ocelot will wait for no one when he is ready to go."

Keane looked for Tanya in the crowd that had gathered, but she was not among the women who had come to see their men off. After leaving Ten-Moon, he'd gone to the Tower House to gather what he'd need for the journey. She hadn't been there, nor anywhere in sight. He glanced up at the Tower House windows for the hundredth time, hoping she had returned and might be standing there watching his departure. Hoping she might give some sign that she loved him. But only empty, dark openings stared back.

It was clear she did not want to see him before he left, and he didn't have time to look for her now. He wanted desperately to talk to her one last time, to not leave this gap yawning between them while they were separated. He'd never been a superstitious man, but Ten-Moon's words pounded in his mind like a litany of fear.

Finally Keane joined the rest of the expedition, a group of about two dozen, milling around in the center plaza, waiting for Ocelot. It was a number large enough to make a good defense should they be attacked by enemies, but not so many that their absence would leave the village in danger.

The group was growing restless by the time Screaming Panther came onto the plaza and gave the signal for everyone to be quiet. He raised his voice so it boomed in the amphitheater beneath the rock overhang. "Ocelot of the Four Winds is not feeling well. He does not wish to delay the journey and tells the men to go without him. He puts our kachina friend, Trevalyan, in charge of the expedition."

Keane silently cursed. The snake-eyed jackal had tricked him. He had probably intended all along to play hooky, to get Keane out of the village so he could be alone with Tanya. And with that thought came another that he was ashamed of thinking, but it was there bursting forth and making him feel as if a knife had been stabbed into his heart. *Was Tanya a part of the plan?* He looked up to the tower window, hoping again to see her, but the window was still vacant. Was she, at this very moment, with Ocelot?

If he didn't fear losing the respect of the people, he would announce that he had decided not to go, but how could he, now that Ocelot had cleverly handed the leadership to him? people might misconstrue his change of mind as a sign of cowardice. He had agreed to go in the first place only because he felt that, should he and Tanya and Swift Blade be forced to live their lives here, they would need to learn the ways of the people, learn to trade, learn to survive. He had agreed, too, because Ocelot was going. He never would have left the village if he'd had any inkling that that weasel would be staying behind.

An uneasy feeling washed over him like a dam bursting its banks. A few weeks had not seemed such a long time before. Now, it loomed before him like a hundred years. Like an animal in a cage, he was trapped. And, remembering Ten-Moon's words, he wondered if Tanya might very well be, too.

Trying not to show the sudden fear of leaving her, he took a forward position. He assigned someone as his second in command and instructed the young man to lead the way. He didn't know the trail himself, but he could not afford to reveal his ignorance. One of the Kachina People might be expected to know all things, based on their superior position of omniscience.

In less than a minute they were trotting down the canyon path, following the river west. He tried not to look back. He failed only once.

Tanya fought the heaviness of her eyelids and the inevitable slumber that would follow. Never had she felt so lost and alone. Even though she'd had the dream intermittently since she'd been here, it had recurred every night during the week Keane had been gone.

The dream was not the same every night, but the underlying tone of it was. Regardless of what scenes played before her mind, there was always the sensation of being watched by some evil entity. It stood on the perimeters of her dreams, watching them, watching her. And ultimately, before the dream was over, it invaded her body and her mind. It was not always the same cat's eyes that were there, gleaming at her from a bed of darkness. Occasionally it was eyes of other animals that she saw. But always the animal appeared ready to devour her at any second. With each night the dreams grew more real, more frightening. She was reminded of what had been said about the Animal People. Was it possible that She Who Sees Far was right? Was it possible, too, that Keane and Swift Blade's male intuition about Ocelot was more accurate than she had wanted to believe?

Tanya didn't know if the dreams were to blame, but she had been excessively tired and disoriented the past couple of days. She *wanted* to sleep, but she feared the dreams enough to fight her drowsiness.

She left her grass mattress and paced her small quarters. The hour had to be past midnight, although she had no way of being sure. She would have to sleep eventually, but not yet. Not until utter exhaustion took over and reduced the possibility of dreams.

Her thoughts had been on Keane almost constantly since his departure. She had walked away from him scores of times over the years. There had been a feeling of emptiness after each time, but never had she felt this extreme loss, as if a part of her was missing.

She should never have trusted him. Should never have allowed herself to love him. But then, hadn't she always loved him in a way? Hadn't she just hidden the truth behind a facade of disdain? On one hand, he was everything she'd always known him to be; on the other hand, he wasn't anything of what she had expected.

She had removed the Turquoise Sun right after he'd gone. She found it now among her things and held it in her hand. After a time, she placed it around her neck and felt its comforting weight against her bosom. It wouldn't keep the dreams away, but perhaps it had some special power that 1 keep away the evil spirits that seemed so prevalent in this realm of the Anasazi. By the poor light of the small torch, she sat cross-legged on her bed and forced herself to work on the basket she'd been weaving. It was terrible-looking, laughable in fact, but it was her first attempt. Her eyes burned, but she forced herself to concentrate on the intricate pattern that needed to be followed and the tucking and pulling of each strand of grass. While she worked, she tried to recall the more pleasant memories in her life. But soon, the heaviness of her eyelids blurred her vision, dulled her mind. If she could just stay awake until dawn, then she knew she could sleep without fear.

Yet, as always, she slumped back on her mattress and the basket fell limp in her hands. Sleep came. And with it, the dreams . . .

Darkness. Sandstone walls. Yawning doorways. Empty corridors. Ten-Moon.

Why are you here, old man?

Where are you going Tanya?

Following the sound.

What sound?

In the old kiva.

Then go inside.

I can't. Ghosts of the old ones still linger.

Who told you that?

An old Ute, from Durango.

Do not listen to a Ute. Go. Go on. You must see what is on the other side. Now, tell me. What do you see?

A ladder, leading down into a kiva. Darkness. Always darkness. Why must I go down there?

Because he's there. He needs you.

But I fear the darkness.

Help me, Tanya.

Where are you, Keane?

Here.

What do you see? Smell?

Darkness. Coolness. Dust of centuries. Tobacco.

Help me.

I can't see you.

I'm here. By the fire. Help me.

I can't. Blood. Pools of blood. Blood on my knees, my hands, my face, seeping out of the rocks. No place to hide. To run.

I'll chant you back. Just go to him.

Help me, Tanya.

I can't. Ghosts of the old ones still linger.

I'll chant you back. You must go to him.

I can't, old man! The eyes are watching me. And the blood is everywhere!

Go. You must go to him. You are the only one who can find him.

Help me, Tanya.

What is it like there? On the other side of tomorrow?

I can't tell you. I can't get there. The knife and the blood . . .

I'll chant you back.

I can't find him. He's too far away.

Tanya, help me!

Go!

I can't see you! Where are you! No, Keane! No!

Keane!

He came awake with a start. The sound of Tanya's voice calling out to him was as clear and as real as if she'd been lying next to him. But it wasn't Tanya he saw in the darkness. In the next split second, a blur of brown skin, ghoulish paint, and a knife came slicing through the darkness toward him.

There was no time to think, only to react. He rolled to the blade intended for his heart, but it caught his shoulder, opening the skin and drawing blood. He kicked out and caught the man in the thigh, knocking him off balance and into the dirt. In another instant the man leaped up again, releasing a bloodcurdling scream. What the attacker saw, too late, was the big Bowie that had sprang miraculously from Keane's scabbard to his hand. The Indian twisted to avoid contact, but was too late. With a startled look and a grunt of pain, he saw the big blade sink deep into his own heart.

The life went out of him almost instantly, and Keane pushed him away and off his knife. Leaping back, Keane expected to engage in battle with others, but he found that the only attacker was the one that now lay dead, his life's blood seeping out onto Keane's blankets.

The man's war cry brought the others from their sleep with weapons in hand. Bleary-eyed, they searched the surrounding darkness for the enemy, ready to fight, but they were met with only silence. Confused, they looked for the sentry, but soon discovered, upon closer inspection of the dead man, that *he* was the sentry, young Sakngöisi. Immediately murmurs began as to why he had tried to kill Trevalyan.

Keane, shaken by the experience and holding his bleeding arm, glanced into the faces of his traveling companions, wondering if others among them wanted him dead. He saw nothing in their eyes except surprise and disbelief that Sakngöisi, who had given no previous indications of dislike for Keane, would have undertaken the job to be his assassin.

"He is of the Bow Clan," someone said.

"That explains it then," another replied. "They fear a power greater than their own."

They all seemed to accept that explanation, but it did nothing to ease Keane's concern or answer his questions. He wished for Swift Blade to possibly give some insight into the murderous act.

With the hope that the attack had been just one man's

aggression, Keane allowed Owl Dancing to prepare a medicinal paste for his arm and to bandage it, while the others searched for a suitable burial place for Sakngöisi. In this case, it turned out to be a narrow crevice in a ledge of rocks, since digging a grave would have been impossible in the rocky soil without a shovel, or at least some sort of digging implement.

While some expressed sadness and surprise over the young man's traitorous deed, most offered no remorse. He was not given the usual burial with prayer and song. They expressed, instead, their apologies to Keane that one of their own kind had tried to kill him. It was decided that two sentries would be put on duty to assure that it did not happen again.

After the burial they settled back around the fire. It was still several hours until dawn and most of the men welcomed their blankets again. Several however, including Keane, found sleep to be elusive and they stared into the night sky, watching the stars slowly make their journey toward the western horizon.

"It is fortunate you awoke when you did," Owl Dancing whispered. "How did you know he was there?"

Keane glanced at the man who had made his bed but a few feet from Keane's.

"My wife called to me in my sleep to warn me."

As Keane suspected, Owl Dancing accepted such supernatural interference as a natural part of life. As the fire danced across his dark-skinned face, there was nothing resembling doubt or suspicion in his eyes. He, like all the other Red Sand People, believed Keane to be a kachina, a spirit sent in human form to help them. This incident would, hopefully, keep that belief fresh and foremost in their minds.

Shortly, Owl Dancing returned to his sleep. Keane continued to toss and turn. He kept going over the incident in his mind and grew increasingly restless. He began to remember the dream he'd been having just prior to the attack.

It was such a strange dream. He'd been back in the kiva, hurt, and he'd been calling out for Tanya to help him. It had been dark and she couldn't see him. When she had at last come into the kiva, she'd gotten frightened over something and suddenly screamed out his name.

He was beginning to wonder if what he'd heard had only been in the dream, or part of some supernatural connection between the two of them. Her voice had sounded so loud and clear, almost as if she'd been right by his side. As the sound of it echoed through his mind repeatedly, he heard something in the inflection of it that deeply troubled him. He began to discern the fear as having a different quality to it. Soon he realized that her cry in the night had been of a dual nature. It had been a warning call, but it had also been a cry for help.

He knew in that instant that he could not continue the journey. By the light of the fire, he collected his things with overwhelming urgency. Before the darkness began to lift, he woke Owl Dancing and the others and told them to go on without him.

"But you do not have to worry, our friend," Owl Dancing said. "No one will try to harm you again."

"It is not for myself that I fear," Keane replied, tossing his bundle over his shoulder. "It is for my wife. I have seen something in a vision that frightens me, and I must hurry back to her before it is too late."

Twenty-one

Tanya dipped the long-handled ladle into the small pool of water. Carefully she transferred the precious liquid to the narrow-necked jar she had made and designed herself. Her hands were shaking again, as they had been for several days, and she spilled half of the water down the side of the jar.

Since they'd first arrived here, she'd shown great improvement at balancing the jar on her head, as long as she was on level ground. She still had to invent alternative methods when she came to the steep path leading up to the cliff dwellings. These past few days had found her task getting harder and harder, due to an extreme weakness in her body. It took all her effort just to walk. She longed to find her grass mattress and lie upon it. If she hadn't just had her menses, she might have suspected pregnancy. She was vaguely disappointed it was not so.

Her lethargy might be due to the dreams. They'd returned the night Keane had left, nearly two weeks ago, and she had had one every night since. She had been unable to sleep, afraid that whatever had been stealing into her dreams was real and lurking in the shadows of the dark room. She had also been terribly thirsty, but she'd had no desire to eat. Her arms ached this evening from carrying so many water jars today, some for herself and some for She Who Sees who was still confined to her quarters.

vift Blade had explained the custom that kept a woman

in isolation after childbirth. "The mother and baby are protected from strong light for twenty days," he said. "Every fifth day the aunts and grandmothers wash the mother's hair in soap from the yucca root and bathe her in water that has been boiled with juniper twigs.

"On the twentieth day the baby's head is washed. A ceremony of prayer then takes place to dedicate the child to the Sun Father. The baby's grandmother, on its father's side, carries the baby to the top of the cliff as the sun rises. He dedicates the child, a name is chosen from those that the aunts and grandmothers have given it."

Tanya tried again to transfer water from the ladle into the jar, wondering if the name she'd given the baby would be the chosen one. She noticed that She Who Sees Far seemed to favor it. Even the grandmothers and aunts occasionally used it.

Since Keane had been gone, the sun had scorched the mesa and the canyon floors with temperatures that felt well over a hundred degrees every day. People were saying that if rain didn't come soon, the crops would be lost. Even the springs were drying up. The water came much slower now, filling the blue shale basin less frequently. She could hear women at the next spring discussing the same matter. They could not see her for the pinyon, juniper, and brush that blocked their view, but their voices came loud and clear. As their conversation progressed, it became evident to Tanya that they didn't know she was there.

"What good is it doing to have Kachina People among us?" one said. "It is even drier than before, and I am not so sure they should be given credit for the one rain that came shortly after their arrival."

"Yes, and they seem to know nothing. The woman has had to be shown how to do practically everything. If they have power and knowledge, they do not share it with us."

"I agree. If the woman had power, would she have paced the plaza while Ten-Moon brought her friend's baby into the world? She does not even have the power to keep her own man. I heard Snow In Summer followed the trading expedition so she could be with He Who Laughs."

A startled gasp came from the other woman. Tanya's hand halted over the water jar, shaking so badly that the water in the dipper spilled to the ground. Suddenly she found it difficult to breathe. She set the ladle down soundlessly, clutching a nearby rock for support. Her head began to swim, but the women's words droned on in her ears unmercifully.

"Her family has been telling everyone that she went to the village up the canyon to see her mother's people."

"Of course they would make excuses for her absence, *and* her behavior. I'm sure she would have several babies by now if not for the special tea she faithfully consumes each morning to rid her belly of unwanted seeds."

"Do you think He Who Laughs will be foolish enough to become her man?"

"She tells everyone that she has already been with him, and that is why he went away without the kachina woman."

"But Snow In Summer brags about being with many men."

"Yes, but have you known a man to turn her down?"

"If so, she does not speak of those. Maybe He Who Laughs is just using her like all the other men do."

"Some believe the Kachina People are really witches from another tribe and that they've come here with their evil tricks to weaken us so the rest of their tribe can conquer us. Some say they are of the white-skinned people from another world across the ocean. Maybe the white-skinned people are all witches with great power."

"Yes, I've heard of them," the other girl responded agreeably. "They have occasionally landed on our shores and then gone again, died, or been killed. There have been a se sailing vessels have broken up in the rocks along of the Big Water, and the survivors were forced to stay among the People for the rest of their lives. But there is also the legend of the Lost White Brother, Pahána, who will come to bring order to the world. How do we know it is not He Who Laughs? He is very pleasant, and very pleasing to the eye. People would follow him, if he said the word."

"He is not Pahána, because he does not bring with him the missing corner piece of the sacred tablet that Másaw, the guardian spirit of the Fourth World, gave to the Fire Clan upon their emergence here."

"I personally am beginning to believe that the rumors might be true that they are witches. And she screams at night. Have you heard her?"

"No, I have not."

"Many have. I, for one."

"Is it possible for kachinas to have nightmares?"

"I would not think so. They should have power over evil demons getting into their thoughts and their dreams. I think her screams are part of a strange and evil ritual she uses to cast spells over people in the village. Maybe she even cast a spell over Pávati and caused him to jump from the cliffs. He was in the room beneath hers. I wonder who will be next."

"Hush, someone is coming."

"Oh, no! It is my mother. Hurry, let us go out that way through the pinyons. She wants me to grind corn, but I don't want to."

They scampered away, leaving Tanya alone with the words of their conversation weighing heavily on her mind. She was so distraught over the news of Snow In Summer sneaking away to be with Keane on the expedition that she wouldn't have cared if the people decided to burn her at the stake for being a witch—or whatever it was they did to witches.

Their words had left her numb. Visions came to mind of Snow In Summer warming Keane's blankets every nigh and making love to him in the way she herself had done as his wife. Her heart ached so badly she wondered if it would stop beating entirely. She didn't care; death would be welcome if it would take away this pain.

She placed a hand over her heart to calm it. Its wild vibration pulsed through her fingers and into her hand and arm. Beneath her fingers, she felt the rolls and ridges of the Turquoise Sun—Keane's marriage gift. His token of love; his promise that he would love only her.

Suddenly she began to gasp, as if all the air in her lungs had been sucked out and she could get no more. The gasps were followed by wrenching sobs. Driven by some force of insanity, she frantically began to fumble at the gold bar clasp behind her neck. If the necklace hadn't been so solid, she'd have ripped it off. She had never felt such pain, such torment of her mind and body. If this was love, then she wanted no part of it, not ever again!

The necklace fell free and into her hands. Her first thought was to run to the river and fling it into the current. But she held it and stared at it through a blur of tears. He'd only given it to her because it was worth virtually nothing here. There were other things to trade that were more important to people in this world. Things like furs, cotton, knives, the necessities of life.

On trembling legs she stood and swiped at her tears until she could see something of the necklace besides a blur of color. Finding renewed strength, she headed toward the village on a determined stride. She never wanted to see the necklace again . . . and she knew exactly what she would do to make certain she never did.

The infant, Kira, gazed up at Tanya. Her solemn black ~~~~ ne brightly with the curiosity inherent to new life. o Sees Far had just finished nursing her and had her to Tanya. Her trusting eyes made Tanya feel close to her, as if they shared an unspoken and special bond of kinship. She also felt that familiar tug of yearning again to have a child of her own. That would be impossible now, at least with Keane.

She spoke to Kira in a soft voice, and the baby cooed a response, as if she understood the meaning of the singsong words. Her little fist flailed and accidentally touched Tanya's cheek. Startled by the contact, her tiny arm froze in place and her eyes grew twice as large as normal.

The baby's warm hand felt cool against Tanya's heated skin. Her condition had worsened in the last couple of days, and it took every ounce of strength just to think and to accomplish the smallest tasks. Tanya feared that she might have a strange disease that Kira could catch, although a sixth sense told her the illness was isolated to her own body.

A fever seemed to rage inside her, although her skin was cool to the touch. Her thirst could not be abated. Along with an increasing, inexplicable fear came a growing paranoia that she was about to be swallowed up by an invisible but beastly force. She trusted only a handful of people; Swift Blade, She Who Sees Far, and Ocelot. She had even avoided old Ten-Moon, for when she looked into his eyes, she saw—or imagined she saw—a knifelike gaze penetrating the very center of her mind, seeing things he shouldn't see. Knowing things he shouldn't know.

Swift Blade had been worried about her and was never far away. Nor was Ocelot, who had been extremely kind. He had made sure she had plenty of water and insisted that she not make the trek to the spring herself until she felt better. Today he had filled her water jars himself, even though it was considered woman's work. No one in the tribe dared question his actions or his attentions towards her. They might gossip about a relationship developing in the absence of her husband, but none dared openly to confront either of them. He was, after all, the future leader of the Bow Clan, and she was of the Kachina People.

Tanya appreciated his concern, but as each day passed and she seemed to feel worse, she yearned for Keane's laughter and his teasing remarks, his playful eyes. She longed for the friendship that had been between them. The love.

She wanted nothing more than his arms around her at night to protect her from the nightmares. She feared sleep more than ever. The dreams were mostly senseless, intangible. Just bits and pieces of the past; cameos of people's faces. Of more concern was the feeling that something was inside her mind, slowly stealing her thoughts, her knowledge, her past, her memories, and everything that she was or had been. She feared that one day she would wake up and her mind would be completely devoid of anything but space. And there were strange colors flashing in her head, night and day. Occasionally she felt as if she were hallucinating. Many times she would see things that were gone in the next blink of the eye.

Nevertheless, she was reluctant to believe what Keane had said about Ocelot. There might be a witch at work—it was something she could no longer disallow—but could it really be Ocelot? He had practically forsaken his own life to look after her in Keane's absence. She just couldn't believe there was evil behind his kindness.

Kira's tugging on her hair finally drew Tanya back to the present. Her mind was slower to respond than usual. Carefully she extricated the baby's fingers from her hair, numbly realizing at the same time that her head was hurting ferociously from the child pulling on her hair.

She Who Sees Far took the baby and settled her in the curve of her arm. The baby immediately found a nipple, sucked a few times, and fell asleep. She Who Sees Far lifted her eyes to Tanya. A worry line creased her young brow.

"I believe you should see Ten-Moon, Tanya. At first I you were only lonely for Trevalyan, but I can see it ails you is something deeper and more dangerous than loneliness. Your eyes are sunken with dark circles surrounding them. Your skin is the color of ash. Your smile wanes like the full moon. These symptoms are very dangerous. They are elusive like those of the ghost sickness."

Tanya didn't know what that was, but she didn't want to reveal her ignorance. She looked at the sleeping baby in order to conceal any thoughts that might be discernible in her eyes. "I will be fine. Ocelot is taking care of me."

"You should not believe what they are saying about Keane and Snow In Summer," She Who Sees Far said sternly in a tone that contained a warning note. "Do not turn to Ocelot in your loneliness. He is one to take advantage of a woman."

Tanya knew she'd been chastised, but like the entire conversation, the words seemed faraway and part of another layer of awareness she could see but not reach. She did vaguely wonder, however, why she was always attracted to men who were of the kind to use women and then discard them. Then the thought slipped away, as elusive as all the others floating through her mind.

She Who Sees Far continued, but not on the subject of Tanya's illness. She looked through the window and out to the rock wall across the canyon. The distant look entered her eyes. "You are still having the dreams," she stated. "But I have been having dreams, too. They are strange dreams that perplex me and to which I can put no meaning. I thought that since you are one of the Kachina People, you might be able to answer some questions I've had concerning these troubling images."

Tanya feared her ignorance on such supernatural matters would become evident, but she gave her consent for She Who Sees Far to continue.

"There is something about our home here in the cliffs that disturbs me," the young mother said. "In my dreams I see this village abandoned and in ruin. In another vision I see many people here. Thousands. But they do not stay

They come and go as if only here out of curiosity. They are dressed strangely, even more strangely than you and He Who Laughs. Some wear funny things over their eyes, as if to protect their eyes from the light of the sun. They wander through this place, this room where I live, and they look and they wonder. I sense their questions about who the people were who built these dwellings in the alcove of this canyon wall. They try to imagine what life here was like. But they cannot, for they are too far removed from it. Some of them search in the dust for pieces of pottery and arrowheads, but the plazas are swept bare. All that remains are the silent remnants of these dwellings and the ghosts of those who lived and died here—Pávati, Screaming Panther, Ten-Moon—"

"Ten-Moon?" Tanya's head came up with a jerk. "You see the old man dying? When does this happen?"

She Who Sees Far eyed her curiously. "I do not see the exact time that he dies. I only know, in my vision, that he has. Nor do I believe I will die here. Something tells me I will leave this place along with many others before that happens.

"Do you remember before Kira was born and I had the dream of losing something very dear to me? Well, I have that feeling again, and it frightens me a great deal. I believe this new dream signifies what my loss will be. This dream seems to be a premonition. It tells me that I will leave this canyon. When that time comes, I will lose a way of life and everything associated with this place that has been so dear to my heart. My youth, my best memories, my first love.

"You have seen the future, my friend," She Who Sees Far continued. "Can you explain this vision to me? Can you tell me where I go, and why I leave here? Who will ___ ___re in the future? A few? Or many? Or only ghosts? ___ the only movement along the canyon floor will be ___lows of the clouds being chased by the wind."

Tanya lifted her eyes slowly, becoming increasingly aware that they hurt with the slightest movement. She had listened with great interest to her friend, and yet her words were hard to remember. She could not concentrate. She did not know what question, if any, had been posed her.

"It is not for me to expose the future to you," she replied in a way that sounded exceedingly lame, at least to her. "It might change the course of events that should take place naturally."

She Who Sees Far captured Tanya's gaze and held it. Hers was steady and knowing. "One of the Kachina People would know the future, just as would one who has come *from* the future. Someone such as yourself, Tanya Darrow."

Tanya heard the words and knew they were important, but she couldn't grasp the depth of meaning. "What are you saying?"

"I am saying that I do not believe you are from the spiritual realm, sent here in human form to save our people from this drought. I believe you are a woman just like me, only you come from a time that is not yet. I do not understand how you got here, or how you will return. I only know it is dangerous for you to stay much longer, pretending to be a kachina, especially if certain ones should learn the truth."

Tanya's dulled brain was slow to absorb the full meaning and impact of her friend's words. She rubbed her temples. A cold chill washed over her body. Had she said something to inadvertently give herself away? If She Who Sees Far had guessed the truth, would others as well? Would these Anasazi, who believed so heavily in the supernatural, not find it unusual for people to travel through time? But regardless of how She Who Sees Far had learned the truth, Tanya was too weak to deny it. Too tired.

"How do you know this? I don't remember telling you."

"You did not tell me. The answer came in a vision. I did not understand it at first, but gradually it became clear."

"Do others know?"

"I do not believe they do, and your secret is safe with me."

Tanya stood up and moved to the window. The scene before her blurred. She gripped the window sill for support. She Who Sees Far came to her side and put an arm around her waist. "Lie down, my friend. You are very ill. I am afraid you have the ghost sickness. If I am correct, then only a *túhikya* can remove the evil spirit in your body that was put there by a *powáqa* of great power."

Tanya reclined on the grass mattress. It was cool in the room, but she still felt afire inside. "I *am* of the future," she finally admitted. "Probably six or seven hundred years from now. Your vision of the dwellings in ruin is the way I found it when I first came here. Ten-Moon's chant somehow brought us here, and the old man does not know how to get us back. As for your vision of many people walking along these paths and through these corridors, looking but not staying . . . I am sorry. Perhaps it is in a time beyond even my own.

"Now, tell me, She Who Sees Far," Tanya continued. "Am I going to die here? Will my people find my bones in the crevice of the rock alongside those of Pávati and the others?"

She Who Sees Far knelt next to Tanya. She touched her forehead and cheeks with the back of her hand, checking for fever and looking puzzled when she found none. Setting back on her heels, she said, "I do not know the answer to your question, my friend. I only know your strength has been stolen by an evil spirit. With Keane gone, your heart is lonely and vulnerable. It is easy for a witch to put the ghost sickness inside you. I must get Ten-Moon or you will die."

Tanya reached for her arm. "No, not Ten-Moon. I'm not sure I can . . . trust him." Even as Tanya said the words and heard them in her own ears, she wondered what had induced her to say them. Ten-Moon was a friend, wasn't he?

"Ten-Moon would never harm you." She Who Sees Far's brow knotted with concern. "Why would you think otherwise?"

"I . . . don't know." Tanya rubbed her head in a vain effort to clear the confusion from it. "Someone told me not to trust him . . . I don't remember who. Maybe it was only in a dream . . ."

The worry deepened in She Who Sees Far's black eyes. "My mother's house is just around the corner. I will call her to come here, and tell her that she must get Swift Blade to carry you back to your quarters. Then I'll have her send for Ten-Moon. I would get them both myself, but I'm not to leave my room for six more days."

"I can walk back to my quarters."

"Are you positive?"

"Yes."

Tanya wasn't sure how she did it, but she found enough strength to get to her feet and move to the small door opening.

"You *will* have Swift Blade go for Ten-Moon, won't you?"

Tanya nodded. "Yes, of course. Don't worry about me. I'll be fine. And, She Who Sees Far—"

"Yes?"

"You will not give away my secret?"

The black eyes met hers, steady and true. "A friend does not endanger the life of a friend."

Tanya left the room, walking in a daze. She wound her way through the corridors by sheer instinct. In the plaza she was intercepted by Ocelot.

"You do not look well, Eyes of Sky," he said, slipping a hand beneath her elbow to support her. "Circles shadow your eyes. Can you tell me what is wrong? If you would confide in me, then perhaps I can help. I know something of the medicinal plants. My mother was a medicine woman."

Tanya appreciated his help and his kindness, and when she looked into his concerned eyes she saw something familiar. She couldn't put a finger on what it was, but it was as if she'd met a kindred spirit. She knew instinctively that she could trust him more than she could trust Ten-Moon or anyone else in the village, even Swift Blade. She glanced up at the Tower House, feeling uneasy about returning to her own room. Something lurked there in the shadows, waiting to infiltrate her mind and her body in the most evil of ways.

"I think I would like to find a cool spot down by the river."

Ocelot helped her down the path and through the trees. He took her to a secluded place where there were no other people. The last hundred feet or so, she found herself lifted in his arms, but she raised no objection for her legs felt as weak as grass in the wind.

He lowered her to the shade beneath some pinyons. Soon she found her head pillowed by his muscled thigh. The brilliant colors swam in her head again, but she was too dizzy and too tired to open her eyes. Besides, the glare of the sun was less appealing than the images flashing in her brain.

"Would you like me to bathe your skin with the cool water?" he asked softly.

Nothing sounded more wonderful. She was positive her body was on fire, eating away at her from the inside out. Yet, an inner voice warned her against letting Ocelot become too intimate. "I'll be fine. I'd just like to rest for a minute."

She closed her eyes. Ocelot stroked her head, like one would stroke the fur of a kitten. It was such a pleasant feeling that she almost purred with contentedness. She must have dozed off, too, for suddenly Ocelot's words jarred her awake. But no significant amount of time had passed. She saw the sun still shining through the same two branches in the pinyon tree.

"You are not wearing the Turquoise Sun," Ocelot was whispering from a faraway place in her mind. "I hated to lose the necklace to Trevalyan, but he won it fairly. More importantly, he gave it to you. It is what I would have done myself. The instant I saw you, I thought how wonderful the necklace would look against your fair and beautiful neck. It was made for a queen, a goddess. One of the Kachina People. But, tell me. Why have you removed it?"

Tanya wasn't sure she could remember why. She seemed to be falling farther and farther from reality, and from life, with each breath she took. A memory hung in her subconscious about why she'd removed the necklace, but she couldn't grasp the particulars. If Keane was here, she could ask him, but she wasn't sure where he was. He'd been gone a long time, or so it seemed. She remembered things about him—his lovemaking, his flirtatious smiles and words, his joking manner. Things that had always lightened her heart and given her hope and joy. His absence sent pain crashing over her, like waves crashing the beach, pushing her deeper into wet sand, as if she were no more significant than a tiny seashell soon to be buried forever.

"I overhead what those girls were saying about you that day by the pools," Ocelot continued. "You should not allow their foolish words to trouble you, Eyes of Sky."

He still stroked her head. The motion was hypnotizing and she found it more difficult to focus on his words. Vaguely, she remembered the instance he spoke of, but it was irrelevant, senseless. "I didn't see you . . ."

"They had upset you very badly, but I didn't want to interfere. Pay no attention to the women, Eyes of Sky. They talk too much because they have nothing else to do. They do not understand that the gods sometimes make people suffer in order to teach them to be more dependent on the Creator for their needs. They do not understand that the

Kachina People have never been among the mortals for any reason other than to help and guide and to convey messages to the gods. The gods can choose not to answer if the people are not living in accordance to the laws first set down by the Creator. The kachinas have their powers, but it is not for them to take matters into their own hands. Am I not correct?"

His words reached her mind in a pleasant, singsong sort of way. Some of them she heard; some she didn't. All that really mattered was the soft, warm glow of his eyes. He was such a kind man who was always there when she needed help.

"Yes, Ocelot. Others sometimes do not understand the position of the Kachina People as well as you do." She lifted her hand and placed it on his forearm. "Thank you for helping me. I am most grateful for your kindness."

"I fear you worry about what the people will think of your estrangement with Trevalyan. Do not let it trouble you. It is not unusual for men and women to separate and find other mates who are better suited for them. This is true of Kachina People as well."

She was estranged from Keane? How odd. She couldn't remember . . .

She tried to get up, suddenly agitated because she could not remember. She was still dizzy, but forced herself to a sitting position. "I need to go now."

Ocelot placed his hands on her shoulders with just enough pressure to prevent her from rising. "I will bring Ten-Moon," he said. "You are very ill and I fear you will die."

"No. I'll be fine. Ten-Moon is old and needs all his strength to . . ." she faded off, vaguely aware that there was something about Ten-Moon and the chants that she wasn't supposed to tell anyone.

"He needs his strength for what, Eyes of Sky?"

She rubbed her temples. Her thoughts had gelled.

"I don't know. I can't . . . remember."

"I think you don't want him to come because you don't trust him," he said soothingly. "Isn't that correct?"

"Yes. Yes, that's it. I have been told he is a witch."

Ocelot laid a cool hand to her forehead. It felt so refreshing. She drifted off again, onto the edge of sleep. She heard a female voice say . . . *you have the ghost sickness. Only a túhikya can remove the evil spirits . . .*

"I think Ten-Moon is the one who has put the sickness in you." Ocelot again. "He is powerful indeed, but possibly dangerous. If you do not trust him, would you trust me?"

"Are you a . . . *túhikya?*" she mumbled.

"My powers are as great as Ten-Moon's. Maybe greater."

She rolled her head on the soft grass and looked into his black, waiting eyes. There was only kindness and concern there. "All right. Help me, Ocelot . . . if you can."

Twenty-two

Tanya offered no resistance when Ocelot lifted her into his arms. Nor did she care where she was being taken. Occasionally she was forced to walk, to climb through a confusing maze of rocks and narrow trails. Then he was carrying her again. She closed her eyes and rested her head against his chest. She dozed, and when she awoke, she was in a small, dim place far from the village. She knew this because she saw no torches glowing orange, nor heard any sounds except the moaning and creaking of the rock. He laid her on soft furs. Water was placed to her lips and she drank until it was taken away, much too soon. The beautiful colors in her mind returned with even more vigor. She welcomed them and the wonderful euphoric feelings that came with them, as well as the feelings of power, strength, and sexual desire.

She saw a spiral of light twisting and swaying, casting erotic shadows on rock walls. A cave. He had brought her to a cave. Shortly, her clothing was removed by gentle hands and a cool cloth glided over her naked body, reducing the inner heat. She sank into the mesmerizing pleasure and the monotonous sound of the words.

Where do you come from, Tanya Darrow?
Boston.
Where is Boston?
Faraway. To the east.
Why do you come here?
To observe the Anasazi.

The Anasazi?

Yes, it is the name some have given to the Red Sand People.

There were more questions. She didn't know who asked them, if she answered them, or if she only thought she had. It was not important. She looked beyond the spiral of light into the shadows. Something hid there, waiting for the right moment to step into the quivering, red light.

"Keane? Are you here?"

"You must relax, Eyes of Sky," came a whispered male voice. "I will protect you from your enemy, Trevalyan. I am your friend Ocelot. Remember?"

"There is something in the shadows. It's watching me. Where is Keane?"

"It is only your sickness that makes you see things. I am the only one here. Close your eyes. You must trust me to take the sickness from you. I won't hurt you."

Tanya did as she was told. With her eyes closed, she couldn't see the shadows and couldn't feel the strange presence beyond the firelight. She drifted away from the questions and the faint rustling noises surrounding her. She was with Ocelot. He was preparing some sort of ritual, painting his face, putting feathers in his hair. But where was Keane?

She heard the beat of a familiar song, a chant from somewhere in her memory, her past. It was faraway, so distant she could not grasp it. It rested just beyond the edge of her mind, one inch beyond her reach. She'd heard something like that a long time ago, in another lifetime. Except that the words were different. These were from an ancient language she could not understand.

Then she drifted away from it completely, falling into a void of euphoric weightlessness. Into the dream . . .

Ocelot sat back on his heels and allowed the chant to fade away slowly and softly. Eyes of Sky did not stir. The extra drug he'd given her in her water would take her into her own dreamland, and he could do anything with her he pleased. He would keep her here until he had all the answers he needed, and until he had sated his sexual desire for her. Then, when there was nothing left in her mind, he could extend her life through the drug for weeks, months, even years if he so desired. In the event that he might grow tired of sexual intercourse with her, he would increase the amount of the drug until she died. He would bury her in the crevice of the cliffs next to Pávati and cover her body with rocks. No one would be the wiser. Just as no one was the wiser that Snow In Summer had gone nowhere, except on the Road to the Stars. That little *powáqa* had made the mistake of threatening to betray him in order to get her way. She had learned quickly that no one threatens Ocelot of the Four Winds.

From the times he'd been inside Tanya Darrow's mind, and from the questions she'd just answered, he felt confident that she was not of the Kachina People. She might not even be a *powáqa*. If she was either, he wouldn't have been able to so easily inflict the ghost sickness on her, or get into her mind. He had feared what his eternal reward would be for killing a kachina, but those fears were abated now. She had power, but it was of a different sort. It was *human* power.

The images he'd stolen from her mind told him that she was a strong ruler from another world faraway, a place where there were more white people than there were stars in the sky. She came from a place where magnificent palaces were filled with splendid wonders and riches, where animals and people did her bidding. He was positive she was here to control the Red Sand People, to win their confidence, steal their lands, and take them away to the cities to be slaves.

Through her thoughts, he had seen her in the canyon below the village, but the dwellings were in ruin, vacant. The Red Sand People were gone. He did not understand this at first, then realized he'd stolen a piece of what the future was going to be. He'd stolen a piece of time. The scenes he'd seen of her walking through the ruins were images of her evil intent. What he'd seen was her idea of what the canyon would look like when she had captured the people and taken them away as her slaves to this place she called Boston.

In her mind he had also seen white slaves digging in this village, after it was abandoned and in ruins. They had been searching for pieces of what the Red Sand People had left behind. Searching for treasures like the Turquoise Sun. He suspected it was her goal to bring in an army and lay waste. He had originally planned to kill Screaming Panther and old Ten-Moon, but the woman posed a greater threat. Destroying her must come first.

She was powerful, for a woman, and held a position of great authority. Still, he knew he could destroy her and Trevalyan both without repercussions from the spirit world. It had always been his goal that if anyone was going to rule the Red Sand People, it would be him and the Bow Clan. This woman would not get in his way. When he was in control of all the tribes here in the mesa land, he would join forces with the powers to the south and they would locate this Boston of hers and lay siege to it. The lands and riches she ruled were going to be his. And, if perchance she became his woman willingly, then he would not have to kill her, but would rule alongside her. He need not worry about Trevalyan; he was already dead at the hand of Sakngöisi.

There was much no one knew of his powers, and he had a powerful urge to tell someone. He would have liked to tell her, but her mind was as fertile with the drug as spring earth. Whatever he told her would remain in her subconscious, influencing her waking considerations and actions. Therefore, the only thoughts he had put there, and *would* put there, were the ones he wanted her to remember and to believe.

So he gloated only in his own mind of how he had killed Pávati and planned the raid. He had been so clever. He had had his own followers from the village and all the surrounding villages paint their faces to conceal their identities. They had struck fast and then left quickly, washing their faces in the river. He had made sure they gathered up the dead bodies of their own and hauled them away. Any dead from Screaming Panther's village were washed of their paint and then counted as part of the Red Sand dead. No one had been the wiser.

He had done it in the name of desire. He had never wanted a woman the way he wanted this one. He had tricked Trevalyan into leaving, then he had put the drug in Tanya's water so her mind would be more open to his suggestions. It was a new drug from a plant found in the tropics, and it worked very well. By getting into her mind without as much resistance he had been better able to convince her, through mental suggestion, to distrust Ten-Moon and turn to him instead.

"It is time for you to be my wife," he spoke aloud now, wanting his words to sink deep into her subconscious. "Trevalyan betrayed you, remember? As we speak, he is with Snow In Summer. Come to me. Open yourself to me. You will not regret it. You will understand what I have done. You will share with me a physical experience unlike any you may have had before. We were meant to be together. You will soon understand this."

He moved closer to her, to the pale skin that so fascinated him. He ran a hand along the flat of her stomach, lifted a perfectly shaped breast into one palm, and stroked the golden length of her hair with the other. She stirred slightly, then sank back into her drug-induced sleep. He felt his manhood hardening and knew that, at long last, he would satisfy his sexual need for her with no interferences.

He ran his hands along the inside of her thighs and gently
spread her legs. Outside, the sun had set. Twilight settled
over the canyon. Here in the cave darkness had already
fallen. The firelight touched on the golden mound between
her legs and he feasted his eyes on her pale-toned womanhood. The blood began to pulse through his veins, pumping
hard in his loins. He had never wanted a woman as desperately as he wanted this one. She had toyed with his mind,
distracted his purpose. She would pay for that.

He untied the leather breechcloth around his waist and
cast it aside. Unrestricted, his shaft rose high and hard. He
spread her legs even farther and positioned himself between
them.

"You will be mine now, Eyes of Sky," he whispered.
"You may dream of Trevalyan being inside you, but it will
be me you open yourself to. And soon, very soon, you will
forget about him. You will come to me, even in your
dreams."

*She could see nothing. She could only feel. And she felt
his warmth in the darkness. He moved next to her, molding
his naked length to hers. She felt the rough pads of his
fingertips on her skin, caressing the curve of her waist, her
hip, the sensitive area between her legs. His warm breath
tickled her.*

"When did you come back, my darling? I missed you
so."

He answered with a kiss, and she settled into the sweet
darkness. It didn't matter when he had returned. It only
mattered that he had.

The hair at the nape of his neck was long. It had grown.
And it was coarse. She could not remember his hair having
been that coarse. It had always been soft and silky.

His lips closed fully over hers. Cruel, rapacious lips. She
tried to open her eyes again, fighting the darkness and the

peculiarities in his lovemaking which she could not remember from the times before. But something powerful held her eyes closed. The only thing she saw were the brilliant, soothing colors that hypnotized.

His extended shaft moved up along her thigh toward the yearning part of her. She gripped his buttocks, pulling him closer. Why did he not hurry? Didn't he feel the same desperate urgency? Why did he seem to purposefully be tormenting her by making her wait?

Then she heard a small voice somewhere outside herself. *"Remember, Tanya, the dream always starts wonderful. But don't forget the way it ends. Remember the cat. Remember the eyes."*

Yes, the cat. How could she have forgotten that beastly creature of evil, whose spirit had tried to enter her body through sexual intercourse, just as it had tried to plunder and steal her dreams and her memories. She could not let it conquer her. She had to open her eyes before it stole her life, her soul.

The scream echoed through the canyon, sounding and resounding against the rock walls until Keane had no idea of its point of origin. Then suddenly it ended. The echoes ended, and all was deathly silent.

The twilight touched the cliff walls but faded rapidly as darkness moved up from the canyon floor devour it. Up ahead perched the village on its rock ledge. A few torches had been lit. The scream had not come from the village, but somewhere closer to the left of where they stood. Three men from the trading expedition had returned with him, and they huddled around him now, terrified of the blood-curdling sound, but possibly more disturbed by the eerie silence that had followed.

"What is happening?" Owl Dancing cried. "Is the village under siege?"

"No. It's Tanya! I told you she was in danger. We must find her, and quickly. Are there caves in the cliffs where she could be?"

"Yes, many. But they are small and high on the canyon walls. The darkness will make it difficult to find her."

Keane tossed his pack into the brush, trying to pinpoint where the scream had originated. Suddenly a rock came tumbling and bouncing down the side of the mountain right toward him. He saw it in time to dodge it, as did his companions.

"Either somebody is trying to kill us," he told the others, "or they're running from something."

The place where the rock had fallen was in the vicinity of where he had first heard the scream. He held up his torch and began lunging up the side of the canyon, slipping in the sandy soil, tripping over rocks, flailing through brush, dodging the branches of pinyons and junipers.

"Tanya! Tanya, where are you!" Like the scream, his shouted plea echoed through the canyon. His words were tossed around and around, slamming against the canyon wall and back into his own ears. A response came, but it was caught in the vibration of his own voice and he couldn't pinpoint where it had come from. He waited for silence, listened.

"Keane!"

The voice was closer, just above him now. He craned his neck to look up the side of the canyon. And then he spotted a ledge of rocks barely visible in the dusk. If there was a cave inside them, there was no outward indication, but following a hunch he struggled upward, being forced to take a serpentine route because of the tough terrain.

He called Tanya's name again and then he saw her standing on the ledge of rocks. Her blond hair tumbled onto her shoulders in dishevelment. She had something wrapped around her, but her arms and legs were bare.

My god, what was happening? Had someone hurt her? At least she was alive.

"I'm here, Tanya!"

She saw him a moment later, then suddenly crumpled to the ground. By the time he found a way to the ledge of rocks and pulled her into his arms, she was sobbing.

"He was there again, Keane. You were right about him. He's so evil. Wicked."

"Sweetheart." He brushed the strands of hair from her face. "It's all right now. I'm here."

"The dream . . . I opened my eyes . . . he was . . . there . . ."

"Ocelot?"

"Yes." She shuddered and dug her fingers into his shoulders for support. "At first I thought . . . it was . . . you. Thought you'd . . . come back. I screamed and he . . . hit me. Then he heard you call my name and he ran. I . . . can't think clearly. My mind is so . . . muddled."

"How did you get here?"

"I was ill. He said he could cure the ghost sickness, so he brought me . . . here."

"I'll kill the bastard."

He tilted her head and looked into her eyes. What he saw shocked him beyond belief. She looked barely an inch from death. Her eyes were glazed, dull and distant, like those of people he'd seen who were on opium. Her pallor was the same gray as the dusk. What had happened to the vibrant woman he'd left here just over two weeks ago? How could her health have deteriorated so rapidly?

He pulled her into his arms, wanting to give her strength and protection. He searched the coming darkness for Ocelot. He heard and saw no movement save that of his traveling companions struggling up the canyon wall, cutting a path through the dark shadows of the trees and rocks.

The opening that led into the cave was barely a foot wide. From his position, he could see the faint red glow of a fire inside. When Owl Dancing and the others reached him, he pointed to the opening. "Ocelot had her in there as his prisoner. But he heard us coming and ran. See what you can find, will you? I'm going to get her back to the village and to Ten-Moon. Oh, and Owl Dancing, one more thing."

"Yes, Trevalyan?"

"If you find Ocelot of the Four Winds, you have my permission to kill him if necessary. But if possible, I'd rather you save that honor for me."

Swift Blade came with Ten-Moon and Long Scar to the Tower House and insisted that they take Tanya to the Sacred Kiva for the ritual that would purge her body of the ghost sickness. Wrapped in blankets and once again in Keane's strong arms, she was carried across the plaza through the darkness, too weak to resist. Her mind was still dulled, her head filled with colors. She could not get enough water, despite the cup Keane frequently lifted to her lips.

The village knew of her sickness and many of the people followed behind them and the medicine men, forming a procession of worried well-wishers. They murmured among themselves over who had done this terrible thing to *her,* one of the Kachina People. They sent out their own prayers to the Creator that she would not be taken from them by this evil spirit threatening to claim her soul.

Ten-Moon prepared his *páhos* and his sacred cornmeal and began his chanting. The people knew the song could go on for hours or even days. It would last until the sickness was purged from her body. They also knew that if the *powáqa* who had cursed her with the sickness was too powerful, Ten-Moon and Long Scar would not be able to conquer it. If that happened, she would die. They wondered, too, why the gods did not intervene.

One by one, they left the Sacred Kiva and returned to their duties. Keane was forced to leave, too. Because he was not a kachina, and because he was too close to Tanya in heart, Ten-Moon knew he could be of no use to them in the ritual. His presence would only interfere with the full concentration needed to drive the evil spirit from Tanya's body.

Keane, reluctant to leave his wife again, joined Swift Blade and She Who Sees Far in the plaza. At dawn, the young woman brought him food which he nibbled at, water which barely passed his lips. All day he paced the stones that formed the plazas and the roofs of the many kivas until he fell into exhaustion in the afternoon shade of the rock walls. There he sat with nothing to do but watch the infant, Kira, nurse at her mother's breast.

In those moments of utter despair, he pondered his relationship with Tanya. Would they be able to recapture what they'd had as man and wife? Would she someday have a child of his? And if she carried a baby of his at this moment, would the sickness harm the child? Above all else, he was tormented by not knowing what her kidnapper had done to her. Ocelot had not yet been found. But when he was, he would not survive the wrath of the people, nor the vengeance of an angry husband.

Keane honed his knife on the pumice stone until it was sharp enough to split a hair. He then lathered his beard with soap from the yucca root. Wishing he had a piece of the obsidian mirror, he settled for his watery reflection in the pond and proceeded to shave and trim his hair.

Feeling human again, he donned the buckskin chaps he had designed, which She Who Sees Far had sewn for him. He covered his loins and buttocks with a leather breechcloth. Lastly, he pulled on the moccasins that had been a gift to him from an old woman named Song of the Morning.

His own clothing hung on tree branches to dry from the scrubbing he'd given them. The trading expedition had taken its toll on both shirt and trousers, leaving them torn and shabby. He decided the native attire would be more appropriate on this day, when he wanted to look his best for Tanya.

The chanting had finally ended after three days. A weary Ten-Moon and Long Scar had emerged from the Sacred Kiva, announcing to the village that the ghost sickness had been purged from Tanya's body. Swift Blade had given her his first floor apartment in which to recuperate and had helped Keane transfer her belongings. Keane had carried her to the Tower House under the watchful eyes of the entire village. She Who Sees Far and her mother, Masavehma, had ushered the men out of the room so they could bathe Tanya and wash her hair. Keane had taken the opportunity to go to the river and do the same to himself.

Now he nervously wondered how Tanya would react to seeing him again. Would she still be angry over the discord Snow In Summer had caused? Everyone had been surprised when Snow hadn't returned with the trading party, and more surprised to learn that she had never been with them. It was rumored now that the young woman had either run away to another village and to relatives of her father's clan, or she had met with an accident—and probably death—while trying to catch up to the trading expedition.

Keane heard movement in the brush and automatically reached for his knife. Upon seeing Swift Blade emerge from the willows, he relaxed. They had agreed that Swift Blade would go first to see Tanya; now he was returning. As soon as he was close enough for conversation, Keane asked him how she was doing.

"She is weak," the young Hopi replied solemnly, "but her mind is clear, although she does not remember much of what took place over the past few weeks."

"Did you tell her I would be seeing her soon?"

"I did."

"And what was her reaction?"

"She said nothing. But do not be troubled. She is very tired. I'm sure she will be looking forward to your visit."

Keane nodded, but did not have the same confidence.

Swift Blade's gaze traveled over Keane's new attire. A dubious expression eased onto his face, then shifted to amusement. "Perhaps I know nothing, my friend, but aren't those leather leggings going to be too hot? And the hat doesn't look quite right with your new attire. Maybe I should get you some beads and feathers."

Keane repositioned his Stetson, anchoring it more firmly on his head. "If you think you're going to talk me out of my hat, you've been in the sun too long."

Swift Blade grinned. "It was worth a try."

Keane turned to go. "Would you hang around here with my clothes until I get back? I don't want somebody thinking they're gifts from the gods."

"I cannot imagine anyone wanting them, but yes, I'll stay until you return—or until they dry. Whichever comes first." Keane thanked him and hurried back along the path to the village.

At the Tower House, he removed his hat before stepping through the squatty door. Tanya was sitting up in bed. Kneeling behind her, a young girl of about ten was gently combing through her freshly washed hair. Tanya wore a jerkin made of the soft hide of mountain goats, tied at the waist by a sash woven from black and gray dog hair. Her legs, folded beneath her, were concealed by a cotton blanket. Even though her customary tan had faded, and the dark circles still smudged the area around her eyes, he considered her the most beautiful woman he'd ever seen. And she was his wife, a fact that was still sometimes too incredible to believe.

Both Tanya and the girl looked up at his entrance. The young girl came to her feet immediately, lowering her gaze respectfully. Tanya's gaze, however, locked firmly with Keane's. He couldn't fathom the thoughts that roiled beneath the surface of those eyes, but he sensed a dissipation of the discord that had raged between them a few weeks ago.

Tanya touched the young girl's hand. "You may go now, Kaeuhamana. I must speak with my husband."

Keane stepped aside so the young girl could make her exit, which she did, very hastily. Then his attention returned to Tanya, whose eyes still glowed enigmatically. What should he say to her? *You are looking much better. I'm glad to see you're feeling better. I'm happy to be with you again. I missed you. God, how I missed you. I should never have left you here alone with that damned Indian. Can you ever forgive me?*

"There was never anything between me and Snow In Summer."

He surprised himself with the words that finally spilled from his mouth. He hadn't intended to leap into the very cause of their estrangement. But perhaps it was just as well. It had to be resolved before they could resume being man and wife.

He watched Tanya's expression closely for some indication of her sentiment. He thought he detected a subtle softening in her eyes. Then, with a great deal of effort, she lifted her hand toward him. "Come to me, Keane," she whispered. "Please. I have missed you more than you can possibly know."

Twenty-three

Keane did not hesitate. In the next moment he was across the room and gathering her into his arms. "Sweetheart, can you ever forgive me for leaving you here alone? When I think of that bastard Ocelot, I want to kill him with my bare hands."

Tanya clung to him, pressing her face against his cleanly shaven jaw. She breathed in the essence of him, absorbed every nuance that made him the man she loved. She would recognize him even in the dark, and in her dreams. That recognition of his touch, his scent, his kiss, the feel of his body beneath her caressing hand had been the only thing that had saved her from becoming Ocelot's victim.

It was several minutes before she set herself away from him, and then only reluctantly. "It's I who needs to ask forgiveness," she said, wiping aside tears that had fallen onto her cheeks.

"What is it, Tanya?" A knot of worry tightened in his stomach. This was not the confident Tanya Darrow he had always known. He detected uncertainty and perhaps even guilt in the way her eyes avoided his. He had the sinking feeling that she was about to tell him something that could be devastating to his heart.

She moved to the small window and watched the people on the plaza near the Tower House. "I've done something, Keane. Something you might never forgive me for. Understand how hurt I was when I heard that Snow In Summer had gone to be with you on the expedition. Up until then I had tried to think I had merely overreacted. I wanted to believe what you'd said. I tried. Then Ocelot came to me when I was down at the river. He said Snow In Summer had followed the expedition so she could be with you. I felt betrayed. And I did something I truly regret."

Keane's heart skipped a beat. Surely she hadn't made love to Ocelot to get even for what she thought he'd done? God, don't let it be that. But he feigned a careless smile to hide his fear and to cushion the impact of what was to come. "Come on, sweetheart. It can't be as bad as you're making it sound."

Her solemn expression only deepened. "It is. You're going to hate me forever. I . . . I . . . removed the Turquoise Sun from my neck and I . . . I thought about throwing it in the river." Shame flushed her face scarlet.

His heart skipped two beats and he laughed nervously. "You didn't, of course."

"No. I came back to the village and I . . . gave it away."

His heart stopped. She'd given away the Turquoise Sun? For the love of everything sacred, how could she have done such a thing? Not only was it worth a fortune, but it had been his wedding gift to her. If he'd given her a diamond ring, would she have given it away, too? Had this token of his love meant no more to her than that? Suddenly he felt very sick.

She was facing the window again, waiting for his response, which didn't come. All the words swirling in his head had stuck in his throat in a mass large enough to choke him.

"I gave it to Kira," she whispered. "I'm so sorry, Keane. I know how much it . . . was worth. I know now that Snow In Summer was only trying to separate us. She Who Sees Far says Snow tried to bed any man who would have her. I shouldn't have listened to gossip. I think She Who Sees

Far would give the necklace back to me if I asked her to, but I don't feel right about doing that."

Keane was numb. That the necklace had been worth a fortune didn't matter now. He had given it to her as a symbol of his love. By giving it to her, he had hoped she would believe in that love. And believe that no other could ever take her place.

Were her misconceptions about him so deeply rooted that she would *never* believe him, never trust him, no matter what he did or did not do? How could they live as man and wife if she believed he was having a love affair with every woman he talked to, or every woman who threw herself at him? More importantly, what could he do to make her realize that their relationship, their laughter and good times, their nights of lovemaking, their future—wherever it might take place—was more important to him than a bauble of turquoise and gold? Words alone wouldn't be enough. If he expressed his dismay, she might think he was upset at losing a priceless artifact. It would merely serve to reinforce what she had believed about him all along—that he was nothing but an adventurer of shallow heart and mind.

In search for answers to his dilemma, his eyes came to rest on the clay jar in the corner containing the jewelry which the people had given them as gifts. Without waiting to contemplate whether it was the right solution, he reached into the jar and drew out the first thing his fingers fell upon—a simple strand of white seashells.

Tanya had turned from the window to see what he was doing. Blue eyes locked with green. He had nearly lost her to the forces of a supernatural evil he could not fully comprehend, and only the power of an old medicine man had saved her life. He would do everything humanly possible to prevent anything from coming between them again.

Without a word of explanation, he slipped the necklace over her head and took her hands in his. "You're my wife, Tanya," he said. "Nothing is ever going to change that.

Nothing will ever change my love for you either. Perhaps, somewhere in time, you'll believe me. As for the Turquoise Sun, maybe God has a purpose for it here with the Red Sand People, a purpose that is not for us to know or to interfere with. There was a time when I never would have believed such nonsense, but being here has changed my ideas about a lot of things."

He drew her down to the grass mattress and into his embrace, breathing deeply of her freshly washed hair and the sweet natural scent of her skin. He lifted the maize-colored length of it away from her shoulder and replaced its warmth with the fire of his kiss.

Her nearness stirred tumultuous desires and emotions he had never felt with any other woman. He shared a bond with her that went beyond the physical and to the very core of his soul. He wanted to make love to her, but knew she would need to regain her strength first.

She snuggled even closer to him and he felt her relax. "I'm glad you're not angry with me, Keane."

"You followed your heart. That's all anyone can do. Now, just rest."

"Will you stay with me?"

"I'll never leave you again."

"Keane . . ." her voice drifted off, as did her mind, toward sleep. It came back in snatches as she tried to maintain consciousness. "I haven't said this . . . before. Haven't dared. But I'm . . . no longer afraid. Keane, more than anything . . . in the world . . . I want you . . . to know . . . I . . ."

He waited for her to finish her sentence, but after a moment realized she had fallen asleep. He eased her back to her pillow where she could rest more comfortably, but he stayed by her side with his arm draped over her protectively. He studied the delicate features that had received his kisses now more times than either of them could count. If he lived as long as Ten-Moon, he would never grow tired of holding her, loving her, looking at her. She was his heart and soul. He wondered what words they were that had died on her lips. Was it at all possible that they had been words of love?

Daylight gently lifted the darkness from the canyon and tiptoed softly through the second-story window of the Tower House. Tanya stirred, feeling the sun's heat on her cheek. She opened her eyes to the new day, feeling fully refreshed from her ordeal. Her heart was light this morning. With the dawning came the memory of the man who had saved her life, in so many ways. She turned her head on her pillow to watch him sleep. That he hadn't been upset about her giving away the Turquoise Sun completely astounded her. Perhaps she had misjudged him all these years. She had never believed he had his priorities straight. Now, she'd been given cause to look at him in a whole new light. Maybe she had not been fair to Keane at all. Either that or he had truly changed after living with the Anasazi.

It wasn't long before her resistance failed and she reached out to fondle a short strand of rumpled black hair. He slept on. She traced the line of his jaw, covered with the shadow of morning stubble. She touched his lips that had held smiles and laughter from the very beginning. Lips that had touched her in ways she could never have imagined they would.

She didn't want to go back to their own world of 1896. She was sure of it now. She feared things would change if they did; that she would lose him. Here, in this world of the Anasazi, their love was safe. Last night she'd found the courage to open her heart, to say the words she'd kept hidden for so long. She had told him she loved him, finally, and then she'd fallen asleep in his arms. This morning she was going to show him just how much she loved him. She leaned over him, laying the whisper of a kiss to his lips.

He reached out for her, pulling her into his arms and into

his dreams. Her kisses gradually awakened him fully, and he opened his eyes to gaze fondly into her provocative smile. "Are you sure you're up to this?" he whispered while scattering kisses along her throat.

She sank gloriously into his touch and his nearness, closing her eyes to better absorb every facet of his lovemaking. "The ghost sickness is gone. I want to make love to you more than anything in the world."

She claimed his lips gently at first, then possessively, and finally with an urgency that surpassed any she'd felt before. A fire flashed up from a deep well within her. Keane rose over her and she lifted her arms to his powerful shoulders, slid her hands over the hard sinews in his back. He abandoned her lips to brand the rest of her body with kisses. She tilted her head back, reveling in the heat of each caress as it incited fire wherever it fell. Likewise, his hands refamiliarized themselves with each curve, line, and angle that was uniquely hers, moving so tenderly as to seem almost reverent.

The leather jerkin, which she had fallen asleep in, was already open to his exploring touch. Easily and quickly it was removed. Sometime in the night, Keane had removed his own clothing, too, so she was confronted with no barriers. Lying on his side, he held her loins to his. She pressed even closer to his muscular thighs and extended shaft. His kisses continued to fall like flower petals along her shoulder, then he moved down. Beginning at her toes, he feathered kisses up both legs, across her hips and taut stomach, over her rib cage and breasts. He paused, tasting each rosebud peak with the tip of his tongue, cupping and lifting the perfect mounds to make them more accommodating to his purpose. At the point of her womanhood, she eagerly welcomed his soft, stimulating touch. She could have taken him then, so powerful was her need, but she wanted to cling a bit longer to the ecstasy coursing through her veins like liquid fire. And she wanted to give him back what he had given her.

She took the dominant position, gently pressing him back to the fur pillows. She knew his body well, but her lips never tired of caressing his rugged contours.

"I need you, sweetheart," he whispered. "I can't wait much longer."

"Nor can I." She kissed his lips, long and slow, parting his mouth and sampling the unique taste that was his alone.

"Then come to me."

His shaft lifted to her wetness and she eased down over him, feeling a special bonding with him that she had not allowed herself to feel before. She had given him her body many times as his wife in those two weeks before their estrangement, but now she willingly relinquished her heart and soul.

They moved in rhythmic unison. The dance lifted their spirits upward beyond the Tower House and beyond the red rock canyon walls. Like the sun, they rose high enough to claim the sky above and beyond the clouds, beyond even time itself. This moment, and this bed of fulfillment, would never be forgotten.

The sun had chased away any trace of dawn by the time Keane and Tanya awoke in each other's arms. Tanya's stomach released a tremendous growl. Laughing, she apologized for its less than romantic overtones.

Keane just grinned and traced her cheek lovingly. "I guess it's time for this caveman to go find a mammoth for his wife to eat."

"I'd settle for something that would fit in a clay bowl." She grinned back, feeling a freedom of heart and soul she had never before felt.

"I'll see if I can arrange it." He leaped up and reached

for his breechcloth and leather chaps. "Stay put. I'll be right back."

"Keane." Suddenly apprehension stole her smile. "Find out what happened to Ocelot, would you? I'd feel better knowing he had either skipped the country or been taken prisoner."

"I'd feel better knowing he was dead," he said flatly.

"Why do you think he did it?"

Keane was moved by her desolate expression. He had never felt so helpless as he did where Ocelot was concerned. "I don't know, Tanya. We can talk to Ten-Moon and see what he thinks. All I know is that if Ocelot ever shows his face in this village again, he'll answer directly to me."

"Be wary, Keane. He's clever."

He kissed away her concern. "Don't worry. I won't turn my back on him. Now, stay put and I'll rustle up something around here to eat. Boy, what I wouldn't give for a big, juicy sirloin steak."

After he was gone, Tanya found that worm of fear crawling inside her again. Where was Ocelot? Was he somewhere right now, trying to get back into her mind? What could she do to guard against the infiltration of the witch? And why was he so determined to destroy her? Would he put the ghost sickness inside her again without her knowledge? She would most certainly talk to Ten-Moon to see if there was anything she could do to protect herself.

She was very relieved when Keane returned, bringing a bowl of steaming, rabbit stew. It was mostly broth, but she devoured it and would have eaten more had Keane not warned her to ease back into things gradually.

He changed back into his own clothes, which Swift Blade had rescued from the tree branches. He spent the day with her in the room, talking and laughing about other adventures, other expeditions, other times. They made love and, late in the afternoon, Tanya slept. Keane dozed, but not for long. He mostly sat and studied her face in repose and wondered how he could keep her safe from Ocelot. The Indian hadn't shown his face in the village, but Keane sensed he was still near, lurking not far from the cliff dwellings. He wondered if Ocelot was somewhere right now spying on them by way of sorcery, delving into their minds each time they slept.

When Tanya was in a deep sleep and appeared to be resting comfortably, he left the room and sent a child to bring Ten-Moon. They sat outside the Tower House, always in sight of the doorway, and they discussed the possibility of trying the chant again.

"Her life is in danger here," Keane said, glancing nervously back at the room. "Until Ocelot is dead, or gone far away from here, I won't rest easy."

Ten-Moon nodded in the somnolent way that indicated he was giving something his greatest consideration. "Yes, the presence of danger gets as strong as the scent of decaying flesh on the wind. Tomorrow night, when she is stronger, we will try again. But you must think back on everything you did upon entering the tunnel. Everything you did *inside* the tunnel. The time of day might even be important. And the phase of the moon."

"Perhaps you should sing the chant exactly as it was sung the first time, with no variations."

Ten-Moon's old lips pursed thoughtfully. "That may be what I am doing wrong. I will not try to reverse things. I will simply repeat the chant. But I think it is time that I ask for the aid of the other priests."

Keane's eyes met the old man's. Silent understanding spanned the distance between them. They did not have to mention the risks again; they were both very much aware of them. Keane nodded. "Very well. I'll tell Tanya and Swift Blade."

Keane watched Ten-Moon hobble back to his quarters, wondering if he would live until tomorrow night. With the thought heavy on his mind, he returned to Tanya's side. He felt a weariness like that which he'd seen in the old medicine man's eyes. Sleep came to him quickly, and in his dreams danced sirloin steaks, cigars, and a Great Bear who saw everything in his tiny, obsidian mirror.

Keane opened his eyes to a darkness that was eased only by the plaza torches. He had come awake with a sense of something having disturbed his sleep. He listened, but heard nothing out of the ordinary. He was about to shift to his other side when a shadow moved across the doorway. Instantly he reached for his knife, only to be halted by a low and sinister voice, hissing like a snake from the darkness.

"Give the knife to me, Trevalyan, or you will find mine embedded in your heart. Then who would protect your woman?"

Keane, having little choice, obliged. Ocelot stepped from the shadows, ridiculously dressed once again in the finery of the yellow silk corset. In a flippant gesture, he tossed his own knife onto the mattress. His voice never rose above a whisper. "My gift to you, Kachina. For what good it will do you now."

Three more people stepped through the narrow opening. One of them was shoved and fell face down onto the grass mattress, jerking Tanya rudely from her sleep, confused and frightened. Ocelot's threatening tone reached them again. "The knife will fly through the darkness to your heart before you can give a scream of warning to the village, Eyes of Sky, so I suggest you remain as silent as death itself."

Swift Blade was the one at the foot of the mattress struggling to right himself. It became apparent that his hands were tied behind his back, and the plaza torches revealed a face covered with bruises and fresh blood. Tanya gasped, automatically reaching out to help him to his knees. Ocelot grabbed a hank of his hair and shoved him at the other two men who had squeezed into the tiny room.

"What have you done to him?" Tanya demanded, coming to her feet and gripping a blanket to her nakedness.

Ocelot's gaze slid over her long legs, exposed below the blanket's rough hem. "I tried to get some information," he replied mockingly. "But your One of Many Words suddenly had none at all."

"Why didn't you just go into his mind and *steal* what you needed?" she snapped vehemently. "You're good at that."

"It takes time to steal thoughts, and time is running out."

"What do you want?"

His smile reminded Tanya of the devil's own. "I want the Bow Clan to rule over the Fourth World. I want all the Bear Clan witches dead. I want their hearts bleeding at the end of a sharp stake, Eyes of Sky . . . and I want *your* heart to be the first."

Twenty-four

Tanya and Keane were allowed to dress, then they were led from the village and down the path to the river. Tanya prayed with each step taken that someone would awaken and see what was taking place, but the village slept on. She considered yelling for help, but Ocelot seemed to have read her mind. At the exact moment the thought sprang to consciousness, his fingertips bit into her arm, while the tip of the Bowie dug into her back.

They stumbled through darkness, aided only by the light of the stars and the moon. They were taken to a secluded place farther upriver than Tanya had been before. There, circling a small campfire like a pride of hungry lions with gleaming eyes, sat at least two dozen youths from the village. Their eyes appeared glazed, drugged. Tanya saw the reason quickly enough when she spotted the *peyotl* buttons filling numerous wooden bowls. The young people came to their feet, stepping back to allow Ocelot and his assistants to shove the prisoners into the center of the circle with their backs to the fire.

Ocelot took a commanding position in front of them, and elevated his voice so all could hear. "I have brought you three witches of the Bear Clan. They were sent to this world in a pleasing disguise so that you might be deceived and thus submit to their will. Ten-Moon, the oldest and most powerful witch of the Bear Clan, tells you these three are Kachina People, summoned from the realm of the gods. I say it is a lie. They claim responsibility for bringing the first rain, but if they were truly kachinas, why have they not brought the second rain we so desperately need? And you have all surely heard by now that this one, Trevalyan, killed our beloved Sakngöisi while on the trading expedition."

A shout rose up from the group. For a moment the trio feared they would be charged and killed immediately in retaliation. But Ocelot held up his arms to calm them. They sank back, looking resentful that they should have to wait to spill blood. "The Bear Clan is working in force to destroy every person of the Bow Clan," he said. "But we will stand strong against their evil, and we will destroy them. We will start by taking the hearts of these impostors. We will appeal to our deity, Sáviki, with these sacrifices. When we have the power of their blood flowing through our veins, we will rise up against the leaders of the Bear Clan and put an end to their autocratic rule, to their very existence. Now, let us begin."

The circle broke to the left of the prisoners. Ocelot's cohorts moved aside, like a curtain being drawn away from a stage. Behind them, the trio saw a large slab of rock balanced on four flat stones, giving the appearance of a table or altar. The young man named Tuwálanmomo stepped forward. "It is ready, my Chief."

The hair on Tanya's head prickled. She moved closer to Keane, drawing comfort from his presence even though she knew the three of them were grossly outnumbered. This group would do Ocelot's bidding and never question it. A thirst for blood shone brightly in their eyes, and the weapons they carried were crude but deadly enough.

Keane's hand curled around hers and she heard him whisper. "Don't worry, sweetheart," he whispered. "We've been in tighter spots. Remember the time down in South America?"

"How could I forget?" she replied grimly. "I don't suppose you've got a plan for getting us out of this one, have you? Personally, I'm fresh out of ideas."

"Well, not just yet, but I'm working on it."

Ocelot whirled and strode up to the two of them, glaring at the smiles on their lips that slowly faded under his disapproval. He placed the tip of the Bowie at the base of Keane's throat. "What is it you say behind my back in this strange language of yours that brings the two of you such amusement? I can tell you, you will not be amused at what is about to happen to you."

Keane released Tanya's hand and in a movement almost imperceptible, moved away from her by a few inches. The smile that had been on his lips shifted until all that remained of it was a snicker. "I said you were a coward who is afraid to prove his strength against an adversary. That you hide behind a group of children."

Ocelot's hand jerked. Keane flinched, and a drop of blood began a slow trickle down the blade to the handle. "Your foolishness knows no bounds, Trevalyan. One more reason why you couldn't possibly be one of the Kachina People."

"Would a true kachina not have superior strength?"

Ocelot's eyes narrowed suspiciously. He took a new grip on the knife handle and glanced at Keane's blood staining the blade. "A true kachina sent by the gods would not bleed."

"How can you be sure? Have Kachina People lived among you in your lifetime?"

Ocelot's eyes narrowed, but he gave no reply.

"They were with you only at the Emergence into this world. They have not come since until now."

"You have done nothing," Ocelot countered. "If you were truly of the Kachina People, you would have been sent here with a purpose."

"Our purpose will not become evident until we are gone."

"There is nothing you can say that will make me believe

you. Your tongue is like a snake's that separates at the end. I have seen the woman's plans to lay waste to our village and reduce our people to slaves. If they become slaves, Trevalyan, it will be under *my* rule, not yours."

"You have clearly misunderstood what you saw in Tanya Darrow's mind. If this village was in ruins, it was because you saw the future in her mind, and you saw that the Bow Clan destroyed it with their own evil ways. We were sent here to observe your strength," Keane lied. "To see the power you held over the people and to prevent you from taking control. The Creator had hoped the Bow Clan had changed in this Fourth World, but we can attest to the fact that they have not. It would seem that there are those who never learn from their mistakes."

"And you will die from yours."

"Death? I am not of this world, Ocelot," Keane bluffed. "I only inhabit this body until the return to my own world. You can kill my body, but you cannot kill my soul."

"Your heart is your soul, Trevalyan. Without that, you are truly dead. *If* you are a kachina—which you are not."

"Then try to take my heart, Ocelot. I challenge you to do so. The truth of the matter is that you're afraid to dirty that pretty yellow corset."

"I am not afraid of you or anything. Least of all that you could be the victor in a battle with me."

Keane smiled inwardly. It had been easier than he'd thought to maneuver the fool right into the position he wanted him to be. "Then tell your people that you and I will fight until one of us is dead," Keane said. "Tell them, that if I'm the victor, they will surrender their weapons to me. They must agree or they will suffer the wrath of the gods. Tell them."

Ocelot could not pass up the challenge. To do so would be an indication of fear or cowardice, or an admission that he was incorrect in his accusations. He reiterated Keane's demands to his followers. But in their drugged state of mind, they believed him to be invincible and were not troubled that Keane would win. One began to chant and soon the others joined in. "Kill him, kill him, kill him." The gleam of blood lust deepened in their eyes.

Ocelot turned back to Keane. "I have your knife, Trevalyan. What do you have?"

"I have the power of the gods. Are you sure you don't want to change your mind while you still can?"

Tanya thought perhaps Keane had lost his mind. She watched him back away from Ocelot, and away from the fire, slipping off his shirt as he went. For an instant, fear flashed across Ocelot's eyes, but he corralled it swiftly and replaced it with an evil appetite to destroy. Taking a crouching position, he gripped the Bowie tightly in his fist.

In English, Keane said to Tanya, "If you get the chance, I want you and Swift Blade to get the hell out of here and go for help."

"I won't leave you."

"Damn it, Tanya. There's no point in standing around watching me get my heart cut out and waiting for your turn. Let me be the martyr. You can be the heroine and save yourself and Swift Blade. Get Screaming Panther and his warriors. I'll try to stall him and you might even get help in time to save me."

"All right. I'll watch for my chance."

Their conversation unsettled Ocelot as his eyes darted from one to the other. "Speak so I can understand you!" he shouted.

Keane's upper lip curled with derision that further unsettled his opponent. He switched languages again. "I was just telling my wife to think about the big celebration we're going to have after I bury that knife right in the center of your belly. I'm not going to put it in your heart, Big Wind. No, that would be a death too quick and easy for a witch who has brought drought and sickness and deception to his village."

"You speak big for one who is unarmed."

"I will not be unarmed for long."

The two men began circling now with more intent. Keane drew Ocelot away from the fire, the light. The youths focused on the ensuing battle and lost interest in Tanya and Swift Blade as they followed the movements between Ocelot and Keane. But the two young men assigned as guards had apparently not been ingesting *peyotl*. They stayed close to their prisoners, anticipating that Ocelot would win the battle and they would have more blood to draw.

Tanya and Swift Blade watched helplessly as Ocelot struck out at Keane with the knife. Keane leaped out of the way, the wide arc of the blade missing his naked chest. Tanya wondered if he had a chance. He was a bigger man than Ocelot and more powerful, but Ocelot moved as agilely on his feet as a cat.

The knife blade gleamed in the firelight. Sweat beaded on the two men's chests. Soon it rolled in rivulets down their torsos. The Bowie sliced the air again and caught its target. Blood sprang to the surface of Keane's chest and was soon commingling with the sweat. The youths saw the blood and one shouted, "Take his heart, Ocelot! Take the impostor's heart!"

Keane, undaunted, began to taunt his opponent. "Make the next one count, Big Wind. You'll never do more than nick me if you don't come a little closer. What's wrong? Are you afraid I'll grab that knife and turn it against you?"

If Keane felt fear, he revealed absolutely none. The daredevil in him sprang to the fore. He egged Ocelot closer, closer, then danced from the slashing arc of the Bowie. Ocelot grew braver and took a lunging step. It was the moment Keane had been waiting for. He grabbed the Indian's wrist in an iron grip, forcing the hand that held the knife upward and away from him.

The youths' chanting stopped. A roar of disapproval went

through them as they realized their leader was not invincible and might very well lose the battle.

With superior strength, Keane continued to lift Ocelot's arm up until it was over his head. Then swiftly and skill-fully, he kicked the Indian's feet out from under him. Ocelot landed hard on the ground on a rock, screaming out with shock and pain. The knife flew into the brush, lost to the darkness. Simultaneously, Keane came down with both knees in the center of the Indian's stomach, knocking the air from Ocelot's lungs in one long gush. Tuwálanmomo, seeing his leader losing the battle, suddenly lifted his spear and shouted, "Capture him!"

He gave a war cry and raced forward. The others fol-lowed.

Tanya screamed Keane's name in warning, but the youths' death chant drowned her words as they surged forward. The guards grabbed her and Swift Blade, yanking them back to prevent them from interfering. Keane was captured and dragged to the altar, where they tied his hands and legs with cotton ropes.

Ocelot, still gripping his stomach but able to breathe now, pushed his way through the crowd. Blood seeped from a rock wound on his back, staining the yellow silk corset. But he had found Keane's knife in the bushes and once again brandished it with authority.

Tanya struggled against the guards that still held her arms behind her back. "You said I would be first, Ocelot," she challenged. "Are you not a man of your word? How can your people believe anything you say? How do they know that you won't lie to them on other matters?"

"God, Tanya. Don't," Keane moaned.

Ignoring Keane, Ocelot stepped up to Tanya. The fire of hatred in his eyes for Keane quieted ever so slightly when his gaze enveloped her. "Perhaps you are right, Eyes of Sky. I will make him suffer even more by being forced to watch what we are going to do to you before we kill you.

What *I* am going to do to you. Something I started once before." He turned to his followers. "Guards! Tie her between those trees—there, where Trevalyan can see what her fate will be."

Tanya tossed her head back defiantly, but walked with all the pride and courage she could muster to what her death would be. She hesitated as she went past the stone altar where Keane would watch her fate, her misery. She only hoped they would kill her before she had to watch his.

"I guess I should have kept my mouth shut," she said as she paused beside Keane.

"You and I have never been much good at that, have we?"

"No, I guess not."

The smile faded from his lips. His green eyes sought hers out, touching her in the way his hands could not. "We'll be together again, in another time, another place."

"Don't tell me you believe in reincarnation."

"I believe in love, T. D., and love always finds a way."

Ocelot grabbed her from the guards and hauled her to the spot where he planned his defilement. He began barking orders again. Two men scrambled forward with more rope to tie her arms and legs. Ocelot reached out and jerked at the buttons that held her trousers.

"You'll be mine now, *powáqa*. And when I'm done with you, every man here will have his fill as well."

What happened in the next few minutes was a blur. Warriors suddenly sprang from the darkness, from behind trees and rocks, screaming battle cries and attacking the Bow Clan rebels with spears and primitive knives. Tanya recognized Screaming Panther, Long Scar, Broken Spear, and many of the other men of the village. She saw Ten-Moon coming up the river as quickly as his old legs would carry him, assisted by She Who Sees Far.

Confused by the assault, Ocelot was momentarily paralyzed. Tanya, seeing her chance, kicked out and caught him in the groin with her knee. Doubling over, he dropped the knife and grabbed his injured genitals. Tanya retrieved the knife, and, as added incentive, placed her booted foot on his skinny rump and gave a hard shove, knocking him the rest of the way to the ground.

Fearing for Keane in his helpless state, she shoved her way through the mêlée. At his side, she quickly sliced through the cotton ropes that held him captive. He took the knife from her and leaped off the slab, preparing to be engaged in combat. Instead, they were surprised to see the short battle already coming to an end. The young rebels, their minds and senses dulled with *peyotl,* were no match for the experienced and older Bear Clan warriors. In a matter of minutes, the youths were subdued.

It was quickly evident, however, that only about a dozen of the young rebels remained. None had been killed, but the remainder had mysteriously vanished with their leader into the darkness.

"Where has he gone?" Screaming Panther demanded. "Did anyone see where he went?"

"They have fled to safety," Broken Spear replied.

"But what will happen now?" Tanya asked, afraid of a counterattack.

"I can tell you what will happen!" came a voice from behind them. They turned to see Ten-Moon, followed by She Who Sees Far. The old man stopped a foot from them. "Ocelot will keep trying to kill you. He will be back, eventually, and I suspect he will recruit more followers from his father's clan upriver. You are not safe. We must go swiftly to the Sacred Kiva, and we must once again perform the ceremony that will return you to your own world."

"He's right," added She Who Sees Far. "If you stay among the Red Sand People, you will never be safe from Ocelot and his warriors again."

"This rebellion has been long in the making, my friends," Ten-Moon continued. "It is not your battle and you were not meant to die here in this land, in this time. Your purpose is in the future, where you can tell others about Those Who Came Before. Now, we must hurry. There is no way of knowing when Ocelot will try again to kill you."

"Just tell me one thing," Tanya laid a detaining hand on the old man's arm. "How did you know we were here and in danger?"

Ten-Moon's old eyes shifted and came to rest on She Who Sees Far. In their ancient light and knowledge gleamed respect and pride. "I did not know, but She Who Sees Far saw it in a vision and she came to me. I know now who will take my place, for she has power even greater than Long Scar's. Even greater than my own. Now, hurry. We must not delay another moment."

A small fire burned in the Sacred Kiva. Ten-Moon's *páhos* and other fetishes were already assembled. "Go into the tunnel, quickly," he said, waving a hand in that direction. "She Who Sees Far will assist me. She knows the chant, although I don't know how she learned it." He gave her a stern, disapproving scowl.

"I have listened to it since I was a child," she said without apology. "There are many shadows in the cliffs in which a young girl can hide and listen to male secrets."

"A nosey child," he snorted. Then, having already forgiven her, he turned back to the three time-travelers. "When you get into the tunnel, try to remember everything that you did the first time. It could be very important. Leave nothing out."

Keane lit the lantern with a burning twig from the fire, but hesitated at the tunnel entrance.

"Well," Ten-Moon said impatiently. "What is it, Trevalyan?"

Keane turned back to the old man, seeing something of regret in his eyes and feeling it in his own heart. He pulled his Bowie from its scabbard one more time and held it out, hilt first, to the old man. "I want you to have this, Ten-Moon. Your people have given us many gifts. Now, I give a gift to you."

Ten-Moon could not find words for several moments. Finally, he lifted his chin proudly and said, "I am honored, but I cannot accept such a powerful weapon. I cannot be sure where you will go when I send you away from here. It may not be to the place where you want to go, and you might need the knife for your survival."

Keane refused to be swayed. He continued holding the knife out to the old man. "If you fail—as you have done before—I'll return. If that happens, you can give it back to me if it'll make you feel better. Agreed?"

Ten-Moon stiffened with slight indignation. "There is no need for you to point out my failures, Trevalyan. I am fully aware of them. But, when you put it that way, I suppose I can keep the knife for you." He accepted it gingerly, giving it the respect it deserved. "I will cherish it always. She Who Sees Far will see that I am buried with it, along with my other possessions, should you actually find your way to the future."

Keane gave She Who Sees Far his gratitude for her help and wisdom, then led the way into the tunnel. Swift Blade also took a moment to express words of thanks and appreciation to both medicine man and apprentice. When his feet disappeared behind Keane and the lantern's fading light, Tanya turned to Ten-Moon, surprising him with a hug and a kiss on his leathery cheek. She did the same for She Who Sees Far and held onto her friend's hands a moment longer. Their eyes met in understanding of the special relationship they had shared.

"Take good care of Kira."

"You can be assured I will. Your name will live on in the legends of my people."

"You speak as if you are positive she will not return,"

Ten-Moon said wryly. "Remember, I have tried this many times before, only to be met with failure. There are no guarantees."

She Who Sees Far smiled coyly at the old man's skepticism. "You did not have me to help you."

The old man's only response was a disgusted snort.

"If it doesn't work," She Who Sees Far continued, "then so be it. But one must say what is on one's mind, for one never knows what tomorrow will bring.

"Now, you must go, Tanya Darrow, so this old *túhikya* and I can begin the chant. The warriors will try to track Ocelot and kill him, but as long as you are here, you will never be safe from him and his followers. He could steal into the village again and kill you. He could inflict the ghost sickness again."

"But what of the rest of the village?"

"We will manage, as we always have. But it is as Ten-Moon has said—your destiny is not here." She squeezed Tanya's hands. "May the gods lead the way across the barrier of time."

They hugged each other, then Tanya followed Keane and Swift Blade into the tunnel.

Everything was the same as it had been the times before. Their footsteps, as carefully placed as they were, still echoed back in the darkness beyond the circle of light. The bundles they'd brought earlier were still lined up in front of the stone table. The awesome stillness of the stately canyon had a calming effect, and they nearly forgot that death could be nipping at their heels. Here, all worlds were easily forgotten, both the one they'd left behind, and the one they hoped to travel to.

"He said to retrace our every move." Keane's voice sounded loud and hollow as it bounced back to them off the rock walls. He lowered it to a whisper. "What did we do differently that first time than we did the others?"

They each thought back, trying desperately to remember

some small thing—anything—that they might have forgotten. It was Swift Blade who commented first. "We struggled over the mirror."

"Yes!" Tanya's eyes gleamed with excitement. "That must be the missing link." She moved swiftly toward the stone that had served as a table for the vase and mirror. By the time she reached it, she could barely see. "Bring the light forward, Keane," she said, motioning for him to join her.

When he didn't move and didn't respond, she glanced over her shoulder questioningly. "Keane? Is something wrong?"

In the distance, the chanting had begun, sounding farther away than it actually was.

"You won't find it there, Tanya." His gaze lifted to hers and held. She could never recall seeing Keane Trevalyan sheepish, but he definitely was now. "It's . . . hidden."

"What?"

Sighing resignedly, Keane circled the stone table and bent down behind it. When he returned to his full height, he had the vase in hand. "I came down here shortly after our arrival," he said softly. "I hid it."

Tanya said nothing, only looked at him with knowing eyes that shifted perceptively with disappointment. She knew he had deceived her, that he'd planned to have it for himself. But so much had happened since that day. So many priorities had gotten shifted around in his mind and in his life. He could try to explain it all to her, but he doubted she would ever believe him now, and they really didn't have time to discuss it anyway.

So he told her the simple truth. "I hid it because I planned to sell it if we ever got back. But someone was here before me, and I found the mirror broken."

Tanya wasn't surprised, although she was greatly disappointed. Not that he had planned to sell it—that didn't surprise her at all, because she had figured in the beginning that he would try to do exactly that. She was only hurt that he had deceived her after all they had shared. But deciding this was not the time nor the place to dwell on it, she said, "Why would someone do that, Keane? Who would have come in here besides us? The villagers were too superstitious about the Sacred Kiva and the underground kingdom of the gods to venture into this cavern."

"It could have been Ten-Moon," Keane replied. "He spent a lot of time in the Sacred Kiva. But I'm more inclined to think it was Ocelot, and that he broke the mirror intentionally. The fragments were scattered, as if someone had broken it and either ran away out of fear, or because they simply didn't have enough respect for it to pick up the pieces."

"But why would Ocelot do that?"

Swift Blade offered a plausible answer. "Because he's a witch, looking for power. Therefore he is afraid of all powers greater than his own."

Tanya's hope trickled away like a streambed going dry. It mattered little what Keane's plans for the mirror had been. If the mirror had been a crucial factor in moving them through time, then their chances of repeating the process, or reversing it, were gone.

She looked at the vase and the strange material that was neither glass nor metal, but something incredibly strong. Something definitely of the future, beyond even their own time. Did the vase of futuristic material and the mirror of ancient obsidian represent the earth's span of existence? Or the existence of this, the Fourth World? Perhaps it represented *all* time, from the creation to the very end.

"I put the broken pieces inside the vase," Keane offered.

Tanya, thinking they were gone forever, tipped the vase and watched the pieces slide out into her hand. As she stared at the pieces an idea came to her. "Perhaps—" her face screwed up and she shook her head. "No. That would be stupid. I doubt it would work."

"What?" Keane touched her arm. "What is it? Don't be afraid to place your bet on a hunch. It might be the difference between us getting back or staying here."

She lifted her gaze to his. She wasn't sure she wanted to go back to the future. He loved her in this world. Would he love her in the next? Or would other women more beguiling turn his head and eventually win his favor? If only she could find the answer in his eyes, but she saw nothing of the future in the green depths. Did she dare risk the known for the unknown?

The chanting continued on from the Sacred Kiva.

"I'm afraid I'm not much good at gambling."

"What have we got to lose, Tanya?"

She fingered the fragments of the mirror. "More than you can know."

"Tanya—"

She sighed. "All right. There are three pieces of the mirror. We'll each hold a piece and then join hands, form a continuous circle. It will connect us as we were connected that first time when all of our hands were on the mirror's handle."

Keane planted a swift but sound kiss on her lips. "Thank God for brilliant women. Now, come on, let's get going before Ten-Moon falls asleep again. Or dies."

Tanya returned the vase to the stone table. Forming a triangle, they each placed a fragment of the mirror in their right palm and then closed their hands carefully around each other's and over the sharp bits of obsidian.

"Let's hope this works."

"Now you will die!" came a shout in the ancient language of the Anasazi.

Ocelot suddenly sprang from the darkness like a snarling cat. In his hand was a bow and a nocked arrow. He still wore the corset. The flight from Screaming Panther's warriors and the journey through the tunnel had taken its toll on it, leaving it dirty and torn. Regardless, he maintained a posture of absolute self-confidence.

"I cannot understand your ugly words, Trevalyan," he said, "but I see by your expression and the tones of your voices that you are wondering who broke the Great Bear's mirror."

"I take it you know?" Keane's lip curled disdainfully as he switched once again to Ocelot's language.

Ocelot lifted his head proudly. "It *was* I who broke it. And when I broke it, the power of the Great Bear was destroyed. If you hope to get assistance from him to escape this place, you will be sorely disappointed."

"And so might you, when you face the Great Bear's retribution for such a devious act."

Only a flicker of fear crossed Ocelot's face and then it was gone. "I destroyed his power. He can do nothing to me now."

"How did you know we were here?" Tanya demanded.

Ocelot smirked. "After the battle with the Bear Clan warriors, I knew you would hide here like the cowards you are. So I arrived first. And after I've spilled your blood on these rocks, I will kill the other witches, Ten-Moon and She Who Sees Far."

Tanya gripped Keane and Swift Blade's hands tighter until she felt the obsidian cut into her flesh. So he couldn't understand, she switched back to English. "Don't listen to him. Don't move. Don't break the circle. Great Bear . . . please help us. Help us—"

Her appeal was cut short by a cold wind that rushed past them, extinguishing the lantern as it had done that time before. Again, Tanya experienced disorientation as if suspended in space. She could not see the others, and wondered if they felt it, too. The chanting from the Sacred Kiva grew louder, louder. Then suddenly it began to fade, until it slipped beyond tangible existence and fell into a place that seemed to exist only in a distant corner of her memory.

As swiftly as it had come, the eerie feeling passed. The three stood in the darkness, remembering how this perplexing situation had happened before and where it had taken them that first time. If Ocelot was still with them, they heard no sound from that direction. They *felt,* rather than saw, empty space where he had been. The biggest concern now that loomed in their mind was what they would find this time when they stepped out on the other side of the cavern. Would Ten-Moon still be there in the Sacred Kiva, trying to fine tune a mystical rain chant? Or would they find prehistoric beasts? Futuristic monsters? If the key to time travel was the Great Bear's mirror, what was the key to controlling it? Or did the Great Bear maintain complete authority?

"If I had a match, I'd light the lantern," Keane said, his whisper echoing in the cavern.

"Do you think he's still here? Ocelot?" Tanya murmured, afraid he would be and that another arrow would flash through the darkness when he heard the sound of their voices.

They listened again, but heard only the drip of water into a distant subterranean pool. The chanting, too, had ceased.

"What do we do now?" Swift Blade asked anxiously.

As if in answer to his question, another breeze skipped past them, brushing their faces and hair with ghostly fingers. Suddenly the lantern wick flickered, flared, then leveled out strong and steady.

"I'll be damned." Keane stared down at the lantern.

"Be careful what you say," Tanya warned. "You might get your wish."

Slowly they released each other's hands. Each looked to the spot where Ocelot had stood. They were alone. At their feet, however, was an arrow. It had fallen just to the left of them. Keane stooped and picked it up. It was clearly old. Ancient, in fact.

And then he knew—they all knew—that Ten-Moon had succeeded.

Twenty-five

The kiva was as they had found it the very first time. No *páhos* or altars remained. No bowls of sacred cornmeal. No jugs of precious water. No fire glowing in the fire pit. Mice skittered across the broken withes in the ceiling, causing particles of dust to filter down into the musty air. The *sipapuni* was covered over with centuries of dirt. The chant of Ten-Moon and She Who Sees Far was now only a memory on the wind.

For all appearances, Ten-Moon, with the help of the Great Bear's mirror and possibly the talents of She Who Sees Far, had been successful in once again moving them through time. The question now was which century had they been taken to?

Feeling skeptical and anxious, they took the short tunnel to the outer kiva and up the rickety ladder to the plaza. Regardless of how thoroughly they had prepared themselves for what awaited them, they were nonetheless dumbfounded to see university students dressed in dusty clothes, sifting through mounds of debris. The closest was Georgia Murphy, logging in a piece of pottery she'd just found. No one acted as if anything was out of the ordinary.

"He was successful," Tanya said, dismayed. "I never dreamed he could actually do it."

"He was aided by the Great Bear," Swift Blade put in. "And the power of the mirror."

"And possibly the fact that we had to leave or die, and we all knew it. He said we had to *want* to go."

"That may be, but I can tell you one thing," Keane put in. "I never would have given that old *túhikya* my Bowie if I'd thought he wasn't going to fall asleep at the helm again. I think he just needed some incentive to make the proper pleas."

Tanya glanced at the half-smile on his face, but heard the sentiment in his voice. She sensed he was going to miss the old medicine man, as they all would. She would miss She Who Sees Far, too.

"Now that we know how, we could always go back," she whispered, sounding perhaps a bit too anxious.

Keane didn't seem to notice her sudden reluctance to return to their own time. His grin widened. "Not before I get a case or two of cigars!" Then he circled her hand with his. "Come on, sweetheart. Let's see how long we've been gone."

They took the path, sidestepping the rubble. Swift Blade followed quietly, saying nothing, but looking sad and slightly lost. Perhaps like them, he was sorry to leave the Red Sand People, knowing they would never see them again.

Georgia Murphy was the first to notice their approach. She came to her feet, dusting her backside with an exaggerated swing of her hips. Tanya sensed the provocative move was for Keane's benefit. Georgia's gaze slid over Keane appreciatively. She seemed not to notice whose hand he was holding.

"Hey!" she called, flashing him a smile. "Where've you three been? We've been looking all over for you for hours. We were beginning to think you'd been captured by Indians."

Tanya's heart sank to her toes and stayed there. They had returned to their world—the real world. The world of beautiful women that Keane had never yet been able to resist.

Would he still honor the marriage vows they'd made in the Tower House? Would she still hear his whispered words of love? Or would he return to the wild side?

Her gaze shifted to the stately structure of the Tower House they'd shared as husband and wife. Now she knew why it had given her such a feeling of *déjà vu* the first time she'd seen it.

She heard Keane say, "We were just exploring up on the mesa, Georgia. How long have we been gone anyway?"

Georgia shrugged, and her heavy bosom pressed even tighter against her shirtwaist. "No one has seen you since last night," she replied. "We figured you'd spent the night in the kiva. When we didn't find you there, we didn't know what to think. Miles just told us to keep digging. That you'd come back sooner or later. I guess he was right. But you'll have people talking, Miss Darrow, if you keep spending your nights with two good-looking men. Whatever would your daddy say?"

Tanya ignored the sassy reprimand. She hoped Keane might say something in explanation, but he didn't seem to have heard the barb. Instead, his attention had become riveted to a commotion going on over at the other side of the ruins. "What's that all about?"

Georgia perked up again. "Oh, it's that mummified body we found. You know, the one back where the turkeys roost. The old man was buried with all his possessions—which I guess is normal for Indians—but believe me, he had a bunch of *strange* things. Some of the boys think he was a medicine man or something. The peculiar thing about it is that he also had a knife, and it looks just like the one you carry, Keane. A Bowie. Only its rusted up and rotting, of course. How he got it is beyond me, unless some explorer put it there to play a joke on a bunch of poor archaeologists. Or unless the body isn't as old as we figured. Come on, you've got to see this to believe it. It's the *strangest* thing."

She grabbed Keane by the hand, pulling him away from

Tanya. He glanced helplessly over his shoulder while Georgia dragged him away, chattering, "Zeke is fit to be tied. He even went out riding to see if he could find some sign of you three. He's the one who figured you'd been captured by the Indians. He assumes that you're stew meat in somebody's pot by now. Oh, Keane! I forgot all about your ribs. I'm *so* sorry. We can go slower if you'd like."

"Don't worry," Keane replied. "I seem to have made a miraculous recovery. Tell me more about the old man's body."

"It's in amazingly good condition. And there was also a leather scroll with some pictures painted on it. It's the *strangest* thing. On the scroll, there's this man with the head of a cat, and a long tail. He's wearing a peculiar yellow garment that greatly resembles that corset I loaned you, Keane. He seems to be being eaten by a giant bear that's coming out of a star-filled sky."

"Does the cat look like an ocelot?"

"Well . . . maybe. What does an ocelot look like?"

Georgia giggled. Keane laughed along with her. Tanya rolled her eyes. She didn't miss the way Keane looked down at the buxom little flirt. Suddenly she stopped dead in her tracks, feeling like a fool trotting along behind the two of them. Keane wasn't her husband anymore. Not in this world. She had to accept that things would go back to the way they had been. Promises made during dark nights lit by Anasazi torchlight would be forgotten now.

She decided to look at the mummy later. From the information Georgia had gushed, she was already almost one hundred percent positive it was Ten-Moon's body. And she wasn't ready to see the old medicine man in death. Not yet. The scroll would be interesting, though. It sounded as if Ten-Moon had kept his promise of having She Who Sees Far bury him with all his possessions. He had said he would do it in case they should find him in the future. It seemed clear to her that he had left them the scroll, a picture message, to inform them of what Ocelot's fate had been. But being eaten by a giant bear? That translated to her as the Great Bear of the Night Sky. Could it be possible? If it was true, then Ocelot hadn't succeeded in killing Ten-Moon or She Who Sees Far, because he had died first.

Swift Blade, loyal guide to the end, had stopped next to her, waiting for her next move. Pulling herself from her thoughts, she said, "I think I'll go back to camp and let Zeke know we're here, so he can quit worrying. I'll take a look at the mummy later."

Concern creased Swift Blade's face. "Miss Darrow, are we going to tell them where we've been?"

Tanya sighed and pushed her hat to the back of her head. "I don't know, Swift Blade. My people are not like yours. They cannot accept supernatural things. I'm afraid they'd think we had all lost our minds, or that I was trying some publicity stunt to bring myself fame and fortune. At the very least, they would think it was a tremendous joke."

He nodded. "Yes, you're probably right. Well, I guess I'll go see what they've found." He turned to leave, but then hesitated. "Miss Darrow." The runnels in his brow deepened. "Are you going to be all right? I mean, what about you and Keane now that you're back?"

The young Hopi was only concerned, but why did he have to mention the marriage that was, and now wasn't? She swallowed hard and forced a smile that quivered at the corners. "Circumstances lead people into things they might not otherwise do. I'll be just fine, Swift Blade. Please, don't worry about me. And would you join me in an hour? We'll get the items in the cavern that were gifts from the people. We might sift through them and keep a few for ourselves, log in the remainder. One way or the other, we need to get that tunnel sealed up again. It's too dangerous to leave open."

* * *

Tanya and Swift Blade had no problem sealing up the tunnel without interference. Everyone was too busy working on the mummified body of Ten-Moon to notice the two of them missing again. She'd gone over to join the others only long enough to take a look and to listen to the conjecturing about who he was, and how a modern-day Bowie had come to be buried with him.

The preservation of the body was incredible. The hair was still intact; most of the skin as well. The heavy hide robes he'd been wearing were only partially decayed. The scroll, too, was in excellent condition. The leather hide it had been painted on was stiff and dry, but the colors were still vivid enough to differentiate. The scroll had presented a great mystery that had thoroughly puzzled everyone. When her opinion had been sought, she had merely exchanged glances with Keane and Swift Blade and said she had not the slightest clue.

She had returned to her tent to be alone. Keane didn't join her all day. He appeared in camp only briefly for supper before returning to the dig. Georgia Murphy stayed with him the entire time. If he minded, it wasn't apparent. Tanya couldn't remember when he had been so engrossed with his work. For the first time in his life, he seemed almost obsessed.

Georgia returned to camp around dark, announcing that Keane would be along shortly. "He's really fascinated by the body of that old man and the things we found buried with him." She shrugged and gave Tanya a smile, or perhaps it was more of a smirk. Tanya's jealousy flared. She wondered if the two of them had actually been up in the ruins engaged in some intimate act rather than in the business of archaeology.

By the time campfires dotted the river and most of the students were asleep, Keane still had not returned. Tanya sat outside her tent and studied the stars. They were about the only thing that didn't appear to have changed. Her gaze wandered over the starlit canyon. She remembered the times she and She Who Sees Far had gathered water, collected plants for medicines and dyes, giggled and laughed with the other women during pottery-making sessions, and bathed in the pool. The pools had fallen into disrepair now and were hardly recognizable.

Where had the people's migrations taken them when they'd left here? How had they died? Where had they been buried? She wondered if these were questions whose answers would remain forever elusive.

A footstep disturbed her thoughts. She looked up to see Miles coming to join her. They sat for a while, just listening to crickets and nightbirds, to frogs on the water's edge, and to the occasional rustle of a small creature in the brush. In her memory, she heard the screams again, echoing through the canyon the night of the raid. Keane had killed for her that night—and had almost *been* killed. He'd come close to dying during the expedition, too, and there at the end when Ocelot had taken them prisoner. She didn't know how she could go on if he died. She supposed that in all honesty, she would rather see him with another woman than to see him dead.

"I don't imagine you'd care to tell me where you three really went," Miles said. "Had us spooked, you know. I figured I'd be taking these students out of here myself if you didn't show up real soon."

Tanya glanced at the trees where Keane had first kissed her. He had seemed so sincere, and she had so desperately wanted to believe his words of love. Since they'd been back he'd kept himself busy, away from her. She guessed it was his way to ease out of their "marriage."

"Like we said, Miles, we just went exploring. Looking for ruins on the mesa. To be honest, we sort of went too far and got turned around. We had a time getting ourselves back on track. These ruins are hard to see from up on the mesa. I suppose that's why the Anasazi put their village here in the first place."

He eyed her skeptically and followed her gaze to the ruins tucked away so neatly in the rock amphitheater. "Maybe you ought to go up there and make sure he hasn't fallen through another kiva. His supper's gonna be plumb ruined."

That he knew Keane had been on her mind surprised Tanya, but the suggestion was all she needed for an excuse to join him. She didn't want to crawl to him. She didn't want to beg or plead for his love and attention, but she wanted to know where she stood now that they were back. He'd spoken words of love, but that had been in another time, another world. They'd shared intimacies and promises, but that had been when they had believed they would be with the Anasazi until their deaths. And, of course, she wanted to make sure he *hadn't* fallen through another kiva and found some other tunnel to worlds beyond.

She rose to her feet. "I'll go check on him."

"That would be right wise, Missy. And take your Colt, just in case. Fire it off if you find he's been snake-bit or something. 'Course, I can come with you, if you want me to."

She managed a smile, recalling that she'd lived this scene before, or one very similar. It seemed there were a lot of scenes that kept resurfacing in her life. "Kid me, Miles, but not yourself. The last thing you want to do is climb up to those dwellings."

He grinned sheepishly, recalling, too, having heard those words before. "Guess you're right about that, Missy. I prefer riding. You take the revolver anyway. You never know what you'll disturb in those ruins."

She studied the dark cliffs, remembering the way they had looked in the soft glow of torchlight. "The only thing in those ruins now, Miles, are ghosts."

"Didn't think you believed in such nonsense."

"I didn't—yesterday."

She retrieved her holster and Colt from her tent and strapped it on while he watched. She honestly didn't feel it was necessary, but she did it to satisfy him. She took another minute to light a lantern. Then, telling him good night, she headed out along the trail.

Once in the ruins, she spotted the glow from another lantern. It took her to the first floor of the Tower House, the room that had been Swift Blade's and Pávati's; the room where she had recovered from the ghost sickness.

Keane was there, sitting cross-legged in the middle of the ancient room and staring down at bits and pieces of the life they had shared for a moment in time. Navajo blankets nearly covered the floor, and artifacts were neatly lined up along the blankets' colorful stripes. Everything else in the room was gone except a ladder propped up in the hatchway leading to the second floor. Keane held a bow in his hands, stroking it in a reverent way. If she wasn't mistaken, he looked as if he had just been humbled by something.

He saw her then and the humility was quickly replaced by his usual devil-may-care grin. "Would you look here, T. D.? Ten-Moon was buried with this bow. Do you recognize it?"

She stepped through the high-silled doorway and knelt next to him, touching the old wood that had miraculously not turned to dust. "No, I'm afraid I don't."

"Okay, how about this?" He carefully set the bow aside and picked up a small mug. Her insides rolled over with a wave of nostalgia as he transferred it to her waiting hands. She turned it over and saw her own initials engraved in the bottom, just where she had put them.

"It's mine," she managed to say around the lump in her throat. "I made it. Where did you find it?"

"It was in Ten-Moon's grave with this bow—the one I made for myself. He had these things of ours buried with him, Tanya. He did as he said he would, hoping we'd find them."

"Maybe it was his way of telling us goodbye," she replied. "But they'll have to be logged with everything else to avoid suspicion. If we kept them, we'd be accused of being thieves of time, although I suppose you could get a good price for that bow back in New York. As well as the scroll. Any of this stuff would bring a fortune. Maybe enough for you to live off of for years."

She wasn't prepared for his piercing look. "First off, these items belong to your expedition, Tanya. But even if I had a right to them, I couldn't sell them. These things are *ours*. And Ten-Moon's. I'm not sure I would want to see them handed over to a museum either."

"Then let's not. We wouldn't have to log these items. I could make some personal arrangements for them."

His eyes ovaled with surprise. "Am I hearing words from the lips of Tanya Darrow, *the* Professor of Extreme Moral Integrity?"

She assumed a nonchalant expression. "It's safe to say that the Professor Darrow you speak of has either matured or loosened up. Or both."

He grinned mischievously. "I like loose, mature women."

Their eyes locked as each thought of the intimate moments they'd shared. Tanya wondered if he saw in hers the warm glow of desire she recognized in his. But where would it lead them now? Did they have a future here?

"The students found some pottery today, too," he said very seriously now. "It was made by She Who Sees Far. It was all I could do to keep from telling them the truth when they started noticing how different her work was from that of the others. They said it must have been made by a woman who came in from another tribe. One student even had the notion that it had come from another group of people who'd moved into the dwellings after the first group left. I wanted to tell them that the woman who designed it was just unique; that she had unprecedented visions. I doubt I'll ever be able to look at another potsherd without wondering about the woman who made it. Damn! I really miss those people and their simple way of life."

"We could always go back. Tonight. Right now." Tanya was startled by the urgency in her voice. Or was it desperation? Desperation that if they stayed here she would lose Keane to Georgia Murphy, or another just like her? That fear compelled her to continue with the foolish notion. "Swift Blade and I mortared the tunnel back up, but we could take it down easily enough. What do you say, Keane?"

His reaction was not what she had hoped it would be. He merely picked up the scroll again and studied it. "If we returned, it would change things, Tanya. Our purpose is here, as Ten-Moon and She Who Sees Far said it was. It is our job to see that their lives spent in these dwellings are never forgotten. And, if we can, we need to try and remove at least part of the mystery surrounding them, so people from now and the future will better understand them."

She released her hope on a sigh of resignation. He was right, of course. She had to face reality, no matter how harsh and undesirable it might be.

"So what do you think the scroll signifies?" she asked.

"I believe it's Ten-Moon's message to us that Ocelot was swallowed by the Great Bear."

"I interpreted it in the same way. But how could it be? And how would Ten-Moon know? The Great Bear was— *is*—only a supernatural being."

"Could it be possible that when we were moved forward in time, Ocelot was also moved to another time? But because he wasn't connected to us by means of the mirror, he ended up in a totally different time?"

She frowned. "But how would Ten-Moon have known what happened to Ocelot if he just disappeared?"

"When we didn't return to the Sacred Kiva, Ten-Moon might have gotten curious and gone into the tunnel and the cavern. You know he was itching to find out what was in there. And being a *túhikya,* he's been in contact with the spirit world before so he wouldn't have been as frightened of it as other people might have been. Once inside the cavern, he would have found the vase and the pieces of the mirror. He might have found that arrow that belonged to Ocelot, too. Who knows? Maybe he found something else of Ocelot's that would have given him an indication that he'd been there, attempting to kill us."

"Yes." She nodded slowly, seeing the plausibility of the idea. "And maybe Ocelot's accomplices were caught and they verified that Ocelot had gone to the cavern to lay in wait for us, knowing we would try to escape through the same tunnel in which we had appeared. He went there to kill us, but then vanished when we did, never to be seen again."

Keane picked up the story again. "Ten-Moon then drew the picture on the scroll, showing Ocelot being 'swallowed' by the Great Bear. In his eyes, we were probably swallowed, too, when we stepped beyond the veil of time."

"I like that theory," Tanya said with a satisfied smile lighting her face. "I especially like the idea of Ocelot stepping out of the cavern into a time other than his own."

Keane chuckled. "His witchcraft wouldn't do him much good against a saber-toothed tiger or a man-eating dinosaur, would it?"

"Or against a mob of curious people from the future. She Who Sees Far told me that in her visions she saw thousands of people in these ruins, people just wandering around, wondering about Those Who Came Before."

"That would serve Ocelot right," Keane replied. "They would probably put him on display in a museum along with the rest of the artifacts. And wonder where he'd acquired a yellow silk corset from the nineteenth century."

Tanya enjoyed a good laugh picturing that scenario. Then she said, "Unfortunately, we'll never know for sure. But at least we have a better idea of why the Anasazi left and where they went."

"Yes. And their migrations need to be understood. People need to realize that it was never their intention to stay in the cliffs forever. They were here only as a stopover on their migrations, and until the Creator directed them to the final place of settlement. The place where the Hopis now reside on Black Mesa."

"But who will believe us?"

Keane shrugged. "We'll have to find proof. Build a theory as solid as we can build it. And, speaking of proof—I've been thinking a lot about that position that was offered to me at the Prescott Institute of Natural History. If I took it, it would allow me to head expeditions in this area. To find the proof we need. I already know where many of the tribes lived; I visited a lot of them on the trading expedition.

"I don't think I can walk away from this, Tanya," he continued in earnest. "It's too much a part of me now. I know you'll probably want to put all these things in a museum, but I'd like to keep Ten-Moon's belongings in my personal collection. He gave me the respect of an equal and a true friend, and yet he was like a father to me, too."

Tanya couldn't believe her ears; Keane Trevalyan, playboy and adventurer, thief of time, was actually talking about taking an honest job, dedicating himself to the history of the Red Sand People—the Anasazi. And putting priceless artifacts in his private collection instead of on the auction block. It revealed a moral conscience she had always hoped he had, but had never allowed anyone to see in the old days.

But it appeared that this was the final break. This was his way of telling her that their paths would separate now. He'd found a new purpose in life, and she wouldn't be part of those plans. Why should he return to a primitive lifestyle with the Anasazi when, unlike herself, he could have anything, anybody he wanted right here in 1896?

At least his experience with the Anasazi had made him

realize no price could be put on the vestiges of someone's life. Being with the Anasazi had made her realize a few things, too. She no longer begrudged those individuals who had bought artifacts at exorbitant prices for their private collections. Nor did she hold it against Keane any longer for finding those artifacts and making them available to collectors. She did not fault him for sequestering Ten-Moon's possessions for himself, because she would like to keep She Who Sees Far's piece of pottery, too.

She understood now why people would pay small fortunes for artifacts to stock their mantels and curio cabinets. She realized that they didn't do it for the money or the prestige, but out of sentiment and respect for history and the people who made it. They wanted to hold a piece of the past and be a small part of it in the only way they could be. They loved the past as much as she did. They merely had a different way of showing it. And most of the time, the only way they could acquire fine antiques was through people like Keane who did the work and took the risks to find them.

She choked back a rising wave of emotion and forced a smile, hoping that if he saw her lips trembling he would think it was just sentimentality over finding Ten-Moon's body and his belongings. She never wanted Keane to know how devastating his announcement had been.

She stood up and edged to the door, knowing she had to get away as quickly as possible before she crumbled right in front of him. "The job at Prescott sounds wonderful, Keane." She gave him her brightest smile. "I hope it works out for you. Now, if you'll excuse me, I need to get back to camp. I'm way behind on my journal entries. And I need to write a letter to . . . to . . . Edward."

She had one foot through the narrow doorway when Keane's voice came back to her, low and almost threatening. "Not so quick, *Mrs.* Trevalyan. The only letter you'll be writing to Edward is a letter of farewell."

Twenty-six

Defiantly, Tanya faced him. "I get it. It's all right for you to continue your relationships with women like Georgia Murphy, but I'm supposed to be faithful only to you."

"You're not a stupid woman, Tanya. Don't try to be one now, just so you can pick a fight with me and cause us to break up. That's what you want, isn't it? You want us to separate now that we're back in our own time, so you can continue your long-distance relationship with that stupid Englishman who has long since forgotten about you! The only problem is, you don't know how to jilt me gracefully, so you figure you'll lay all the blame on me."

"Ha! Now you're turning the tables on *me*. You were flirting with Georgia. You've spent all day and half the night with her, even to the point of acting as if I no longer existed."

He shook his head in disgust. "I think you must have brought along some of Ocelot's *peyotl* buttons and you've been nipping them on the side. You're hallucinating, Tanya *You're* the one who took off and made sure you stayed away from me. I was only trying not to be rude to Georgia. I you'd have stuck around instead of running off in a huf and a sulk—and if you'd *trusted* me—you'd have seen tha I didn't encourage her. You'd have seen that she finally gav up and went back to her tent—alone!"

He ran a frustrated hand through his hair. "Damn i' Tanya. We made a commitment to each other, and I pe sonally don't care if it was technically over six hundred years ago. I intend on honoring it, even if you don't."

Tanya wanted to believe him. She really did. But he was just another Frankie Locke, full of promises and pretty lies he had no intention of keeping. "I know why you turned to me and made me your wife," she said, trying not to cry. "Because we were alone in a world we never thought we would get out of. But there's no need for you to feel committed to either me or to the vows we made under totally different circumstances than what we face now. The rules we lived by with the Red Sand People do not apply anymore."

"Maybe rules change," he snapped. "But vows and promises, and true love, survive the passage of time."

There *were* some things time could not change, like the way his nearness and his touch ignited passions too easily disturbed. But they weren't married in this world, and there were consequences she would pay if she continued a love affair with him. For all his pretty words, he was offering nothing that resembled a legitimate marriage proposal. He was offering only another night or two of sexual bliss, pretending to be man and wife, until he took off for Prescott Institute.

"Is it really true love, Keane?" Her voice suddenly turned weary. All the fight fled her body. "Or is it only *convenient* love? The Anasazi are gone, and with them their way of life. *Our* way of life as husband and wife. We did what we had to do to survive, and we did what felt right at the time. In this world my heart needs promises that will last a lifetime, not just until this dig is over, or until you find another woman you'd rather share your bed with. I suspect that's why you want to take that job at Prescott. It's an easy way out. A way for you to put distance between us, just the way Edward did with me, until the distance itself breaks us up. Apparently I'm not the sort of woman that men want to spend their lives with. So please, Keane. There's no need to prolong the inevitable."

She ran from his bewildered green eyes that seemed, in that last instant, to contain a deep anguish. She didn't try to examine that look. It was better for her heart to end their relationship now, rather than to love him more with each new day and then face having him walk away from her later.

Running blindly, she left the Tower House and headed for the only sanctuary she knew—the Sacred Kiva.

Keane started to follow her, then stopped suddenly in the middle of the plaza. Like a fool, he was still chasing after a dream. Discouraged, he returned to the Tower House, settled back on the Navajo blankets, and stared at the artifacts surrounding him. He thought of all the times he'd held Tanya in his arms after making love to her, and the way she would fall asleep, contented. But he wasn't content, and he doubted he ever would be again.

He had followed her around for years, hoping to win her affection and to make her his wife. In the end, he'd only accomplished that dream by taking her to a world where she'd had little choice but to turn to him for every aspect of intimacy, companionship, friendship, and protection. Now she was clearly trying to end their relationship. But he wasn't ready to go his separate way, or to let her go hers. If she left his life now, there would be no way to ever draw her into it again.

She had never said she loved him. Neither had she said she didn't. Only one thing was certain—she didn't believe his love for her was genuine. She insisted on comparing him to that no-good Frankie Locke and assumed that he was not capable of being true to one woman. Now, she was even comparing him to Eddie Chatham, of all people! Suggesting he was using Eddie's tactic of separating them in order to break them up. Granted, he'd been known to do that before with certain obnoxious women that had clung to him like sour perfume, but all he'd ever done with Tanya was try to position himself on her back doorstep at every opportunity. Well, maybe he'd become sour perfume to her.

Nevertheless, he wasn't ready to give up yet. He remembered the way she had made love to him, and he refused to believe she hadn't cared something for him. He still believed that Tanya Darrow had simply been hurt one time too many by love and relationships, and she was positive he was like those who had hurt her. He had to do or say something that would convince her otherwise. He'd succeeded once, when he'd given her the Turquoise Sun. It seemed unfair that he was being forced to prove himself again, but he was willing. If only he still had the Sun.

But maybe he did. Was it possible that the necklace was still where he'd left it before they'd gone back in time? Or had its course been altered when Tanya gave it to Kira? Was there any possible way it could have come full circle?

His heart began to pound with new hope and excitement. Quickly, but cautiously, he scaled the ladder that led to the second floor and the original quarters he'd shared with Tanya. He was thankful the students hadn't started excavating here in the tower, for it was here that he had temporarily hidden the Turquoise Sun from Tanya and her field crew.

The second-story floor creaked and sagged when he stepped out onto it. Pieces of mortar fell to the room below, and he hoped it wouldn't give way beneath him. Up above, bats stirred in the storage area of the third floor and fluttered about, disturbed by his intrusion. The ceiling, which was also the floor for the storage room, was riddled with large, gaping holes where mortar had cracked, shrunk, and fallen out. Several timbers had rotted and broken in half and were held in place only because their ends were still wedged into the outer walls.

He reached up into a pocket between the rotting timbers

and withes of the ceiling. There, his hand fell on the bandana he'd wrapped the necklace in. He didn't fully understand how, but the Turquoise Sun had indeed come back to him.

He plucked it from its hiding place, appreciating the solid weight of it in his hands. Then he removed it from the bandana and fanned it out on the stone floor. Its condition was as perfect as it had been when Ocelot had brought it from his trading expedition, except for the initials Keane himself had scratched on the bar clasp. And suddenly he wondered if the initials had been there when he'd acquired it from Hooting Owl, or if . . . but there was no way of knowing, nor of understanding their journey back in time and the consequences it might have had on the future.

Retracing his steps, he left the Tower House and went directly to the Sacred Kiva. Perhaps he was a fool to persist in his love for Tanya, but he was also a gambler, and a gambler couldn't acquire the pot if he didn't risk every coin he owned. What did it matter if she crushed his heart? It was lost now anyway if he didn't try.

He burrowed his way through the short tunnel that led to the Sacred Kiva. Tanya was sitting cross-legged in front of the fire with her back to him, staring at the dancing flames. She knew he was there, but she didn't turn around.

"Can't a person ever have a moment's peace around this place?" Something in her voice suggested she had tried to sound harsh, but it came out sounding more like a plea.

"There's something I need to tell you, Tanya."

"Won't it wait? I'd like to be alone for a while."

"No, it won't wait. And I don't care if you do want to be alone. I've got something to say to you."

She turned her head just enough to look up at him, but her expression was muddled and he couldn't fully separate and identify the emotions flowing across it. He gripped tighter the necklace he held hidden behind his back.

"All right," she said. "I'm listening."

"I don't think you've ever listened, Tanya," he said flatly.

"What are you talking about? Of course I've listened."

"No, you've listened to rumors and gossip, and you've based your opinion of me on the same. You've hidden the truth of your own desire for me behind the assumption that I'll hurt you the way Frankie Locke and Eddie Chatham did."

"Eddie didn't hurt me."

"He left you and never came back. He never wrote to you once. He left you with uncertainty."

"It doesn't matter. I never loved him. I know that now."

"Then you know what real love is?"

She avoided his eyes, focusing on the fire instead.

"I, too, know what real love is, Tanya. I know that I really love you and that I've loved you for a long time. I don't know the exact day it happened. Years ago, I woke up one day and realized I'd been tagging you all over the country not just to crash your digs and get in on some good artifacts, but because I was in love with you. Being your husband has only made that love deeper and stronger. It's rooted in my soul, Tanya, and I'll love you forever, no matter where we are in time, whether we're together or apart. If I take the job at Prescott, it would only be contingent on whether you would go with me. It was something I had planned on discussing with you, if you had given me the chance. Now, do me a favor and close your eyes."

Tanya could do little more than stare at him. He'd left her no opening for retaliation or even a response. No opportunity to spill the feelings that were overflowing inside of her. The amazing thing about it all was that she believed him. She suddenly wondered how she could have ever *not* believed him.

"Have I ever mistreated you?" he continued. "Lied to you? Deceived you? Intentionally hurt you? For once, just trust me. Trust me with your heart."

Finally she found her tongue. "Why do I keep getting

these feelings of *déjà vu?*" she said, meeting his earnest green eyes. "We've been through this before."

"Yes, in another time and another place. But this is *our* time, and we can't let the rest of life get away from us because of tiny pebbles in our shoes. Do you understand what I'm saying, Tanya? We can't allow anything to come between us. So I'm going to say it all over again, even if you've heard it before. Hold out your hands and close your eyes."

With her curiosity thoroughly piqued, Tanya obliged.

Keane watched until her long lashes fluttered down and her eyelids hid her view. He studied her face in that moment when she couldn't see him, and he thought his heart might burst from the sheer love exploding inside him. Could he truly succeed in making her believe that she was the only woman he would ever love? The only woman he wanted to share the rest of his life with? Perhaps he wouldn't be able to, but he had to try.

"Put your hands closer together, sweetheart."

She obeyed, and carefully he placed the necklace in her waiting palms. It more than filled them and draped down over her slender fingers.

"You can open your eyes now."

She did, and they grew as large as silver dollars. "Oh, my god, Keane," she whispered in dismay. "The Turquoise Sun! But . . . how? She Who Sees Far must not have given it to Kira after all, but left it here for me. Where did you find it?"

"I found it where I left it."

"Where *you* left it?" Her brow furrowed as she met his expectant gaze. "I don't understand."

"No, I didn't expect that you would. You see, this necklace keeps popping up in my life. Do you remember those Utes who were after me?"

"The ones who beat you up and chased you here? But

who—according to you—had no good reason for wanting you dead?"

He grinned a lopsided grin. "Yeah, those are the ones."

She smirked. "Why do I get the feeling that they *did* have a good reason to want you dead? And why do I get the feeling that it all had something to do with this necklace?"

He feigned innocence. "Because you're a very perceptive woman, sweetheart."

"Let me guess. They had the necklace and you wanted it?"

"Right again. I convinced them to convince Hooting Owl—the Ute who owned it—to gamble it. If one of them won, they got everything I owned, including my horse. Well, none of them won. They seemed to think I cheated."

"Did you?"

"Of course not."

Her lips curved into a knowing smile. "Come on, Keane. You can tell me the truth. You *did* cheat them out of the necklace, didn't you? The same way you cheated Ocelot out of it."

He laughed. "I didn't cheat Ocelot. He was just stupid. As for the Utes—I didn't cheat them either. They were drunk and a little dull-witted."

"And I suppose you're the one who got them drunk?"

"I certainly didn't discourage them, if that's what you mean. I merely took advantage of the situation and played a better hand of poker."

"The truth at last." She shook her head. Her lips lifted into a full smile of amusement. She studied his face for a moment, forgetting the ups and downs of their relationship. He must truly want it to work or he wouldn't be here again, offering her the necklace that would give him financial security for the rest of his life. He would have just packed his bags and left the dig, taking the necklace with him.

She knew in that moment that she'd been an unadulterated fool. Why had she found it so hard to believe him? So hard to see the real Keane Trevalyan? Years of love and happiness might have been hers had she not spent them running away from him but toward him.

Slowly, with tears forming in her eyes again, she slipped her arms around his neck. He took advantage of the move and curved her body closer to his. Her heart swelled anew with a love she could not deny no matter how hard she tried. She tilted her head back and he scattered kisses along the curve of her neck. His intimate ministrations rattled her concentration until she could think of nothing but his nearness and other more intimate possibilities. Once again, she was a prisoner of love and of her own desire.

"How could the Sun have possibly ended up in your possession again, Keane?" she whispered. "It's a miracle."

He slid his hands across her shoulders and down her arms, then twined her fingers with his. "Kira must have given it to her daughter and so on and so on. Then about twenty or thirty years ago it was passed to Hooting Owl. He gambled it to me. He told me it had belonged to an Anasazi maiden, and that it was very old and very sacred. I didn't think much of it at the time. I could only see how much it would be worth back in New York. I wouldn't be surprised at all if our initials had been on it all along."

Tanya looked at it dangling over one palm. "There are a few things in this world that I would pay a price for in order to keep them in my possession. The Turquoise Sun is one of them."

Keane lifted it from her hand and secured it around her neck. "I thought it was lost forever when you gave it to Kira. But I'm giving it to you now, as I did before, as a token of my love. I made a marriage vow to you that I had no intention of dismissing or breaking. Nothing, least of all time, can change that. Now that we're back in our own world, we'll ride up to Durango, find a preacher, and make our marriage legal by today's standards."

Tanya wiped at the tears of joy falling freely now from her eyes. She had never heard sweeter words. He had said everything she had yearned for him to say. She wanted to return his words, but a lump of sentiment the size of the sun—the real sun—was stuck in her throat. All she could do was nod her head and squeeze his hands. He pulled her into his arms and held her tightly to his wildly beating heart.

"I don't have much to offer you, Tanya. And I can't promise you I'll change much. I'll always love to travel and find rare artifacts, go on adventures and probably land myself in trouble. I'll always want you right by my side, if you want to be there. I will admit, though, that living among the Anasazi has made me look at things differently. These pieces of life have suddenly taken on new meaning. They'll be going to museums from here on out."

"Except for the ones we're going to keep, of course."

"I've totally corrupted you, haven't I?" He tried to sound penitent, but amusement twinkled in his eyes.

She, too, suppressed a smile and fingered the necklace. "You can't take all the credit. I'll bet you didn't know that I've had a collection of antiques and artifacts for years. Of course, it's just a *teeny* collection."

His hoot of laughter echoed throughout the kiva. When it faded, his grin stretched from ear to ear. "Ah, the truth at last."

Tanya elevated her chin indignantly. Her lips formed a pout. "I never said I was perfect. That was your assumption."

He leaned closer, running his fingertip along her cheek. "Well, sweetheart," he said. "You *are* perfect—in my eyes."

He kissed the end of her nose and then her lips. Reverting to seriousness again, he searched the depths of her eyes as if he hoped to find answers hidden to questions he had not yet spoken.

"What is it, Keane? Something's still troubling you."

He nodded. "Yes, I guess it is. You haven't said what you think about me taking that job at Prescott."

"How do you feel about it? You've been used to being on your own, going where you want to go, when you want to go. Is it something you could be happy with?"

He gave her question a moment of consideration, but Tanya could tell he'd already given many hours of consideration to the job offer and how it would change his life. His answer was confident. "If it's still available, I'd really like to have it. I'd like to be the director over the excavation of these ruins. I'd make sure you and your father stayed in charge.

"But you never said if you would come with me, Tanya. I'm concerned about your job at Wellesley. I won't take the job at Prescott if you don't want to move out here. I'll understand if you don't want to give up that position. I know how much it means to you and how hard you've worked there. I'm sure I can find something in Boston. And this country is wild, rough, not the best place for—"

Her lips closed over his, effectively silencing him. She pressed him back onto the Navajo blanket. After a moment, she lifted her head just enough to whisper against the corner of his mouth. "I think you've said about enough, Keane Trevalyan. I'd leave Boston and Wellesley in a heartbeat to live in New Mexico with you and be able to run these excavations. When I first rode my horse down into this canyon, I felt as if I'd come home. I didn't understand it then, but I do now. I *was* coming home—to the first home we had ever had together."

He searched her eyes. "Then your answer is yes?"

"My answer has always been yes. I was just waiting for the question."

"There's something I've been waiting for, too," he whispered. "Something I've been waiting to hear you say for six hundred years and then some."

Perplexed, she looked into the solemn green depths of his eyes. Shining bright and clear, she saw there a need and a yearning identical to that which had been hidden in her own heart all her life. In that instant, she realized what he wanted, needed, but had never received from her or any other woman. She'd not only been a fool, she'd been a blind fool. While she'd been thinking of her own desires and pain, her own fears and needs, Keane had been suffering in silence with the same lonely affliction of the heart.

She kissed the contours of his face, touching every angle, every perfection, every flaw. "Six hundred years is a long time to wait. It probably wouldn't be wise to make you wait any longer."

He closed his eyes, sinking into the delicious sensations of her touch. "M-m-m-m. I sure hope you don't."

Tanya rose up on one elbow and gazed down at Keane Trevalyan—adventurer, playboy, husband, lover, friend. "A few minutes ago, I said that there were a few things in this world I would pay a price for in order to keep them in my possession. Well, the Turquoise Sun is one of those things. Your love is another. Nothing will ever come between us again, Keane," she whispered. "Nothing."

His eyes locked with hers, but that longing had not been fully satisfied. "Say the words, Tanya," he pleaded softly. "I need to hear them more than you can ever know."

Her pulsed quickened. It was crazy to be so afraid to say three little words that had been in her heart for years. And when she said them—*if* she said them—there would definitely be no going back. But then, she didn't want to go back. She wanted to go forward into the future with the man she held in her arms at this very moment. That would never be possible unless she finally, after all these years, made the ultimate commitment. It was time to take chances, to gamble. To trust.

She swallowed hard and took a deep breath, then plunged

into the future with those three little words. "I love you. I have always loved you, Keane Trevalyan, and I always will."

He grinned and pulled her closer. "And I'll make sure you never regret it, sweetheart. I promise."

Epilogue

"Keane Trevalyan! Are you up here or have you gone and run off again! Answer me!"

Keane groaned and sat up, raking a hand through his hair and getting his bearings. Tanya sat up next to him, wincing from sore spots she'd acquired after a night of lovemaking on a hard floor.

"What's that horrible sound?" With bleary eyes she looked at the sun shining through the tower window.

"I believe it's Georgia Murphy."

"Why did I ever bring her on this expedition?" Tanya's tone lifted with utter dismay at her own shortsightedness.

"Because God knew you were going to need her yellow silk corset to bind up your future husband's broken ribs with," Keane replied matter-of-factly.

Tanya accepted that answer as a plausible one. It was too early in the morning to think of a better one. "Well, what does she want?"

As if she'd heard their question, Georgia's voice came back loud and clear, screeching an answer in the highest possible pitch. "If you're in these ruins somewhere, you'd better come out and make it quick! There's three angry-looking Utes down in camp, and they say you've got something that belongs to them. A necklace."

"Oh, hell." Keane moaned again. "Is there a back door out of this place?"

"Only through the cavern."

"I'm not sure I'm ready for another time-traveling adventure just yet." He reached for his shirt. "I need some coffee first," he continued. "And a cigar."

Tanya fondly touched the necklace lying on her clothes next to where they'd been sleeping. "I guess it *is* rightfully Hooting Owl's."

"I think we could argue that point. We had it six hundred years before Hooting Owl, and it has our initials on it. Besides, I won it fair and square. He's just a sore loser."

"How could we explain it to him? He'd never believe us."

Keane, cigar between his teeth, searched his pockets for matches and found none. "What's with my luck?"

"Who needs luck when you have love?" She grinned at him impishly.

His scowl lifted and he tossed the cigar aside. Pulling her into his arms, he kissed her soundly. "You're absolutely right, sweetheart. I didn't want that old cigar anyway."

"Keane Trevalyan! Come out of those ruins!" Georgia hollered again. "They said they wouldn't kill all of us if you gave them back the necklace."

Keane's lips compressed into an annoyed line. "Those boys are really serious, aren't they? Guess I'd better forget the back door. I wonder if they would consider a trade. I could give them my horse and ride double with you. That would be cozy, wouldn't it? Yeah, I like that idea."

Tanya traced one of the larger turquoise stones in the necklace. "It seems it wasn't destined to stay in our possession."

Keane gathered up his cigar out of nervousness and searched for the matches again. "Well, if we can't strike some sort of bargain with him, or at least convince him he's a damned Indian trader, then I'll buy you a ring with a lot of diamonds and rubies. I figured I would anyway. I mean, you can't wear the necklace everyday. It isn't practical."

Tanya sighed. "Let's give it back and get it over with before I get any more attached to it."

They dressed. Tanya decided to wear the necklace one last time and positioned it so everyone could see it over the outside of her shirt.

They found Georgia and followed her down the trail back to camp. As they approached the Utes, Keane took Tanya's hand in a protective gesture, just as he had done the night they'd stepped out to face the Anasazi for the first time. Then unexpectedly, the Utes dropped to their knees, lowered their heads, and began mumbling something in their native tongue.

"Oh, my god, not again." Keane rolled his eyes skyward. "What's with us and Indians? You fellows can get up." He motioned to them with his hands. "And before you get any ideas, we're not gods and we're not messengers of the gods."

Hooting Owl was the first to look up, his eyes still pinned to Tanya and the Turquoise Sun. If he or the others had heard anything Keane had said, they made no indication of it. Finally Hooting Owl rose to his feet, but with an air of extreme deference. Buffalo Belly and Talon Hunter followed. Keane stepped behind Tanya and began working the long bar clasp to remove it.

Hooting Owl thrust out his hand; his eyes rounded with alarm. "No! You must not remove it!"

The bystanders leaned closer, perplexed by this unexpected development.

Keane placed his hands back on his hips in an aggravated stance. "Listen, Hooting Owl, don't play games with me. Do you want the necklace or not? You guys beat the crap out of me, accused me of cheating, risked coming into these haunted ruins, and now you say you don't *want* it? Then what *do* you want? I've got a good horse and saddle, but that's about it—outside of my hide. And I think you already took your fair share of that."

Again, Hooting Owl ignored everything Keane was saying. "Who is this woman?" he demanded. "This one with hair the color of corn and eyes the color of the sky?"

Keane took a deep, sustaining breath, then released it. He tried hard not to blow sky-high, but these Utes were getting on his nerves. "She's Tanya Darrow. My wife and head of this expedition."

A gasp went up among the students, but Tanya and Keane were too intent on the Utes to worry about the shocking impact of their announcement.

"Maybe that is who she is to you," Hooting Owl replied, almost indignantly. "But it is clear to us that she is the one who has come to complete the circle of time, to close the gap left open many centuries ago."

Keane's patience was about gone. "This is utter nonsense."

"No," Hooting Owl insisted. "There was something I did not tell you when I gambled the Sun. You see, the necklace carries with it an ancient legend. I can see now that the Creator had a hand in my decision that day we played cards. It was His way of seeing that the necklace was returned to its rightful owner."

"Go on, Hooting Owl," Tanya prodded, very curious now.

Hooting Owl nodded, eager to honor Tanya's request. "Long ago, three people were sent from the future to live with the people of these ancient dwellings," he said. "These three were summoned by a powerful medicine man, for only they had the ability to expose the witch who had brought a terrible drought to the land. The witch was doing these evil deeds to turn everyone away from the Bear Clan leaders. He wanted them to follow him and make him the leader, hence bringing the evil Bow Clan back into power. But the Future People tricked the witch with their superior knowledge, and he was swallowed up by the Great Bear of the Night Sky in a dark cave no one has ever seen since that time.

"One of the future people was a young Indian man who could speak many tongues. They called him One of Many Words. The other man was a very handsome one, it is said, and a smile was always on his face. His name was He Who Laughs. But the woman was the one for whom the necklace had been made by the gods themselves. Her hair was the color of corn and her eyes the color of the sky. Those Who Came Before called her Eyes of Sky."

"Please finish your story," Tanya said. "I want to know what the legends say."

Hooting Owl nodded. "He Who Laughs loved Eyes of Sky more than life itself. The story goes that he would follow her to the ends of the earth, crossing all barriers of time just so he could be with her. And, because he loved her, he gambled everything he had for the necklace so he could give it to her as a wedding gift. This is how the necklace came into her possession. It was the way the gods had planned it since the beginning of time. But she doubted her man's love, and before they returned to their own time, she gave it to a child of the People. The child was a female whom Eyes of Sky gave a name at birth. That name was Kira. Kira later became an important medicine woman and helped lead her people to their new and final settlement on Black Mesa.

"But He Who Laughs and Eyes of Sky have been separated for centuries searching for each other. It is said that during the time when Eyes of Sky finally returns to this earth, the necklace will find its way back to her. As proof of her rightful ownership, it will bear the initials of her new name on one side of the bar clasp. He Who Laughs will also have a new name. His initials will be on the adjoining clasp.

"We have seen these initials and we know that they match your English names. The love between you is sealed now because of the necklace, and you will never be separated again. We have kept the necklace in safekeeping for you these many years, Eyes of Sky—Tanya Darrow. Now it is yours. The prophecy has been fulfilled."

The Utes, having no more to say, gave one last respectful bow to Tanya and Keane, then mounted their ponies and rode away.

The students gathered around to stare at the necklace hanging at Tanya's throat, to touch and admire it, to marvel at the strange story.

"What were those crazy Indians talking about?" Miles spat tobacco on the ground and watched the receding figures of the Utes as they wound their way out of the canyon and to the mesa above.

Keane took Tanya's hand, holding it tightly. In her eyes shone the love that had, and would, withstand centuries. He read something else there, too, that told him what his answer should be.

"Oh, I think it was all just a coincidence, Miles. A very lucky coincidence."

Author's Note

Shortly after the Spaniards arrived in the Southwest, explorers reported the discovery of ancient ruins belonging to a lost civilization in southwestern Colorado.

The first report to gain public notice came after an important discovery by two cowboys in December 1888. While out searching for stray cattle, Richard Wetherill and Charlie Mason stumbled upon the largest ruin which they named Cliff Palace.

The Smithsonian Institution and other museums had been sponsoring expeditions into the Southwest since the 1880's. With the discovery of Cliff Palace, the interest shifted to Mesa Verde. Both official and unofficial excavating was conducted in the area until Mesa Verde National Park was established in 1906.

Many people have theorized on the disappearance of the Anasazi. When I read the history of the Hopi Indians, however, I felt that the question had been satisfactorily addressed by their historians. I chose to use their creation myths, legends, and some of their religious beliefs to provide the basis for this story about the Anasazi.

Studies also reveal that the Anasazi gradually abandoned the cliff dwellings during the same time-frame that the Aztecs, or Aztlans, rose to power in Mexico. Some scholars believe that the Aztecs (whom history records as having come from "caves in the north,") might have been descendants of those Anasazi who left the hard life in the San Juan River region for the easier life in the tropics.

Castillo Blanco is a fictitious ruin fashioned after Cliff Palace, Square Tower House, and Spruce Tree House. Prescott Institute of Natural History is also fictitious and not intended to depict an actual institute. Nor are the religious rituals and ceremonies in this book intended to be authentic portrayals of those conducted by the Hopis, but only a basis for those used by the ancient culture of the Anasazi.

The Turquoise Sun was a very interesting and challenging book to write. The similar cultures of the Hopi and Anasazi were fascinating subjects I regrettably put behind me, but I hope the story will live on in your hearts, as it will mine.

I always enjoy hearing from readers who share my love for the Old West and its many stories. If you would like to know about my previous or upcoming releases, or would like your name added to my mailing list for future mailings, please send your letters to me, with a legal-sized, self-addressed stamped envelope to:

Linda Sandifer
P. O. Box 293
Iona, ID 83427-9701

ROMANCE FROM FERN MICHAELS

WATCH FOR THESE ZEBRA REGENCIES

LADY STEPHANIE   (0-8217-5341-X, $4.50)
by Jeanne Savery

Lady Stephanie Morris has only one true love: the family estate she has managed ever since her mother died. But then Lord Anthony Rider arrives on her estate, claiming he has plans for both the land and the woman. Stephanie soon realizes she's fallen in love with a man whose sensual caresses will plunge her into a world of peril and intrigue . . . a man as dangerous as he is irresistible.

BRIGHTON BEAUTY   (0-8217-5340-1, $4.50)
by Marilyn Clay

Chelsea Grant, pretty and poor, naively takes school friend Alayna Marchmont's place and spends a month in the country. The devastating man had sailed from Honduras to claim his promised bride, Miss Marchmont. An affair of the heart may lead to disaster . . . unless a resourceful Brighton beauty finds a way to stop a masquerade and keep a lord's love.

LORD DIABLO'S DEMISE   (0-8217-5338-X, $4.50)
by Meg-Lynn Roberts

The sinfully handsome Lord Harry Glendower was a gambler and the black sheep of his family. About to be forced into a marriage of convenience, the devilish fellow engineered his own demise, never having dreamed that faking his death would lead him to the heavenly refuge of spirited heiress Gwyn Morgan, the daughter of a physician.

A PERILOUS ATTRACTION   (0-8217-5339-8, $4.50)
by Dawn Aldridge Poore

Alissa Morgan is stunned when a frantic passenger thrusts her baby into Alissa's arms and flees, having heard rumors that a notorious highwayman posed a threat to their coach. Handsome stranger Hugh Sebastian secretly possesses the treasured necklace the highwayman seeks and volunteers to pose as Alissa's husband to save her reputation. With a lost baby and missing necklace in their care, the couple embarks on a journey into peril—and passion.

Available wherever paperbacks are sold, or order direct from the Publisher. Send cover price plus 50¢ per copy for mailing and handling to Penguin USA, P.O. Box 999, c/o Dept. 17109, Bergenfield, NJ 07621. Residents of New York and Tennessee must include sales tax. DO NOT SEND CASH.